THE MEDICI MURDERS

THE MEDICI MURDERS

David Hewson

**SEVERN
HOUSE**

First world edition published in Great Britain and the USA in 2022
by Severn House, an imprint of Canongate Books Ltd,
14 High Street, Edinburgh EH1 1TE.

Trade paperback edition first published in Great Britain and the USA in 2023
by Severn House, an imprint of Canongate Books Ltd.

severnhouse.com

British Library Cataloguing-in-Publication Data
A CIP catalogue record for this title is available from the British Library.

ISBN-13: 978-1-4483-0656-5 (cased)
ISBN-13: 978-1-4483-0770-8 (trade paper)
ISBN-13: 978-1-4483-0771-5 (e-book)

All Severn House titles are printed on acid-free paper.

Typeset by Palimpsest Book Production Ltd.,
Falkirk, Stirlingshire, Scotland.
Printed and bound in Great Britain by
TJ Books, Padstow, Cornwall.

ONE

The Capitano's Demand

The morning I was summoned to unravel a murder was bright and icy and full of pigeons. They were everywhere as I walked from my home in Dorsoduro, across the Accademia Bridge, through San Marco and past the cafés in the Piazza, where a grey and busy flock kept buzzing a group of Carnival-goers foolish enough to eat their pastries outside.

The Romans feared the owl, Edgar Allan Poe the raven. An old farmer I knew when I was a child in Yorkshire used to claim a robin flying into the house foretold a coming death. Unless it happened in November, in which case you might live. Pigeons, rats with wings, are perhaps too common, too greedy and annoying to be portents of death. In any case, they were late to the party. The corpse was on the slab already, which was why I was making my way across Venice that February day, all too aware of the noisome creatures flapping and pecking around me. It almost felt as if they were cooing a warning: *This is Carnival, icy cold, full of strangers hiding behind masks. Nothing here is real or settled, fixed or safe. Beware.*

Though doubtless that was my imagination. Something about Venice always sparks flights of wild and random thoughts.

My destination lay just beyond the tourist mecca of the Doge's Palace and the great Byzantine basilica that is the city's time-worn heart. The small square of Campo San Zaccaria was, as usual, empty. Few among the crowds milling aimlessly in the piazza around the corner seemed to know what lies along a narrow side alley from

1

the Riva degli Schiavoni waterfront, with its much-pictured view across the bay of the Bacino San Marco to the stately campanile of San Giorgio Maggiore, marooned on a small island of its own.

There's the charming San Zaccaria church, where early doges remain interred within a dark and atmospheric crypt that often floods with the waters of the lagoon. Appropriately, since three of them were assassinated in the streets around the *campo* by angry mobs and conspirators. Once, the area was home to a group of nuns who, under pressure from the then doge, sold off their nearby orchards so that the state could build the Piazza San Marco. The small seat of worship that remains pre-dates its celebrated basilica neighbour. It's named after Zechariah, the father of John the Baptist, murdered by Herod's soldiers during the Massacre of the Innocents, who is supposedly interred in the crypt too. Since he also has tombs in Azerbaijan, Constantinople and Jerusalem, Zaccaria – to give him his Venetian name – seems a well-travelled sort of chap, though to most outsiders he's simply a stop for the vaporetto.

I've spent most of my life dealing with history one way or another. From what I've seen and learned, the past in Venice is much like that elsewhere, fluid, malleable, easily changed to suit the viewpoint of the narrator. Only larger, grander, more ambitious. Remember, always, that in Italian *storia* means both 'history' and 'story'. The gap between truth and fable is slender, sometimes barely visible at all.

San Zaccaria's altar boasts Bellini's *Madonna Enthroned with Child and Saints*, one of the city's great masterpieces, as wonderful as it's ignored. Works by Tintoretto, Van Dyck, Palma Vecchio and his great-nephew Il Giovane decorate the chapels and nave walls. I make a lone pilgrimage to those pews from time to time. Just to sit there, an atheist enthralled by visions of paradise and a world of quiet order and settled belief. Though that day all my head was filled with was the rattle of pigeons, shuffling and grunting on the roof.

*   *   *

NO SOLITARY VIGIL IN the belly of San Zaccaria's nave lay in wait that dazzling, bone-chilling morning. My destination was more mundane: the Carabinieri headquarters, a charming old ochre building next to the church, perhaps something clerical at one time. I don't know and I wasn't minded to ask. I've never had many dealings with the police, apart from the one time our Ford Escort was vandalised outside the house in Wimbledon, and a lot of use they were then. But I had been summoned, by a captain it turned out. A woman, mid to late thirties, with the alert, intelligent face of a university lecturer paired with the trim figure, painted nails and perfect hair of a fashionable middle-class Venetian lady. She wore the standard Carabinieri uniform, dark blue with red flashes, cut very neatly it seemed to me, perhaps custom-tailored. The jacket and trousers looked as if they'd come straight from the press of a dry cleaner that morning, and their owner fresh from the beauty salon.

'Signor Clover,' she said in a low and confident tone that was dry but not unfriendly. 'Do take a seat.' There was only one, opposite her desk in a small office, just the two of us, a phone, a computer. It didn't feel like Scotland Yard. 'Thank you for coming.'

'I wasn't aware I had a choice.'

'No,' she said. 'True.'

I hoped I wasn't trembling. I'd been living in Venice for three months. My papers were surely in order after all the many meetings with rubber-stamp-wielding bureaucrats I'd suffered. No need to fear any of the routine hazards that sometimes befall the foreigner in Italy. All the same, something about this woman made me uneasy. My only knowledge – if it could be called that – of police interrogations came from dramas on the TV. They seemed, well, more *dramatic*. This encounter had a close and personal air about it, which somehow made the atmosphere more uncomfortable.

'Capitana . . .' I checked the nameplate on the desk, 'Fabbri.'

That got me a hard, judgemental stare.

'Capitano. The title describes the job and has nothing to do with gender. I thought your Italian was better than that.'

Valentina Fabbri had a direct and laser-like gaze to compete with that of my late wife. I felt myself wilting beneath it in that stuffy, overheated little room.

'My Italian was not the problem. It was my comprehension.'

'Call me Valentina if you find it easier.'

'I was wondering why you—'

'Please, Arnold! You surely know. I have a corpse on my hands,' she said, as if the idea greatly annoyed her. 'At least in a fridge in the Ospedale Civile. A bloody corpse. That of a famous English historian. A lord.'

'A knight,' I pointed out. 'It's not the same.'

'I stand corrected.'

Something that didn't happen often, judging by the tone of her voice.

'How may I help?'

'It's Carnival. We have our hands full dealing with drunken foreigners in stupid costumes fighting one another and winding up in canals.'

'That's what happened, isn't it? A tragic case of street violence.'

She appeared outraged. 'Here? In Venice? No! This would appear to have all the hallmarks of murder, foul and deliberate. Yet the only murders we have are those committed in the ridiculous fictions written by foreigners. It's unthinkable. Unacceptable. This is a city of beauty, art and culture. And of seeing as many tourists as possible pass through Piazzale Roma then leave as quickly as we may dispatch them.' She leaned forward. 'Alive.' A jab of her painted fingernail. 'Always . . . alive.'

'A reasonable wish your visitors would applaud, I'm sure.'

'You and I both understand no local killed your famous historian. You and I both know the answer to this riddle lies in – what do you call it? – your Golden Circuit.'

'Gilded Circle.'

'Exactly. Well, they've been in the cells since yesterday. Along with the young American woman who accompanied the fellow here and his son.'

'I believe Miss Buckley was meant to be his producer.'

'Meant to be. None of those I hold in custody seems consumed by grief.'

I kept my peace.

'You don't seem surprised?'

'I'm sure they have their reasons.'

'Precisely! And this is what I would like to understand. Their reasons. The truth of the matter. I am owed it. Luca Volpetti, a man I like and respect, not least because he once stepped out with my cousin, tells me you're an intelligent, resourceful fellow, and you know them all.'

Thanks for that, Luca, I thought. 'I know *of* them. Though not the American woman much, or the son.'

She checked some notes in front of her. 'All the same. You have more experience *of* these people than anyone else. You're English too. So perhaps you have some insight into the dark maze of their minds that I lack. Volpetti says you've been involved in this odd business the dead man had here.'

'As has he, but—'

'Let me be perfectly clear. I wish this problem gone. You and I will apply our minds to solving it. Immediately. By this evening I would like the matter resolved.'

I was, by now, expecting the first part. Not the deadline. 'Don't murder investigations take much longer than that? I mean . . . forensics? Science? All the things you see on television?'

She groaned in a way that told me the question was preposterous. 'This is Venice. Carnival time. Not television. I want this settled by tonight. My husband, Franco, runs Il Pagliaccio, the restaurant. The Clown, as you say. Near the Accademia. You know it?'

The fanciest and most expensive hip establishment in the city's most fancy and expensive *sestiere*.

'A touch beyond my budget from what I've heard. Also . . .' I gestured to my clothes. A tweed jacket at least fifteen years old. Beneath that a lumberjack shirt, red tartan, a Christmas present from God knows when. Tattered jeans, a budget supermarket brand. And on the hook behind the door, the duffel coat I'd brought from Wimbledon, a good decade old. 'I never felt I'd pass the dress code.'

'He's experimenting with a new menu this evening. I am duty bound to taste it and tell him what he's got wrong. Seven thirty. By then it would greatly suit me if this case was . . . dealt with.'

'So quickly?'

'I'm an optimist. Aren't you?' She hesitated. Slowly a smile emerged, then vanished seconds later. 'Help me, Arnold. Together let us establish the facts. Then you may join me for dinner. Wear your pyjamas for all I care. Cuisine from the lagoon, every item on the menu. *Risotto di gò*, with the little fishes prised from deep mud. *Moeche*. Soft-shell crabs.' She snapped her fingers. '*Canoce*, the mantis shrimp with claws so fierce they can break your finger. Wine from the best vineyards in the Veneto that would cost you a fortune if you were paying. You like fish and wine? For free?'

Mostly, on my budget, I lived off supermarket takeaways, pizza and an occasional kebab. 'That would be nice.'

'Nice?' She stared at me. 'Then we must get to work and solve this bloody riddle.'

I looked around the small room. There wasn't a sound from outside. The Carabinieri headquarters seemed remarkably relaxed. 'On our own, Capitano?'

'Valentina, I said! On our own. How many people do you think my husband's going to give free food? We can do this. A dead man. A handful of suspects, all of them reluctant to speak a word of truth. A portion of pastry, as you English say.'

'A piece of cake.'

'Speaking of which . . .' She picked up the phone and rattled off some orders. Very quickly a young man in uniform came in and deposited two cups of strong coffee on the desk along with four tiny shell-like Neapolitan pastries, *sfogliatelle*. 'These are your favourite, filled with zabaglione.'

'They are indeed. How . . .?'

'Volpetti, of course. Think, Arnold. Make connections. Let us pick apart this tale with logic. That's your calling, or so Luca told me. Now I need your faculties more than ever.'

'I see.'

'Start at the beginning. Tell me everything you know. About Marmaduke Godolphin and his Gilded Circle. Why they're here. How they get on with one another. Let us explore these people with the same incisive intelligence a pathologist friend of mine is using to explore our unfortunate cadaver in the Ospedale Civile.'

The beginning. People always ask for that. Yet I was never entirely sure where stories truly originated. One could usually see the end, and the middle was clear enough. But the seed, the spark that generated them, so often stayed hidden in the shadows of the past, unwilling to make itself known. Or, just as often, distorted by individuals determined to place their own stamp on history and obliterate the marks of others.

Outside I heard church bells chime nine. Pigeons cooed behind their dying toll.

'I am waiting,' she muttered as she rapped her scarlet fingernails on the desk.

'Very well,' I told her. 'But I must warn you. This may take a while.'

WHILE I GENERALLY ADHERE to Donne's maxim that each man's death diminishes me, it must be admitted that some diminish one rather less than others. Sir Marmaduke Godolphin, a man of barely hidden shallows despite a plethora of academic gongs, a dodgy knighthood and – this surely mattered most – fame as one of Britain's most-watched TV historians, remains a case in point. Not that I was in any way delighted that one cold February night he should be found floating face down in the grubby waters of the *rio* San Tomà, bewigged and bejewelled, made up like a Renaissance gigolo seeking custom, the costume of a doge around his plump form, a stiletto blade in his chest, his life bleeding away into the foul grey shallows.

Why should I be? Until his final few days in Venice I barely knew the man any more than he and his Gilded Circle of adoring acolytes were conscious of me. Our paths had crossed only in passing at Cambridge, where Godolphin was the glorious academic of the hour, a handsome fellow, popular with the women, especially after the BBC made him the face of their lightweight documentaries on the empires of Greece and Rome and beyond. A few years after I graduated, he ceased to be Marmaduke Godolphin, Professor of Classics, and was transformed into Duke Godolphin, minor pedagogue turned major media star. *Duke on Persia. Duke in the Footsteps of Caesar. Duke Dissects the Tudors.*

Like Roman crowds rushing to the Colosseum for bread and circuses, the public flocked in droves to his breezy, abbreviated retelling of history. I watched with bemusement. It seemed humdrum, pop-documentary stuff, full of dubious theatrical 'reconstructions' in which our charismatic chap bestrode the world with aplomb while wearing his trademark denim jacket, safari boots and glittering smile. The accompanying best-selling books only added to his celebrity and fortune. Marmaduke Godolphin was the public face of the past for millions.

I, on the other hand, a decade younger, was a state-aided student from a council house in Rotherham, a commoner with a stutter and a northern accent to boot, far too impoverished and, more importantly, proletarian to join his glittering clique. Not for me Eton and a family lineage traced back to the Norman Conquest, certain destiny for Oxbridge and future eminence. Instead, I was headed for a 2:1 in history and English, which, in the early 1980s would serve as an entry point into the quiet and anonymous world of a professional archivist, first at the Historical Manuscripts Commission, then, when we merged with the Public Records Office, the National Archives at Kew.

Duke Godolphin built his dazzling career through the time-honoured English means of an upper-class chumocracy. As he worked his way from studio to studio and bed to bed across the fragrant media landscape of London, my working day was spent in the suburbs, deep in volumes of correspondence concerning British foreign affairs, from the private diplomatic dispatches of the Plantagenets to the secret files of foreigners in the employ of our spymasters from Elizabeth through Victoria.

As a young man I sometimes dreamed of advancement, though primarily because I relished the idea of one day receiving the title 'Keeper of the Public Records'. 'Keeper of the National Archives' did not, for some reason, possess quite the same ring. In any case, when annual assessments arrived I was invariably informed that while diligent and insightful as a practical archivist, Arnold Clover, loyal servant to the institution all his adult life, lacked the leadership qualities that were, it seemed, more important. The stutter, while now only occasional, doubtless didn't help any more than my inability to shake off my Yorkshire twang.

By the time I approached retirement, Marmaduke Godolphin was a very visible knight of the realm, forever on the box and radio, venting loudly on everything from current affairs to history, morals and religion. A self-declared polymath, a braying controversialist willing to spout on everything from capital punishment to cancel culture for any newspaper, TV show or radio programme that sought his forcefully expressed opinions.

The TV work had become less frequent over the years, perhaps because of changing tastes. Godolphin was 'old guard', and proud of it, a chap who appealed to an aged audience fond of hearing reassuring tales about the greatness of England's past. In his mind, it seemed, he was a populist, odd given his lineage, wealth and clear distaste for any he regarded as hoi polloi. While rumours of his fevered love life found their way into the tabloid gossip columns from time to time, he remained, on paper at least, happily married to Felicity, a former student turned senior producer at the BBC. The woman who gave him a leg-up in his TV career, turning him from one more talking head into the star of his eponymous series.

By now in his mid seventies but as energetic as ever, he was a man to be reckoned with, holding board positions in industry and public bodies open only to that exclusive English cabal known as the Great and the Good. A sure thing for the House of Lords, one might have thought, if the swirls of rumour about his private life and occasional lapse into dubious financial transactions hadn't snatched away the ermine at the last moment. Or perhaps he'd just never got around to bunging the right politicians. It doubtless rarely concerned him. He was a man of substance, with a son, Jolyon – no ordinary names for the Godolphins – who'd taken on the mantle of television historian in his stead. In the odd way the British have at times, his admirers continued to love his progression from television academic to national pundit, a raffish character who liked to portray himself as a loyal and patriotic Englishman brave enough to say what others never dared. He was the 'voice of the people', not that he'd deign to spend a moment in their company unless it was to scrawl a quick signature on a book of his they'd bought before rushing off to feast and drink and argue in the Garrick.

I, meanwhile, was about to end forty mostly happy years wreathed in the daily ritual of paper and parchment, wax and ink. One never tires of the delights of ancient documents. The smell, the soft feel of old vellum, the visual pleasure of so many kinds of calligraphy and printing, the stains of age, of wear and fire. Above all, the realisation that so many hands – the touch of monarchs, statesmen, archbishops and all the many homicidal monsters among them – held these same frail pages before.

Even now, from Venice, I miss the intimate pleasure of picking up those precious documents in the quiet corners of Kew, though long before I left it was apparent that the days of holding them in your hands were numbered. The horrors of digitisation were upon us. Soon, the perpetually enthusiastic young of the IT department predicted, we'd never again need to recover an ancient item from its home among Kew's sliding double cabinets. Except for the documentaries made by the likes of Jolyon Godolphin, following in the footsteps of his father, and then they'd probably get some underpaid actor to do the work. A keyword, even a snatch of metadata, was all that was needed to retrieve a scan from the data store. Not the skill and cunning of a professional archivist built up over decades, an expert – that derided calling – who knew where to look and what document connected with another, sometimes far away among those serried ranks of files.

The creation of an interdependence of descriptors, a few my own, mostly those of others, many long dead. That was what my job entailed. Building a web of reliable links throughout the vast store of material in our care, making items, some deeply obscure, available to those who needed them even though our customers usually arrived on our doorstep with only the vaguest idea of what, in truth, they sought. An archivist maintains an entire library in the mind, shelf upon shelf, reference upon reference, page upon page. I can still close my eyes and see the whole of the foreign affairs section of Kew, tracing mental lines from the Field of Gold to the Raj, Lepanto through to World War Two.

I met my beloved Eleanor over a seemingly anonymous account of Agincourt, which she, being infinitely brighter, spotted immediately was a rough crib from Holinshed. At the time she was the lowest level of archivist, and in the way of public institutions, it was a position from which she never much progressed. The one sop they gave her was foreign liaison, so the two of us would make the odd trip to the great libraries of Europe, Eleanor on business, me occasionally tagging along as a happy traveller paying my own way. Always appreciated, never promoted, that was my wife's fate, doubtless because she had a forthright manner and didn't suffer fools in any sense, least of all gladly. We were married within the year, rarely well off on our civil service salaries, not that it mattered. She was a woman of sound sense when it came to life in general and money in particular. Especially for planning for the future we'd build for ourselves once the daily round of work in Kew was over.

There were no children – an accident we learned to accept. No close relatives or domestic ties. A move abroad in retirement seemed not just sensible but inevitable. We were firm Europhiles who loved to travel on our modest budget, by train whenever we could since you saw so much more.

We learned Italian at night school, she more quickly, naturally. Before long, the two of us began to make research trips to search out suitable destinations. After rejecting Rome as chaotically expensive and Florence as too touristy, we settled upon a modest cul-de-sac at the edge of Dorsoduro in Venice as the place we'd spend our mutual, loving dotage. With our savings and the proceeds of our terraced house in Wimbledon, we could, she assured me, afford a compact one-bedroom ground-floor flat in a quiet area away from the crowds, live off our pensions and explore all the delights Italy had to offer.

Eleanor had never been happier.

It felt as if we were walking through a dream.

We were.

THREE DAYS BEFORE OUR joint retirement party, seven weeks from taking possession of the ground-floor flat she'd found around the corner from San Pantalon, Eleanor collapsed at home. The sound of her falling to the floor was terrible, so loud, so heavy, I'll never forget it. I found her at the foot of the stairs, gasping, eyes glazed, mouth flapping for a second or two, and then, as I struggled to think what to do, what to say, what to think, she fell silent. In outright panic I called an ambulance, but she was dead already and I knew it. A heart attack, the consultant said, a pre-existing condition. She'd been making occasional visits to the hospital, more than I knew about, it appeared. A minor ailment, she always said. Nothing that need worry me. It was only later that I discovered the doctors had warned her months before that she was suffering from an untreatable cardiovascular condition that was dangerous and untreatable. Had I known that, we'd never have sold the house, never have contemplated fleeing cold and bitter England for the paradise we thought awaited us in Italy. As Eleanor doubtless understood.

There was a cremation: a few colleagues from Kew, one distant cousin I'd never heard of who turned up in the hope there might be something in the will. As if. Before I knew it, still in a blur, I was on a plane to Marco Polo airport and a life that was new in ways I'd never wanted. It's not as if I had much choice. The contract on the tiny flat was signed; inescapable, the Venetian estate agent said, except at great cost. Just as importantly, we'd sold the Wimbledon house to a lovely young couple who would have been heartbroken if I'd pulled out. There was sufficient hurt in my life at that moment; I'd no wish to spread it around. Besides, what was left for me in England?

Those first few weeks remain hazy as I struggled to cope with my loss and a strange new home. Shopping and bureaucracy baffled me, as did the accent, so different from night school in Wimbledon. The Venetians are often characterised as cold and unwelcoming to strangers unless you come bearing money. This is unfair and mistakes cautious reticence for rudeness and being offhand. Since my Italian was passable – even though I was occasionally scolded for speaking 'like a Roman' – I conversed easily in shops and cafés. Soon I established a regular round of places to visit for coffee, the occasional drink and cheap lunch, and before long found myself being acknowledged as a regular. A resident foreigner, not a tourist. The distinction was important.

As life began to settle, an old friend from Kew emailed me with news from home and an early Christmas present so generous and apposite I stared at his message in tears. He'd used his connections to cadge free reader tickets for all the main libraries of the city – the vast shelves of the Marciana; the unique and somewhat eccentric Querini Stampalia, a historic palace with a more modern element courtesy of Carlo Scarpa; the Fondazione Giorgio Cini on San Giorgio Maggiore. Even a small museum dedicated to the history of the Lido on the other side of the lagoon.

Best of all, I was provided with unrestricted access to the State Archives of Venice, housed for the most part in the former convent annexed for the purpose by Napoleon. It was next to the great basilica of the Frari, no more than a two-minute walk from my little home. More than seventy kilometres of shelving in all, along with its satellite buildings, rich with original documents that dated as far back as the seventh century. So many of them that some remain unread for many a long year. Heaven for the likes of me. A home from home. Paradise regained.

The staff there warmed to me once I explained my background in Kew, Luca Volpetti, a charming senior archivist who lived on the Lido, most of all. Venetian born and bred, he was a bachelor who knew every bar, café and local restaurant and soon took me under his wing. Luca showed me corners of the city few outsiders knew existed, wondrous palazzi open only to those invited through their doors, tiny societies dedicated to music, books and the arts. And on a practical level, since he was also a fellow fond of the table, where to eat wonderfully for a pittance.

With his encouragement, I became a volunteer at the State Archives, showing round the occasional English visitor – it was not a place that sold itself to the public – and on occasion helping with advice on how we might have approached some of the daunting collection issues the Archives faced had we been in the more egalitarian location of Kew, rather than the grand if faded former home of a minor order of friars. As the year turned, I found I rarely thought of England, an angry, distant place, much at all.

Yet England was to find me.

THE COUNTDOWN TO THE strange demise of Marmaduke Godolphin began with Luca Volpetti on a February Thursday during Carnival. This was my first experience of the seasonal festival that is, next to the Biennale, probably the city's most famous event. In the tourist areas of the city, visitors were wandering around in masks and costumes, most traditional, some deliberately exaggerated, a few quite bizarre. It never seemed to occur to many newcomers that northern Italy by the Adriatic might be cold. As a result, a good few turned up in flimsy summer outfits and soon found themselves shivering at night when the temperature rarely rose much above freezing. I was determined not to be sniffy about fleeting tourists, however ignorant, noisy and annoying they were at times. They brought money into the city then swiftly left. Both, it seemed to me, were welcome.

Luca had called me at home and, with an air of enthusiastic mystery in his voice, suggested we meet for lunch somewhere there'd be none of that sartorial nonsense: the Osteria Ai Pugni, a discreet little bar near Campo San Barnaba, popular with locals, especially staff from Ca' Foscari, the nearby university. All around were tourist traps where a plate of simple spaghetti might cost fifteen euros or more. In the cramped tables at the back of the Pugni, the knowledgeable could find a range of pasta dishes changing daily for half that, and a good glass of Veneto wine for a pittance.

For once my new friend was late. When he bustled through the door, black *tabarro* cape flying, he was gasping for breath.

'Are you all right?' I asked as the waitress delivered my plate of winter radicchio, gorgonzola and walnut pasta along with a glass of red.

'I fear not. I am excited. *Over*excited. Normally I'm the most unflappable of creatures, as you know.' This was not even close to the truth. 'It's worrying in our line of work, isn't it?'

'Rare, I would have said. Uncomfortable. Perhaps unwelcome. Wine will help.'

'No ordinary wine. Anna!' He called the manager over. 'A bottle of Prosecco for Arnold and me if you will. The Vigne di Alice.'

She was a smart young woman who always looked after us on our regular visits. 'The Vigne's twenty-seven euros, Luca. Have you won the lottery?'

He thought for a moment, frowned and ordered a radicchio pasta just like mine. The dark red chicory came from Sant'Erasmo, Venice's vegetable island. It was bound to be superb.

A dapper dresser as well as a man of great charm and a sweet and cheery temper, that day Luca was wrapped in his dashing cape, a silver clasp at the neck, an arty floppy hat against the winter cold and a scarf so long it reminded me of a far-off Doctor Who. All of which he deposited on the adjoining seat with a flourish that said, 'Now down to business.'

While coveting the bachelor life, he made no secret of the fact that he was friend and lover to two lady professors at Ca' Foscari, one of them married, the second widowed, both aware of each other and quite content with the arrangement. As, it seemed, was the husband, who was an occasional visitor to the widowed professor among other ladies in town. Venice was quite different to Wimbledon, at least the Wimbledon I knew.

'Not in the sense you mean,' he told Anna. 'But yes. I have won the lottery in a way.' He smiled across the table and took my hand. 'So has our friend from England. You'll never guess what I have a sniff of now. It is the most amazing discovery ever, Arnold. Simply stupendous! Come. We eat. We drink. Then I give you your homework. After that, tomorrow, you meet a great countryman of yours. Sir Marmaduke Godolphin.'

The name left me quite flabbergasted, and I said so, in English, which only left him confused.

'I do not know this word. What is the meaning of "flabber"? Or the verb "to gast"?'

'Rather surprised,' was all I could suggest in its place.

'He is a knight, Arnold. On the TV. You are familiar with him?'

'A little. We were at Cambridge at the same time, though I doubt he noticed me. I was a humble student under the wing of someone he despised; Godolphin was a starry professor. I'd say I know of him mostly. He hasn't been on the TV so much of late. At least not fronting a history series. Mostly political stuff. Opinion pieces. A talking head. A bellowing head, if I'm honest. That kind of thing.'

'Well, it's history he's after now.' The Prosecco arrived with his food. Anna poured us two glasses. 'The fellow's coming to Venice with a great project in his head. An extraordinary discovery lies ahead of us.'

He chinked his glass against mine in a toast. Together we took a sip of the most expensive wine I'd tried since arriving. It was a distinct cut above the ordinary: dry, perfectly chilled, not too fizzy. He glowed with pleasure, then stabbed the deep red chicory and cheese on his plate. 'We are to host a meeting of starry academics. Some of the most famous names in the field. All assembled to hear Godolphin's discovery.'

'*His* discovery?'

'An amazing one, or so the man says. And you are mistaken, my friend. He does remember you.' He raised his glass in a toast. 'The fellow requested your assistance in person.'

I was briefly lost for words. Then I asked, 'What discovery is this?'

'That would be telling.'

'It would indeed, Luca. So . . . do.'

His arms flew about the way they often did. 'I don't know beyond a few morsels he's let escape! He's keeping his cards remarkably close to his chest, as you say. His secret remains a secret until he reveals it. And to his former pupils too, I imagine. Since they are the illustrious authorities he's summoned for the occasion.'

I thought back to Cambridge all those years before. The Gilded Circle. Godolphin's chosen ones. They were inseparable, always following him around the college and the faculty like tame puppies. His magic had rubbed off too. Their careers had flourished around the world, though none to the extent of his. 'I don't suppose by any chance they might be called Caroline Fitzroy, Bernard Hauptmann and George Bourne?'

Luca stared at me in awe. 'How did you know?'

'I guessed. A dreadful habit in an archivist, I imagine.'

'Pah.' He waved a hand and took a second sip. 'I guess all the time and never tell them. We all do. Let's not pretend. Yes. Those three.'

'And his wife? Felicity?'

His eyes narrowed. 'The fact that a man should come to Venice in the company of his wife is not *so* unusual. That is not a guess at all.'

I'd vaguely followed their careers. Felicity, of course, had married her old tutor and helped propel his career upwards in the world of broadcasting. Caroline had joined the Sorbonne. Hauptmann, the American, was another to choose the safety of academic tenure, at Harvard. George Bourne, the most congenial of the lot, if I recalled correctly, bumbled his way into publishing and seemed to labour with a middling career until he took on Marmaduke Godolphin's TV tie-ins. On the back of Felicity's felicitous promotion of her husband's many series, Bourne's star rose too, with Godolphin's pop offerings selling as Christmas titles on a regular basis. It's not just archivists who build and maintain their links, you see. As a result of such commercial success with his former professor, Bourne now held a senior position and a fancy title with one of the big international companies.

'I glimpsed them at Cambridge when I was there,' I said. 'The whole gang seemed awfully close, a clique. How much of that was genuine affection and how much ambition I've no idea. The successful tend to stick together even when they come to hate one another. I can't say I'm terribly surprised to discover they're still at it forty years on.'

'Hmm.' Luca didn't seem to know how to take that.

'I'm an archivist, I will always be an archivist. I seek connections everywhere. As do you. I may be retired, but you can't stifle the habits of a lifetime.'

'Good!' He opened his leather valise, a battered old thing, quite fetching in its decay. 'We will need your habits. I have my orders from Godolphin. Yours too. And before you ask . . . yes, we will be paid. Three hundred euros a day each, a minimum of five days, in cash. I talked him up from a hundred. Told him our time was precious, which it is. I hope you agree.'

More money than I'd made daily in my life. Godolphin must have had his fingers in some precious pie. 'For what exactly?'

He retrieved two books from his case and spread them out on the table amidst the plates and glasses. Histories both, about the Medici. 'For doing what people like us do. Panning for historical gold. Godolphin has uncovered a collection of material that is on its way here now. He has good reason to believe that there are two items hidden somewhere within it of immense interest and importance. Revelations that will change the way we see history. Or at least a vital part of it.'

'What kind of items? What part?'

He sipped his fizz and smiled. 'I've no idea. The fonds first, the discovery after. You know the routine.'

Fonds. There was a word I hadn't heard in a while. In archival terms it stands for the broadest form of a catalogue, the top level, usually the person or institution from which the records came, later to be sorted into series of related records, then files, which are numerous items relating to a single subject, and finally the individual document itself.

Imagine. A trolley load of boxes containing the correspondence of a monarch. A fonds.

The boxes that pertain to a particular year. A series.

The collection in that year that covers correspondence with his prime minister. A file.

A single letter expressing his displeasure about something or other. An item.

Fonds ➜ Series ➜ Files ➜ Items.

There's much more to cataloguing than that, of course, but this is the heart of the process.

'What fonds?' I asked.

Luca raised his glass in a toast again.

'A set of previously unseen state papers belonging to Gian Gastone de' Medici, Grand Duke of Tuscany. The last of his line.'

The idea seemed incredible. 'Surely everything about the Medici is known and filed in Florence already? Where on earth would a man like Marmaduke Godolphin—'

His hands started flapping again, so wildly he almost hit the woman on the table behind him. 'I don't know, and I don't care! He says he has acquired the items by private means. They're being placed in a locked room in the Archives shortly. Everything is quite undocumented. Untouched, it seems, since that last, sad Medici expired fat and drunk in the pit of his bed. Godolphin is convinced there's real gold in there. It's our job to mine for it.'

'When did Gian Gastone die?'

He pulled out a small notepad he kept with him constantly and checked. 'July the seventh, 1737.'

Anna, always an observant presence behind the bar, noticed that a sudden silence had descended. She came and cleared away the plates as we ordered coffee.

'Some state documents of the last Duke of Tuscany have lain untouched for three hundred years?' I said. 'And now they're in the possession of Marmaduke Godolphin?'

'Correct,' Luca replied while making sure he didn't look me in the eye.

'Why can't he find what he wants for himself?'

He made that gesture the Italians love so much, a frown with corners of the mouth downturned and a little shrug of the shoulders. 'Perhaps he thinks it's beneath a great man like him. Sorting through piles of dirty and dusty papers. Or the discovery will appear more theatrically significant if it's made by the likes of us on his instructions. One step at a time. First, we must work. The treasure trove he's delivered is not so large, it seems. All we need to find is the two items that interest him. As well as the money, our prize is that he'll donate the entire collection to the Archives. Imagine!' He chuckled. 'The academic opportunities apart . . . Florence will be furious!'

There was an old rivalry that had survived the centuries.

'And for him?' Marmaduke Godolphin had surely never performed a selfless act in his life.

'A TV series? The chance to revive his career if, as you say, it's been quiet of late? Yet more fame? Money? I don't know. Who cares? This is fun, my English friend. This is what we're made for. Finding things ordinary mortals miss. With a tidy reward to boot. But first . . .' He pushed the books across the table, 'we must, he says, read. And read. And read.'

'About what?'

He opened the nearest book and stabbed his finger on a copperplate engraving that filled the page. It portrayed a struggle, a desperate one, two men at each other's throats, daggers in hand, fighting for their lives. 'About cut-throats. Killers. Assassins, near and far.'

TWO

The Gilded Circle

'You do talk like a Roman,' Valentina Fabbri said as the church bells chimed ten.

'I believe our teacher came from there.'

'See?' She pointed her pen at me. 'Making links. It's what you do. It's what I must do too.'

A call went out to the front desk. Two more little cups of coffee appeared. I wondered how many I might be expected to consume before this odd day was over.

'Have you heard from the hospital?' I asked.

'About what?'

'About the autopsy. You said he was being, well . . .'

I heard Eleanor's voice laughing in my ear. Once I fainted when I cut myself shaving.

'Dissected, Arnold. Cut apart. It's what happens in such circumstances. Godolphin had been drinking, he was wounded, he was dead in the *rio*. They will conduct tests that doubtless tell us many other facts in time. These, I think, are enough for now.'

'The weapon?' They always asked that in crime books and I was suddenly keen to know more. 'Have you found it?'

'It was in his chest. A dagger. A stiletto, a very fancy one Godolphin had been given by a mysterious admirer. You know of it already, I think.'

'I'm a bit squeamish,' I admitted, feeling it as well.

'A slim blade. Long. The man suffered two blows. The first minor, a cut to his arm. The second much deeper. It seems a stiletto in the heart is what we must deal with in order to resolve this mystery.'

'In the heart?' I gasped.

She gave me a curious look. 'None of this has been made public yet. All the press have been told is that he was injured.'

I sipped half the coffee and all the tiny glass of water that came with it, wondering who she thought I might tell.

'Do you know how Godolphin came to find you here?'

'I only know what he said when we met.'

'Which is?'

By now I'd had sufficient time to think through how I'd tell this story. My way, that was important. 'It seems my name was mentioned by a man called Wolff, who sold him the material in question. It appears the fellow had some connection with Kew and discovered I'd retired to Venice.'

'Who is this Wolff?'

'I feel we're getting ahead of ourselves.'

'You mean the fact that you knew Godolphin at Cambridge was a coincidence?'

'As I said, I didn't know him. Cambridge takes in thousands of students every year.'

'Did you envy him, this professor?'

An odd question. 'Why would I?'

Her frown was much the same as Luca's, and the quick shrug of the shoulders. 'He was famous. He had riches. Women, young women at his behest, it seems. An academic reputation.'

'I believe you'd find a good number of true academics who might debate that last point.'

'All the same . . .'

It was important to get this clear from the start. 'I have never envied anyone. I was fortunate to pass a pleasant working life in the company of a woman I loved more than anything on this earth. Now I'm lucky enough to be here, a widower in the place of our dreams. Without Eleanor it still feels like home, which is how she'd wish it. Even if Marmaduke Godolphin weren't lying in the Ospedale Civile all cut about by scalpels and saws, I would never have exchanged places with him. Not for one second.'

She finished her coffee. 'Continue with your story, please. I find it . . .' she gestured, 'intriguing.'

LUCA VOLPETTI APPEARED UNABLE to shed more light on our strange commission. Instead we enjoyed the rest of our lunch in genial banter about the city, the weather and local politics. Finally Anna brought us a couple of portions of almond and honey cake as an apology for the expense of the wine. After that, my friend threw on his *tabarro* with a melodramatic flourish, then his floppy hat and scarf, and sped off to an assignation with the lady lecturer in Middle Eastern studies, who lived around the corner. Her husband, it seemed, was away in Milan for a few days and she longed for company.

I was left to mull over the fact that Marmaduke Godolphin, a man I'd last seen in person four decades before, and then only at a distance, had somehow come to pick me out in a foreign land. Why? To offer a very welcome sum for my skills as an archivist in pursuit of two mysterious items hidden somewhere inside an equally enigmatic fonds.

None of this sounded quite right. I'd done some general reading about the sprawling Medici dynasty, as almost anyone with even a passing interest in Italian history might do. Gian Gastone was a sorry individual who spent his last few years watching his great dukedom fall to pieces, mostly from beneath filthy sheets in the Pitti Palace, drunk, obese and incoherent. There he was entertained daily by a series of young men and women dubbed the *ruspanti*, who pleasured him and themselves at their foul master's command.

The idea that such a sorry libertine had much in the way of

interesting correspondence seemed fanciful. Luca was incorrect in calling the old fool the last of the Medici. He had a sister, Anna Maria Luisa, who was there at his squalid deathbed and inherited everything. In an astonishing act of generosity, she willed the lot to the Tuscan state on condition nothing be removed from Florence. The *patto di famiglia*, or family pact, that she signed in October 1737 explains why so much of the city's cultural heritage remains in place today. Everything of note was surely in the local archives. Though given the chaos of the fellow's final few years, perhaps it was possible some documents had escaped the Pitti Palace into private hands. This was all idle speculation until Luca and I had sight of the material Godolphin was bringing to Venice, and the chance to ask him where on earth he had found it.

MY FIRST TASK WHEN I returned to my apartment near San Pantalon was to take a good look at the two books Godolphin had demanded we read. They were serious tomes, not the popular history for which he was famous. Expensive academic volumes with arcane terms instead of plain language, pages of endnotes, bibliographies and other appendices. Dull as ditchwater to the lay reader, frankly.

To give Duke Godolphin his due, he could tell a good tale for the popular market. I'd skimmed a couple of his books over the years and found them readable if decidedly loose with even quite well-known facts. The man gave thrilling voice to so many dubious stories – the evils of Nero and Caligula, the wickedness of Richard III, the idea that Caravaggio had to flee Rome over a fight after a game of tennis – as if they were gospel, rather than the invention of authors with an axe to grind, often writing years after the event. Still, this casual approach to historical fact did nothing to stem his sales. Every series on the box was accompanied by a bestseller in the charts.

The heavy volumes Luca gave me came with the kind of price tag that said no one outside a university library was destined to be a customer. But at least you might be guaranteed something that hoped to stand as academic truth, or a passably honest stab at the facts. My experiences as an archivist dealing with the people who produced these books, popular and academic, were, I must say, mixed. Some were diligent researchers who approached our fonds with open minds. Others simply knew what they were looking for and were determined to avoid any conflicting material that might challenge their version of events.

Quite where these two books stood on that front, I'd no idea. The most interesting aspect of both titles was the names on the covers.

Caroline Fitzroy and Bernard Hauptmann.

I could still picture them back in Cambridge, when we were young and they, at least, were carefree. Caroline was a vigorous woman, rushing everywhere, sporty, so she went rowing and threw herself into any society – political, cultural, argumentative – that would have her. No nights in the union bar or crawling the town pubs, at least as far as I could recall. Work, the encouragement and company of Godolphin and a path to that much-longed-for first – which she naturally attained – were all that mattered.

It was taken as read that she was sleeping with him. In that she was far from alone. No one batted an eyelid back then, or if they did, they made sure to keep quiet. Today, Godolphin would be hounded out of the university for his sexual antics and the way he clearly rewarded favours between the sheets with academic achievement. At the time, behaviour like this was, if not approved, swept under the carpet, left to undergraduate gossip, one of the rites of university passage. Academics had been talking their students into their beds for centuries. We were a historic college. Why kick up a fuss? Especially if being a bit on the side meant a better degree, more career opportunities, networking connections that could be mined and used later in life. As I said to Luca, archivists aren't the only ones to forge links.

Felicity, his future wife, was among his many conquests. She, I recalled, was quiet, a little shy, though she came to the bar and parties from time to time, not staying long, but looking as she wanted to if only she could pluck up the courage. Tall and slim, gazelle-like to my mind, she was prettier and more striking than Caroline, though not as quick or smart, or so the gossips said. A 2:1 like mine was all the future held, but ten years or so later, when she was working at the Beeb, she married her old tutor, visibly pregnant as she walked down the aisle. So perhaps, in the end, she got the prize she longed for. Though I rather doubt it was one many others wanted. Men like Godolphin, it seemed to me, are never cured of their habits. He was a womaniser, quite shameless about it. Later in life, some dark rumours had dogged him about sexual advances that had exceeded the lax norm of the time. A few paragraphs appeared in the papers. Two young women came forward to complain to the authorities, were listened to then dismissed as troublemakers, flirts incensed by Godolphin's rejection. The scandal never caught fire. Soon, another TV series came along and the shady stories were forgotten. Though not, perhaps, by Felicity.

Then there was Bernard Hauptmann. Tall, handsome, athletic, very American and another keen rower – he nearly made the crew for the Boat Race – he was the self-appointed captain of Godolphin's Gilded Circle (I so wish I could remember who invented that term, it was so perfect). He had a first-class brain in a first-class body and was sure to let everyone know. If I recalled correctly, there was a rumour he'd hitched up with both Caroline and Felicity, perhaps alongside Godolphin – literally even. None of us in the common herd really knew what went on with that lot. We were excluded socially and intellectually from their private delights. An audience in the stalls with the curtain firmly drawn across the stage.

Hauptmann got a first too, and was soon back in America teaching at Harvard. My archival activities only involved one trip across the Atlantic, to a boring convention in a boring city – St Louis if I recall correctly – never to be repeated.

Yet here they were again. Godolphin and his Gilded Circle assembled in Venice for some revelation in which I was to be a part.

Caroline's book was entitled *Alessandro de' Medici: A Duke Besmirched*. It was handsomely produced and priced that way too, with Vasari's portrait from the Uffizi on the cover: the doomed fellow, dark of face and demeanour, in heavy armour seated at a window, looking out at a distant view of Florence and the Duomo.

Bernard's seemed a little cheaper, in production if not cost. Its title was *A Medici Murderer of Merit*. The cover was a portrait of a bearded man in medieval dress, side on, presumably chosen for looks rather than accuracy, since, as the inside flap conceded, no reliable portrait of Lorenzino de' Medici could be found.

I poured myself a glass of wine from Danilo, the vineyard shop in San Barnaba, another tip from Luca Volpetti – a few euros a litre if you brought your own plastic bottle. Then I began to read.

Godolphin was notorious for setting his students against one another, allowing them to argue two sides of a disputatious case as if their very lives depended on it. I thought it a pretty good guess that in summoning his acolytes to Venice, he'd returned to his old trickery. Caroline Fitzroy and Bernard Hauptmann had, you see, approached the same story, two spectacular and controversial assassinations, and reached entirely conflicting conclusions. There were heroes and villains in both versions. Different ones, their gallantry and wickedness stated with such conviction that each title ridiculed as idiotic the idea that any other interpretation of events might be believed.

Caroline was convinced that Alessandro was a decent ruler of Florence in difficult times, and that his cousin Lorenzino slaughtered him through nothing but jealousy, personal and sexual. That Lorenzino – 'little Laurence' – was really, as his foes dubbed him, Lorenzaccio, evil Laurence, a beast, a killer, barely human.

Hauptmann believed he had firm evidence to prove the opposite: Alessandro was the monster Lorenzino claimed, a violent rapist, slaughtering his enemies in the city without trial, stealing their riches like a latter-day Caligula. Lorenzino, on the other hand, was a noble artist, a poet and author of elegant literature, including a heartfelt explanation of his reasons – good, republican ones – for slaughtering his cousin in bed. They couldn't both be right. In the heady, confined academic circles in which these two moved, side by side these rival tomes appeared tantamount to a declaration of war.

Here, it seemed to me, was the real reason Godolphin had summoned them to Venice. He was about to perpetrate some new trick on his old students, one that might set them at each other's throats again, as they surely had been four decades earlier. Then, if he was true to form, ridiculing the pair of them with the revelation – *his* revelation – that they were both wrong. And he, the great Duke Godolphin, knew the real story.

Luca's far assassins were Lorenzino and the street thug who'd stabbed and gouged Alessandro to death in Lorenzino's bedroom in another Piazza San Marco, Florence's this time. The near ones were the men who eleven years later hunted down the fugitive assassin in Venice and cut him to pieces on the Ponte San Tomà, just a few steps away from the Grand Canal and a couple of minutes on foot from my home.

There would be a third death in the story, the puzzling and bloody end of the great popular historian himself. The principal narrative hiding behind its predecessors, as it were. But I get ahead of myself. Behold, the archivist demanding logic and a linear appraisal of the known facts, from A to B to C. Admirable as this is, rationality and a direct approach to the strange death of Marmaduke Godolphin may tell you half the story if at all. It was vital I break the habit of a lifetime and duck and dive between people, days and the events of this curious week in a freezing Venice of outlandish regalia and multifarious masks, some obvious, some hidden, to the wearers themselves at times.

First, I told Valentina Fabbri, I must introduce the cast. After that, we would return to examine the Venetian assassination that went before, the Passeggiata of Blood, as Marmaduke dubbed it, unaware that his own would soon spill into the filthy grey waters of the *rio* San Tomà.

TWO DAYS AFTER MY lunch with Luca, I found myself invited for afternoon drinks at the swish hotel – boutique is, I'm told, the word – where Godolphin had placed himself and his guests. The party had booked all the available rooms in the Locanda Valier, a small establishment on the Grand Canal between the palazzi Giustinian Persico and Pisani Moretta. The location was quite deliberate. The places of the principal story Godolphin wished to explore, that of the assassination of the murderer Lorenzino de' Medici, were within walking distance, from Campo San Polo, where the fugitive lived in hiding, to the bridge over the narrow *rio* San Tomà, just around the corner, where Lorenzino – and almost five hundred years later, Marmaduke Godolphin – died on a cold, dark, bloody night.

The Valier was a fancy establishment, named after Silvestro, the 109th Doge of Venice, who supposedly lived there for a while. Unlikely, it seemed to me, given its modest proportions – the fellow's vast tomb in Giovanni e Paolo is almost as big as its dining room. But Venice has a long record of varnishing her history for visitors. Behind the freshly painted facade on the Grand Canal, which provided every guest room with a view, was a garden set with tables and, in winter, outdoor heaters among the slumbering palms and weedy lemon trees. Here was where we were ordered to meet to find out what was on the great man's mind.

The weather wasn't much above freezing. That morning I'd seen frost and ice on some of the water leaks in the *corte* where I lived, behind the Scuola di San Rocco. In the square around the corner where I went for a morning coffee and seasonal pastry, the Carnival folk were out already, strangers in a foreign city, wondering what to do. There was no sign of a Harlequin, Plague Doctor or Pulcinella in the Valier garden that afternoon. Only a shivering waiter in a white jacket trying to smile as he worked an outdoor cocktail stand. I felt quite out of place, and Luca, who met me on the way in, seemed sniffy about the establishment's general air. The international he could handle; it was the fake Venetian that offended him most. He had strong opinions on the subject. Only once do I recall hearing the man swear, and that was when I asked him if he'd ever set foot in Harry's Bar.

My friend had turned out in his flying black cloak and floppy hat. As usual, I was wearing my old duffel coat bought years back from Debenhams, when it still existed. We'd spent the morning preparing a spare room in the State Archives for the material our leader wished us to examine when it arrived from an unknown location on Monday. Two computers at separate desks were installed for us, both with views onto the empty convent courtyard between the Archives and the Frari church. I've no idea what it felt like to be a monk back when the place was an adjunct of the great basilica next door. All the same, sitting with Luca in that room, so quiet, so spare, the plain walls ruffled with damp blisters and a powdery white, I began to gain an inkling. It seemed a place for quiet contemplation and focus, a refuge from the busy city outside. A sanctuary where for centuries men and women might have peered at the seemingly small and insignificant in the hope of finding meaning. Or so we might have prayed. Both of us, as we trooped into the garden of the Valier, were perplexed by the task ahead.

Our great leader had yet to appear. Still, Luca insisted, we could always do what the English did best. Mingle, he said, which convinced me he barely knew us at all.

I had a good idea what Marmaduke Godolphin would look like when he deigned to join us. Along with millions of others, I'd followed his TV career across the years, first as a tall, rangy, almost thuggish fellow of film star appearance, traversing the globe in what was meant to appear hardship and occasional danger. Then, as he mellowed and his girth grew, his travelling style became more opulent, while his hair, always carefully coiffured for the camera, turned first salt and pepper and later acquired a shade of silver so perfect I had to wonder if it was dyed. He just wasn't on the TV as much as he used to be, and when he did appear it was often as an acerbic, angry talking head in an opinion slot, rather than fronting his history programmes of old.

'Why on earth can't we be inside?' Luca whispered as we assembled by the cocktail stand. 'It's bitter out here.'

My friend had no knowledge of Godolphin then. We were all at the great man's disposal. Placing us in some discomfort while waiting on his tardy presence was one means he had of reminding us of the fact.

To hell with him, it was the others that fascinated me.

Luca soon fell into conversation with George Bourne as the latter – now twice the breadth I remembered, with jowls that would have suited a Shar Pei – heard the magic word 'Negroni' and the two of them began to peruse the many fancy bottles behind the counter. Felicity was the one I couldn't take my eyes off. Back at Cambridge, she was the only member of the Gilded Circle I wanted to get to know. Perhaps even, in my embarrassed, stuttering northern tones, to ask quietly if she'd like to go for a bike ride somewhere. Or a drink perhaps. All a pipe dream, of course.

It wasn't just that she was the prettiest. She always looked so deeply sad, for reasons I could only guess at, reasons I thought I might dispel with a kindly word, a half of bitter in the Eagle and the tale of how Crick and Watson had once bounced in there to announce their discovery of DNA. It was never to happen, and she doubtless knew the Crick and Watson story anyway. But I was naïve back then. All that mattered to the young me was her face, so beautiful but rarely, in my experience, broken by so much as the shadow of a smile. She reminded me of paintings of Botticelli's maidens I'd seen in an art book, and later for real in the Uffizi. Pale skin that was almost translucent, features of seemingly perfect geometric proportions, set on a long, swanlike neck, though not quite as exaggerated as his Venus rising from a scallop shell. Her eyes were memorable too, blue, always wide, alert, seeking something just out of sight, which was why she never seemed to blink.

Four decades on, not much about her had changed. She stood, just as skinny as I recalled, leaning languidly on the brick wall next to a gas heater, alone with a glass of white wine, watching Caroline Fitzroy as she joined Luca Volpetti and George Bourne at the booze stand. There was canned music, Vivaldi as usual, from speakers wired through the trees. Her dark winter coat clutched her slender figure with the sheer cut and elegance that, to me anyway, spelled expense. Her hair, still chestnut brown, was shorter and sparser. Rings glittered on her bony fingers and a double string of pearls hung around her taut, slender throat.

I swallowed a slug of gin, vermouth and Campari then plucked up the courage to do something I'd wanted to do forty years before and never dared.

'My name's Arnold Clover,' I said, holding out my hand.

She took it and for the first time briefly smiled. A lone ray of winter sunshine broke through the clouds to cast its wan light on the freezing cold of the Valier garden. Unseen on the Grand Canal a vaporetto honked its horn. Somewhere inside the hotel a woman laughed, while overhead a raucous gull let out a squawk. I felt a little giddy, the way one does when distant past and present recognise each other from afar and realise they're not such strangers at all.

'You won't remember me, but I was at Cambridge at the same time as you. A different tutor. A different . . . set.'

That smile again, then, after shaking my hand with as little effort as possible, she said in a voice I thought somewhat croaky, 'Arnold

Clover. I do remember you.' She looked me up and down. 'You're not much different. You must have led a more monastic life than the rest of us.'

I was speechless for a moment. 'You look just as I recall, Lady Godolphin.'

'I'm too old for flattery, darling. And for pity's sake don't give me the lady crap. Everyone calls me Fliss.'

'Do you like that?'

'After a while you're not given much choice.'

'You have one now.'

She laughed and said, 'Then call me what you like.'

'I wasn't trying to flatter you. I don't think we ever spoke.'

'Yes, we did.' She took my arm and leaned forward. I could smell perfume, sweet and exotic. 'You asked me to dance at one of those dreadful evenings in the union bar. There was some godawful band on. I said no.'

Much as I racked my brains, I couldn't remember that. 'Sorry. How uncharacteristically forward of me. And ignorant to have forgotten.'

She frowned. 'I'm sure it was you. I think. I hope you didn't take it badly. The music was some appalling progressive rock nonsense. All dissonance, pretentious lyrics and strange time signatures. The idea anyone could dance to it . . .'

'I probably wasn't really asking for a dance.'

Another brief moment of amusement.

'I probably wasn't saying no because of the music. I was screwing my professor. Or rather he was screwing me. At least we're at the stage of separate rooms, so I won't have to deal with that again. Life was complicated enough back in Cambridge. I wouldn't have been doing you any favours.' I got the once-over again. 'And you wouldn't have wound up looking as . . . normal as you do today.'

'Normal meaning boring.'

'I don't know you. How could I tell?'

'Sir Marmaduke seems quite well kept for his age.'

'Are you married too?'

'My wife died last year. We were going to retire here together. I decided to come alone. It was the right thing to do. Nothing left for me in England.'

'Sorry to hear that,' she said automatically, then finished her glass of wine and held it out.

Without a second thought, I went and fetched another.

'Do you have the faintest idea what this circus is about, Arnold Clover?'

'You don't?'

'I wouldn't be asking, would I?'

Ah, the sharpness. That seemed new.

I recounted what Luca Volpetti had told me. There was a fonds, a collection of historic material Godolphin had somehow acquired. The two of us had yet to examine it, but some part was believed to be connected to two infamous assassinations in the Medici clan: Lorenzino's savage killing of his cousin the duke, Alessandro; and Lorenzino's own murder here, close by on the Ponte San Tomà. Who was the hero, who the villain? Who ordered Lorenzino's murder in revenge? That was still in doubt. There, it seemed to me, lay the puzzle. Opinions differed. Particularly among her fellow former students, Caroline Fitzroy and Bernard Hauptmann.

Her husband was of the firm opinion that an important new revelation lurked somewhere among the material he'd acquired. What it was, neither of us could guess. I was to join Luca Volpetti in searching through the collection sent to the State Archives, trying to find the proverbial needle in what my Venetian friend, ever more nervy as the moment of truth approached, suspected might prove a rather impenetrable haystack.

'I'm through with history,' Felicity said. 'Gave up on all that when I married him.'

'You make those TV programmes of his.'

She touched my arm again and there was, very briefly, something coarse in her manner. '*Made*. Duke hasn't managed to get a series greenlit for eighteen months. It's driving him nuts. I was executive producer, for him and others. Which means he's the only one out of a proper job right now. All I do is hire and fire and sign off the invoices that cross my desk. That's show business, love. More business than show, as always. Don't mistake it for anything else. The days of educational television are gone. Now we're shovelling shit to the masses, handing the proles their soma. What did you do before you fled?'

There was a cynicism in place of what I thought of as her innocence back in Cambridge. But perhaps that was my naïvety again.

'The kind of thing Marmaduke seems to have searched me out for. I was an archivist. I found things. Documents. Hidden links. Truths that lurk beneath the surface, perhaps.'

'And that's what you're going to do for Duke? Be a kind of . . . researcher?'

'Possibly. Until we receive clearer orders, I haven't a clue. You'll be handling this new series of his and you don't know what it's about?'

That laugh again, cynical and cold this time. 'If there is a series. My husband always likes to keep his cards close to his chest. It doesn't matter anyway. I'm done after this.'

I didn't know what to say. From what I recalled, she was quite senior in the BBC.

'You're retiring?'

She cackled. '*Being* retired. The face no longer fits. Unlike my husband, I'm considered "woke". Or to put it differently, I oppose hanging, lying, cheating and blaming foreigners for every misfortune we've happily brought upon ourselves these last few sorry years. Nor do I have the Union Jack flying in my office. The flaggies rule, in case you hadn't noticed. There's a purge worthy of Stalin going on. Don't you read the papers?'

'Not any more.'

'No matter.' She was doing well with the wine. 'Apart from the *Guardian* and the *FT*, they wouldn't tell you half the story anyway. And who reads those? The rest are on side, as they say. This last piece of Duke's nonsense I'll see out if he manages to sell it. Then I resign. Once they organise a suitable pay-off and agree to honour every penny of my pension. Not that anyone will notice or care, nor will I be able to talk about it or else they'll snatch my money back.'

'Perhaps you could work for someone else.'

She glanced back at the hotel, as if expecting her husband to make an appearance. 'Too old, too set in my ways. Too . . . unalluring. Besides, I fear I'm getting shoved out of the creative side altogether. A while back I caught him on Zoom talking to some starry-eyed young thing from America. About producing. Seems she's flown here from New York. I assume the poor mite's familiar with the extracurricular duties Duke expects of his female assistants. Oh look. Another face from the past.'

It took me a moment to recognise Bernard Hauptmann as he hobbled out of the hotel. Gone was the steely athlete of his youth. In his place was a man who looked decidedly ill, limping into the garden wincing with some pain. His hair – always fashionably long in Cambridge – was now reduced to a monk-like fringe around a shiny bald pate. Still, Felicity Godolphin looked pleased to see him.

'Now, *he* certainly won't remember me,' I said.

Hauptmann caught her eye, beamed like a man suddenly relieved of a discomfort and waved a hand. A gesture, a smile from Felicity in return. I was trained to notice small details. It wasn't hard here.

'You kept in touch?' I asked, trying not to sound disappointed, because, to be honest, I wasn't, not really.

'Very much so.' She winked. 'Duke's not the only one who can play those games.'

The Gilded Circle, it seemed, still lived their lives on a different plane to the rest of us.

'Do you know Venice well?' I asked.

The question seemed to surprise her. 'Not at all. He always brings one of his floozies when he comes here. I used to be the room-mate for Paris and Rome, but those days are gone. I told you. Separate beds. I wonder why he asked me along at all, if I'm honest.'

'There's a painting I'd like to show you. Well, a series, to be more accurate. I love them. They're easily missed. If you had time tomorrow? They're in the Accademia. Not far to walk. Sunday morning. The place will be quiet first thing.'

Another smile, the warmest yet. 'Is this revenge for me turning you down on the dance floor forty years ago?'

It was my turn to laugh. 'No. You're married to a knight of the realm. I'm a widower living here on a modest pension enjoying what the Italians call *dolce far niente*.'

'Staying amused while doing nothing. I always wondered if that wasn't just a way of trying to paint an acceptable face on boredom.'

'That's because you've not spent enough time in Venice. You speak the language?'

'A bit.'

'I'm never bored in Venice. It's impossible. I thought you might like a break from present company. They are beautiful paintings too. I go back once a month to look at them.'

She was peering at the hotel again. 'My son was supposed to be here. He's probably had another flaming row with his father.'

'Don't they work together on his programmes?'

She snorted and spilled some wine. 'Jo's in mortal fear of him. Duke thinks he's a useless fool. There is . . . history between the two of them. Not the kind you might think. I'll leave it at that.'

I maintained what I trusted was a discreet silence.

'Sorry, Arnold. The Godolphins don't do family ties. Never have.' She touched my hand. 'Apologies. It's rude to inflict that on a stranger.

If your paintings are really that good, and they won't get in the way of your work . . .'

'As I said, I don't know what my work is. Any more than you, it seems. Besides, the collection hasn't arrived. Sunday's still different here. A day of rest. Contemplation. Monday is when the fun begins.'

'If it is fun,' she murmured.

There was a commotion at the hotel door.

The man himself, finally. Silver hair; it *was* dyed surely. An immaculate dark blue pinstriped jacket and matching white shirt with a scarlet silk neckerchief to add a raffish touch. And, so help me, jeans and desert boots, just as he wore thirty-odd years before when he was starting out on his TV career.

'Seems you're about to find out,' Felicity said. 'Nine o'clock too early?'

No, I told her. It wasn't.

'Well, I need to talk to an old and much-loved friend. Before we all get our orders.' She waved. 'Bye, bye, Arnold Clover. Perhaps we'll have that dance one day. Who knows?'

AS I EXPECTED, GODOLPHIN did not deign to address his audience upon his immediate arrival. Instead, he was distracted by a nervous young woman, thirty or perhaps younger, very blonde, very chic in a fake fur coat. Patricia Buckley. The tentative producer from New York Felicity must have been talking about. From the way the fellow fussed around her, speaking to no one else for quite a while, his wife's suspicions appeared well founded. Godolphin must have been four decades her elder, not that it seemed to trouble him.

I took the opportunity to grit my teeth and do what did not come naturally: attempt to socialise. But with an aim. If I could be a kind of tour guide for Felicity Godolphin, there was no reason I shouldn't offer the same service to our host's other guests. George Bourne looked happily stuck into the drink, stumbling around the company. Caroline Fitzroy seemed less content. I remembered her as a dark-haired woman, Mediterranean-looking or so I'd thought. When I mentioned this that night in the Valier garden, she smiled and complimented me on my memory. So much better than hers, she said. Which was her way of telling me she hadn't a clue who I was. It turned out her mother was Greek and her father something in shipping. She'd been brought up in Surrey and rarely set foot in her mother's homeland. After Cambridge, she decided to specialise in Italian Renaissance history and found a professorship in Paris at the Sorbonne.

The bright, determined and distinctly ambitious young woman I'd seen in Cambridge was just about visible in her now. She looked jaded, dressed in old, shabby clothes that didn't fit too well, smoking constantly, her face fuller, very lined, her eyes tired. Age sucks the energy out of you, of course. But it seemed to me Caroline Fitzroy had lost it more than most. I asked the question I'd determined to put to all the Gilded Circle: was there anything in Venice they'd like to see? Something obscure, perhaps? An object, a sight, a memory that might not be easily found in a guidebook? If so, I might try to locate it for them.

She thought about this for a moment, then, idly, not expecting an answer, said she was thinking of working on a book about Renaissance courtesans. Not the whores, the street prostitutes, but the classier ones who slept with counts and kings, discussed philosophy, wrote poetry, were part of the establishment and paid their entrance fee in bed.

'It's just an idea,' she added. 'I haven't done a stroke of research.'

Perfect. I knew just the place to start.

'How about a look through the *Catalogo de tutte le principal et più honorate cortigiane di Venetia*? A quite formal directory of the principal high-class Venetian courtesans of the mid sixteenth century. They include a woman little known outside this city called Veronica Franco. She was, for a short while, the mistress of Henry III of France, an early proto-feminist and an acclaimed poet in her time who wrote in *terza rima*, which is—'

'I'm aware what *terza rima* is,' she snapped. 'I was reading Dante at school.'

I waited.

'You have all this here? To hand?'

'And much more. Monday. When the Archives reopen. I'll have the documents ready while we work on Godolphin's project. I'm sure you'll find them fascinating.'

'How much is this going to cost me?'

With that I looked deeply offended, which wasn't hard. 'Free of charge to someone from my old university. Even one who doesn't remember me. Though . . .' I put on my best smile, 'if you'd care to buy me a plate of eight-euro pasta afterwards, I'd happily show you the best place to find that too.'

Just for a few seconds she smiled, and I saw the years vanish, glimpsed a fleeting ghost of the bright and forceful young woman I used to see striding across Christ's Pieces. Suddenly I felt rather old and a little sad. Time can be cruel in its revelations as easily as it may be kind when it comes to recollections we'd rather forget.

'I really don't remember you, Arnold Clover,' she said. 'I'm starting to think that's rather remiss of me. Monday it is.'

'WE CROSSED PATHS IN Cambridge,' I told George Bourne, unable to think of anything original.

'Can't say the name rings a bell.'

He was ruddy-faced, swaying, half-cut – or perhaps three quarters – already.

'No reason it should. No reason at all.'

I told him as little as possible about my own past, only how I'd admired Godolphin's close little clique from a distance.

'The Gilded Circle,' he said. 'That's what they used to call us, or so I was led to believe. Did you . . . What's the name again?'

'Clover. Arnold Clover. I do recall the term. It was a long time ago.'

'Buggered if I can remember a tenth of it, frankly. Pissed or stoned most of the time. Or both. Served me fine, though.'

'You were in the Gilded Circle,' I said without thinking.

Bourne looked me up and down, trying to work out if that was a sly insult. 'Back then, I was rather clever. I do believe that stood me in good stead as well. It wasn't just Duke Godolphin's magic dust.'

'I never meant to suggest it was. And now you're at the very pinnacle of publishing.'

Bourne was a man who wanted to talk about himself, at length and in the fullest detail. I had to listen to a summary of his career, from photocopier boy to editor to publishing director, and how important he'd been in furthering Marmaduke Godolphin's career as a bestselling author.

'He owes everything to me, you know.' He ordered up another Negroni. 'Yes, the man can churn out a tedious academic paper. No denying his knowledge and his presenting skills on the box. But write intelligible prose for ordinary mortals?' He chuckled and spilled some of the drink down his shirt, barely seeming to notice. 'God, no. That's my voice you hear, my prose that sells him.'

'Should you not have an acknowledgement then?'

He grunted. 'First book I did for him he fawned all over me. Second, I was a paragraph. Third, a line. Nothing since. Takes all the credit for the writing and barely a sentence is his. All done for him, the research, the planning. Poor Fliss has been handling that side of the job for years and she never gets so much as a bunch of flowers from Tesco.'

I told him I never bought Eleanor flowers. She always said they were a terrible waste of money and often imported from Africa, which only added to pollution for no reason at all. Bourne didn't know how to respond to that until, after a little thought, he said, 'My husband doesn't like flowers either.' He waited to see if I was shocked. 'I wasn't joking, Clover.'

'I assumed you weren't. I'm a firm believer that happiness and contentment are everything. How people find them is their business. I was wondering . . .' The approach. It had to be made. He was heading for fresh drink before long and, I imagine, more interesting conversation. 'I live in Venice. If there's anything in particular you'd like to see, it's possible I can open doors.'

He laughed. Then he raised a fat finger and said, '*Death in Venice*.'

'It happens.'

'You know what I mean.'

Of course I did. But I wanted him to say it. George Bourne, it turned out, had a fascination with the film. Not the Thomas Mann book, which was, as he said with a sniff, only a short novella that scarcely counted as real fiction. The film was different. When starting out in publishing, he'd met Dirk Bogarde, the star, who was by then writing his memoirs. The two had got on famously. Bogarde had told him such stories about the shooting, and how Visconti's decision to change the profession of Bogarde's character, Aschenbach, from author to musician so improved the story and gave the director the opportunity for the film's gorgeous score of mostly Mahler.

'I would,' he declared, 'like to see the location.' He cast a glance around the Valier garden. 'Is it close? Doesn't look like anything this.'

'It's on the Lido. Across the lagoon. Nothing like round here.'

'There then, Mr Clover. Take me. How about that?'

The Hotel des Bains and the stretch of perfect sand with its cabins and sunbeds staring out at the long grey line of the Adriatic. So different now from the time Bogarde sat on the beach with his deathly white face.

'Bit cold for sunbathing in February,' I said.

Bourne stared hard at me. 'I think I do remember you. Did you play table tennis?'

'Never.'

'What the hell. I know every moment in that film. I want to see what the place is like now.'

'Tomorrow. We can take a boat late morning. There's an exceptionally good fish restaurant in the vicinity, though it's not cheap. A little beyond my budget, if I'm honest . . .'

'You can be my chickadee . . . That's not the right word, is it?'

'Cicerone.' I held out my hand. 'Do call me Arnold.'

He smiled at that, and we shook.

'I'll pay,' he cried, then pulled out a corporate Amex card. 'Or rather *they* will!'

I WAS DETERMINED TO tick off all the members of the Gilded Circle. To make a connection, an offer, to invite myself into their lives if you like. Forty years before, they'd appeared remote, untouchable, aloof. Now they looked like a bunch of upper-class tourists of a certain age, summoned to a city they barely knew for reasons they failed to understand. Perhaps it was altruism. Or a selfish desire on my part, a wish to get close to them and feel myself their equal finally. I'd downed a couple of Negronis too. Motives could wait until the morning.

Bernard Hauptmann was the last. I had to wait until Felicity left him to talk to her husband and the young American, quite fiercely by the looks of it.

'You won't recall me from Cambridge,' I said, for what I trusted was the last time that evening.

To be fair, Hauptmann did at least seem to try, and apologised when he couldn't.

'Getting old,' he said. 'Getting sick. Memory's going. Faculties. Losing it . . .'

'I've been reading your book about Lorenzino de' Medici. It didn't sound like something put together by a man who was losing anything at all.'

I'd omitted saying this to Caroline Fitzroy; hers was so dry and dull I didn't want to pretend I'd found it interesting. Hauptmann's at least had a spark of life.

'Spent ten years on that. Ten long, painful years. And? Be candid.'

'I thought it was well done. Carefully researched, well argued. It had . . . heft.'

'Heft?' His eyebrows were almost on his scalp. 'But not *entertaining*?'

'In its own way.'

He didn't like that one bit. 'Don't patronise me. I'm an academic, not a showman. That's what the old man always reaches for. The common herd. While the rest of us linger in his shadow talking to one another.' He watched Godolphin chatting away to his female associate, seemingly ignoring his own wife. 'Six months or a year he spends on the nonsense. Most of the drivel's the work of his private army of barely paid researchers anyway. He chose to be a performer. I'm not. If I wanted, I could pull his trivia apart in five seconds.'

'But you don't.'

He hesitated. 'Only once. I wrote a review of some piffle he produced about Dante. Absolute bilge. Put a little review in what I thought was an arcane historian's newsletter with barely a circulation to speak of. Two days later, I have him on the phone, furious, saying if I didn't pull every word, he'd kill me.'

I blinked. 'Really?'

'A few days after that, I get another call from someone on high reminding me that academic tenure can, in exceptional circumstances, be revoked.'

This was news to me. 'How could a review in a small journal possibly count as exceptional circumstances?'

'Duke Godolphin has a fragile ego and friends everywhere,' Hauptmann said with another dark glance in the man's direction. 'Or rather, not friends but people who owe him. Or maybe they're scared. I've kept my opinions to myself. For now. The time will come.'

I made my offer. To search out something special for him in Venice.

'Why would you do that?' he asked.

'B-b-because . . .' Damn the stutter. It returned whenever it felt like. 'Because I love this place. I like to think people leave it with some distinct memory, other than San Marco and the endless crowds of the Rialto.'

'Duly noted. I have other plans.'

'Wh-whatever time suits . . .'

'Are you hard of hearing as well?'

'No.' I was starting to take a dislike to Bernard Hauptmann.

'How long have you lived in Venice, Clover?'

'Three months.'

'For fifteen of the last twenty years, I've been a visiting lecturer at Ca' Foscari. A month or more each year. And you're offering me a sightseeing tour?'

Godolphin was on the hotel steps, tapping a cocktail glass with a spoon.

'Nice talking to you,' Hauptmann muttered, then wandered off in the direction of a furious-looking Felicity, now on her own, gripping a wine glass as if, on this chilly Venetian night, it was the most important thing in the world.

THREE

The Passeggiata of Blood

'Very generous of you,' Valentina said, 'to offer to show them round the city. There are tour guides who do that for a living. I have a cousin, Paola . . .'

I was to learn she had an entire battalion of cousins.

'I'm sorry if you feel I'm stealing Paola's business. It's just that they all looked a bit downcast.'

That shrug again. 'Some people are made that way.'

'Made. Exactly. I had an inkling it might be a good idea to get them out of Godolphin's orbit, as it were. As I told Bernard Hauptmann, I really don't like the idea of people going away from here disappointed. Many do, you know?'

She waved a dismissive hand. 'Only the dull and the idle. And anyway, we don't want them back. That's all there was to it? A kindly offer on your part?'

I wondered what to say.

'Arnold?'

'F-f-forty years ago, I was a scruffy, impoverished grammar school kid watching them all strut around Cambridge as if they owned the place. Affluent, starry, privileged and they wouldn't give me the time of day. Now they were here. A place I know better than any of them, Hauptmann apart. Perhaps I felt I was making the point that I was finally their equal. I don't know. It just seemed the obvious thing to do.'

'As if they'd make you an honorary member of the Gilded Circle?'

'That,' I said rather snappily, 'could never happen. I'd had a few drinks. I was expected to talk to them. It was all I could think of to say.'

She scribbled something on her pad.

'You still like the wife? Felicity? You find the lady alluring after all these years?'

More coffee arrived. I pushed mine to one side. 'She's a very striking woman. A memory from the past. I may have dreamt about her mildly before I met Eleanor, but that was long ago, and she was always well out of my class. I was simply sorry to see she still seemed miserable.'

'You find women who look despondent attractive?'

That was uncalled for. 'Not at all. I don't like the thought of people being unhappy. Men or women. There's too much pain in the world already. I particularly dislike it when they're made that way by others, especially those who are meant to be close to them. You see it so often. Broken families. Marriages dead yet kept on life support. When both parties would be free and happy if they simply arranged an amicable divorce.'

She made another note, of what I couldn't guess. 'You are aware, Arnold, that most murders are committed in a domestic setting? A man kills his wife. A wife murders her husband or pays another to do the job. Lovers. Relatives. Those closest to you are always more dangerous than that hooded stranger in the street.'

'A *masked* stranger here right now, I believe.'

Carnival. Half the city seemed to be walking around in disguise.

'True,' she said. 'Godolphin still had his mask when they found him. A plain *bauta*. White, originally. Full face, no hole for the mouth. Only the eyes. Not something one wears for a party since you can't eat or drink. Would you like to see a photograph from the mortuary?'

I almost jumped out of my seat and shrieked, 'Must I?'

She shrugged. 'The thing was collected from a local maker two days before. By this American assistant of his, Miss Buckley. Along with masks for all the others, all ordered ten days ago. He had the event well planned, it seems. He hired all the costumes. He'd even asked people for their measurements.' She checked her notes. 'A variety of dresses and old-fashioned male outfits. Then, at the last moment, for you.'

'And Luca,' I added. 'We were staff. The others were his guests, I suppose. He changed his mind.'

She flicked through the pages. 'Scaramouche for Volpetti. Yours was the Plague Doctor.'

I was starting to sweat. 'Possibly. We didn't wear them, as it happened.'

'We've a witness, the only witness, a worker from one of the bars going home. Around midnight he saw a man who could only be Godolphin arguing with someone near the San Tomà bridge. Someone wearing a black cloak and hood. That's all we know.'

This was news. 'But you think Godolphin was wearing his *bauta*?'

She turned the computer screen to face me. A white mask, stained dark red around the eyes and mouth, splatters on the cheek. I think I must have shuddered. 'You're not good around blood, I see.'

'No. The reason I mention it is . . . if Godolphin was wearing a mask, how could someone be sure it was him?'

The frown again. 'The thing has a lanyard. It was round his neck when he was found, not on his face. How many men were hanging round there that night dressed as a doge?'

I had no answer to that. 'Perhaps someone was simply out to commit a murder. The first victim they met.' She seemed unwilling to divulge any more details, so I had to ask. 'You seem reluctant to consider this might just be a lunatic cut-throat. The kind of street thug who killed Lorenzino de' Medici.'

She thought for a moment, then said, 'True. I am reluctant. This is not the Wild West. We no longer have cut-throats. Your Medici was killed on purpose, by an assassin who stalked him, not a lunatic at large. My present corpse happens to be an English aristocrat with many enemies, a good few of them here. Please, Arnold. Does it make the least bit of sense that a stranger would kill a man this way for no good reason? Here? In Venice?'

'I don't know. I'm an archivist. Retired. Not a detective, whatever you may feel. I must say . . . if you've never dealt with murder, shouldn't you call in someone who has? Someone with experience?'

That amused her. 'Touché. A lack of experience is not the same as a lack of understanding. I can read. Files. Statements. Procedural reports. This case is not complicated. It's merely . . . foggy. An unexplained death. A conundrum, something we are long familiar with here. Between the two of us, I believe we can blow away these mists. If I fail to make headway, then perhaps someone else outside will be brought in. I doubt that's going to be necessary. A culprit will be found soon enough.'

Ah, I thought. So that's why you're so anxious to put a name on the charge sheet in a matter of hours. Nothing to do with your husband's menu. If you don't, they'll call in someone from the mainland to take over.

There was the sound of voices beyond the door. Men, joking in coarse Venetian. Valentina went and looked. Two young officers in uniform were holding up a drunk in the costume of Pulcinella, black mask, red scarf, tambourine in one hand, vomit down the front of his baggy white suit.

'What did he do?' she demanded.

'Can barely walk,' said one of the officers, holding him at arm's length. 'Keeps throwing up. Hotel's kicked him out.'

'Fine the idiot,' she ordered. 'Take him to a cash machine and get the money. Then put him on a bus out of here with a warning that if he comes back, he'll answer to me.' They saluted. 'And make less noise. I'm busy.'

'Capitano!'

They dragged their prisoner down the corridor.

'Carnival,' she grumbled as she went back to her seat. 'Bad enough at the best of times. And now I have your English mystery to deal with.'

'It's not actually mine, is it?' I said with what I hoped was an indication of annoyance.

'Then whose? Hauptmann never took up your invitation?'

'No. He seems to think he knows the place already.'

'No one knows Venice completely. Not even those of us who were born here. *Non basta una vita.* One lifetime isn't enough. And the others?'

This seemed exasperating.

'I fail to understand why you're throwing all these questions at me. Surely they'd be better asked of Godolphin's guests?'

She tapped something on the keyboard then wheeled round the screen of the computer. There were six video frames frozen there: Felicity, Caroline Fitzroy, Bernard Hauptmann, George Bourne, Patricia Buckley, and Jolyon Godolphin, Marmaduke's son.

'I've interviewed them all. More than once. To no avail. We have statements. I have no reason to believe any of them. A good officer always checks one story against another. Now continue with yours. Only the relevant parts, please. We have one day, remember?'

I found that amusing. She looked surprised.

'Did I say something funny?'

'How do I know what's relevant? How, for that matter, do you?'

Her head bobbed from side to side, accompanied by a quick frown. Another Italian gesture I'd come to recognise ... *fair point.*

'I feel your free supper slipping away from you, Arnold Clover. But carry on. Tell me about our dead man's piece of theatre.'

* * *

THE LIGHT WAS ALMOST gone, a winter evening falling all around. Godolphin was ready to make his great announcement. Patricia Buckley stood by his side, still nervous, shivering in her heavy winter coat, a large placard in her hands, the back turned towards us. Felicity watched from the wings, Hauptmann alongside her. Caroline Fitzroy had started talking to Luca. Bourne was at the bar. Then I saw a new figure emerge from the hotel, young, angry, marching forward into the little gaggle. Jolyon Godolphin, I recognised him from the TV. He had less hair than his father, forty or so years his senior, less presence too. On the box he never looked quite comfortable. Nepotism was not, it seemed, a good way of casting TV documentaries.

We waited in the cold, glasses in hand. Godolphin, at least, seemed oblivious to the temperature. Part of the act: the world traveller, used to roughing it.

'I assembled you all here for a reason,' he declared with a wave of his arm, in the same booming voice he used on TV.

'A reason?' George Bourne called out. 'That's a disappointment. I thought you were paying us all back with a freebie finally.'

The man from publishing looked distinctly unsteady on his feet. No one laughed. Godolphin glared at him with a cold and supercilious malice, then, with a dramatic flourish in that aristocratic stentorian tone of his, boomed, 'The Passeggiata of Blood. This is what I have for you tonight. The opening episode of an entertainment that we will conclude when our archivists . . .' to my surprise, he gestured first at Luca and then, with a quick wave, in my direction, 'have done their work.'

With a curt gesture, he motioned to the young woman by his side. After a twitchy shake of her head, she flipped round the card. It was a design for the titles of the TV series: Godolphin in a straw gondolier's hat, a dark Venetian alley behind him, a bearded man wounded, blood around his throat, crouched over what looked like the bridge around the corner, a masked villain thrusting a dagger into his chest. The title was in a fancy script. One oddity: no mention of the BBC there, only the name of one of those new American networks.

'The Passeggiata of Blood shall be my most ambitious, my most earth-shattering work to date.'

Bourne choked on what looked like a fresh Negroni, then yelled, 'Earth-shattering? It's history, dear boy. Pop history at that. Also, never use foreign words in the title, Dukey. The English hoi polloi won't have a clue what you're talking about.'

'Caroline.' Godolphin ignored him and instead raised a glass to his old pupil. She, without a smile, did the same. 'Bernard. What I intend to reveal shortly will shock you. Will shock the world when it becomes public. Reputations . . .' he stared at them and smiled, 'will be redrawn. Of the living and the famous dead.'

Felicity stepped forward, another full glass of wine in her hand. 'Oh for God's sake, Duke. You're not on the box now. Say what you have to say and let us off the leash. Some of us have tables booked for dinner.'

'All in good time, my dear,' the great man said with a nod. 'First we must walk in the footsteps of murder.'

LUCA AND I HAD an idea what Godolphin was up to that night, though we'd not the faintest clue he'd go about it in such a hammily dramatic fashion. It was that old tour-guide trick. Following in the footsteps of historical infamy, in this case the assassination of Lorenzino de' Medici, or Lorenzaccio depending on your point of view.

As an archivist, I'm familiar with the idea that most history is received third hand. Rarely is it written by contemporary observers who have witnessed the events let alone participated in them. Much of what we think of as historical record is distilled instead from evidence and guesswork years after the incidents in question. First-hand accounts, the words and thoughts of the protagonists themselves, are sadly rare.

In the case of the assassinations at the heart of the present tale, however, we possess two extraordinary documents written by the hands that wielded the bloody blades. Lorenzino's apologia after he'd slaughtered his cousin in bed we'll come to in a while. Godolphin was focused entirely on the remarkable account of one Francesco Bibboni, the hired killer who slew the unfortunate fugitive a short walk away from where we began our journey that dark and bitter night in the Valier garden. Bibboni, who died safe in bed at the age of eighty, wrote down every step, from the men he murdered before coming to Venice with a fugitive Medici in his sights, to his narrow escape from the bloody deed itself.

As we walked out of the hotel into the shadowy lanes that led to the Rialto, Godolphin took us through the man's flat and unrepentant retelling of his quest to hunt down and kill the elusive Medici noble. Lorenzino knew he was a wanted man. He'd spent four careful years hiding out with close friends in Venice, a city at social and political odds with Florence where, in the commentaries being written by Medici hagiographers, he was nothing but a murderous villain, harboured by enemies.

Marching ahead in full TV mode, Godolphin grew into his showy narrative, his voice thunderous with thespian power and certainty as he told his tale. Bibboni was, it seems, a careful and professional hit man, taking weeks to choose the moment to pounce, determined to slay the wanted Medici then escape the equally vengeful Venetians as quickly as he could once the job was done.

Twice, Godolphin explained, he and his accomplice saw the opportunity to kill Lorenzino but backed off for practical reasons. Once was during Carnival, on 3 February 1548, when the doomed Lorenzino dressed as a gypsy woman to join a party on horseback jousting in one of the *campi*, an event too public for Bibboni's liking. Later they came across their intended victim as he headed off for a romantic assignation, only to decide they lacked the correct weapons for the job.

All this Godolphin recounted in true TV historian fashion as we walked through the stygian alleys towards the Rialto. The way ahead opened out. I recognised the doorway to the church of San Polo to our left. This was the *campo* of the same name, full of noise and Carnival-goers, many of them in costume. It might have been the sixteenth century again.

'It is the second Sunday of Lent, February the twenty-sixth,' our leader declared. 'Imagine.'

As I sat in Valentina Fabbri's office remembering that evening, I couldn't help but shiver. The twenty-sixth was a Sunday this year too. Duke Godolphin would die a few days later.

Timing. He possessed it to the very end.

We came to a halt just after the church, at the point where the square opened out into the broad piazza it had been for centuries.

Godolphin gestured towards the figures there, most of them in medieval costume, milling among the electric lights, spilling into the shadows. 'The Passeggiata of Blood begins.'

CAMPO SAN POLO IS one of the city's larger squares, crossed by locals and tourists on their way between the Rialto, the Frari and the Accademia. But this was February, Carnival, and the place was more animated than I'd ever seen. Strings of fairy lights dangled from the trees and the walls of the taller houses on the three sides facing us. A busy temporary ice rink occupied a good portion of the far end. Around it stalls sold drinks, beer and mulled wine, hot food, salumi and cheese. Small dogs dashed through the forest of legs, yapping constantly, chased by giggling children, happy in the holiday night.

Godolphin brought us to a halt outside a café close to a broad and shadowy *sotoportego* that led to the Rialto. The bar was packed, all the tables outside occupied, almost everyone in costume. George Bourne was the only one in the party who pushed his way through to the bar to grab a drink. In my thick winter duffel coat, jeans and a fisherman's woollen hat bought from a cheap shop in the via Garibaldi, I still felt freezing. My sense of foreboding was not helped by Luca staring right at me with a look that seemed to say: what have we let ourselves in for?

The lecture – or rather the TV episode in its draft script form – continued. 'Almost five centuries ago,' Godolphin declared, 'this same café was a shoemaker's shop, a place where the sly Francesco Bibboni had made himself welcome over the previous weeks. The villain was an organised, methodical man. He had a reason. The tall building to our right was where Lorenzino had come to live, still cautious, hiding away with a bodyguard and another escapee from Florentine justice, the rebel Alessandro Soderini. From the cobbler's, Bibboni had a good view of his target's home and was able to build a picture of his comings and goings.

'In fear of his life he might be, but Lorenzino, an arty fellow in his own mind, was no monk. He'd been carrying on an affair with a famous local beauty, Elena Barozzi, a married woman who'd borne a child, a girl believed to be his, not her husband's. He'd also formed a firm friendship with Giovanni della Casa, the papal nuncio to the city and a fellow poet, a useful ally in his bid to stay one step ahead of his pursuers. In a city like this, no man can hide for ever. Behold.'

We followed the line of his outstretched arm to the first-floor windows of a terraced house to the side, overlooking the stalls. There was a dummy behind the glass: a man in period costume wearing a tricorn hat. I felt even colder then. Our host was good at spiking anticipation.

'On that chilly day, Francesco Bibboni hid in the shadows where we now stand and saw Lorenzino come to this very window, towelling his wet hair. Ready to go out. To see his mistress, Elena Barozzi, without a doubt. The mother of his child, an infant he loved deeply and—'

'Oh for pity's sake,' Hauptmann cried. 'You're taking everything Bibboni wrote as gospel. Why? The fellow was a self-confessed liar, a crook, a thug who went round Italy killing for whoever paid him. Too cowardly to be a good soldier, just a hired assassin wielding a dagger in the dark. Nothing but a vile monster . . .'

A man was getting up from one of the tables. He was huge, six foot six, clad all in black, the costume of a pirate or a thug from a child's story, a scar on his cheek, fake or not I couldn't tell. With a slow and menacing certainty, he withdrew the long, narrow blade of a stiletto from his right sleeve, then marched over to Hauptmann, pushed up close to the puzzled American's face and placed the sharp edge of the weapon tight to the man's cheek. In gruff and heavily accented English he announced, 'My name is Francesco Bibboni, worm. Insult me one more time and after I've cut your throat I'll tear your head off and shit down the hole.'

There was that strange pregnant silence that comes before an act of violence. The only noise to break it was the screech of a metal table leg on ancient cobbles. Someone getting to his feet close by. A shorter fellow, stockier, also with a scar, this time dressed in what looked like an old soldier's uniform, worn and stained with God knows what. He had an ugly face with a scraggy beard, a spotted kerchief at his throat, a floppy round hat, the seams pinched, much like the one worn by the man still with his knife to Hauptmann's cheek.

'I am at work. Do not interrupt me, Bebo,' the one who called himself Bibboni spat at him. None of us moved. Godolphin watched, highly amused.

'Blow me, mate,' the newcomer cried. 'Why are you wasting time on this idiot?' He waved a fist at the pools of darkness untouched by the party lights of the Carnival. 'We've got better brains to spill than this pipsqueak's. Look up there. Our bloke's preening himself up for his tart. We got him this time, I reckon.'

Every eye turned to see where he was pointing. The dummy at the window on the first floor was gone. In its place was a man, tall, bearded, handsome. No shirt, a muscled torso, pale white. He had a towel round his neck and was running his fingers through his wet hair, looking out at the busy *campo*, scanning right to left as if worried by what he might see.

A man. Just an actor. And this was show, not real. Still, I confess I found myself shaking and shivering as if an icicle had fallen down my spine. I doubt I was alone.

Bibboni released his grip on Hauptmann. 'You know the game,' he said to his mate. 'We've practised it enough. You go off to pretend you're godly. That felon's bound to pass by the church headed for his bit of skirt. Bebo up front. I follow on behind. When you see me coming up quick, then . . .' He made a gesture, the blade crossing his throat.

Bebo rushed into the square and headed towards the church. Bibboni brandished his stiletto one last time at the American, then chuckled a villainous cackle and headed into the crowd.

Bernard Hauptmann cast a hateful glance in Godolphin's direction. If the man noticed or cared, he didn't show it.

Instead, he walked forward, removed the glass from George Bourne's hands – it was almost empty anyway – and placed it on the nearest table.

'O for a Muse of fire, that would ascend the brightest heaven of invention,' he proclaimed in that grand and so very English voice. 'A kingdom for a stage, princes to act . . . Why tell a story when you can show it?'

He gestured at his killers, now scattering through the night. 'Come. Our entertainment has begun.'

*   *   *

BEBO WAS GONE, SCURRYING in the direction of the church. The door to the building on the right opened and the man we'd seen at the window emerged, dressed in a dark velvet medieval jacket and trousers. A ginger-haired fellow, some years older, followed in much the same kind of outfit.

'Alessandro Soderini,' Godolphin said as he stood at our backs. 'Lorenzino's uncle. A hater of the Medici. Detested by them in return.'

At his urging, we began to follow behind the two doomed men, who were walking in line like dark cranes, just as Bibboni said in his later confession. The assassins were nowhere to be seen.

Luca nudged my elbow. 'This Englishman friend of yours likes to put on a spectacle, doesn't he?'

'Indeed he does.'

'Why?'

My friend was an expert in unanswerable questions. 'Because he's in show business, I imagine.'

The church of San Polo has little to admire from the outside, and barely seems a religious building at all from some angles. Within, there are paintings by Veronese, Tintoretto perhaps, the Tiepolos, and a spectacular timbered ship's keel ceiling over the nave. 'Of no importance', Ruskin declared with a sniff, though anywhere else in the world it might be thought spectacular. All the same, most visitors walk straight past to the more thrilling glories of the Frari. Not our reborn Lorenzino and his uncle. They dodged inside the door on the street. And here I had to remind myself once again: *storia* is both history and story. In Bibboni's colourful tale of the murder, which I'd read in full in Hauptmann's book, the villain's fellow cut-throat, Bebo, had hidden in a second door of San Polo and signalled to his mate when their victim re-emerged. But if there was a second door, I couldn't see it. Perhaps the church had been rebuilt – possible – or Bibboni's account was not as accurate as it appeared. The point Bernard Hauptmann had tried, and failed, to make.

Godolphin brought us to a halt a short way from the church wall. Then he began to retell a story that by now I knew very well. The background to the murders we were about to witness, the slaughter of Alessandro de' Medici in Florence eleven years earlier, the time Lorenzino spent on the run, living off the favours of the Medici's enemies. Time he spent writing flowery poetry and a lengthy, self-serving and at times quite contradictory apology for his crime, pleading that it was the fair and justifiable assassination of a monstrous, cruel and bloody tyrant, an enemy of the republican democracy Florence would become if only the Medici gang would allow it.

'He rattles all this off as if everything's accepted fact,' Luca whispered in my ear.

'I believe his point is that it isn't. And we're expected to confirm it.'

He tugged my sleeve. 'This, Arnold, is the strangest job I've ever taken on. Where are our murderers now?'

If it were 1548, they'd be thinking beyond the swift and deadly act about to take place and how they might escape with their lives. For me, the most striking part of Bibboni's tale wasn't the murder itself, which was told in a plain, matter-of-fact fashion, as if slaughtering men in the street was an everyday occurrence. As it was, it seemed, for the thugs involved. Far more extraordinary was what came after. These were now wanted killers, due for torture in the secret quarters of the Doge's Palace, followed by a cruel death between the columns by the waterfront outside the Piazza San Marco. Every employee of the Venetian state – no friend to Florence at that moment – would be searching them out, anxious for the reward that would surely come if they were seized.

Bibboni had found himself fleeing twenty city guards just minutes after he struck down Lorenzino. The two villains raced to the church of Spirito Santo on the Zattere and hid in the nave as armed men patrolled the lane and jetty outside hunting for them. Then, as the net closed, the pair raced to the Punta della Dogana and grabbed a gondola for the short trip over to San Marco and the Ponte della Paglia, the spot so usually crowded with tourists. After that, Bibboni hid out with an old acquaintance, explaining the blood on his clothes as the consequence of a street fight. Finally they were taken under the wing of the Spanish ambassador, an ally of Cosimo Medici, who would smuggle the pair out of Venice and across Italy to eventual safety and a fat purse from a grateful Florentine duke. It seemed a miracle that they escaped at all. Something that could only be done with planning and the connivance of others with power and money. Francesco Bibboni was merely the hand that wielded the sword in a long and complex trail of connections leading from who knows where to a pool of blood on the cobblestones by the Ponte San Tomà.

'Look,' Godolphin ordered. 'By the food stalls.'

There they were, Bibboni and Bebo, hats pulled firmly down over their brows, just two more Carnival-goers out for the night, or so it seemed, though both were watching the door of San Polo like eager hawks.

All this was rehearsed, timed like an abbreviated performance in an outdoor theatre. I saw Godolphin pick up his phone and tap the screen. Bibboni said something to his mate and Bebo wandered off down the alley towards the Frari. One ahead, one behind. Just as it was in 1548. At the front of the church there was a commotion. Lorenzino and Alessandro Soderini – part of a rich republican clan exiled, occasionally on pain of death, by successive Medici dukes – emerged, glancing up and down the lane. Then they moved off, the way we'd come. Through the shadows, Bibboni and Bebo began to follow. As, at a distance, did we.

WE WERE HEADED BACK towards the Ponte San Tomà. Perhaps for the evident reason – this was where Bibboni and his accomplice, Bebo da Volterra, cut down Lorenzino de' Medici that distant night. Though I couldn't help recalling that Godolphin had never built his career on the obvious. He was a debunker, a controversialist, a man always looking for the next argument, never frightened of confrontation or portraying wild theory as plain fact. Nothing pleased him more than being able to say, 'Everything you believed till now is wrong . . . Now let me put you right.'

The night before, wondering where Godolphin was leading us, I'd been scavenging my books and a variety of online sources – the reliable ones, of course. By the side of the bridge is a handsome ochre palazzo known today as the Casa Goldoni, the house of the playwright Carlo Goldoni, who was born there in 1707. It's one of the oldest substantial buildings in the vicinity, nothing much from the street but beautiful if you stand on the little bridge where the Gothic windows and arches, three storeys of living quarters, an iron water gate for visitors and a single very Venetian funnel chimney are visible. Around the corner is the small rectangle of Campo San Tomà with its restaurants and shops and constant lines of travellers to and from the nearby vaporetto stop. A short walk through the narrow alleys and you're by the vast basilica of the Frari.

Today, the Casa Goldoni is a museum dedicated to the city's most famous dramatist, with an eighteenth-century puppet theatre to maintain the dramatic connection. It's a slim tie, frankly. Goldoni was to die, impoverished, in Versailles, cursing his native city after a feud with another Venetian writer, Carlo Gozzi, whose work is now pretty much forgotten except as the inspiration for Puccini's *Turandot* and Prokofiev's *The Love for Three Oranges*. But I digress – forgive me.

The original name of Casa Goldoni was Ca' Centanni. Lorenzino would be familiar with the place since, a century and a half before the birth of Goldoni, it was home to his lover Elena Barozzi and her cuckolded husband, Antonio Zantani, a seemingly fey and moneyed aristocrat with a career in music and the arts that was nothing like as flourishing as he wished. Elena, on the other hand, was a woman of note in the city, a legendary beauty. She'd been painted by Titian among others, seen verses dedicated to her looks, supposedly those of a classical goddess. Small wonder, then, that Lorenzino, a ladies' man all his life, was enamoured of her. Though I was always puzzled by how the accounts I read of his murder – Hauptmann's among them – never mentioned the fact that he died almost on her doorstep.

I was duty bound to approach whatever new tale – or fabrication – Marmaduke Godolphin had in store for us concerning the death of the fugitive Medici with a degree of scepticism. Nevertheless, it was apparent to me there were holes in all the stories we'd been fed: Caroline Fitzroy's, Bernard Hauptmann's, even – perhaps especially – the memoir of the murderer Francesco Bibboni.

It was around three hundred metres from the door of the church of San Polo to the San Tomà bridge. Godolphin's actors froze in the street lights ahead, Bebo tucked behind the low, short crossing over the *rio*, Lorenzino and Alessandro Soderini in the middle on the steps, Bibboni a few paces short of them.

'Act Two,' Godolphin declared as we came to a halt, an audience for the drama about to unfold. 'A time for weapons.'

Lorenzino and his uncle heard and patted their waists. There were blades there, short, broad swords in scabbards strapped to their belts.

'The hunted and the hunters,' our leader continued. 'Differentiated by class, high and low. Differentiated by their arms too.' Lorenzino and Alessandro reached to their sides and withdrew their swords. 'A man who's being sought must make his willingness to fight clear and threatening. He carries his principal blade about him like a badge. Here, the *cinquedea*, a sidearm for self-defence, nothing else. Medici and Soderini, being nobles, have the finest, made by the Missaglia merchant-armourer family in Milan.' Lorenzino swept his through the icy night air. 'A short sword? Or a long dagger? Take your pick. This is made more for cut than thrust. You grasp your man, you wrestle, slash and stab. The blade is broad and heavy and will slice deep, through fabric, never armour. No soldier bears this weapon. It is protection for the shadows of the street, a device against cut-throats and killers in the dark.'

Bibboni stepped forward and withdrew from his right sleeve the dagger we'd seen before.

'A stiletto,' Godolphin continued. 'It could scarcely be more different. Our killer has about him a knife upon his belt – no man wouldn't in these desperate times. But the deadliest weapon an assassin carries stays hidden, in the fellow's capacious sleeve, waiting on its moment. The point as keen as a surgeon's needle, the cross-section here a diamond shape, only lightly sharpened. It is the tip that kills, a spike that can find gaps in a knight's armour, penetrate chain mail to enter the flesh within. One deep thrust may run right through a man's liver, open his guts, carve a fatal slice through a beating heart.'

A slash through the air. A cry. Bibboni shouted, 'Hey, Soderini. Take to your heels if you know what's good for you. It's your nephew we've come for, not you.'

Angry cries echoed off the walls of the Casa Goldoni, danced down the narrow canal, drowned in the grey water sparkling in the street lights.

'Bibboni and his accomplice have fine knives, above their station,' Godolphin carried on calmly, regardless. 'Double-edged fullered blades, damascened scrollwork on the pommel behind the wire-bound grip. Weapons beyond curs like them, one stolen from an aristocrat they murdered earlier in Vicenza, a paid job to settle a local vendetta. Bibboni's is the fancier . . .' He snorted. 'The provenance of that I'll save for later. By way of caution – why kill a man once when you might do it twice? – he has, with heavy-gloved fingers, smeared dried viper venom on his, a trick he learned in Rome from assassins once in the employ of the Borgias. Days hence, Alessandro Soderini will die of the poison in agony, bleeding constantly from his wounds, screaming his hatred for Cosimo Medici, Venice and the world.'

He took a step nearer the bridge. The actors knew their moves. They closed on one another.

'Lorenzino Medici, a fugitive for eleven years, will die here, steps away from the safety of his lover's home. In the arms of his mother, who will seem remarkably unmoved.' Godolphin waved a professorial finger. 'But listen carefully to his final words, because there the true story begins.'

He turned to his actors. '*Avanti!* Act Three! The climax of our tale!'

I FOUND IT HARD to watch, though the others seemed engrossed, even my good friend Luca. Violence, even when it's fake, disturbs me. Not just for the brute force, rarely necessary, but the way it grasps the attention, demands the spectator observe in horrified fascination. We love it, we hate it. We struggle to look away, and when we do so, we often half turn around and peek back through trembling fingers.

Bibboni went for Soderini first, screaming foul abuse in slang Italian I dimly recognised. Bebo blocked the exit to the bridge, waving his weapon, keeping Lorenzino there to await his fate. There were cries of anger, screams of pain. When I could bring myself to look, the one who played Soderini was limping off into the shadows towards Campo San Tomà.

Lorenzino was the star of this show, after Marmaduke Godolphin. His sword clattered on the stone steps, beyond reach, useless. We gathered round as Bibboni tried to deliver a convincing fatal blow with that long stiletto that seemed all too real. A stab meant to look like a thrust to the chest, though the chap clearly took the weapon under his shoulder. A cry then, too theatrical to be real, and his assailant vanished after his mate.

Had the real Lorenzino died this way? There was no way of knowing. Nearly five centuries separated us. But he did die, and on this very spot.

'Well, that wasn't exactly the Royal Shakespeare Company,' George Bourne said, staring at the groaning man clasping the railings of the bridge.

A woman shuffled through us, exercising her elbows against our ribs the way only a Venetian matron knows how. She was the mother, it seemed, Maria Soderini, sister, too, to the fatally wounded Alessandro, now elsewhere. A stern-looking figure in a black dress and veil, she stood over the dying man. The deed was done. The hunter had found his prey.

Godolphin ushered us close and mouthed the order, 'Listen.'

'Mamma, Mamma.' Cough, splutter. 'Now in this cold dark street I die. Forgive me. Bless me as I go to my grave . . .' It was amateur-hour acting, in reasonable English, an amusing little tableau of the kind one might have expected from a tourist show.

'We all die,' the woman said with a shrug and a quick frown. 'Best get on with it.'

'A little sympathy, please,' he begged then, with pleading, histrionic eyes turned to us all. 'Light a candle. Say a prayer, friends. I am so very young and noble. An artist and a patriot. I die in the name of freedom, and the man to blame . . .'

Godolphin stood over him, waiting. This was close to slipping into melodramatic comedy, and that, I gathered, was the last thing he wanted.

'The creature who brought me here . . .' Lorenzino cried, wiping his brow with what must have been fake blood. The red, just visible in the street lights, stained his forehead, and remembering his script, he dabbed some on his neck.

'Who?' the mother asked. 'Say his name.'

'The one who set me on this path in Florence eleven years ago. Talked me into killing sick, mad Alessandro. Promised me a safe passage here if only I stayed low.'

The mother booted him in the shin and got a squawk of furious pain in return. 'Instead, you father a child on some local slapper and walk round with your uncle like you own the place.'

'A little pity, Mamma! Blame the cruel villain who sent me. Who master-minded the killing of Alessandro and provided this . . .' He picked up the fancy stiletto in front of him. 'The same blade that takes my life. Who promised me so much then betrayed me to save his own skin . . . Aahhh.'

Much disgusting hacking and spitting ensued.

'A name!' the mother asked, just before Godolphin seemed ready to step in and demand the very same thing. 'Say his name!'

Lorenzino's throat cleared miraculously, and he declared, with the rhythm and clarity of a well-prepared speech, 'No. Great as I am, a poet, a philosopher, he is greater. For all his weaknesses, the boys, the perfidy. Genius comes with a demon in the blood. I fear to speak it for the danger such knowledge might bring you . . .' Another bout of coughing. 'As I leave this mortal life, to stain his memory with the truth, even though he kills me . . .'

'Go on,' Mamma said, and fetched him another kick that would have done justice to a pantomime dame. 'You know you want to.'

The dying man rolled towards her on the freezing steps and said, 'If you insist, dear heart. Buonarroti! Lodovico Buonarroti! Michelangelo as they call the villain now that he lives a life of luxury and fame, glorying in the light of the Pope's patronage and the adoration of the masses! This Michelangelo is the dog who lured these killers here and silences me now to save his miserable skin. I swear it. I can prove it, Mamma. Just look for the letter . . .'

He clutched his chest, then, with a final cry and a choking cough, expired.

Though not for long. With a jolly cry, the thespian sprang to his feet, wiping away the fake blood from his brow, bowing to his audi-ence. The mother too, and shortly after, newly returned, her brother Soderini and finally, with a flourish of their weapons, our two assassins.

We applauded, though out of surprise, appreciation or pure bewilderment I wasn't quite sure. Lorenzino passed round business cards for a theatrical troupe, the Commedia dell'Arte Padovana. Then Bibboni walked over and handed the dagger that had supposedly killed him to Godolphin.

'It's a fine weapon, sir,' he said with another bow. 'I was careful not to stab my friend for real.'

'A great and expensive blade,' Godolphin agreed, and secreted the knife up his own sleeve. 'A gift from a dear friend. We will see you later in the year. For the re-enactment in earnest.'

'The BBC!' Mamma cried.

Then the whole crowd of them were around us, holding out their hats for tips. I put in a few coins. So did Felicity Godolphin. The rest . . . I never saw. I couldn't take my eyes off Bernard Hauptmann. He looked ready to explode.

WE KEPT QUIET UNTIL the actors had vanished into the night, happy with their work and the money I imagine Godolphin was sending their way. Later, on my way home, I'd see them laughing and joking outside a charming little bar at the edge of Campo San Tomà, ridiculing the whole performance, from what I heard. Michelangelo, perhaps the greatest artist the world has ever known, a schemer and murderer? Who could possibly have imagined it? Or that the BBC of all people would broadcast such a ridiculous suggestion?

Yet great artistry often went with terrible, violent character. Just look at Caravaggio. And then there was the extraordinary Benvenuto Cellini, very much a part of this tale. The idea that genius was accompanied by madness and an almost psychopathic sense of distance from ordinary mortals was scarcely new or rare.

But back to the Ponte San Tomà. After our players had departed, Godolphin puffed out his chest and looked ready to speak. Hauptmann got in first with as slow and sarcastic a handclap as I've heard. 'You brought us all this way for a barrel load of bull? Come on. Michelangelo? Seriously?'

Godolphin sighed the way he must have done when he was disappointed by their student ideas all those years before. 'I regret to say, Bernard, your fantasies about Lorenzino are about to be exposed. As are those of poor Caroline. I doubt you need worry much. So few people bought your books, they're hardly likely to ask for their money back. Within academia, of course . . .' He coughed into his fist and smiled.

'You mean we're here to be humiliated?' Caroline Fitzroy asked.

'You're here for the truth.' Godolphin sat on the bridge railing, and I wondered if he was tempting someone to push him in. 'That's what we all want, isn't it? Personal humiliation is nothing next to that moment of epiphany when the past becomes clear and real. The truth is that Michelangelo, a firm republican, as we all know, was a part of Lorenzino's plot to murder Alessandro de' Medici. Later, our genius made his peace with Cosimo, Alessandro's successor, and the Pope, of course, and engineered the downfall of the fool he'd set up in the first place. He was a man of priorities, you know. There was work in the Sistine Chapel to be finished, *The Last Judgement*, appropriately enough. By the time our fugitive Lorenzino was hiding out in Venice, Michelangelo was the architect of St Peter's, with a great dome to design along with much else. But he still owed Cosimo in Florence a debt. An apology for arranging the murder of his predecessor and—'

'Evidence!' Felicity cried. 'You can't just pull all this out of the air, Duke. It's never been suggested, has it?'

'Not for a second,' Hauptmann said. 'The whole idea is ridiculous.'

Godolphin smiled and opened his arms wide, as if to say: really? 'Oh Bernard. Always so prosaic. Always so lacking in imagination. It was once ridiculous that a king of England, killed on the battlefield, might be found buried beneath a car park in Leicester. It was ridiculous that that same king, Richard III, was a hunchback, an invention of Shakespeare's, until they found his crooked bones. The world's full of the ridiculous until we dig up something that shows it's not. But I understand you're a doubting Thomas.'

With that, he smiled and gestured towards me and Luca by my side. 'You require proof. Our friends here will soon provide it.' He shuffled off the iron railing. 'So please don't think of departing Venice until you see the evidence for yourself. I am paying for your stay, aren't I? And we shall have a glorious evening, a *ridotto* no less, with masks and music, to celebrate the final revelation. Oh . . .'

There was another polished TV touch to his performance. The pause, the expectant hiatus before a revelation.

'Just so you know, Felicity. This is much too important a story for the domestic drones and budget of the Beeb. I'm selling it to the Americans, through Patricia here.' The young woman nodded and looked deeply uncomfortable. 'She will take full charge. Your services will not be required. Nor yours, Jolyon. I've never been a believer in nepotism anyway and it's time you both flew my well-feathered nest.' He turned to George Bourne. 'As to handing over a prize of this immensity to a piddling little British publisher with piddling little British aspirations—'

'What the hell am I supposed to do, Dad?' Jolyon Godolphin yelled.

Godolphin looked baffled by the question. 'Whatever you choose. Time to strike out on your own. Do like I did. Begin at the beginning.'

As if the Godolphins started in the same place as the rest of us.

'You're a charlatan,' Hauptmann declared, quite furious. 'You always have been. How you got away with your goddam tricks all these years. The lies. The things you stole and never gave credit for. The women.'

'The women?' Godolphin demanded. 'I never had any complaints.'

'Because they didn't dare,' his son shouted back. 'Christ, I—'

At that moment I recalled what Felicity had said about history between the two of them. His mother was soon on him, arms round his shoulders, shushing him into silence.

It was the strangest atmosphere. Part family feud. Part dark, surreal theatre.

'I'm out of this,' Hauptmann said. 'Plane home tomorrow.'

As he turned to go, Godolphin strode across the bridge, faster than any of us might have expected, and placed himself in his way, just as the fake Bibboni had earlier. He withdrew the long striking dagger from his sleeve and held it up to Hauptmann's throat, then, with a grin, flipped it round so it shone beneath the bright street light. 'Want to admire the workmanship? The design?' he said. I saw the weapon close up later. Godolphin must have flourished it to every one of us, he was so proud of the thing. It was handsome, ornate, convincing, the proportions perfect, blade to hilt, the patterns of the damascened work and the decorations as dainty as any piece of jewellery. 'This is part of the story too, Bernard. Something from the pen and mind of Michelangelo. Remember what he said? When someone asked him how he looked at a piece of marble and imagined it might turn into a David?'

'Tell me.'

'He doesn't. The statue's there already, waiting inside. The job of the sculptor is the same as that of the true historian. Not to create something. But to reveal it. You're not leaving. You want to see what happens next. You all do.'

The blade waved from side to side, at us as much as Hauptmann. Duke Godolphin stood there grinning like someone who'd just won the world.

I still struggle to erase that picture from my memory. The doomed man brandishing his fine stiletto, the point sparkling like something magical in the bright yellow radiance from the iron lamp above him.

A short time hence, that same sharp blade would aim for what passed as his heart.

AFTER A REVELATION LIKE that, Luca and I were expecting a briefing or at least an explanation from Godolphin before we set about our task. Which appeared to be proving that one of the most celebrated figures in history was, unknown to anyone for centuries, party to two infamous murders. Instead, he merely wandered over in the packed bar of the Valier – a wedding party had turned up and lent the place a cheerier air than it might have had otherwise – and told us he'd speak at greater length when the consignment he called the Wolff Bequest was in place in the State Archives the following Monday.

Luca appeared somewhat daunted by the man. I was determined not to be browbeaten.

'You won't remember me from Cambridge,' I said for the umpteenth time that day.

'You're right, Clover. I don't. But the late Grigor Wolff assured me you're good at your job. That's all I need to know.'

'Never heard of him.'

He shrugged and murmured, 'Doesn't matter. He'd heard of you. Monday morning. I'll give you more detail then.' He smiled and withdrew the stiletto from his sleeve again. It struck me that he must have had some kind of sheath for it hidden away there. As if he wanted the thing at hand for some reason. 'All you two need do is find me the original design for this. The letter that goes with it. And a later missive when the man changes sides. Both in the hand of Michelangelo himself.'

Luca edged forward. 'But how can you be so sure they're there?'

That smile again, and a wave of the dagger as if it was proof.

'I am. That's all you need to know.'

*   *   *

THE DARKNESS OF VENICE is quite unlike that of any other place on earth. A never-ending black emptiness that feels as if it might swallow you forever. The evening was raw, the cobbles so icy workmen were placing sand and salt on the bridges to stop people slipping. If one stumbled into the water on a night like this . . . It didn't bear thinking about.

Luca declared he'd make the long walk down to the Zattere to catch the night boat to the Lido. The Number 1 was closer but slower and would be full of the Carnival crowd.

We walked through Campo San Tomà to the Frari and from there past the shadow of the great church. There'd been a food stall or something outside the railings. Rubbish was on the ground, and nearby a bunch of English drunks leant against the wall eating pizza and swearing like troopers.

The corner of Calle San Pantalon, next to the cake shop of Tonolo, was where we customarily parted. The apartment Eleanor had found was just round the corner. My friend would carry on through Campo Santa Margherita and San Barnaba on to the Giudecca Canal. It was one of my favourite walks in Dorsoduro and another night I might have accompanied him to the vaporetto stop. But something about the evening had got to us both, and it wasn't just the manner and character of Marmaduke Godolphin. This bizarre quest had an edgy feeling about it. The atmosphere of anger and hatred lurking beneath the surface of Godolphin's party was unmissable. It was as if there was something malevolent lurking just beyond our reach, and we were meant to be the instigators of its revelation.

Luca stopped to stare into Tonolo's window. The following morning the shelves would be full of grand torte and chocolate creations. People queued outside for ages to buy a treat for lunch. Sunday still had a special feeling about it in Venice, in Italy really. There was a separation between the worldly and the personal we'd lost back in the place I used to call home.

'What have you led me into, Arnold Clover?' he said, gazing at our reflection in the glass.

'I . . . I . . .?'

With a smile, he clasped my arm and pointed to the counter, dimly lit inside. 'I was joking. What happened to that famous English sense of humour? On Monday I will arrive with *frittelle*. The only thing about Carnival I find worthwhile.'

'Doughnuts—'

'They are *not* doughnuts!'

'If I may finish . . . doughnuts have nothing on *frittelle*. Especially when they come filled with zabaglione.'

'Well recovered, sir. I will say one thing more about our business and then tonight is done. Your Englishman is either a genius or completely crazy. Or both.'

Or neither. It's funny how people always forget that possibility.

'Perhaps, Luca. But we're trapped, aren't we? We agreed. We said we'd go along with whatever madcap scheme he's cooked up. Too late to back out now. Also . . .'

He was a smart man. He knew what I was about to say. He nudged me with his elbow. 'Also, we both of us want to know if he's right, don't we? Like he said to that American. If what he says is true, we're about to be part of an amazing revelation.'

'Or a fantastic debacle.'

He nodded. 'Soon, I think, we'll see.'

FOUR

The Far Assassins

Sunday morning just after nine, rime frost like icing sugar dappling the railings of the Accademia bridge, wisps of thin mist wafting along the Grand Canal. A Number 1 vaporetto was making a graceful demi-tour towards the jetty. By the steps, handing out pamphlets for a concert that evening, stood a miserable-looking girl in a tired gold wig and grubby Carnival dress, the kind where the hips are exaggerated with some sort of hidden support. The few tourists around were taking pictures of her, naturally. She tried to smile but still didn't get a cent, just them taking her leaflets, doubtless to be dropped in the nearest bin soon after.

Felicity said no to a pamphlet but still handed the kid a couple of notes. 'God, what it must be like to be young these days,' she grumbled when we were out of earshot, heading for the bridge. 'I want to see the view.'

'Hard times,' I agreed.

'Harder than you know.'

It felt even chillier on the exposed rise of the bridge, the wind whistling through the canal mouth, the heavy form of Salute ahead of us, a grey ghost wreathed in the lagoon's soggy breath. The city had a smell to it that morning, never the noxious one the ignorant complain of – which is usually the work of a cesspit boat emptying a *pozzo nero*, or an accident of low water. This was Venice in winter, salt air, damp but fresh as the ocean, clear and so cold it felt like ice settling in your lungs.

She'd come dressed for the weather, a thick padded coat, dark wool trousers, a posh-looking beanie, and dark glasses, either to keep out the low winter sun or hide a hangover after what I assumed was a late dinner rendezvous with Bernard Hauptmann. The night of Godolphin's Passeggiata of Blood had taken its toll. The bill the old man was going to get for booze alone would have made me want to wear shades for days. Not that he seemed to mind. I've rarely seen someone enjoy inflicting pain on others quite so much.

My offer to Felicity, Caroline and Bourne did not come from altruism alone. Four decades on, something about the Gilded Circle continued to fascinate me. Why did they remain so connected to one another? Was it Godolphin's abuse that kept them together? Could they never escape the man? As a group they still seemed in some ways as distant and incomprehensible as they had in Cambridge. Yet here they were, in Venice. On my doorstep. Perhaps there were answers to be had. It was prurient, even shameful to try to pry into their lives and their private troubles like this. But curiosity was at the heart of everything I'd done throughout my professional life. I sought answers, truths, a logical explanation of events. Gaps and forgeries and broken links always troubled me.

Still, I hesitated that morning by the Accademia bridge. Then, in the deep breath of a stiffening winter breeze, Felicity Godolphin said, 'Let's get on with it, Mr Clover. Show me why I'm here.'

ELEANOR AND I HAD found the room by accident twenty-odd years before. It was our first visit, a penurious one but a revelation nonetheless. We stayed in a tent on a campsite across the lagoon in Treporti, taking the boat to the city. Ten days passed in a flash. Much of the time we were delightfully lost, taking the wrong vaporetti, forever wandering round the alleys, the squares, trying to make out the signs, to find some logic and sense to where we were and where on earth we might be headed. Venice seemed to know no compass, no concept of north and south, east and west, up and down. Only an endless tangled nexus of streets, lanes, passages and turnings described with strange terms – *sotoportego* and *rio terà* – that meant nothing to us then and appeared nowhere in our simple tourist Italian dictionary. We felt like children who'd sneaked through the gates of a hidden paradise only to find ourselves stumbling through an Eden we'd never imagined, knew we'd never conquer.

Even today, settled here, I sometimes find myself lost, especially in the tangle of streets that run west of the Rialto into a web of tiny twisting alleys populated by small shops and bars that seem little changed in decades. Part of the process of adapting to this city, of allowing it to work its way slyly into your blood, is that you accept being rudderless in its grip. No one truly visits the place: Venice allows you in and holds you prisoner. Only by abandoning yourself to the unknown shadows, the alleys yet to be explored can you hope to encounter the many recondite pleasures hidden from the light of day.

The nine canvases devoted to the story of the entirely mythical St Ursula are for me one of the greatest of those pleasures. They run round the walls of their own small room hidden away in the heart of the old religious charity building, the Scuola della Carità, that is now the Accademia, the greatest art gallery in a city rich with treasures. We hit upon Ursula by accident on that first visit. In the ensuing time, the gallery has undergone many changes, which meant that when I finally returned to live in San Pantalon, I had to ask directions to find her again. The paintings hadn't moved, though everything around them seemed to have shifted, which was a very Venetian thing to do. Every canvas had been restored so beautifully the gorgeous colours now shone more vividly than ever. It was as if the faces, the people and the story those works told were all real, contemporary, alive.

Felicity, who thought she'd been to the city twice, perhaps three times in her life, and then only briefly, stood in Ursula's small sanctuary inside the Accademia as amazed as we'd been when we discovered it. For me, the nine canvases of Carpaccio always seem like a fifteenth-century cinematic melodrama played out in dreamy scenes by characters who might be fellow passengers on the vaporetto; gateways into a medieval landscape that turns Europe, the rich background for the story, into a mythical Arcadia of palaces and throne rooms, great galleys and, in the end, a spectacular battlefield of slaughter.

'Tell me the story,' she demanded, and took my arm at the beginning of the cycle.

I'd no need. It was spelled out on the walls. Ursula, a beautiful Christian virgin, daughter of the king of England, is betrothed to the son of a pagan ruler in France. She agrees to the marriage on condition he converts. The two are blessed in Rome by the Pope. On their return, they're slaughtered by the troops of Attila the Hun outside Cologne, along with eleven thousand virgins accompanying them.

'That's an awful lot of virgins. Where did they find them?' Felicity said as we reached the great martyrdom canvas, Ursula on her knees praying as a rather handsome knight prepares to take her life with his arrow.

'Different times,' I suggested.

She had her finger to her cheek and was bent down to examine Ursula's sad face closely. The expression there always shocked me: acceptance, resignation, defeat. Felicity shook her head and said, 'The poor girl seems very fatalistic about her end, I must say. If it was me, I'd be screaming my head off and trying to scratch the bastard's eyes out.'

'Martyrdom. I never really understood it. Perhaps as an agnostic I never will.'

'Pluck up your courage, Arnold, and turn full-on atheist. It makes life so much easier.'

I imagine it would. Life without doubts must be comforting, if a little narrow.

'It reminds me of another scene from Venice,' she went on. '*Othello*. When he's about to kill Desdemona. That foul ingrate Iago's poisoned his mind against her, remember?'

I felt a shiver.

'All those vile whispers, none true, and the fool's going to murder his own wife for an infidelity she's never committed.'

'I wonder why Iago did that.'

She looked at me, puzzled. 'Why? All that matters is he did. And what was Desdemona's reaction when her idiot husband came to smother her? She forgave him. "Commend me to my kind lord: O, farewell." All over a bloody handkerchief. I'd have scratched his eyes out too.'

With a little effort I managed to prise her away from the violence and drama of the final slaughter and return to the earlier painting, a tamer one, that always fascinated me more. It was Ursula in bed, eyes closed, dreaming. A beautiful winged angel has entered her room, a bright and supernatural light behind him, and he's staring at her as she lies beneath the sheets.

'What's that in his hand?' Felicity asked. 'It looks like a gigantic pen.'

'A palm frond. It's the symbol of coming martyrdom. The implication is that once she's had this dream, she knows she's going to die if she chooses to carry on. Violently, with immense cruelty, which sort of went with the role.'

Felicity took a step closer and peered closely at the young woman painted so delicately by Carpaccio more than half a millennium before. The same face as the one waiting on a bloody death a few canvases along the wall. The face that so fascinated Ruskin when he was writing *The Stones of Venice* that he went half mad beginning to believe it was that of his dead lover. Though I spared Felicity that disturbing story.

'Here's what's bothering me, now you mention it,' I said. 'If she knows she's going to die . . . why doesn't she do something?'

'I imagine you can't scratch out the eyes of an angel in a dream.'

'No. But she has a choice. To acquiesce. Or to fight. Or simply turn back. Save her own life regardless of what others think. To be herself. Not a part of someone else's plan. Even God's.'

It occurred to me then that Felicity was starting to understand why I thought this place might interest her.

She unhooked my arm from hers and I wondered if perhaps I'd gone too far. 'You've led a simple life, Arnold. A humble one. Please don't take that as an insult. Or a criticism.'

'I won't.'

'The humbler you are, the more invisible, the more choices you have along the way.'

That seemed frankly ridiculous. 'We never had much money. We were never poor. But there was never quite enough. Our choices were limited, I guarantee it.'

'I'm sure that's true. But ten clear choices are worth much more than a hundred fuzzy ones. I'm not a victim, you know. I stuck with Duke because I wanted to. Regardless.'

I shrugged. 'I'm sorry. It's just that last night I got the impression there were victims. That he likes that fact. Enjoys creating them. He as good as fired you. Perhaps more, for all I know. Fired his son. Told Caroline and Bernard Hauptmann he was going to make them look fools in the academic circles that for them are all that matter. And gave George Bourne his marching orders too. Quite a performance.'

'Everything is with my husband. He's an actor manqué.'

She walked out of the Ursula room, down the stairs into the front of the gallery. Then straight out into the cold day. Perhaps it was the sudden glaring sunlight after the dark inside, but when she removed her sunglasses and, just for once, blinked, I thought her light blue eyes were glistening.

'Does the name Julie Dean mean anything?' she asked.

'No. But I could use a coffee.'

'Julie Dean. There was the briefest of mentions in the papers before Duke called his chums and got it all stifled. Three years ago. I can still remember the day.'

'I'm sorry . . .'

'She was a runner on the series I was producing for him. One more hopeful thinking they'd get a break into TV if only they worked their arses off for free. God, the way we treat those poor kids. I hired her. If you can call working for bus fares a hire.'

'Pretty?' I asked, not that it was needed.

'I suppose. And quite naïve. Her predecessor had been rather left-wing and vocal about it. I wanted someone who was, if I'm honest, unremarkable, even a little mousy. Duke sometimes admires resistance. It turns him on. Especially if it's physical. Conflicting opinions are another matter, a proper turn-off. Or at least they were.'

'I don't imagine you agree with him much.'

'I was young, impressionable and stupid. And kept my mouth shut. What little spark there was died the moment I brought Jo into the world. That's why he wanted me. To keep the line going. He needed a son. Once that was done . . .'

'Julie Dean.' I shook my head. 'No. Sorry. I was never one much for reading the news. It always seems so depressing.'

'Jo was on the team by then, trying to learn how to take over from his father. He rather fancied Julie, not that he managed to pluck up the courage to do anything about it. Once he understood that, Duke had no such qualms. Shy little Julie Dean went on his hit list. I suspect he enjoyed trying to pluck a young prize like that out of his son's shaky fingers. I don't know the details. I've never wanted them in the past. The stupid girl never came to me. Instead, she finally plucked up the courage and went over my head to one of Duke's mates in the hierarchy. Before I knew, it was over. He was absolved. She was out on her ear. If only . . .'

Time was getting on. I was due to accompany George Bourne to the Lido and his appointment with the ghost of Dirk Bogarde before long.

'I doubt she was the only one,' I said. 'Men who behave that way—'

'She was the only one who killed herself.' There was steel in her voice now, and hatred too. 'As far as I know, anyway. When no one, not a soul, would listen to her, she threw herself under a Tube train. Oxford Circus. Just a stone's throw from Broadcasting House. I've no idea whether the idiot girl was hoping to make a point, but she failed miserably. If there was a suicide note somewhere pointing a finger at Marmaduke Godolphin, someone dealt with it. Nothing but a voice over a speaker by the eastbound platform of the Central Line talking about "a person on the track".'

'You can't blame yourself.'

She glared at me. 'I don't. I blame him. I also know he'll always get away with things like that. Because getting away with it is what Sir Marmaduke Godolphin does. Just as he'll get away with whatever circus he's planning for here. It's not just about these pieces of paper you're looking for. It's the return of the great TV historian to our screens, bigger, bolder than ever with his new American pals. While the rest of us are reduced to our true role as lowly mortals, lucky to be in his shadow.'

I looked at my watch and said I was sorry, but it was too late to stop for a coffee now. And would she like me to guide her back to the hotel.

'I can find my own way, thank you. I have done for most of the last forty years.' A smile and she touched my arm. 'I know you mean well, Arnold. I can feel it. I know what you think when you see poor Ursula, who never existed, dreaming of her angel with a martyr's palm . . . praying in front of her murderer. Passive. Not doing a thing.'

'You said you'd scratch his eyes out.'

'I did. And perhaps I'd try. But then another chap would be along with his blade and his bow and arrow. They win in the end. They always win. I know that men, real men, *kind* men, think we have choices. But you don't understand. Because you're still men all the same. Nothing's quite that simple. If it was, my husband would be in jail. God knows how many young girls he treated the way he did pathetic little Julie Dean. I don't even want to think about it. Or he'd be dead. I think I'd prefer that. In fact, of all the possible options, all the outcomes, as they say, I sometimes think none would be more satisfactory than seeing his smug face in a coffin. Even he can't rise from the grave.'

VALENTINA LISTENED IN SILENCE to my retelling of the night of the Passeggiata and our visit to the Accademia. It must have been approaching eleven in her office. Time was starting to drift in my head.

She read a message, then tapped something into the keyboard. A reply, I suspect, judging by the way she hammered the return key at the end. Then she said, 'I'm pleased you know how to pronounce "Medici". It drives me nuts when I hear "Me-DEE-chi". The same with Capri. "CapREE". Why do foreigners never listen?'

For the same reason we don't call Venice 'Venezia', Florence, 'Firenze', Titian 'Tiziano'. Because we're foreigners. Not that I said it. Instead, I asked for directions to the toilet and found her back on the computer when I returned, reading something at length.

'Is it possible Felicity Godolphin was jealous of this young American?' she asked. 'Deeply offended by her husband's decision to fire her and move broadcaster? Enough that she might murder him? Or engineer his murder by another?'

'I . . . I really don't know.'

'Was she sounding you out for the job?'

I laughed, couldn't help it. 'She seems a very sensible and intelligent woman. I'm a retired archivist trying to live as quiet a life as possible.'

'Just the kind of man I'd pick. Who'd suspect you?'

This was beyond ridiculous. 'Valentina. I'm so squeamish my wife had to take a mouse out of the trap if we caught one.'

She tapped her pen on the desk. 'I wasn't suggesting you killed him. I was wondering if it might have occurred to Felicity Godolphin that you could be persuaded. And if not you . . . then who? She said she wanted him dead.'

'Wishing for something and making it happen are vastly different things.'

'Married to a philanderer and abuser of women. Thrown out of a job she loved . . .'

No. This was wrong, surely. 'Felicity didn't seem to be so exercised by his predilections, only the consequences when they went too far. How could she be after all these years? I'd be surprised if she felt that way when she married him. Everyone knew the kind of man Godolphin was. I wouldn't say he flaunted his affairs, only because he would have regarded that as common. If you can call sleeping with your students for favours affairs. He certainly never made a secret of what he was up to.'

'All the same . . .'

It seemed a good time to take a sip of the cold coffee in front of me, even though I didn't want it. Outside, the bells struck, though what the time was I didn't notice. No pigeons, though. Not now.

'If you want my honest opinion, I suspect any of them might have wished him dead. Felicity, Caroline Fitzroy. Hauptmann. Even George Bourne. Either by their own hand or that of another. I also believe he gave them all reason enough to feel that way. Whether they were capable . . . you must judge. Not me.'

She nodded. 'I will. What do I need to know next?'

That, I thought, was obvious. Godolphin, in his own theatrical way, had relayed to us the tale of the near assassin the night before with his hired *commedia dell'arte* company from Padua. But the death of Lorenzino was only half the story, the final act as it were.

'You need to know what happened when I took George Bourne to the Lido so he could chase a few memories of his favourite film.'

WE HAD TO TAKE the Number 1, of course, because Bourne was insistent he see the Grand Canal. The boat chugged from stop to stop, all the way from San Tomà past the Accademia, Salute, San Marco, the Arsenale, Giardini and Sant'Elena to the outer island of the lagoon, where I would see my first motor vehicles in weeks. He was equally insistent I recount to him the other murder in Godolphin's coming work. We'd all heard the curious version of Lorenzino's murder the previous night. Now Bourne wanted to be told an equally dark and bloody story: the tale of what had prompted it, Lorenzino's sly assassination of his cousin Alessandro, Duke of Florence. This, he said, was to prepare him as editor for the receipt of Godolphin's draft manuscript, and the months of rewrites and editing to follow. He dismissed entirely the threat the previous night to take the book to another, larger publishing house.

'Money will sort that out,' he declared as we barged and banged our way into the Arsenale stop. 'It always does. While our imprint may be small – exclusive is the term I prefer – our parent . . . far from it. Like most authors, Duke knows nothing about what really goes on in publishing. Nor should he. The arrogant sod should just get on with writing the same old tosh he's done for years and leave me to clean it up. I own the ungrateful bastard. He's going nowhere.'

The complexities of the book world are, I'm delighted to say, quite beyond me.

As our half-empty vaporetto made its way along the waterfront and across the lagoon, I recounted for him the story as I'd read it in the books Godolphin had provided, with a few scraps of information from my own research as well.

It begins on a freezing January evening in 1537, the fifth, the night before Epiphany, when the folklore witch La Befana flies through the dark on her broomstick delivering gifts of sweets to good children and lumps of coal to the naughty. Benvenuto Cellini, goldsmith, accomplished musician, inventor of tales, rapist of men and women, genius, thug and murderer, an inveterate liar and braggart who claimed to have raised demons through witchcraft in the Colosseum along with much else, is doing what he'll do at regular intervals in his melodramatically violent life: fleeing. Cellini was a friend of Lorenzino de' Medici, and the two will meet when the supposedly patriotic hero has committed murder and headed for the road himself. But that lies ahead. Our belligerent genius has concluded that Florence under the leadership of Alessandro de' Medici has become too hot for him. Rome will be no better when his crimes catch up. Jailed for a while in the Castel Sant'Angelo, he'll be lucky to escape with his life. But luck always seems to favour Cellini. Eight years hence, he'll find himself back in Florence, in favour with Alessandro's successor, Cosimo I de' Medici, working on the astonishing and violent bronze that would become *Perseus with the Head of Medusa*, a grisly wonder that still graces the Loggia dei Lanzi today. For now, he simply wishes to be free of the city of his birth, where the political temperament has become feverishly perilous as Alessandro turns upon his many republican foes.

Benvenuto Cellini's extraordinary autobiography was a work I'd read in translation more than once. The night before, I'd found the relevant section concerning Alessandro's death and copied it to my phone. As the vaporetto made its sluggish way across the lagoon to the Lido, I read out the part in which Cellini recalled the moment he bolted from Florence for the south in the company of a friend.

'We mounted and rode rapidly toward Rome; and when we had reached a certain gently rising ground – night had already fallen – looking in the direction of Florence, both of us with one breath exclaimed in the utmost astonishment: "O God of heaven! what is that great thing one sees there over Florence?" It resembled a huge beam of fire, which sparkled and gave out extraordinary lustre. I said to Felice: "Assuredly we shall hear tomorrow that something of vast importance has happened in Florence.'"

Benvenuto Cellini was an inveterate liar and fantasist. No one else reported comets in the sky that night. Nor was Alessandro de' Medici, just twenty-six years old, a new Caesar, the kind of great statesman who merited momentous heavenly events to mark his passing. Florence was a city in love with independence, constantly flirting with the rule by oligarchy that Venice enjoyed, repeatedly finding its natural republicanism crushed by the Medici and their allies. Alessandro was imposed upon the city at the age of nineteen by the Medici Pope, Clement VII, who may well have been his real father. A decent young man, honourable, trustworthy, pious according to his hagiographers. A monster, raping women, torturing and executing his enemies, ruling by force and fear in the eyes of many others.

'WAIT . . .' VALENTINA BUTTED IN. 'You're saying Alessandro was the son of the Pope?'

She did like her interruptions.

'It's one possibility. The lad was known as "Il Moro", the Moor, because he had a dark complexion. Almost black. His mother was reputed to be an African servant in the Medici household in Rome. Officially he was the bastard of Lorenzo, the Duke of Urbino. But many believe that Clement – whose real name was Giulio de' Medici – was the real father.'

'And this is important because . . .?'

'I don't know if it is.'

'Then why are we discussing two murders almost five centuries ago?'

That question surprised me. 'May I remind you, Capitano, of your words when we first met? You asked me to tell you everything I know about Marmaduke Godolphin, his Gilded Circle and why they're here. Are these facts pertinent to his death? I've no idea. I do know they lie at the heart of this story, however. Without them the man would never have laid on this performance. He might still be alive. You're the detective. You tell me.'

Valentina muttered something under her breath. Her computer sounded. She read another incoming message then tapped her watch.

ON THIS WINTER NIGHT, the Duke of Florence lay half asleep on a bed in the apartment of his cousin Lorenzino in the Piazza San Marco, waiting on the promised arrival of a lady he'd long lusted after, Caterina de' Ginori, Lorenzino's aunt. She was one of the city's beauties, a woman renowned for her virtue and her fidelity to an aristocratic husband. But he was away and Lorenzino told his cousin he'd approached her on Alessandro's behalf. Caterina, he said, was willing to please her lord however he wished, but only in secret. That meant she could not risk going to his well-guarded home, the fortress-like Palazzo Medici, two blocks away in the centre, where she might be seen. A private assignation in Lorenzo's apartment must suffice instead.

Expectant, the sybaritic Alessandro waited on the divan. When the door opened, there was no clandestine lover, only Lorenzino with a hired thug.

'Are you sleeping?' Lorenzino asked his cousin.

Without waiting for an answer, the two pounced, stabbing with sword and dagger, ignoring the duke's pleas for mercy. Alessandro de' Medici did not die easily. He did his best to fight back, biting his cousin's finger down to the bone. Then the hired hand plunged a sword into his throat and the slaughter continued, cut after cut on a man already dead, spilling his blood and guts on Lorenzino's sheets.

Here was the assassin's opportunity. To declare himself to the people of Florence as their liberator, slaying the dictator to free them from his tyranny. Instead, Lorenzino de' Medici ran, and kept on running until Bibboni and Bebo caught up with him on the Ponte San Tomà. In the meantime, he chased women, wrote poetry and penned his 'apology' for Alessandro's murder, in which he offered not an ounce of regret, only justifications. The man, he claimed, was a new despot, Caesar reborn. And Lorenzino was the noble Brutus, murdering him for the greater public good. Not that I imagine he saw himself suffering Brutus's grim fate when he penned those words.

Either way, both were dead within the space of eleven years, Alessandro to a family tomb in San Lorenzo, Lorenzino somewhere I'd no idea at that moment. While Florence was in the hands of another Medici, Cosimo, and would remain under the clan's iron thumb for another two centuries.

I FINISHED MY TALE as we headed out from Sant'Elena, prow pointed at the sleek modern vaporetto terminal of the Lido.

'It was all for nothing,' I said as we approached the jetty. 'Blood and pain and death . . . a waste.'

'You have a very prosaic view of matters,' Bourne replied. 'Well, which was it then?'

'Which what?'

'Was Alessandro the beast deserving slaughter? Or the innocent, a sacrificial lamb?'

Oh for an answer. Long years spent among old documents have left me firmly convinced that when they contradict one another over great matters, the truth often lies somewhere in between. I told Bourne that. And that there was plenty of documentary evidence to back the opposing viewpoints of both Caroline Fitzroy and Bernard Hauptmann on which of them was the angel and which the devil.

'Duke won't go for the established story,' Bourne replied. 'He never does. His entire reputation – his act, to be more precise – is based upon the idea that he has greater knowledge and insight than the rest of us, and he'll prove it by turning history on its head.'

That seemed to sum the man up. Naming Michelangelo, an artist known for his piety and gentleness, a scheming murderer certainly fitted the pattern.

'Does it never worry you that you're still tied to him?' I asked. 'So long after Cambridge? I don't get the impression it's down to affection.'

Bourne laughed out loud. 'Affection? Duke doesn't know the word. As for me . . . he was my golden goose. No denying it. He could be again. That book's going to make a fortune. I mean . . . Michelangelo. It's like outing Lewis Carroll as Jack the Ripper. I'll kill the evil old sod myself if he doesn't let me have it.'

'Bit extreme, George.'

He looked at me as if I was a fool. 'You don't know this business. There's not an editor out there who's never wanted to murder an author from time to time.'

'Perhaps there are authors who feel the same way about you?'

He found that amusing too. 'Rubbish. Between books they don't even know I exist. To them I'm just a corporate drone. One who posts a payment into their bank account from time to time if they're lucky. No one would want to harm a publisher, old man. They wouldn't think us worth it.'

Our destination lay on the far side of the Lido, where the endless beach looked out onto the Adriatic, chilly and grey in the depths of winter. There was nothing going east for a hundred kilometres until the coast of Croatia appeared. Bourne dismissed the offer of a taxi immediately. He was an energetic chap despite his weight and lifestyle. In truth, I had to struggle to keep up with him as he marched towards the seafront, turned the corner, spotted the hulk of the famous hotel from his beloved film, then sat down, disconsolate, on a bench by the road.

'I did warn you it was different,' I said, catching up.

'What in God's name . . .?'

The Hotel des Bains had long since shut up shop. It was now an off-white elephant, dead to the world behind scaffolding and harsh metal shutters. There was no longer any call on the Lido for a massive five-star hotel catering to the upper classes of Europe. The sands where Bogarde's German had eyed his beloved boy with such longing were closed too, a private place, locked up for the winter.

'You said you wanted to see it. Well, now you have.'

'Bloody cinema. All they do is lie to you.'

He looked desolate until I reminded him that I knew somewhere excellent for lunch. 'Bait the hook well. This fish will bite.'

I shook my head and said, 'Sorry?'

'Shakespeare.' He turned and gazed again at the beached concrete corpse of the whale behind us. Without its glitzy clientele and busy uniformed bellboys and waiters, the Hotel des Bains was a sorry sight. 'Literary nonsense that shouldn't trouble the mind of an archivist. Or anyone these days for that matter. It's money that counts. Only money. It wasn't always like this. Not quite. The bugger is, Duke adapted. I never quite managed it. I'm the not-quite man. Always on the cusp, never quite getting to the very top.' He turned to look me up and down. 'What did you do for advancement in the civil service?'

'Stayed quiet, anonymous, subservient and blindly loyal. And told everyone what they wanted to hear.'

He nudged me with his elbow. 'How come you never rose to the heights then?' He winced, then came a guilty grin. 'I'm sorry. That was cruel and unfair. The Godolphin in me speaking. He does this to you. Brings everyone down to his own mean-spirited level. Do you get lonely here? Being on your tod?'

'I'm not . . . on my tod. Eleanor's still with me in a way. We spent most of our adult lives together. Someone doesn't just vanish. Not after that. I have friends too. One in particular, Luca Volpetti. The archivist helping me with Godolphin's quest.'

Bourne stared one last time at the sad hulk of the hotel, then groaned as he got to his feet. '*Avanti*, cicerone! Let us feast!'

'**WHERE DID YOU EAT?**' Valentina wondered.

I was taken aback that our lunch seemed more significant than George Bourne's dark ramblings. All the same, I told her: a charming local place in the old Lido market, one that ran its own fish stall and *cicchetti* bar by the side.

'You could have taken him to Il Pagliaccio.'

'I believe that would have been rather more expensive.'

'He had an Amex card! His company was paying.'

'Sorry. Another time, should the opportunity arise. He enjoyed it. Two bottles of Ribolla Gialla, mostly down his throat, and—'

She tapped the desk with her pen. 'And he spoke these very words? You'll swear to it. He said he'd kill the evil old bastard if he couldn't get the book. You squeezed it out of him, Arnold. Quite the detective really.'

'I didn't squeeze anything out of him. He volunteered it.' That just got me a sceptical stare. 'This is the kind of thing the English say. My dear Eleanor, if someone moved her coffee mug at work or something, used to stare them in the eye and growl, "Do that again and you're dead." To me too sometimes. It was a joke. They're not real threats.'

'The English, it seems to me, say an awful lot of things they don't actually mean. All the same . . . those words were his. And now Godolphin's dead.'

The church bells rang once more. I don't know if Valentina Fabbri felt we were getting anywhere. I certainly didn't.

'What was his mood?' she asked.

'Gloomy. Resigned.' I thought back to the way he'd talked about his old professor turned TV star. 'Betrayed. He felt he was a big part of Godolphin's success. An essential element in the man's career.

But I can't imagine an important fellow in publishing would kill someone for ingratitude.'

That earned me a dismissive glance. 'You should read the case files I've seen. Not from here, naturally, but Rome, Naples, Milan. Men, and sometimes women, will commit murder for the smallest of reasons. A slight. A long-held grudge. The wrong word at the right time. Especially when alcohol's involved. You said he liked his drink.'

'No . . .'

'You said—'

'I mean no, I don't believe he would kill someone. It's unthinkable.'

'You wouldn't say his mood was murderous then?'

There was a conversation we had, and I wondered whether to repeat it. Though on reflection, I rather imagined Valentina would get the truth out of me in any case.

'If anything, I'd say his mood was close to suicidal. It was the film, you see.'

'The film? I don't know it.'

I told her briefly what I thought it was about, at least what George Bourne believed. An old, frail man finds himself in the Hotel des Bains, looking lovingly at a beautiful teenage boy. Desperate to talk to him, to be with him. Perhaps to do nothing more than enjoy his company – which got a snort from my Carabinieri *capitano*.

'George seemed to identify with Gustav von Aschenbach. Bogarde's character in the film. To see himself as someone who had held back from making bold decisions out of nothing but reticence and fear. Whether that was to do with his career, his personal life, something else . . . I've no idea. He said . . .' the words were so odd I think I recalled them near perfectly, 'there's a lesson for me here, Arnold Clover. You can dye your hair, rouge your face. Play the fool all you wish. But if you leave things till they're too late, you're dead anyway. I should retire to a small cottage in Tuscany and drown myself in wine.'

Valentina put her hand to her cheek and gave me a look that, were she not a police officer, I'd have called coquettish.

'Your response to that was . . .?'

'What I would have said to anyone in the circumstances. Nothing ventured, nothing gained. I could have stayed in Wimbledon, mourning my lovely wife. But where would that have got me? Instead, I caught a plane, half asleep, and found myself here, making a new life for myself. In a new world, one that was alive and full of wonder. It was the best thing I could do. Far better than drinking oneself into a lonely grave in Tuscany, even if I had the money. And I don't.'

'Which, of course, you told him?'

'In a roundabout way. The man's a leading publisher. He's enjoyed the kind of success I could never achieve. The money too, I imagine. It would be remiss to think I could lecture him about much at all. Though he did seem thoughtful, a little melancholy on the vaporetto back.'

She took her hand away from her cheek and scribbled something on her pad.

'They're all on my list,' she said. 'The wife. The son. The girlfriend. Your two academics and George Bourne.'

Like Luca, she seemed to feel I was somehow responsible for every foreign suspect in Venice at that moment. There seemed no point in objecting further.

'Enough of your publisher, Arnold. Move on. Tell me about Godolphin's marvellous discovery.' She checked her phone and then her watch. 'After that, we will head out for a little light lunch. Somewhere I know. Somewhere you will not.'

FIVE

The Wolff Bequest

At eight on Monday morning, I met Luca for coffee and the promised *frittelle* outside Adagio, one of his favourite cafés by the Frari. He was in full excited-puppy mode once more.

'It's possible, Arnold,' he said with a conspiratorial wink as we walked in from the bright, freezing day. 'I've been up half the night. It is indeed possible.'

I was still half asleep after lots of reading myself. 'What . . .?'

'Michelangelo! I know it sounds quite bizarre. Insane even. All the same . . . Godolphin may be on to something.'

I then received a brief history lesson I didn't need since I'd travelled down the same path of discovery myself in the small hours. It all came down to the feverish state of Florence in the second decade of the sixteenth century. The Medici, as close to monarchs as one could get without the title, had been expelled from the city, which was endeavouring to set itself up as a democratic republic following the kind of model set by Venice. I use the word 'democratic' loosely, of course, since it was scarcely one man, one vote, and women barely counted except in the kitchen or beneath the sheets. Though as dear Eleanor was wont to point out at frequent intervals, our own modern claim to the term had lately come to be viewed with scepticism in more than a few quarters.

Pope Clement VII wanted the Medici back on their throne, for good family reasons – as we've discussed, he was born Giulio de' Medici, son of Giuliano, who'd been murdered during an earlier uprising against the family known as the Pazzi conspiracy.

Clement enrolled the support of Charles V, the Holy Roman Emperor, Archduke of Austria and King of Spain. Florence found itself besieged for ten months, finally capitulating in August 1530. Michelangelo was in a very awkward position. All artists seek patrons to pay their bills – how else can they live? He'd been a favourite of the Medici before their expulsion in 1527, working on the design and construction of their magnificent chapel in the Basilica di San Lorenzo, the mausoleum for the family's most celebrated figures. But when the brief republic emerged, he sided with the forces who wanted the grasping clan gone for good and went so far as to take charge of the fortifications that would keep out the besieging forces for so long.

When the city fell, the leaders of the republican movement were rapidly rounded up and many executed. A fearful Michelangelo, a fellow keen on designing instruments of war but never using them himself, vanished. Where, no one had a clue. The triumphant Clement installed Alessandro as the new duke, placing the Medici back in charge of 'their' city. In October of that year, the Pope let it be known that the elusive Michelangelo would be forgiven, provided he returned and completed the half-finished chapel in San Lorenzo. Message received, the obedient genius emerged from his secret hiding place, tail between his legs, a servant of the family once more, and got on with the job.

Five centuries later, an accidental discovery revealed where he'd been skulking out of sight of Alessandro's killers: a secret chamber in San Lorenzo close to the Medici Chapel itself, which he'd decorated with idle sketches to pass the months he spent trapped there. All that was in the past. Michelangelo was working and demonstrating his brilliance again, and so he was forgiven. By 1534 he would be in Rome, where Clement would order him to paint the massive *Last Judgement* in the Sistine Chapel.

'Let us imagine,' said Luca, 'that Michelangelo remained a private republican. Imagine, too, that he resented Clement's dying demand that he undertake such a vast task, one that would occupy the next seven years. And that would embroil him in great controversy.'

The nudity in Michelangelo's work had scandalised the more conservative elements in the Vatican, who saw parts as bordering on the obscene. There was even a suggestion from a particularly virulent and imaginative critic that the painter had portrayed two saints having sex in one scene. Not long after Michelangelo completed the work, other artists were being employed to paint over the elements the offended clerics found most upsetting, adding cloaks and changes in posture and appearance that are still on the walls and ceiling of the Sistine Chapel today.

'It still doesn't make him an accessory to murder.'

'True. But we know for sure that he feared Alessandro, who might well have had him killed. Why else did he hide? It's conceivable, my friend, that he still hated the fellow and sought revenge. I say no more.'

This Michelangelo is the dog who lured these killers here and silences me now to save his miserable skin. I swear it. I can prove it. Those were the words Duke Godolphin's script placed in the mouth of the Paduan actor playing the dying Lorenzino. They could be interpreted in one way only.

'Let's accept the idea that Michelangelo may have been a player in the original conspiracy to slaughter Alessandro in Lorenzino's bed,' Luca went on. 'Eleven years later, in 1548, he is part of the Papal establishment. Newly appointed architect for the great dome of St Peter's. Still slaving over *The Last Judgement* and much else. Forever falling out with his masters and others.' He tapped my arm. 'Writing homoerotic poetry to his chums at a time when sodomy could get you killed. And Lorenzino is at large, knowing full well that the fellow was part of his conspiracy to kill the duke. That his paintbrush and his sculptor's mallet and chisels were stained with noble blood. Knowing about Michelangelo's sexual habits too, I imagine. A dangerous man to have abroad.'

'If he had the chance to silence the fugitive . . .'

In his excitement, Luca spilled the last few crumbs of his pastry on the counter. 'He'd be a fool not to take it. Wouldn't he? And whatever he was, he was no fool. As I said, it is conceivable – I say no more – that your English historian is on to something here.'

Equally conceivable, I thought, that Godolphin was stringing us all along with a farrago of half-truths and inventions that might get him back in the headlines. It wouldn't be the first time.

'We need evidence,' I said.

'We do.' My friend finished his coffee and stared at the empty cup. 'After another macchiato.'

'IT'S NOT "CONCEIVABLE",' VALENTINA said, clicking the button of her pen repeatedly, a gesture of mild outrage I now recognised. 'It's downright ridiculous.'

'I understand you might see this as a dreadful slur on a great Italian icon.'

'That's nothing to do with it! How could such a secret be kept for nearly five centuries? Michelangelo is one of the most celebrated men in history. People seem to think they know everything about him. If he were a treacherous murderer—'

'He isn't. He wasn't.'

'We know that now, don't we? My question is how could anyone – a famous British historian – believe it in the first place?'

I tried to explain that Godolphin was no serious historian and hadn't been for years. He was a TV personality, a storyteller, a raconteur of fables and myths. It didn't matter whether he truly believed what he was saying. Only that it caused sufficient commotion to get him back on the box and sell a good number of books.

'Now,' I concluded, 'if you will allow me to get on with my story.'

She was barely listening. Another message had come in on her phone.

'Am I really being of some assistance here?' I asked, faintly hoping she'd say no and let me go.

'More than you can imagine. Though we have still some distance to travel.'

'I would have thought interviewing your suspects, if indeed they are—'

'They're suspects.'

'Then—'

'Arnold! Are you listening? I have interrogated all of them repeatedly. If I do not charge someone soon, I will have to let them go. Perhaps I may be unable to keep them in Italy at all.' Ah. Another reason for the haste. 'They offer nothing of any use. No one saw a thing. No one heard a thing. None of them expresses much in the way of grief for Godolphin's bloody end. Though that in itself is not a crime.'

She was, it seemed to me, beginning to get desperate. I could only wonder what gambit she might try next.

Then, to my surprise and, I thought, hers, she said, 'They're all lying. I can feel it. They all have something they don't wish me to know. Perhaps when we are nearer a solution, I will bring them into the same room and the two of us will unseal their secrets.'

'You surely don't think they *all* murdered Duke Godolphin? That they somehow conspired . . .?'

I got the gimlet stare. 'I don't know. Do you?'

Somewhere close by, on the roof, pigeons cooed and clattered across the tiles.

'It seems a little Agatha Christie,' I suggested.

'She was very English too, wasn't she? Never mind. We will get to the bottom of this. I have another idea.'

'I'm glad you have, because—'

'Lunch,' she announced.

'I'm not sure I'm terribly hungry.'

'Don't eat anything then. Volpetti will meet us.' She smiled, and something in that seemingly genial expression made me think I'd rather not have Valentina Fabbri on my heels if I were a criminal myself. 'The three of us can discuss this over a glass of wine and *cicchetti*. Now . . .' the smile disappeared, 'carry on with this tale of your . . . fonds.'

OUR FIRST SURPRISE WHEN we entered the State Archives was to discover we were now housed in an entirely different part of the building. Instead of the small, quiet academic office Luca had reserved for us, we'd been shunted off to a chilly, draughty storage area far away from the street.

The Franciscan friars evicted by Napoleon, first for his soldiers, then for the Archives, had enjoyed quite a fine home for a good four centuries or so. They owned two great cloisters, one, adjoining the Frari, dedicated to the Trinity and kept in smart fashion since it was just visible to the public from the chapter house. The second, named for Sant'Antonio, was rather shabby in comparison, the paving stones mucky with moss and grime, the porticoes more time-worn, the well at the centre stained with soot and pigeon droppings. A corner the Archives never much used, it seemed to me. Our original home looked out onto Trinity, which gave it a cheery, bright air in the February sun. This new place lurked in constant shadow and had the feeling of neglect. A red child's balloon was bouncing across the courtyard when I turned to look, chased by a couple of bored pigeons. I had a bad feeling about the place, about Godolphin's project and what was expected of us. Judging by the look of surprise on my friend's face, he felt much the same.

This, he said, as we crossed the courtyard, was a part of the complex he rarely visited. I imagine it had once been a refectory for the Franciscan friars, a place they could eat in silence, the minor ones in all probability. Now it was a kind of warehouse for unwanted office material – old computers, printers and desks.

'I do not understand, Arnold,' he said as he unlocked the door. 'Your Godolphin has some explaining to do.'

The reason we were there, not in our original office, was obvious straight away. The Wolff Bequest had arrived, and it was simply enormous. A collection of large furniture removal boxes, all stamped with the name and trademark of a Berlin transport company, stood lined up against the walls, covered in transit labels that described each one as 'household goods'.

'Interesting,' I muttered, anxious to take a closer look. There were mysteries here to be investigated, I felt sure. And mysteries were my business.

There were footsteps behind us, then a nervous cough. I turned. It was Duke Godolphin with his son, Jolyon, the one doing the coughing.

'Well,' said Godolphin, clapping his gloved hands against the cold, his breath misting in the freezing morning air. 'Time to get to work.'

Before I could respond, Luca stepped up to him and said a word I suspect Godolphin heard rarely.

'No.' He walked over to the nearest packing case. 'First you must explain what this is. I count thirteen boxes.' I got my friend's drift, took out a penknife and zipped open the tape on the box. We all looked inside. Pile upon pile of envelopes. 'Thirteen as full as this will be a nightmare for two people.'

Godolphin patted his son's arm. 'That's why I brought him along.'

Luca was glancing at me for help. 'Before anything happens, we need more information from you,' I said. 'These are the State Archives of Venice. Not some back-street antiques shop. Who is this Wolff? What exactly are we looking for? We need . . .' Time to make a threat, something I'd rarely done before but I found myself enjoying it. 'We need you to be frank with us. If you're not, I'm out of this game and so is Luca. We're agreed. You can hunt through all this yourself.'

I got the kind of stare he must have reserved for students who'd disappointed him.

'Jolyon,' he said, 'make yourself at home. These gentlemen and I are going for a little chat.'

THERE WAS A CAFÉ round the corner, opposite the canal. We took a table away from the busy crowd by the counter. Godolphin seemed a little awkward. It struck me that the nature of the Wolff Bequest was a surprise to him too, not that he wished to let on.

After the drinks arrived and we were alone, I let Luca leap in. The problem was not simply the extent of the task in front of us. There was also the question of provenance. The State Archives were an official organisation. Every item that passed through its doors needed to have a listed source stating where it came from and how it had been acquired.

'It came from me,' Godolphin said. 'And I acquired it.'

I'd rarely seen Luca cross, except when we'd encountered annoying tourists. Now was different and he was determined to let it show.

'That's not good enough!'

'Far from it,' I agreed. 'You know that as well as we do. From what I've seen, these items have been shipped here by a simple removals company. No proper documentation. No sign they come from an academic facility at all.'

'That,' Godolphin replied with a quick smile, 'is because they don't. Grigor Wolff didn't work in those circles. He was a man after my own heart. An antiquarian who maintained a private collection. More focused on results than bureaucracy and paperwork. You met him, surely?'

That seemed to be a question aimed at both of us.

'I never heard the name till now,' I said.

Luca shook his head.

'Then he must have dealt with others who knew of you. Listen.'

Listen we did. It sounded an odd tale to say the least.

Godolphin's story was that a few years before, he'd received a message from Berlin, an antiquarian named Grigor Wolff who'd heard he'd been searching for new material on the secret service under Elizabeth I. Wolff proved a reclusive character who would communicate by email only. Godolphin was understandably reluctant to begin with, believing he was dealing with either a crank or a conman.

'But the fellow knew my work going back years. He was an ardent fan. He saved me enormous amounts of time and money finding the material I wanted. For example, he alerted me to the existence of a dispatch from Francis Walsingham about the Armada that had somehow got ignored in the depths of the General Archive of the Indies in Seville.'

That sounded odd.

'What on earth was Walsingham doing in Seville?' I wondered. 'The archive there's all to do with the New World, surely.'

'Piracy, dear boy,' Godolphin said with a look that told me I should have known. 'Drake and Raleigh. I take it you never read the book or watched the TV programme.'

'Bit of a busman's holiday,' I replied, which immediately generated a linguistic query from Luca wondering why we were suddenly talking about driving buses and what business I had doing a job like that in addition to being an archivist.

'That was the first of his tip-offs,' Godolphin interrupted before I finished putting my friend straight. 'Later he uncovered some documents about de Sade and his imprisonment in Vincennes. Grigor was able to lay his hands on all manner of interesting documents.'

Luca had his phone out. 'Who is the man?' he demanded. 'Why have we never heard of him? Why is he a mystery even unto Google?'

For once Duke Godolphin was silent.

'You've never met him, have you?' I said.

'There was never the need. The fellow always said he wished to guard his privacy. It was a condition of his doing business with me.'

'But you paid him?'

Again he seemed reluctant to go on. 'Grigor always said he'd invoice me for expenses at some stage,' he admitted when I pressed him. 'His principal interest was seeing the items he'd uncovered gain a wider audience, which was only possible through me. He was an admirer, as I said. You may find that hard to understand. I don't. I assumed it was a hobby. He told me he was a man of private means and had no need of extra income. His reward came in seeing me make use of what he'd dug up. Grigor was the archaeologist, as it were. I was his means to reach the public.' Godolphin finished his coffee and was starting to look bored. I imagine he was rarely asked to explain himself to anyone. 'His only stipulation was that I never thank him in print or in the credits. Anonymity. He demanded it. I was happy to agree.'

Luca was looking right at me, and I knew what was going through his mind. So I said it for him.

'Do you have any idea where the material we're about to look at originated?'

All I got in return was a frown, then, 'Not a clue. I never asked about anything. I merely had the material checked out by one of my researchers, satisfied myself it was as genuine as one could expect, and got on with the job. Which is what I want of you.'

'If it was stolen,' I said, 'you wouldn't know?'

'I have no reason to think anything's been stolen.'

'The material was shipped here as household goods. There's no paperwork. No proper documentation. We must talk to this man. We must hear what he has to say.'

Duke Godolphin sighed. 'That, I'm afraid, is impossible. Unless you know how to raise the dead.'

We were the ones who fell silent then. Godolphin filled in the gaps.

The previous summer, Wolff had emailed him to say that during his travels across Europe he'd located two of the most precious lost documents he'd ever uncovered. On this occasion, he warned, he would ask for money. A cash sum of €10,000, half in advance, paid to an address in Koblenz.

'No turning that down, was there? I took a lady friend along for a cruise on the Moselle. The address was a bar. A woman seemed to be expecting the envelope. She said nothing when I wondered if it was possible to meet Wolff. Koblenz is home to the Bundesarchiv, of course, so I asked after him there. Again, if anyone knew the man, they weren't saying. A little while later, he emailed me to say his doctor had advised him he had at best a month or two to live. He was arranging for the documents to be sent here and wished the collection to be donated to the State Archives once I was finished with them. This was where he wanted them to reside.' He pointed out of the window, across to the great wall of the Frari with its rose window. 'Somewhere in there, in the chapel used by the Florentines, lie the bones of Lorenzino de' Medici, beneath an unmarked flagstone. He seemed to believe it appropriate for the material to be interred nearby.'

'And the rest of the money?' I asked.

Godolphin shrugged. 'He never mentioned it. So why would I? The fellow had read the tedious tomes produced by my former students about the Medici's little falling-out. He was, he said, outraged by their lack of style and fresh insight. So he'd gone hunting in all these arcane places he knew and found something that had escaped Florence. Something that showed that both Caroline Fitzroy and Bernard Hauptmann had been barking up the wrong tree.' He pulled out a large phone. 'This is the right tree. Or at least a part of it.'

There were, Wolff had assured him, two letters somewhere in those packing cases. One from Michelangelo to Lorenzino offering his support for the murder of Alessandro. The second, eleven years later, from the artist to someone in Venice setting up Lorenzino's assassination here.

He fiddled with the phone and pulled up a photo. I let Luca take the first look, watched the expression on his face turn to amazement. Then he passed it to me. It was a photograph of part of an old document, a letter scrawled in a near-impenetrable hand, the design of a dagger at the top, next to it one word in old, scribbled writing: 'Cellini!'

'Wolff sent me this. I've had it checked against specimens of Michelangelo's hand and it matches. It's a portion of a letter written by Michelangelo to Lorenzino offering his support for the assassination of the duke. The weapon to do the job too. The promise of a stiletto to perform the task. A commission he would hand over to none other than Benvenuto Cellini.'

Godolphin looked round to make sure no one was watching, then withdrew from his left sleeve the dagger we'd seen the actor playing Bibboni brandish on the San Tomà bridge. Close up, the thing was beautiful and frightening at the same time, the long blade a tapering sharp needle made to take a life, the hilt a turned-baluster grip, both decorative and, one imagined, easy to hold. It looked brand new but stained with black ink to give the appearance of age.

'He also mailed me this weapon he'd had made from the design as proof of the value of his discovery. An extraordinary piece. After that, he upped and died before he was able to give me more details. All I had was a last message from him, in which he sounded quite delirious, saying he was bequeathing me his whole collection and I was to find what I needed there.'

'The second letter?' Luca asked.

'As I said, it's to do with Lorenzino's murder here. That's all I know.'

'When did Wolff die?' I asked. 'Where?'

Duke Godolphin threw his hands in the air, a theatrical gesture he used on TV. 'In Berlin. At Christmas, I believe. What does it matter? No one sent me an invitation to the funeral. The man wanted his privacy. Who am I to deny him that in death? I'd hoped he'd be joining us here and perhaps I could entice him on screen if he was halfway photogenic. Instead, when he knew he was a goner, he gave me your name, Clover. He suggested I might reach you through library circles here. Which, thanks to your friend, I did.'

We stared at our coffee cups and listened to the banter from the bar. The Archives were just across the bridge in front of the Frari, a short way, it seemed, from the buried bones of the murdered Lorenzino. Neither of us was much keen to go back to that room with its packing cases and Godolphin's miserable-looking, put-upon son.

'If any of this material has been acquired unconventionally—' Luca began.

'If you mean stolen,' Godolphin interrupted, 'come out and say it.'

'I mean if any of this material has been acquired in a way that would bring the State Archives into disrepute—'

'It hasn't. I've no reason to believe Wolff was anything other than an eccentric and reclusive antiquarian.'

I put my hand on my friend's arm. 'One way or another, we have to look, Luca. If those letters really are there . . . we can't just walk away. Can we? Lord knows there's far too much important material lying in dusty corners untouched, unread. We have to know.'

Godolphin slapped me on the shoulder. 'Good man! Fliss said I ought to remember you from Cambridge.'

'I don't know why. I was never one of your students.'

'I will see you both prosper from this. I may be a hard taskmaster at times, but I'm always a grateful one.'

Just then, I thought about Felicity's story of the unfortunate young woman he'd pestered. Julie Dean. She, I knew, would not have agreed.

He got to his feet, sniffed, and threw a twenty-euro note on the table. 'Always remember, this is television, not academia. Entertainment. I'm not paying you to deliver me an arcane truth that'll make some ancient professor in his dotage wet his pants. I want you to uncover what I need to tell the tale of my Passeggiata of Blood. Namely that

Michelangelo was a conspirator in murder and a traitor to the man he egged on to the assassination of the Duke of Florence. Front-page news. I've got a pal on the *Sunday Times* all lined up to run it as a front-page exclusive once the cat is in the bag. Is that clear?'

'Perfectly,' I said before Luca could get in another word.

'Best get started then.' Godolphin buttoned up his coat. 'I have matters to attend to. As do you.'

GODOLPHIN VANISHED INTO THE bright and icy morning, tugging his long black coat around him. Luca and I slunk across to the Archives and made our way to the outpost we'd been given at the end of the cloisters. The collection of packing cases seemed even larger when we got back. Jolyon Godolphin was there, sitting beside one munching a cereal bar. He was a quiet chap, younger-looking than his thirty-odd years. His thinning hair was fair, unkempt, in need of a cut, his face striking like his mother's but with none of the same focus or vivacity. There was something bleak and dead about his eyes, and I doubt it had suddenly appeared that weekend when his own father had effectively thrown him out into the street and told him to make his way on his own. From what I recalled, the one book he'd written after his TV series had been slated by the critics for sloppy fact-checking and style. Perhaps, unlike his father, he'd taken the risk of writing the thing himself.

As we eyed the boxes wondering where to start, Jolyon shuffled over and asked what we wanted him to do.

'Have you had breakfast?' Luca asked.

He held up the wrapper of the cereal bar and said he'd been late and skipped the buffet in the hotel.

'First you can go and get yourself a coffee and a pastry, then come back here when we've organised matters somewhat. A good archivist never works on an empty stomach, do they, Arnold?'

'Never,' I agreed. 'Quite unknown.'

The young chap looked grateful, smiled very briefly and vanished. 'Don't be long,' I called after him. 'Lots of work to do.'

We watched him cross the mossy cloisters.

'Poor lad looks like one of life's casualties,' Luca said as he vanished into the arch on the far side.

'I suspect Marmaduke Godolphin has left a trail of those over the years.'

'We're not joining the list, are we?'

I kept staring at the portico across the way. Beyond lay the Trinity cloisters. After that, the Frari and the chapel where, somewhere beneath its flagstones, lay the remains of Lorenzino de' Medici. Or so Godolphin would have us believe. Was it true? I asked Luca. Was one of the most notorious of Renaissance assassins really interred beneath the stones now passed by tens of thousands of tourists each year, visiting one of the greatest basilicas in a city so full of churches?

He nodded. 'Yesterday I mentioned Lorenzino to a friend who works there. It seems the general belief is that he was buried secretly in the chapel of the Baptist to the right of the transept. It was dedicated to Florentines living in the city, paid for by them.' He sighed. 'I know Godolphin comes across as a fraud. But he does seem to put his finger on some interesting connections.'

In that chilly former monk's refectory where we were bound to spend the next few days, I found I could picture the place precisely. There was an extraordinary polychrome wooden sculpture of John the Baptist there, executed by Florence's foremost sculptor of the time, Donatello. The figure wore a ragged animal skin and a golden cape around his shoulders, an agonised, half-crazed expression on his face that reminded me instantly of the same sculptor's skeletal, penitent Mary Magdalene now in the Duomo Museum in Florence. Neither was a work I could look at for long without a shiver and a wish to be elsewhere.

My friend laughed when I mentioned it. 'You know what's funny?

Donatello was commissioned to produce that by the original Cosimo, the one who put the Medici on their pedestal in the 1450s. It was a thank you to Venice for harbouring him and his family when they themselves were exiled from Florence. One minute friends. The next . . . bitter enemies. I keep saying, Arnold. Godolphin may well be on to something. We weren't Italians then. Just cities with warlords fighting for territory in a land scarred by violence, greed and hate.'

I was warming to my Venetian friend more each day. He was so knowledgeable and gave away that hard-earned wisdom so freely to anyone who needed it.

I patted the nearest case. 'Only one way to find out.'

The son came back looking happier for his breakfast. Luca found a pair of scissors and announced that since his father had brought this massive pile of material into the archives, it was surely Jolyon's privilege to begin the task of exploring them.

The young man grinned at that, clearly relieved that his old man was no longer around. He ran the scissors along the tape of the next box along and we peered inside. It was just like the one we'd seen earlier. Envelopes of all sizes, some small and white, some large manila, a few the kind of padded bags people use for mailing delicate objects.

Luca waved at him to begin.

With tentative fingers – delicate, it seemed to me – Jolyon reached inside and retrieved a faded A4 envelope with a cardboard back. The flap was sealed. He ripped it open and withdrew the contents.

The three of us stared at a dessert menu from the Hotel Adlon, Berlin, dated September 1999.

THE NEXT FEW HOURS threw up many such surprises. There were no labels on the packing cases, only numbers, transport stickers and what looked like the odd scribble of graffiti, we presumed written by the logistics company during their work. After a while we gave up on the idea of trying to process them in sequential order and decided to open the lot and take the job from there.

With their lids removed they all looked much the same: boxes stuffed with envelopes of varying kinds, some clearly ancient, a few quite new. The temptation was always to try opening the latter first on the grounds that the late Grigor Wolff must have had access to these mysterious Michelangelo papers recently in order to send Godolphin the snap of the page containing the dagger illustration. This, however, proved quite wrong. The most recent envelopes contained random items of random age: newspaper clippings from the German and Dutch press, most a few years old; more restaurant menus and a few cocktail lists from bars in Amsterdam and Paris; tourist information leaflets for sights across Europe; and a short poem, scribbled in French, on the back of a half-torn Guinness beer mat.

Luca and I were lost as to how to proceed. We'd been promised archive material from an antiquarian. This looked more like a haul of old junk from the house clearance of a recently deceased eccentric. Nevertheless, our archival training prevented us simply diving in, opening the envelopes in a rush and discarding everything that seemed worthless. That went against our training and nature.

After much fruitless searching, we sent Jolyon out to fetch coffee and took a break to decide upon our strategy. We both believed it was entirely possible the enigma we now knew as Grigor Wolff had decided to play a game with Duke Godolphin. Perhaps the Michelangelo letters didn't exist. Or if they did, Wolff had, for reasons unknown, decided to set our TV historian the challenge of unearthing the precious material from amidst the dross. There was, Luca suggested, one obvious reason why this might be necessary: the items were indeed stolen and needed to be hidden from the prying eyes of others. If so, we would do our best to locate them and then, when the time was right, inform the State Archives authorities of what we'd found.

If there were clues in the material we were uncovering, perhaps connected to the boxes from which they originated, it was important to maintain some organisation to deal with their removal. Fonds, we told ourselves. Order must come out of chaos. If we were to have any success at all, we needed to start off arranging the contents of those hundreds of envelopes into a kind of base order that would allow us to narrow things down over time. It wasn't simply a question of burrowing through every case in the hope that those magical two letters might suddenly appear.

The order we decided upon was based on geography. After briefly inspecting the contents of each envelope, we deposited them on the long bench tables at the back of the room according to where they originated. Refinement, if needed to unpick any puzzle left by Wolff, could happen later.

A few hours on, we realised there was some method in the late antiquarian's madness. The boxes were not, as we feared, entirely random in their contents. They came from six countries alone: Italy, Germany, the Netherlands, France, Great Britain and a few from Ireland.

Academic papers, newspaper clippings, old tourist photographs, some still in their frames, movie posters and a good few train timetables now joined the rest of the material on the table.

Nothing that connected with Michelangelo as far as we could see.

The three of us had taken a break around midday. We each had a set of boxes to investigate. By then we still hadn't reached the bottom of the first. This was going to take days. A week or two even. With not a clue how we might find the sensational material Duke Godolphin sought.

I was about to suggest to Luca that perhaps we should call it a day and retire to the Pugni and a consolation meal over which we might consider first, how on earth we got ourselves into such a mess, and second, some way in which we might claw our way out of it.

Then Caroline Fitzroy marched through the door, and I recalled my promise from Saturday evening. A glance at the book of illustrious courtesans that might tempt her into researching the great mistresses of Renaissance Venice.

She took one look around at the mess, then our faces, and burst out laughing.

VERONICA FRANCO WAS BORN to the job of pleasing men. Her mother was a member of the professional trade known as the *cortigiana onesta*, the honest courtesan. This was a million miles from the world of the common prostitutes who clamoured for passing trade around places like the infamous Ponte delle Tette, or Bridge of Tits, in San Polo. There, women were paid by the authorities to display themselves topless in order, the city elders believed, to discourage homosexuality among the working classes. The likes of Veronica Franco served a different clientele altogether, aristocrats local and visiting, who would be amused in bustling artistic salons, listen to her recite her own poetry, play music and sing, then take her to bed. Sex was an important part of the role, as her frank verses confirm. But only with the right sort, among them Henry III of France, to whom she seems to have been presented as a gift when he visited the city.

Tintoretto painted her. The city loved her, until it didn't and she found herself first fighting for her life against charges of witchcraft, then reduced to poverty, abandoned by the same men who'd once craved her company. She died aged forty-five, and after reading of her, and some of her work, I'd become convinced she deserved to be brought to the attention of a modern audience. Many of the opinions she voiced about the strength of women when compared to men and the dangers they faced trying to find their way through a male-dominated world seemed to me distinctly contemporary.

One quotation from her letters I'd stored on my phone, hoping it would spark Caroline Fitzroy's interest: 'When we women also have weapons and the training, we will prove to men everywhere that we have hands and feet and hearts like yours.' She listened to me recite it in the chilly cloister courtyard as I took a break from the work inside. I would, I said, find a friendly archivist in the study room and arrange for her to see all the relevant material, including the fascinating directory of the city's courtesans that the visiting wealthy would browse much as they might peruse the menu of a fine restaurant.

'Very kind of you to dangle all this in front of me,' she said with an unconvincing smile. 'Perhaps some other time.'

Before I could stop her, she was heading for the door to our room. Jolyon and Luca were still sifting through envelopes, looking briefly at the contents, noting the number of the packing case they came from, then placing them in the allotted piles at the back of the room.

'Found Duke's magic papers yet?' she asked.

I explained that it was a complex task involving a vast amount of documentation, little of it relevant. The donor had sadly died before he could offer us the material in a more manageable state.

'Who was he?'

'A chap called Wolff.'

'Who *was* he?'

'I don't know. I'm not sure Godolphin does either. Still, we said we'd look, and that's what we'll do. It may take some time.'

She reached into the nearest packing case, pulled out the first envelope she could find and withdrew a page torn from a local newspaper in Maastricht, a story from 1989 about a cycle race. 'Seems to me,' she said, reaching for her phone, 'you need some help.'

Twenty minutes later, the remaining members of the Gilded Circle, George Bourne, Bernard Hauptmann and Felicity too, were wandering round the room, bemused. Godolphin, it seemed, had taken Patricia Buckley on a boat ride – a private one, naturally. Left to their own devices, it seemed our new assistants couldn't wait to get stuck into our curious collection of ephemera.

What the old man was going to make of it we'd no idea. Nor did we greatly care. This was not the archival exercise we'd signed up for at all. More an odd sideshow to the Carnival that was then beginning to wind down in the streets outside.

That said, we were grateful for the help. I set each up with a packing case and their orders – remove the envelopes, tell us if they contained anything that resembled a Renaissance document, and if not, mark them and place them in the correct geographical pile at the back of the room. They went about the task dutifully, though I must admit, after half an hour of finding mostly tat, the mood had turned quite jocular. George Bourne in particular found the idea that two letters from Michelangelo might be lurking hidden among such junk highly amusing, and chuckled at every new envelope he opened.

This couldn't last, and it didn't.

VALENTINA FABBRI PUSHED BACK her chair, puzzled. 'What you describe sounds decidedly strange.'

To my surprise, I was starting to feel peckish. The prospect of being taken somewhere new and a little secret was enticing. Also, I couldn't wait to get out of the Carabinieri office. The place was pleasant enough, rather more so than expected. If we'd been in the heart of Rome or Naples, doubtless the atmosphere would have been different. But as the *capitano* had declared at the outset, Venice was different. More relaxed. For a police station it felt almost casual.

'It was. I was about to tell you about Godolphin.'

'All in good time. Is this how academia works? With packing cases and boxes of junk?'

Where to start? No, I told her. Usually we received material that came with an audit trail: what it was, where it came from, who had provided it. Luca and I had never encountered anything like the Wolff Bequest.

'What I do not understand,' she replied, 'is why you didn't simply sift through all the junk looking for what you wanted. You seem to have made a lot of work for yourselves. And his guests.'

Not that his guests complained.

I did my best to explain. We were archivists. We believed that every item might be of importance even if at first glance it appeared worthless. Too many precious documents and objects had been discarded over the centuries, lost for ever, when if retained until someone came along who understood them, their true value might have been appreciated.

'Train timetables? Newspaper clippings? Ancient tourist information?'

'We weren't to know what was in the next envelope.'

The pen tapped the desk again. 'And?'

'And we wondered if this wasn't part of some gigantic, complex puzzle. A challenge set by the dead Wolff, perhaps, to see if Godolphin was really the accomplished historian he claimed. We simply didn't know. And when you don't know, you keep every option open, file what you find in a way that means you can retrieve it easily later.'

The door opened. One of the young uniformed officers I'd seen dealing with the drunk earlier was there, looking decidedly uncomfortable.

'What is it?' Valentina asked as the fellow shuffled from foot to foot.

'I regret to report, Capitano, that one of the suspects has escaped.'

At that, I expected to witness an outburst of fury, justified I'd guess. But no. She was not a woman given to predictability. 'Which one?'

'The son.'

'How?'

A stuttered explanation and half-confession followed. It seemed Jolyon Godolphin had asked to be released from his cell to visit the toilet. While he was on the way there, accompanied by a single young cadet, the front door of the station had opened: window cleaners requiring payment. The young man took his opportunity and made a break for it. He was, it seemed, wearing only a jumper and a pair of jeans to face the freezing February weather.

'We have his passport?' Valentina asked.

'Of course.'

'Does he have money?'

The man shrugged. 'Whatever he has in his pockets. The mother is quite furious.'

She got to her feet and went to take a fashionable navy padded coat off the stand behind her. 'Come, Arnold. I feel it's time for lunch.' She glanced at the officer. 'You know what to do.'

A salute and then he raced away.

I was beginning to think I'd never understand police work. In Venice anyway.

'But . . . Jolyon Godolphin's escaped.'

'I heard.'

'Shouldn't . . . shouldn't you be looking for him?'

I shrugged on my old duffel coat, waiting for an answer. None came.

'I mean—'

'How many times do I have to say this? We are in Venice. A city like no other. The young Godolphin has no money. No passport. No knowledge of the place apart from what he picked up on his journey here. It was his first time. I'd asked him that already.'

'And?'

'And where has he to go? The railway station. Or, more likely, Piazzale Roma, where there are buses and taxis, neither of which he can afford. We are an island. A small, enclosed world only a Venetian might escape, and then with some luck.'

She found a woolly hat in her pocket and pulled it over her neat dark hair. No sight of a uniform then. Valentina Fabbri seemed to be one more striking middle-class Venetian lady headed out for lunch. 'He will be here when we return, I feel sure. Of greater interest is why the young man should run when he must know he possesses not the slightest chance of escape.'

It seemed no warmer outside, and the pigeons were back. Four Carabinieri officers, more senior and more serious than the ones I'd seen previously, were talking on their phones in the street. I heard the name 'Godolphin'. Perhaps they had him already.

'Do you like *baccalà*?' Valentina asked.

Salt cod, creamed and spread on bread. A Venetian speciality.

'Very much.'

'Good. You are about to try the best.'

We walked out to the Riva degli Schiavoni, where Carnival figures mingled with tourists, all, like us, enjoying the view across the water to San Giorgio Maggiore. Venice so often seemed to me to resemble a living painting. It was just that the artist changed with the seasons. Canaletto for summer. Turner, now, for the pale, bright sky and the gleaming expanse of lagoon ahead of us.

'Would you say Jolyon Godolphin was an intelligent man?'

He'd been to Oxford, he told me, against his father's wishes. Duke could have eased his way into Cambridge, surely. But Jolyon was having none of it. He wanted, he said, to make his own name, and had only agreed to move into Duke's shoes in TV out of opportunism.

'I believe so. But what, as far as your investigation—'

'Then he knows he has nowhere to hide. Nowhere to go.' Valentina gave me that sharp look of hers. 'Yet still he runs. This is not an investigation, it appears. More a character study of a group of intriguing foreigners.'

I hesitated before asking, 'Me among them?'

She smiled at the endless blue sky and the campanile on the far side of the Bacino, a mirror image of San Marco's to our right. Then Valentina Fabbri walked on.

SIX

Riddles

By mid afternoon, our new research team had reduced the level of the packing cases by about a third. Luca, a man with a sound mathematical brain, had worked out that if we laboured this way for a further two days, we would have opened and examined every envelope in the cases of the Wolff Bequest. The hope was, of course, that we'd find the two Michelangelo letters long before then. But hope was in short supply. The material we kept uncovering looked more like a strange collection of junk from a compulsive hoarder than a promising archive of historical material. Nothing that looked remotely like correspondence from one of the leading figures of the Renaissance.

Felicity and George Bourne seemed delighted by the idea that Godolphin's grand idea of turning history on its head might prove to be the dampest of damp squibs. His son, on the other hand, simply carried on with the task in a glum, robotic fashion. The young man's mental state concerned me, if I'm honest. It wasn't simply that he seemed miserable – his father had long experience of inflicting suffering on those around him, and after the weekend's revelations, it was hardly surprising he was down. But it struck me there was more to it than being thrust out into the cold by an uncaring parent. The poor chap seemed a little disturbed. I thought of what Felicity had told me about how he'd taken a shine to the unfortunate Julie Dean, lacked the courage to do anything about it and watched his father attempt to steal the young woman away for himself. Much the same, it seemed, might be happening with the nervily glamorous Patricia Buckley, supposedly Godolphin's producer, one more successor as candidate for a new squeeze, or so the old man seemed to think.

Caroline Fitzroy and Bernard Hauptmann, somewhat to my surprise, were reluctant to engage with their growing glee. Unlike their former professor, they seemed genuine academic historians, seekers of truth even if it didn't fit their own private beliefs. Both found it highly unlikely that Michelangelo was involved in either Alessandro's assassination or Lorenzino's subsequent murder in Venice. Neither seemed to rule it out completely, for the reasons Luca and I had already uncovered. It was established fact that Michelangelo had made himself an enemy of the Medici for some time, so much so that he'd gone into hiding in the bowels of their chapel in Florence.

Hauptmann, it turned out, had gone back into his university files the previous day and unearthed something that might give Godolphin's wild theory more weight. The American had, through some academic archival system, access to Michelangelo's entire correspondence – the known and verified letters – and come across one that was clear evidence that the man had experience of producing a dagger, perhaps much like the one we'd seen wielded that Saturday night. Some years before Alessandro's assassination, the Florentine aristocrat Piero Aldobrandini had, through Michelangelo's brother Leonardo, demanded he design one for his personal use. The artist had struggled to get out of the commission, complaining *non é mia professione*, this isn't my profession. But Aldobrandini insisted, as did Leonardo, who wanted the money. Besides, Michelangelo wore so many different artistic hats it was hard to imagine what he couldn't do. There was no drawing of the dagger in his known correspondence. His older rival, Leonardo da Vinci, was fond of inventing all manner of war machines and weaponry, but Michelangelo's only known contribution to martial engineering was the plan to build the fortifications of Florence to repel the Pope's forces in 1528, the project that got him into trouble with the Medici in the first place.

Nevertheless, Hauptmann and Caroline Fitzroy both seemed genuinely intrigued by the idea that there might be some truth to Godolphin's conjecture, and happily discussed the possibility with us as we worked. They lightened the atmosphere, if I'm honest, which came as a surprise. Even Felicity and George gave up the sniping talk after a while.

Just after four, there was a booming voice at the door, one I now knew only too well. Duke Godolphin was back, well fed and well watered judging by the ruddy colour in his cheeks. His shirt collar was torn and there was what looked like scratch marks, pink, with raised pale flesh, on his flabby neck.

'What in God's name is this?' he roared, staring hard at the team we'd assembled.

Felicity took one look at him, then marched right up, touched his collar, his neck, and jabbed a finger in his chest. 'What is *this*?' For once, the old man seemed lost for words. Embarrassed. Guilty. 'I thought you were taking your young American friend out for lunch. Where is she?'

'Back in the hotel,' Godolphin grumbled in a voice that was new to me, quiet, low, perhaps even ashamed. 'It was something she ate.'

There came that curious moment when a lie, an uncomfortable one, becomes obvious to everyone who witnesses it without a single word being said.

Luca glanced in my direction, and I knew we were thinking the same thing. A bitter family argument was about to take place. It struck me that Felicity Godolphin appreciated an audience in person just as much as her husband did on TV.

'SHOCKING,' VALENTINA FABBRI SAID with a dismissive wave of her hand as she led me down a tiny alley. 'To engage in flaming rows in front of other people. How histrionic. These television people seem to think they never step off the stage.'

A very adroit observation. My new Carabinieri acquaintance appeared to have a deeper understanding of the dynamics of the Godolphin clan and their guests than I had first appreciated. Which also made me wonder, with some slight trepidation, why she seemed so interested in me.

'May I ask where we're going?'

'I told you. Somewhere for lunch.'

That was it. I gave up and followed along, aware that there would never come a day when I didn't find myself lost somewhere in the snaking labyrinths of alleys that wind like veins and arteries across the city. Valentina was Venice born and bred. She knew every *soto-portego*, *campo*, dead end *corte* and quick shortcut by heart. The leaning tower of the Greek church emerged above the rooftops for a minute or two. We walked through the square of San Giovanni in Bragora, past the modest place of worship where Vivaldi was baptised and – with rather less historical authenticity – the remains of John the Baptist were once interred. After that, I was back to being an outsider, clueless as to where we were, or, for that matter, where we were headed.

In a minute or two we crossed a canal with a bridge I vaguely recognised, Valentina walking so briskly it was hard to keep up. She appeared so focused on something there was no point in trying to spark a conversation. Perhaps it was the missing Jolyon Godolphin, though she'd seemed sure he would be apprehended before long. I glimpsed the white portico of the Schiavoni *scuola* where Carpaccio's St George had been slaughtering unfortunate dragons for a good five centuries and more and started to feel myself on safer ground. This part of Castello I did know, but as soon as I realised that, she took a sharp turn into a narrow and shadowy archway that I would have thought the entrance to a private house. But no. Somewhere between the waterfront and the Arsenale we entered a warren of alleys with a tiny square at its heart. In the middle of the low, shabby terrace stood a set of bright green double doors, above them a hand-painted sign with a crude depiction of a half-full wine glass, *Bar da Ugo* scrawled above it in rough calligraphy.

Ugo was a large, ruddy-faced chap pushing seventy, with a full head of silver hair and a stained cook's apron around his capacious stomach. Valentina's former boss in the Carabinieri, now the owner of a small bar bearing his name. There was much hugging and kissing between them, though it turned out they'd met up only two days before. Being English, I smiled, naturally, and held back. The bar was poorly lit, the walls covered with photographs of locals, some a good couple of decades old. A battered wooden counter looked as if it might have been there when Napoleon's troops were bringing the Venetian republic to an end. At the back, through a pair of rickety French windows, was a tiny courtyard with gas heaters. Ugo led us to a wooden table made from a barrel, then fetched a small carafe of white wine and a plate full of all the Venetian *cicchetti* I'd come to love – *sarde in saor*, sardines in vinegar with onion, the inevitable *baccalà*, aubergine *polpette*, tiny stewed octopus and bread with mountain cheese.

'I'll never find this place again,' I said as we started to tuck in.

Ugo chortled and slapped his belly. He looked more like an out-of-season Santa Claus than a retired cop.

'You're not meant to,' said Valentina.

Our host wagged a fat finger. 'He lives here now, doesn't he? If he can find the place, he's welcome.' He beamed at her. 'Especially if he brings my favourite Carabinieri officer with him. So . . .' He looked about him theatrically, as if checking to see if someone was listening. The courtyard and the bar were, of course, quite empty. 'You finally have a murder, Capitano? Here? In Venice? A famous Englishman?'

She held up one of the *moscardini* and examined the minuscule octopus in the bright lunchtime light.

'Is there something wrong?' he asked, suddenly worried. 'I'm a barman, not a chef. Not like your husband.'

'It's acceptable,' Valentina Fabbri declared, which I thought was probably as high a compliment as she knew. 'Yes. We have a mysterious death.'

'And a suspect?'

'More than I need, thank you.'

Ugo waited. She said nothing more. He got the message and left. It was a delight to be out of her office, to be honest, even feeling a little light-headed after half a glass of Prosecco.

I was about to continue the story of the row when she began examining a chunk of sardine, then said, 'We know Marmaduke Godolphin was setting up his former students – his wife, his publisher among them – for a fall.'

'It looks that way,' I agreed.

'Do you think it occurred to him that perhaps one of them was doing the same to him?'

Her convoluted way of thinking flummoxed me for a moment. 'I'm sorry. You mean . . .?'

'I mean is it possible he suspected that one or several of them invented this mysterious antiquarian Wolff with the express intention of showing him up to be what he truly was, a fraud?'

'But he wasn't. A fraud, that is. He was exactly what he presented himself as. A TV personality. A raconteur. A spinner of entertaining fables that may or may not have been true.'

She looked baffled. 'That is how you saw the man. Not how he saw himself. What would he have done if he'd found one of these people had set a trap for him?'

There was only one answer. 'He'd spring it. With the culprit inside.'

Her phone rang. She listened for a moment, then said a quick *si* and ended the call.

'You've found the son?'

'Volpetti. I've asked him to join us.' She poured out the rest of the small carafe of fizzy wine. 'There are still so many aspects of this story that remain a mystery. Doubtless because I'm not being told them. On with your tale, please. I am, as you English say, all ears.'

'DUKE,' HAUPTMANN SAID, COMING up to the group by the door, hoping to divert the emerging row. 'We're trying to help. To give you the benefit of the doubt. Michelangelo did design a dagger for someone, you know. It's possible—'

'If it's Aldobrandini you're talking about, I'm well aware of what went on there, thank you, Bernard. I was always ten steps ahead of you in Cambridge. I still am. What . . .' he turned to glare at the two of us, 'are these people doing here?'

Luca gulped and went red in the face. Enough. I walked up, put my hand on Hauptmann's sleeve until he stepped aside and faced Godolphin. Forty years before, I might have regarded him with fear. Not any more.

'They're here to help. You never told Luca and me there was a mountain of spurious material to go through.'

'I didn't know.'

'You do now. The two of us can't possibly process all this on our own. It might take months.' An exaggeration, but he wasn't to know. 'Bernard and Caroline kindly offered to give a hand, as did Felicity and George. With Jolyon too, we have a team that should be able to sift and label and sort all thirteen cases – thirteen, every one full to the brim – and find your precious letters within a couple of days. Or . . .' I offered the flimsiest of olive branches, 'perhaps turn them up in a minute or two if we're left to proceed in peace.'

I'd never stood up to the occasional bully I encountered as an archivist. In fact, I doubt I'd confronted one ever. Just then, I wondered why. It was the right thing and it needed doing.

'I am paying you two—'

'Do you want us to continue or not?' I asked with a deliberate effort at a snarl.

'Of course.'

'Then leave us to get on with the job. I will not carry on if you are going to interrupt proceedings with behaviour I consider unacceptable. You can stick your money, Godolphin.'

'Stick it,' Luca repeated, jabbing a finger in the air. 'We are professionals, sir. Not your slaves. Stick . . . it.'

Felicity stepped in front of me. 'I'm not interested in your bloody letters. Where is she? What have you done?'

'I said. The food perhaps . . .' he muttered.

'Jesus, Duke. I know you. I know that look on your face. Outside.'

For once, he obeyed.

It was a fine old argument. Godolphin, Felicity and the son. Lots of shouting. Lots of jabbing of fingers, a welter of accusations, a few weak protests on Godolphin's part, so feeble they carried the obvious stain of guilt. Plenty of ripe language. Something amiss must have happened on his lunch with Patricia Buckley. To Torcello by private boat, it seemed, an outing to the far reaches of the lagoon, which seemed indulgent to say the least. There was a shiftiness to him, a fear behind the anger, I guess. Just as that thought came into my head, I saw Jolyon lose his temper entirely.

'You're a total shit,' he yelled, poking his father on the shoulder so hard Godolphin fell back against the well at the centre of the courtyard.

'Jolyon,' his mother said, trying to take his arm. 'It's not worth it.'

'*He's* not worth it. A total shit to all of us. Why did you bring us here for this circus? Just so you could wallow in humiliating us?'

Godolphin recovered his balance and brushed moss and dirt from the sleeve of his coat. 'Would you rather I fired you by email?'

'I should punch your bloody lights out,' Jolyon shouted, waving a fist. 'You're a bastard to Mum. A bastard to me. We're not going through all this again. Not after Julie. You hear me?'

'Arnold . . .' said a soft voice at my shoulder. It was Luca, of course. 'As you said, we have work to do. Come on. Let's do it.'

Hauptmann patted me on the back. 'Don't let him get to you, old man. It's what he wants.'

More than he wanted the Michelangelo letters? The greater fame that might come his way if he really did manage to show that one of the world's most celebrated artists and intellects was a scheming villain participating in two vile murders? I doubted that. All the same, cruelty was second nature to Marmaduke Godolphin. A part of his character, his persona, much as the occasional stammer was for me. He couldn't help himself, not that it was much of an excuse.

His son returned, dabbing at his face. There was blood beneath one of his nostrils. He was holding his right hand. There'd been a scuffle in the courtyard. From the look on Felicity's face, I guessed she'd had to intervene.

'I think,' she said, 'Jolyon's going to call it a day for now.'

'I'm all right, Mum,' he shot back like a teenager scolded for getting into a brawl.

'You're a Godolphin. You're never all right. Come on. We'll get a drink somewhere. God knows I need one.'

We watched them leave, not a word spoken between us. Then, when they were out of sight, George Bourne boomed, 'A spritz sounds an exceptionally good idea. So long as it comes with a bit of gin and vermouth, and they skip the water and fruit salad.'

'You mean a Negroni?' Caroline Fitzroy said.

He tapped his forehead. 'Correct. I quite forgot. A Negroni. There's a rather fine cocktail bar around the corner I found . . .'

They went for their jackets. Luca glanced at me, hope in his genial face. I'd had enough of work and Godolphin's schemes.

As Bourne led the way out, promising to return the following morning, we took one last look around our newly created archive, such as it was. Then locked up.

'Perhaps we'll find something tomorrow,' Luca suggested, sniffing the icy late-afternoon air. It was dark already and there was little in the way of illumination in this abandoned corner of the archives.

'You really think there's something there?'

He nodded. 'I do. Though what . . . I've no idea. The Aldobrandini dagger. The fact that Michelangelo knew all these people. That he had Benvenuto Cellini to lean upon if he wanted the thing made. There's something to be uncovered here. Can't you feel it?'

Of course I could. I was determined to find it too.

MY LITTLE NEIGHBOURHOOD SAT on the border of San Polo and Dorsoduro. Only tourists who were hopelessly lost made their way into the short *corte* where I lived in a one-bed downstairs flat. They soon realised it led to nothing but the narrow stretch of grey water behind the Scuola San Rocco. The busy hive of Campo Santa Margherita was a few minutes away, and always popular with locals and visitors, day and night, for the bars and restaurants and a few shops. But mostly I met locals on my walks, people working in the city or retired like me. There were, in term time, always plenty of students too, the teeming, transient population of young enrolled at Ca' Foscari, the university headquartered in a doge's former palace on the Grand Canal, or the architecture school in the old Tolentini church complex on the way back to Piazzale Roma. Watching them skip around the city of an evening, hopping from bar to bar, sometimes wearing laurel wreaths and silly costumes as they sang filthy drunken songs to celebrate graduation, a custom going back decades, reminded me of Cambridge, of what it was like to be young and, for a little while, free of the weary doubts and worries of life to come.

They were almost always friendly, if a little raucous at times. One of their favourite haunts was a dark, sparse bar close to Tonolo. The wine and spritz were good and always reasonable, and there were seats at the window with a view out onto the narrow street. Sometimes, when I wanted some time to think, I'd take one and stare out at the queue for the cake shop and the steady traffic tramping between Frari and Campo and towards the bus station. It was a little like watching a moving painting, a Venetian Lowry of engaging ordinariness, the constant motion of everyday life. Calming, especially in those early days when, from time to time, I'd found myself filled with uncertainty about the rash and rapid move from Wimbledon, and my future as a solitary stranger in a place I was only starting to know.

Those kind tickets from London that introduced me to the city's libraries and the friendship of the irrepressible Luca mostly cured me of that brief melancholy. Still, after Godolphin's performance that afternoon, I didn't feel like going straight home, where I knew I'd be lured back into trawling books and academic archives hunting for more information on the blasted Medici and their relationship with the extraordinary Michelangelo di Lodovico Buonarroti Simoni, seeking traces of blood among records of old ink and parchment. An archivist's craving for order and discovery never leaves you. It's an addiction. At least for me.

I ducked into the doorway and took a battered seat by the window. The young woman behind the counter, an arts student who liked to speak English, spotted my arrival immediately and fetched a Campari spritz and a bowl of crisps without being asked. As I took a first welcome sip, I was aware I was being watched. There, at a table near the back, sat Felicity Godolphin, her son and the sorry-looking Patricia Buckley.

Damn, I thought, and wondered if I could throw some money on the counter and make myself scarce. Too late. I'd been spotted. Felicity was up on her feet, striding over as I stared wistfully at the door.

'We need to talk.'

Jolyon nursed what looked like the start of a bruise on his bloody nose. The young American was tearful and appeared divided between self-pity and despair. Felicity Godolphin, nostrils flaring, was consumed with fury. It was, I must admit, quite a spectacle.

'I'm sorry,' I said, before they could get started, 'but I should make it clear. I'm not about to get involved in a family argument. I saw what that was like back in the Archives. It's not a place where an outsider can or should intervene.'

'Dammit,' Felicity cried. 'You haven't even listened to what we have to say.'

True, I hadn't. That much they were owed.

It was quick to tell and entirely predictable. Much like, I imagine, the story of the late Julie Dean's encounters with Godolphin had been. Duke had been cosying up to Patricia Buckley for weeks after the American network dispatched her to come to an arrangement over a new historical series. Jolyon was under the impression she was looking for a job in the BBC, and had taken her to one side, warned her about his father and showed her round London and the sights. All the same, Godolphin senior was not a man to be denied, especially if he felt the prize on offer could be snatched from the arms of his timid son.

Patricia, it seemed, had managed to fend off the old man with as much good grace as she could muster. The American network was determined to steal Godolphin from the BBC. Were she to return home without a deal, she might find herself fired. There was no alternative. She had to stay and get his name on the contract.

Then came the invitation to lunch at the Cipriani in Torcello, a place where Hemingway had worked on his novel *Across the River and into the Trees* while conducting an affair with an eighteen-year-old Venetian countess, Adriana Ivancich. Godolphin explained this to Patricia Buckley in the water taxi on the way back from lunch, and described how Hemingway, then almost fifty, wrote of a dying middle-aged soldier's affair with a young aristocrat. How her youth and compassion dimmed his memories of war and fear of death. The author's relationship with Adriana was mirrored in the plot, though it was never clear how sexual the real-life association was. Hemingway had given her a typewriter and talked to the girl about taking up writing, bought her a camera and helped her learn to use it. He'd even allowed her to design the dust jacket of the novel's first edition, then returned to Cuba and his miserable wife. After a few years, the affair, brought to life one scorching Venetian summer, had petered out. A gift had been passed between young and old in a few brief moments of passion. The pair had, for a while, felt their lives enriched by one another, but not for long.

All this I knew already. I'd set out to read every Venice-set novel I could find when we decided on the move. *Across the River* was far from a favourite, nor was the story behind it as pleasant as Godolphin made out. As with his TV work, he told the tale he wished, not the grubby truth. Poor Adriana had indeed designed a dust jacket for the book, but the publisher turned it down then, under pressure from the writer, amended it to something more professional. Alcohol, heart disease, diabetes and depression took hold of Hemingway. His distant Venetian muse wasn't far behind. She wrote poetry no one much liked, then, after his suicide, a book about their relationship that never found an American publisher. In her early fifties, married and miserable, she hanged herself from a tree in the yard of her home in Tuscany and was laid to rest in Porto Ercole, the place Caravaggio had died, sick and washed up on a beach.

Godolphin told Patricia Buckley none of this. Nor was I about to mention it to the distraught young woman across the table from me in that quiet bar. What had happened in the water taxi back from Torcello was so easily predictable. After regaling her with fanciful tales of Hemingway and Adriana Ivancich's affair, he'd pounced in the most brutal of ways. While the taxi cruised slowly across the lagoon back to Venice – perhaps at Godolphin's request – she'd struggled to fight off the old man's flailing advances on the leather couch inside the cabin.

The details I didn't know and didn't want to. I was struggling to keep the name of Julie Dean and a picture of the Central Line platform at Oxford Circus, a train approaching, out of my head.

'I'm so sorry,' I said.

Felicity glared at me. 'Sorry's not enough.'

'What do you expect me to do?'

'He tried to rape her, Arnold! God knows I've put up with enough from that man over the years. But this . . .'

'Go to the police. Make a complaint.'

Patricia Buckley looked scared. 'I can't do that. New York would terminate me straight away. Besides, it's his word against mine. I did . . . I did go to his room the other night. He asked me. I didn't want him to think I loathed him. He said he wanted to talk about the contract. Kind of . . .'

'Then you should leave.' It was all I could think of. 'Luca and I will tell him we're out of this circus. It won't be a great loss. Something's felt wrong from the beginning.'

'I can't!' she cried, the tears starting. 'Don't you understand? They'll blame me. I can't . . .'

'She's right,' Jolyon Godolphin interrupted. 'It's not the first time, is it, Mum?'

There was a strong note of accusation in his voice at that moment. Once again I heard a Tube train racing out of the mouth of a dark tunnel.

Felicity downed her spritz. 'You must never be alone with him from now on. Leave this to me. I'll deal with it. As I should have done years ago with Julie Dean. I didn't know then. I do now. All of us must keep going.' There was that brief, sharp smile I'd come to know. 'We must let my husband have his moment of glory. His *ridotto*. His apotheosis. Mustn't we?'

She turned to me. 'Patty can't stay in the Valier any more. Find somewhere else. I'll pay.'

'The Al Sole,' I said straight away. 'It's just around the corner.'

She looked it up on her phone, called them, found there was a room going and booked it on the spot. 'Jolyon. You fetch her things. I'll walk her round there. We're agreed then. Duke gets nowhere near her without one of us present.'

Patricia Buckley was crying uncontrollably. Felicity wrapped the weeping woman in her arms.

'The bastard's not doing this again,' she muttered.

LUCA ARRIVED WHILE I was telling my tale at the table in Ugo's courtyard. He looked shocked when I came to the part about meeting the three of them in the bar. I'd kept this to myself until then. Felicity had demanded it. I don't think she fully trusted my Venetian friend, not that I was going to tell him.

Another small carafe arrived, along with a second round of *cicchetti*. Valentina kept glancing at her phone. I wondered if she was feeling less confident about the missing Jolyon Godolphin. But no. When she saw me noticing, she said it was to check the new menu for her husband's restaurant that night.

'The man was a brute,' Luca said out of nowhere, reaching for his glass. 'An absolute monster. If I'd any idea he was such a beast, I'd have turned down his approach at the very start.'

'Then he would have found someone else,' Valentina suggested. 'There's no point in allowing yourself to be haunted by regrets, Luca. What's done is done. You had no great part in it.' She hesitated, then leaned forward and asked, 'Did you?'

He muttered something under his breath, and I realised there was a secret here, shared between the two of them.

'I'm sorry. I don't understand.'

She nodded in my direction and said, 'Tell him. What you told me.'

Guilt written all over his face, Luca apologised profusely. 'I was embarrassed. It seemed a small and unimportant matter—'

'Ha!' Valentina cried, so loudly Ugo popped his head round the door from the bar. 'A fellow asks you to find him a woman for the night, a known lothario, half drunk, lurching down dark alleys at your direction only to wind up dead . . . and you think it a small and unimportant matter?'

'I did tell you in the end.'

'Just as well.'

'Luca. Valentina. I don't understand!'

I knew that after the bizarre and shocking evening of the so-called *ridotto*, Godolphin had taken him to one side. Until that moment, Luca had never explained why.

'The man wanted company. A woman. It was a physical requirement, he said. I was the only local around. I imagine he thought it beneath him to enquire of the concierge. He said it didn't matter how much. He wanted to know where to look.'

I was astonished. The dark side to Godolphin's character seemed quite boundless.

'The wife says he's been doing this on his travels for years,' Valentina explained. 'When they went to a foreign city, he would seek out brothels. Sometimes, when she was younger, she was expected to accompany him and . . .'

She left it at that, thank goodness.

'Good grief,' I whispered. 'What dreadful lives they lead. I trust you told him to get lost.'

Luca waved around his arms the way he liked. 'You met the man! He's one of yours! How could anyone tell a fellow like that to get lost. If that was a possibility, we should have done it earlier.'

'Then—'

'I have no idea where to find a woman of the night. I did what I could to get rid of him. I said to look around Piazzale Roma. A bus station. Cars. Taxis. If there was anywhere to find such a service . . .'

Valentina Fabbri was laughing over the food.

'What's so funny?' Luca demanded.

'That you should think the place to go for loose company is Piazzale Roma. Good Lord. For a chap who's so familiar with women, you have a remarkably poor knowledge of this city's seamier side.'

'I have no knowledge of that kind of thing and no wish for it!'

She wagged a slice of polenta in his face. 'You should have told me this from the beginning. Instead, I had to drag it out of you.'

'I was embarrassed. The man was dead. I couldn't help wonder what his wife would think.'

'I said. His wife was well aware of his habits. I doubt anything he did would shock her.'

No. That was wrong. Felicity had surely warned Duke Godolphin about his behaviour before and expected him to heed what she'd said. The fact that he'd ignored her threat had clearly rattled her.

'I disagree,' I said. 'From what I heard, it seemed the man was breaking a promise to her. That he wouldn't repeat his past behaviour.'

'And she thought,' Valentina asked, 'that he should pay?'

'Possibly. I've no idea. I wasn't privy to their conversations. But again, that's one of those things people say without much thought. It could mean anything. Or nothing. May I finish my story? About our exploration of the Wolff Bequest?'

She was still thinking. 'Perhaps he really did identify with Ernest Hemingway. A great lover. A great artist. A great ego.'

'The last definitely,' Luca agreed.

'Great egos are often made of glass. Hemingway put a shotgun to his head and killed himself. All his dreams, all his passion, all his hope quite spent.' She sighed. 'The foreigners this city attracts.'

We waited for more.

Valentina clicked her fingers at Ugo through the window for the bill. 'Carry on, Arnold. We're running out of time.'

TUESDAY SAW US BACK at work, Jolyon, Felicity, Caroline, George and Hauptmann helping mostly in silence. Duke Godolphin never showed his face. Patricia Buckley planned to stay in her room in the Al Sole, avoiding the man until the planned celebration on the Wednesday evening where the deal with the American network would, once proof of his claims was available, be agreed. Then, Felicity whispered to me as we sorted and sifted Wolff's junk, she would return to New York and ask for someone else to take over production duties on the planned series.

By four that afternoon, working mostly in silence, the six of us had cleared all thirteen packing cases. The contents were neatly stacked in piles – fonds, as it were – on the tables at the back of the room. Modern Venice seemed to boast more shops hoping to flog cast-off bric-a-brac than places selling household essentials, or so Luca frequently complained. The contents of the shadowy Wolff's bequest would have found welcome homes there for those in search of old maps and prints and winsome photographs of tourist resorts from Cornwall to Campania. But there was not a single document relating to the Medici or Michelangelo, or anything close.

Luca and I were, if I'm honest, almost relieved. It saved us the awkward chore of trying to verify anything that might have turned up. Godolphin might have been convinced that his late benefactor had struck pure historical gold. We would be determined to find something akin to proof if we were to attach our names to its credibility. The rest of them were, to my surprise, disappointed. Perhaps it was just that we'd put in so much effort looking for his damned Michelangelo letters, only to come up short. Or in the case of Caroline Fitzroy and Hauptmann, there was genuine frustration that they had nothing to pore over and pull apart the way academics did. George Bourne didn't appear to give a damn either way, and when the last box was cleared, he announced he was off round the corner to down a couple of cocktails in the fancy bar he'd found. The place, it seemed, had rather taken a shine to him. Or, at the ten euros a glass they charged, his money.

'Well,' Luca declared as we wandered up and down in front of the tables, 'who's going to tell our lord and master that the wild goose chase he sent us on doesn't even have a goose?'

'I'll do it,' Hauptmann said. 'If that's what we want.'

I kept pacing the other side of the room, finger to cheek, staring at the empty boxes. There was something odd about them. Something we'd surely missed.

'Best do it now, Bernard,' Felicity suggested. 'Before he's had a drink or two.' Her eyes were directly on him. 'One thing and another he's not in the best of moods, as I'm sure you'll understand.'

'Very well. This may not be pleasant.'

'Wait a minute,' I said. 'Let's not be hasty. We're not done here. I think we should take a look at—'

BEFORE I COULD START on what I thought a thoroughly fascinating segment of my story – the winding route that led us to Wolff's well-concealed letters – Valentina Fabbri was waving me to be silent.

She had her phone out and was tapping a message.

'What is it?' Luca wondered.

'The Godolphin boy. He gave himself up at the train station.'

'I thought you had him in a cell along with the rest of them.'

'Not now, Luca. I'm sure you've work to do. Or a friend to visit. Arnold and I must return to my office.' She beamed at him and he wilted a little beneath her gaze. 'I may require you later.'

She tapped another message on her phone and placed it in her pocket. 'It seems the young man wishes to confess to the murder of his father.'

SEVEN

The Palimpsests

Try as I might, Valentina was not going to allow me to skip the interview in which Jolyon Godolphin so desperately wished to confess to patricide.

'I may need your linguistic skills,' she said as we walked back, the quick way this time, along the waterfront. 'As a translator.'

'Your English seems perfect. Better than a few natives I've met.'

'It should be. I spent three years at Ca' Foscari studying it. And eighteen months in . . .' she thought for a moment, 'Bromley. Waiting on tables in a pizza place with my cousin Giulia.'

I couldn't take my eyes off the Bacino San Marco. That expanse of water running to the Doge's Palace on our side, the campanile and basilica of San Giorgio Maggiore opposite, the mouths of the Giudecca and Grand canals, the sharp, arrow-like spear of the Punta della Dogana with the dome of Salute just beyond. A familiar sight but breathtaking on a clear, icy winter's day all the same. If the streams of pedestrians I watched from the window of the student bar near Tonolo were Lowry, here the city was Turner again.

'Words are only words, Arnold. They do not teach you nuance. Your fellow countrymen, while more rudimentary than they realise, positively drip in nuance. I may notice. Comprehension and insight are more difficult.'

A persuasive argument, or at least it might have been if Valentina – then or since – had asked me a single question concerning nuance.

'How long will it take you to tell me the rest of the story? Of how you found these strange letters Godolphin sought?'

Not so long, I said. Though there were many twists to the tale to follow. She checked her watch, called the office and said to place Jolyon Godolphin in a room with his mother and an officer to watch them. Then wait on her arrival.

'He's hardly a child,' I pointed out when she was off the phone. 'Also, don't you normally keep suspects apart?'

'A coffee,' she declared, diving off to one of the tourist places that line the Riva degli Schiavoni as it approaches the Doge's Palace. 'We must finish this part of your story.'

The waiter clearly recognised her from his jumpy reaction as she grabbed a seat outside beneath a gas heater. I'd never have used a place like this knowing what it would cost.

'I don't understand. You have a man who wishes to confess. Yet you seem in no hurry.'

'Sometimes it pays to let them stew.' Macchiatos and a plate of tiny biscuits. I saw the bill, placed gingerly on the table. Half of what it would have cost me. 'Two days you spent going through that rubbish you called the Wolff Bequest.'

'I wouldn't describe it all as rubbish. And Godolphin called it the Wolff Bequest. Not us. Please stop ascribing to me every action an Englishman has taken anywhere at any time in history.'

That seemed to amuse her. 'But you are the only Englishman I have in my sights right now. Two days you spent delving through all that junk. And suddenly you strike gold. From something you'd looked at already.' Her coffee was gone in two quick gulps. 'How?'

BECAUSE I WAS DETERMINED not to give up. That's how. That Tuesday, when every envelope had been opened and found to be of no interest whatsoever, we were at our lowest. Godolphin had still to arrive. When he did, Hauptmann had taken it on himself to tell him the truth: his treasure chest was empty. The late Grigor Wolff was either a charlatan or a lunatic.

But I couldn't let it go. While they continued to sift through the piles of material in a thoroughly half-hearted fashion, my attention turned to the cases that had carried them to Venice. They were made of stiff reinforced plywood, with paper slips in plastic envelopes, presumably for tracking, stuck to the sides, and a few scrawls in what looked like marker pen. The writing on the one in the middle clearly said 'pal', though what that meant I'd no idea. And I wanted to find out.

Without saying a word to the rest, I walked round all thirteen empty cases, turning them about so that the scrawls were visible. When Felicity asked me what on earth I was doing, all I said was 'Trying to solve a riddle.'

Luca looked even more miserable when he heard that. We'd already been through the possibility that Wolff had somehow sought to hide the Michelangelo letters from plain view. There could, we felt, be only one reason if this were the case. They were, effectively, contraband, either stolen or not meant for export.

I set about checking each box then rearranging them. The rest soon began to understand what I was getting at. The marker pen scribbles on the sides – which seemed random when viewed on their own – now lined up as a message across all thirteen boxes: 'tro-va-pal-in-se-s-ti-lon-dra-3-mil-ano-7'.

Trova is Italian for 'find', of course. *Palinsesti* translates as 'palimpsests', an obscure term for most, though not me or Luca. It means a document, paper or parchment that has been reused, the original writing scrubbed out and replaced by newer text.

The bells of the Frari chimed four. Godolphin was due to pay us a visit any minute. It seemed clear the cryptic line could only mean that one of the letters came from London and could be found in chest three, the second from Milan and was in box seven.

Now you see why archivists are so careful when it comes to what we're supposed to call metadata. Our fonds, such as they were, had been organised on the basis of geography, but each document was still in an envelope on which was marked the number of the box from which it came. Thanks to our careful handling of the material, it was a simple task to find the relevant documents. Made all the easier because there were only two in each fond that carried the magical shipment number. Wolff, it seemed, had planned this very carefully.

Luca and I retrieved them then placed them on a spare desk at the end of the room. The light had almost failed outside. We turned on two study lamps to see what we had. One of the London envelopes contained a miniature of the poster for the Monty Python film *Life of Brian*. The second was a framed print of a sketch I recognised as being by the eccentric artist Louis Wain, famous for his anthropomorphic cats. This was a strange and disturbing image, a shrieking cat with glaring eyes and the message beneath in the artist's handwriting, 'Caught! Keep your mouth shut and let me open your mind for you.'

The first Milan envelope we tried held nothing but a match programme for a home game between Inter and Lazio in 1997. The next, another framed print, an old sepia photograph of a performance of Verdi's opera *Macbeth* at La Fenice the same year, the murderous villain of the title creeping through the dark, dagger in hand.

A palimpsest, I repeat, is a document written over an earlier one. It seemed impossible that any of this material could fit that description if we were to take the hidden message on the packing cases literally.

'Perhaps,' Luca suggested, 'the elusive and dead Wolff has been playing a trick on Duke Godolphin all along.'

'Absurd,' roared a voice from the door. 'Poppycock. Let me see.' The great man entered the room, face flushed – drink, I imagine. Now Patricia Buckley was out of the picture, it was hard to see how he might have any company to keep him amused.

He marched over, looked at what we had and demanded an explanation. I kept quiet, thinking. Luca offered his and concluded, 'I can't see how any of this could be a palimpsest.'

The old man glared at the piles of documents in our fonds. 'Then you'll have to go through it all again and find something that is.'

Luca shook his head. 'No, sir. Not on my part. I've expended as much time on this matter as I'm willing to give you. It's clear Wolff, whoever he was, played you for a fool.'

'No one calls me a fool! You're being paid!'

'*Stick it!*' Luca cried, then grinned at me.

'God,' Hauptmann drawled, 'you Brits do go on. Let it go, Duke. Enough's enough.'

Another fiery argument was on the cards. A prospect I found quite tedious.

I laughed, and that stopped them.

'What?' asked Luca.

I picked up the print of the opera photo, reached for a pair of sharp scissors on the desk and began to remove the brown parchment backing.

'You're all being very literal, if you don't mind my saying. A palimpsest may simply be something that exists in layers, a part of the original still visible. Wolff, it seems, used his imagination. We should use ours. Gloves, Luca?'

He found a pair, white cotton, brand new, in a desk drawer and handed them over.

It was there, behind the poster. A single sheet of yellowed paper, in the corner an ancient ink stain much like the splash of a childish Rorschach test. We all crowded round, breathless.

Ancient spidery writing, and a very precise drawing of a weapon. Godolphin pulled out his phone and found the photo Wolff had sent him. It was the same design of a stiletto, the one Michelangelo was thought to have produced, perhaps originally for Aldobrandini. The text Luca would have to decipher later. For now, one word was very clear, the detail just visible on the photo Wolff had sent Godolphin: *Cellini!*

'O ye of little faith,' the great man said with a triumphant grin.

I'd left the scissors on the desk. Godolphin grabbed them, waved away the offer of the gloves, picked up the second print, the one with the cat, and opened the back. Sure enough, there was a page inside. The same spidery handwriting, the same appearance of aged parchment.

'What's the betting that somewhere in this Michelangelo tells his correspondent to make sure to shut up?' I suggested.

Luca, an eagle-eyed fellow used to deciphering documents from the Renaissance, leaned down and took a look at the handwriting. He pointed to a line at the end and murmured, 'Correct, Arnold. You are quite the sleuth, I must say.'

Godolphin told us to get on with the translation. It would be needed first thing in the morning. There were matters to be discussed with the TV company in New York.

'Where's George Bourne?' he asked, looking round the room. 'Didn't he join you in your efforts to belittle me?'

'Dammit, Duke!' Felicity snapped. 'We've been slaving away on your behalf here for two days. And that's the thanks we get?'

He sniffed. 'You've all had a free trip to Venice at my expense, haven't you? Tomorrow, the *ridotto*. Contracts signed. Deals done.' He smiled. 'New beginnings. For all of us. If any of you see Bourne before I do, tell him I'm adamant. The fool's had the last book he'll get from me.' He pointed at the ancient letters on the desk. 'They've just earned me a fortune. *You* just earned me a fortune. Who knows? I may even give you a mention in the credits.'

He nodded at Luca on the way out. 'On with it, man. I want to be reading this over breakfast.'

*　　*　　*

VALENTINA STOPPED OUTSIDE HER office in San Zaccaria. 'You were the only one who saw the link to solving this riddle? No one else?'

'Eleanor was keen on crosswords. Always looking for the cryptic. She'd often ask me for help.'

'And if you hadn't struck lucky . . . the letters would have remained unfound? Neither Volpetti or the others would have spotted what seems to me a fairly obvious clue?'

In time probably. How would I know? Though primarily we'd all been looking for Godolphin's treasure in brown envelopes, not snatches of an obscure word scrawled on packing cases.

'Godolphin should have been more grateful,' she said and started for the door.

Jolyon was in the place they used for interviews, still with his mother. No one had seen fit to talk to him in Valentina's absence.

'I'd really rather not be a part of this,' I begged again. 'Please.'

Nothing doing. 'I'd really rather you were. Come.'

The room was bare and cold, the fluorescent tubes throwing a harsh light on two miserable people slumped in chairs on the far side of a long grey metal table. I could hear pigeons cooing and shuffling on the roof, then the half-hour chimes. We waited for the sonorous voices of the bells to die, then Valentina took out a pocket recorder, a pen and a notebook and asked, 'Why did you run, Jolyon?'

The question took him by surprise. 'Because . . . because I was guilty.'

'This is Venice. You had no money. No clothes. No ticket anywhere. No way of escape. You must have known that.'

Felicity swore under her breath and muttered, 'This isn't right.'

'Please,' Valentina said. 'Let him answer for himself. Why—'

'Because I was stupid,' he snapped. 'Always have been. Always will be. Dad said that often enough, didn't he? A waste of skin. That was one of his favourites.'

I felt so desperately sorry for the young chap. It was obvious he was in the darkest depths of misery.

'Your father was a cruel man, Jolyon,' I said. 'Crueller than anyone I've ever known. I know this is easily said, but you need to step out from his shadow.'

'What shadow?' he retorted. 'The old bastard's dead. I'm glad of it. I'll dance on his grave.'

'Hard if you're in jail for his murder,' Valentina pointed out. 'How did you do it? Why? When?'

'Why?' He laughed. 'You're really asking why?'

'I am. He's been a monster for years, or so it seems. Why now?'

'Because he was dumping us! Mum. Me. Everyone. No job. No future.'

Felicity reached over and put her hand on his knee. 'We'll never starve, Jo.'

'Not now,' he said with the briefest of sly smiles. 'I had to do it. If there was any justice, he'd be the one here facing jail for throwing himself on Patty.'

'If someone had made a complaint to us,' Valentina replied, 'then perhaps he would have been. But they didn't.'

'He'd have wriggled free. He always does. You don't understand.'

'Very true. Enlighten me. When did you kill him?'

He hesitated for a moment. 'Must have been around midnight.'

'Where?'

'You know where. Everybody knows. That bridge he took us to the first night. The place the Medici was murdered.'

'Yes,' she agreed. 'Everyone does know that. Tell me your movements beforehand.'

That made him falter again. The *ridotto* had ended in such anger and confusion, I'd really no idea where people went.

Jolyon Godolphin, it seems, went for a walk with Patricia Buckley. The two of them had beers and pizza in Campo Santa Margherita. She went back to her hotel. He headed off to his.

'Dad was standing by the bridge. The one from his pathetic little performance. We had an argument. He took out that dagger of his and waved it in my face. I grabbed it, he tried to punch me. Again. So I stabbed him. Then threw him in the canal.'

Valentina wasn't making notes. 'Where? Where did you stab him?'

He tapped his chest. 'Here.'

'How many times?'

'Once. Hard. As hard as I could.'

She closed her notebook, not a fresh word in it, then picked up the recorder and showed it to us. It wasn't turned on.

This was becoming ridiculous, so I decided to jump in. 'Duke was stabbed twice, Jolyon. You're lying and I can think of one reason only. Why on earth do you think your mother killed him? It's ludicrous. Almost as ludicrous as the idea that you did.'

Valentina turned and stared at me, half a smile on her face. 'See, Arnold. You are glad you came.'

'This is a farce. It's obvious.'

Jolyon Godolphin's cheeks turned crimson. 'I . . . I don't think any such thing.'

'What?' It was Felicity.

'Madame,' Valentina went on, 'Signor Clover is correct. It's as clear as day your son never murdered his father. He's no idea how it happened. Only what he seems to have guessed from what he's heard. Yet he ran from here in a hopeless attempt to incriminate himself. He gave himself up to my officers. Then he confessed, though if he really wanted to do that, he could have saved us all the trouble and done so when we first took you all into custody.' She frowned, that familiar expression. 'He could only have done this for one reason. To throw the suspicion off someone else. Who can only be—'

'I didn't kill Duke!' Felicity cried. Her son glanced at her. She slapped him on the hand, the way one might a child. 'Oh for God's sake, Jo . . .'

He looked near to tears.

'You said you'd had enough, Mum. You said after Julie . . . if he did that again. I've never seen you that mad. You said you'd kill him.'

'I've said that every bloody day for the last forty years. If I was going to do it, don't you think I'd have managed by now?'

The *capitano* looked at her watch and sighed. 'Wasting police time is a criminal offence, Jolyon. Be grateful I'm not minded to charge you.' She nodded at the door. 'You may leave.'

He blinked. 'But . . .'

'I said you may leave. I have crossed one suspect off my list anyway. Not that I expected it to be a foolish young man trying to protect his mother.' A flash of a smile. 'Perhaps for no reason.'

'Mum . . .'

'Signora Godolphin will be staying here until we get to the bottom of what happened. What *really* happened.'

Jolyon folded his arms and looked quite cross. 'Then I stay too.'

'No.' Valentina got to her feet and opened the door. 'This is a Carabinieri station not a hotel reception. Go back to the Valier. We will be in touch when there's news.' Another check of the watch. 'Which I trust will not be far away.'

His voice sounded like that of a hurt teenager when he bleated again, 'Mum . . .'

Felicity leaned across and kissed his cheek. 'Do it, Jo. I know you meant well. But . . . honestly. I never hurt your father. That went one way only.'

Valentina summoned one of her officers to take Felicity back to her cell, then marched her son to the reception area and got his coat and jacket. He was a sorry-looking figure as they let him out into the fading afternoon.

'I didn't enjoy that,' I said as we watched him shuffle off towards the piazza, shoulders hunched, hands in pockets, lost to his own thoughts.

Valentina grumbled something I didn't quite hear, then, 'Didn't you?'

'No.'

She folded her arms, cocked her head to one side and shrugged. 'Yet you leapt in unasked, uninvited.'

'It was plain as a pikestaff the chap was making it all up.'

'It was. But thank you for making the point in any case. Come.'

We went back into the station, and she led me behind the front desk into the back of the building. I've never spent much time on police premises over the years, but this felt more like a municipal office than a place to do with law enforcement. Nevertheless, at the bottom of the long corridor there was a double line of cells with flap windows, much as you saw on the TV. Six of them, three on each side, one empty now that Godolphin Junior had been ejected from the place. Valentina opened all the flaps and issued a cheery greeting to the inmates. They each sat there under the thin light of a single bare bulb, a half-finished meal tray on the floor in front of them. A long way from the luxury of the Valier, it seemed to me.

'For God's sake, Clover,' Caroline called. 'Get the British consulate in here or something. This is ridiculous. I need to get back to Paris.'

'And the American embassy,' Hauptmann added. Felicity and George Bourne said nothing. Patricia Buckley just stared at the bare concrete floor, pink-eyed, fresh from another round of weeping, I imagine.

'The relevant authorities have all been informed,' Valentina said. 'A man has died in questionable circumstances. You can't expect us to allow the suspects to roam the streets.'

Caroline got up and came to the window, taking hold of the bars. She shook them, then said, 'How in God's name am I a suspect?'

'You all are, *signora*. You all had a difficult relationship with the victim and, as far as I can ascertain, opportunity.'

George Bourne perked up and came to his window. 'I don't suppose there's a chance of a drink? Medical reasons.'

Valentina gave him a sharp look. 'If one or more of you wishes to confess, the rest can leave straight away.'

Bourne screwed up his rheumy eyes in puzzlement. 'I thought Jolyon told you he stuck his old man. So one of our keepers said.'

'He was lying.'

'Lying to protect me,' Felicity chipped in. 'Not that it was needed.'

'Stupid boy then,' Bourne grunted. 'A spritz and some crisps?'

'We're the Carabinieri, sir. Not Harry's Bar. This is quite simple. I would like to know which one of you met Godolphin by the Ponte San Tomà the night he died.' Silence. 'Or if any of you have suspicions about the others, who that might be. Should someone like to come to my office for a private conversation on that subject now . . .'

Hauptmann groaned. The rest kept quiet.

'No takers?' she asked. 'Oh well.'

We returned to her office. I expressed my amazement that she should coop up her suspects in such conditions. As for the food, it looked quite disgusting.

'Did you not hear my remark about Harry's Bar? One or more of them knows about the death of Marmaduke Godolphin.' She took her seat, placed the notebook in front of her, scribbled something on a fresh page. 'One or more of them, I imagine, invented the absurdity of the Wolff Bequest as a way of luring Godolphin here, I assume with the aim of making a fool of him while he thought he'd be doing the same to them. That can only mean they must know the man very well, which buttons to press, as it were. The wife . . .'

I told her again: I was still unclear how I might be of help in any of this.

'You're a neutral party, Arnold. An observer with no axe to grind, aren't you? Did you find Felicity Godolphin convincing when she denied harming her husband?'

'I thought so. I'm no expert, but—'

'I thought so too. But until our two mysteries, Godolphin's death and the Wolff issue, are resolved, I won't be satisfied.'

A shrug. Outside, the campanile chimed the quarter-hour.

'Now tell me about these so-called letters of Michelangelo,' ordered Valentina Fabbri.

A CONFESSION: HISTORY IS my field, not art. Eleanor was the fan for that, forever wanting to explore any gallery she could find on her travels, the more obscure the better. A place like the Accademia was up my street, especially for Carpaccio and the Ursula Cycle. My dedication did not, however, run to modern installations in distant cities. I'd always tended to the political, governmental and military side of the past, not the cultural. Michelangelo and da Vinci were names I knew, naturally, along with their most famous works, but their characters and their relationship remained a mystery.

Luca found it extraordinary that I'd no idea the two were familiar with one another and bitter rivals for both commissions and fame. It seemed da Vinci, a more sociable fellow twenty years Michelangelo's senior, was in the habit of wandering the streets with a gang of admirers, throwing insults if he met his younger adversary, a largely friendless loner who seemed able to match him in painting, sculpture, architecture and invention. The two are global icons for their genius, a good reason why Godolphin's attempt to paint the younger one as a conspiracist in two murders would, Luca warned, create a storm of controversy. As Duke Godolphin doubtless understood and craved.

It was news to me, too, that Michelangelo could scarcely stop himself drawing and writing with ink or charcoal and making shapes in wax or any piece of stone or wood that came to hand. He was a manic writer of letters, some fourteen hundred of them still around, the last penned four days before his death. As well as correspondence conducted in plain, businesslike language, there were archly formal love poems written after the style of Petrarch, some, controversially, to a young nobleman, Tommaso dei Cavalieri. A mere twenty-three when Michelangelo, more than three decades his senior, took a shine to him, Cavalieri was at his side when the old man died at his house in Rome, just before his eighty-ninth birthday. The love of his life, it seems, a perilous one in an age when homosexuality was meant to be a capital offence. Michelangelo was a reclusive figure, but one not afraid of danger, or so it appeared. Which, naturally, lent more weight to Godolphin's story.

And here the genius was, right in front of us, or so it appeared, as Luca and I sat down to study the two letters from the Wolff Bequest. Calligraphy and the spotting of forgeries were not my field at Kew, though Eleanor had worked a little in that area until she fell out with the manager, an oddly incurious figure she regarded as a gullible fool. Luca had limited experience there too, but he hinted he knew someone who might be able to help if we needed more expert advice. First things first, though. Since copies of Michelangelo's original letters were available to us through the Archives' online links into other academic databases, it was a simple task to pull up correspondence by the master and compare the calligraphy.

Straight away we found ourselves in intriguing territory. Handwriting in Italy in the days before printing, typewriters and computers was an important professional skill, not the lazy scrawl of so many today, me included. Students were trained to write carefully and clearly in a particular style that would be immediately readable by others. If it was illegible, the document – and the fellow who wrote it – was useless.

The script in the letters we'd uncovered was quite extraordinary, a work of art in itself, even more impressive since it came from nothing but ink and a raven's quill. So unusual that Luca was able to find an academic paper dedicated to Michelangelo's handwriting alone. To me, all his letters looked similar. Fortunately, Luca had taken a course in palaeography, the study of old writing systems, and soon began muttering about technical details – majuscule and minuscule, ascenders and ligatures – that went straight over my head. The paper showed that Michelangelo's handwriting had changed fundamentally during his lifetime, providing us with an important clue when it came to dating and fakery.

His earliest personal letters and poems were written in a style known as *mercantesca,* the everyday Gothic cursive script of commerce he would have learned at school, since it was thought the best way to guarantee that a student would find a job in business. Later he made the conscious decision to change to a form called *cancellaresca,* a humanist cursive designed to be more elegant and easier to read, and from what I could gather, more fashionable in cultural circles. The change probably occurred three decades before the period that interested us.

Luca turned a lamp on our two letters, then bent over and peered through a magnifying glass.

'Here,' he said after a long while. 'Take a look for yourself.'

On the computer screen he had an example of Michelangelo's early *mercantesca* style and the *cancellaresca* of the later years. The differences, now that I looked closely, were apparent. The later writing had a more flowing and personal feel to it, better legibility, a sense of artistic class.

'If it's not him, Luca, it's an exceptionally good copy.'

'I agree.'

'What about the paper? The ink? The . . . feel?' I pointed to the Rorschach stain at the bottom right corner. 'And that?'

'Even geniuses can be clumsy with ink, I imagine.' He grimaced. 'We have one expert in the Archives who knows all about this kind of thing. Unfortunately, she's on holiday in Egypt. Lucia abhors Carnival and flees every year. But . . .' he winked, 'I have ideas.'

You usually do, I thought.

'Let's assume these are genuine for the moment and get down to the text.' He punched my shoulder lightly. 'Well, Arnold. What language is this?'

I wasn't falling for that trick and told him: not Italian, a language that didn't then exist in a formal sense, for the reason that Italy didn't either. Michelangelo wrote in the *lingua franca* of the time for someone of his background and class, Florentine. Thanks to the Renaissance, this was to prove the precursor to the modern language we now know, not that I'd ever tried to see how similar the two were. The English of the sixteenth century, which I'd encountered on a regular basis at Kew, wasn't quite as opaque as the language of Chaucer, but it still required a lot of work. Nor was the official English handwriting of the time as clear and careful as the *cancellaresca* in front of us.

The first missive we looked at was the earlier of the two, addressed to Lorenzino de' Medici and dated 30 December 1536, a week before Alessandro's murder. One page, at the top the drawing of the dagger and the word 'Cellini!'

I could understand around eighty per cent of the words as modern Italian immediately, though there were a few odd spellings and the word order in places made no effort to follow the rules Eleanor and I had been taught at night school.

'Godolphin will require a good version of this in English, won't he?' Luca asked.

'I'm sure he will. He wants to brandish it at the Americans to clinch the deal.' The words he'd thrown at us the day before came back to me – this wasn't academic history; it was show business. 'He'll want it pretty sassy too.'

'I don't do sassy,' my friend declared with a shake of his head.

'Fine,' I said. 'Then leave the final version to me.'

Lorenzino, *caro amico,*

Such times we live in. Such beasts rule the world. I hear your anguish. I am at one with your pain. Yet what am I to say to your request? You know me. A humble man of God, enemy of no soul on this earth. Yet you stir such dark thoughts and desires!

Oh friend, oh dear comrade of old. Know this for sure. I long for home. Like you, I ache for a republic such as the Venetians enjoy. We are Florentines both. Free men, not vassals to a king in all but name. Every day I linger here a little of me dies. If I stay in Rome much longer, my own tomb will be made before the Pope's. Yet he will not let me leave. I am a prisoner amidst a plague of vileness, longing for Florence. But what Florence? Those who fought with me against the cruel monsters of the Medici are either dead, exiled or in chains, suffering daily tortures. Only my genius, my wit and artistry save me from the same fate, for now.

Were I to return to my beloved home what would your wicked cousin Il Moro make of me? Thrice before he's threatened my life, forcing me into hiding in the cold and stinking bowels of the Medici's own chapel. Do not mistake power for intelligence, Lorenzino! Had they the brains, they would have found me imprisoned beneath their long, sharp noses, scrawling idly on San Lorenzo's damp and chilly walls.

Yet the stupid and the venal prosper. The tales of the duke's atrocities are everywhere. Not a man in Rome can think him anything but a monster of infamy, stained with the blood of the innocent, befouled by murder, torture, rapine, sins beyond the imagination of the lowest common criminal destined for the scaffold. Such is the beast that rules you. The beast that would, given his head if I returned, take mine.

So here I linger, the Pope's slave, deprived of the money he rightly owes me, half starving, insulted by his prelates, shambling round the Vatican like a beggar with a palette, a chisel and a brush. I am a humble soul at heart, short on choices. You are a nobleman, free to choose your path. I, meanwhile, write, I dream, I build, I create. These are great matters beyond most men. But great deeds of state are for others.

All I have to offer is the gift I have drawn at the beginning of this page. Were you to take it to Cellini, it is possible you might find he has the same drawing, in more detail, with measurements and directions to make a blade that could change our world for the better. Even that Benvenuto has been furnished the money to make such a weapon and will offer it as a gift in the hope you find it of good use.

I wish you well in your endeavours and pray that one day I may return to a Florence renewed.

Michelagniolo (signature)

'I don't understand the signature,' I said, rereading our translation by Luca's side. 'The name's wrong.'

Luca was insistent. 'No. The name's right. It's an old Tuscan version, "Michelagniolo". He never wrote it as "Michelangelo".'

He ran his index finger down the page and stopped on a curious character. 'Look at the way he writes "che".'

I'd barely noticed for trying to make out the words. But it was quite unusual. The three letters 'c', 'h' and 'e', turned into a single new form, the 'h' stabbing down into the top of an extended 'c' below, with a stem across the rising line to form the 'e'. It looked like musical notation newly invented, yet, after a moment's hesitation, was easily recognisable.

'Is that *cancellaresca*?'

Luca shook his head. 'It's him. I remember getting a lecture on it from Lucia when the Accademia hosted an exhibition of his correspondence. This was a device he invented to compress those three letters into one. Michelangelo never stopped creating, you see. It's all very . . .'

'Convincing?' I suggested.

'It seems so. Ordinarily we would start from the position that these documents are fake, and our job is to overturn that verdict.'

That, I thought, was the exact opposite of what Duke Godolphin expected of us.

'The jury is still out,' I said, and turned to the second letter.

It was dated 3 February 1548, just over three weeks before Lorenzino's assassination at the Ponte San Tomà. The handwriting was much the same, down to the unique 'che'. The page was yellowed, like its counterpart. Hardly surprising, I imagined. A raven's feather, a bottle of ink, a sheet to write on; the means of penning a letter couldn't have changed much in a little over eleven years, any more than Michelangelo's handwriting had. The man's circumstances had altered completely, however. Pope Clement VII, the Medici who had freed him from Alessandro's fury on condition he went to work, was dead. The triple crown was now worn by Paul III, who had pressured Michelangelo into finishing his vast *Last Judgement* in the Sistine Chapel, a massive task that would take him four years fraught with arguments and, as we've heard already, result in a work so full of nudity the Church immediately set about toning it down.

So the Michelangelo of 1548 was a different man to the one who seemed to have written the cautious missive to Lorenzino, with a none-too-subtle hint that he was furnishing a weapon suitable for murder from the villainous Benvenuto Cellini. Adored by Paul III for all their occasional disagreements, lauded as the greatest artist the world had known, he now seemed unassailable.

Though the letter appeared to paint a different picture.

Antonio, *amico*,

Your wretched correspondent writes from the pit of sin that is Rome. Expect no good news. I must warn you that I'm barefoot and naked, so to speak, and work for the holy slave master day and night. My life is only hardship and toil, penury and exhaustion. Fame means nothing, nor the dream of love or the simple affection enjoyed by ordinary men.

I have been in this state ever since Florence, and we both know the reason. A man's sins follow him through life. As do those who sin on our behalf.

And now, dear Zantani, you tell me this beast I once favoured is on your doorstep, in your bed, cuckolding you nightly, father to a child who should bear your name. You married a beauty in La Barozza. You should have been content with a plainer woman, one with less ambition and brains, provided she is neither deformed nor mean-spirited.

My own tastes bring me brief respite from all these miseries from time to time, though caution, friend, is always my watchword. In this and so much else, as it must be yours.

Your tormentor is no longer my concern. What intercourse I had with him all those years ago is done, never to be spoken of between us. Though should he find this letter – and I trust he won't – that might change to my detriment. A secret must be well kept. With good fortune it dies with its keeper. The man who cuckolds you could be my undoing. There are still those out there who wish to see me dead.

To that end, and yours, the address in San Polo you provided is now in capable hands. God willing, they will act, and we will both be released from his perfidious presence. If a ruffian who calls himself Bibboni makes himself known to you in the weeks to come, treat him kindly but with circumspection. Venice, I hear, has a fondness for our Lorenzino, and any who engage with those who seek him out may well have much to fear. As to the madrigals and poetry you have sent me, I have no opinion on them and no means to further your wish for their performance and publication.

Perhaps one day I will be allowed to leave this papal prison and visit you in Venice. Though I believe that will not be soon. We must never write nor speak of this again.

You should look to your errant wife and bring her back to the ways of Christ. Then, when we have our satisfaction, SHUT UP. Miserable as this life is, I am too busy to consider the alternative.

Michelagniolo Buonarroti

It was nearly ten by the time we'd finished. There was drunken singing from the passageway that ran behind the Archives, foreign voices, Carnival revellers. Then the Frari bells, the same chimes I heard so often at home. I felt exhausted and longed for bed. Luca looked it too, but there was that manic gleam in his eye. At times he reminded me of a hyperactive schoolteacher chewing on a puzzle in front of his class, more interested in solving it than explaining the thing.

'La Barozza's cuckolded husband. The failed musician and poet Antonio Zantani,' he said, moving the letters into the safety of wood and glass frames for protection. 'Fascinating.'

Translating the neat Florentine hand on the page had been easier than with the earlier document. The anguished, desperate tone of the original had no need of my embroidery to bring it up to the dramatic state Godolphin had demanded. Now both sat in English versions on Luca's laptop, ready to be handed over to the man in the morning.

He'd pulled up a few references to Zantani from the digitised documents held by the Archives. The year before, he'd had call to peruse them while researching an exhibition on famous Venetian women, among them Veronica Franco, the courtesan I thought might interest Caroline Fitzroy. Elena Barozzi was no paid bedmate, but a female celebrity in the city, better known than her husband for her wit, her beauty and her knowledgeable participation in the literary salons of the day. Her daughter openly bore the name Lorenzina de' Medici after her father. The response of the betrayed husband was not, it seemed, recorded, save in a few journals, which noted that it was not unusual for upper-class Venetian women of the time to take lovers quite openly, without any objections from their husbands, who doubtless had mistresses of their own. Zantani sounded a sorry creature from what Luca had turned up, forever trying to interest others in his poetry and music, never finding anyone who thought them much good. Michelangelo included, or so it seemed.

'To think,' my friend went on, 'that Duke Godolphin should have somehow stumbled across two short letters that implicate Michelangelo in a pair of infamous murders. First providing the dagger that Lorenzino used to murder his cousin. Then, eleven years later, tipping off the assassins who were hunting him about his whereabouts, and presumably engaging the help of Antonio Zantani in tracking him down.'

'Can we not just give him our translations in the morning, then leave it to him to decide what to do with them?'

Luca looked taken aback. 'What are you saying? Like it or not, our names are attached to these documents. We have a right – a duty – to query what they suggest.'

What they said – or claimed to – seemed perfectly clear. In 1537, an aggrieved Michelangelo, smarting at being forced to work in Rome instead of his beloved Florence, still full of disgust that the Florentine republic had been handed on a plate to yet another Medici, had offered his private support to Lorenzino along with the weapon the man would use to take his cousin's life. Then, eleven years later, while working on the Sistine Chapel, still miserable and claiming poverty – a state he seemed to be in most of his life – he experienced a change of heart. Fearful that Lorenzino might reveal his part in the plot to murder Alessandro, and expose his own dangerous sexual proclivities, he'd used the information he'd received from Zantani to point Bibboni and his murderous accomplice in the direction of Venice and enlist the aid of the betrayed husband in bringing about Lorenzino's assassination on the Ponte San Tomà.

'I have to admit, Luca, the word that keeps coming to mind is "plausible".'

He scanned my English on the computer again. 'Indeed it is. Which I find perplexing. That's what people want, isn't it? Proof of their own cleverness above all else.'

I had to stifle a laugh. Luca was the most perverse of friends, able to blow hot and cold on an idea in an instant. It wasn't long before this that he was bouncing round the room full of excitement about the idea that the letters might be genuine revelations.

'People like Duke Godolphin, you mean?'

He grimaced and looked briefly guilty. 'Among others. Half the world are actors, performers who crave the spotlight and the stage. While the likes of us provide the scenery and remain unseen, anonymous in the wings. Where I, for one, am happiest. But I apologise for this pompous little lecture. It's been a long day, my friend, and we still have work to do tomorrow.'

'We do?'

'Yes. But more of that later. Now, a drink and—'

The door to the chamber slammed open so hard the racket made us both jump. Godolphin was there, eyes blazing in the harsh ceiling lights, swaying a touch, I thought.

'I couldn't wait,' he bellowed. 'Tell me now.'

AS I EXPLAINED HOW Luca and I had gone about turning the Wolff letters into English, Valentina was once again checking both her phone and her screen for messages. Something was happening, perhaps important, perhaps not. It was impossible to tell from her expression, which was as inscrutable as the face of Carpaccio's mythical Ursula. We'd now been going through the story of the approach to Duke

Godolphin's violent death for a good six hours. I felt grubby and sweaty, even on that freezing February day. Valentina had not a hair out of place and looked as if she could go on for another six without pause, provided the tiny cups of coffee turned up at regular intervals.

'You and Volpetti are good friends?' she asked suddenly, without looking up from her phone. 'You like him?'

I felt myself going red in the face. 'Why do you ask?'

'Because asking questions, sometimes unexpected ones, is my job.'

'Of course. Luca's been incredibly kind to me. Without him I would never have felt at home here as I do.'

'A selfless act on his part, I'm sure.'

My hackles started to rise. 'Yes. A selfless act. You know him better than me. Should I have reason to doubt it?'

She sniffed at that. 'He was once the lover of a friend of mine. Briefly. I don't judge the man for that.'

I'd no idea why the conversation had taken this turn, and said so.

'Because I'm seeking the truth,' she said. 'Which is elusive. Do friends not lie to one another? Don't lovers? Husbands and wives? Volpetti got you into this, didn't he?'

'Yes, but—'

'And this strange engagement with Godolphin. The dead man asking him where to find a woman in Venice. Does that sound convincing?'

Very, I said, from what I knew of the fellow. 'I can't believe you're saying this. Luca is one of the most honest and straightforward men I know.'

She jabbed her pen across the desk. 'Yet I had to prise that story out of him. If it wasn't for the guilty look on his face—'

'Because he was embarrassed. He said so. What other explanation could there be?'

She grumbled something under her breath about there always being another explanation. 'I have four of your Gilded Circle in my custody.

The dead man's wife. Fitzroy, Hauptmann and your bibulous publisher, Bourne. Plus a frightened young American woman. Frightened because she knows something, perhaps.'

'Or she has little faith in your justice system.'

It needed to be said.

'That is possible as well,' Valentina agreed with a nod. She was always full of surprises. 'Though if you heard their stories, fairy stories it seems to me, you might understand my scepticism.'

I groaned. 'As I keep saying . . . I'm not a detective.'

'Oh Arnold,' she replied with a swift, sharp grin. 'I believe you're more of one than you appreciate.' A wave of her hand, tanned, the fingernails scarlet and perfectly clipped. A waft of perfume drifted across the desk. 'Do you know where Luca Volpetti says he was around the time we know Marmaduke Godolphin died? At home on the Lido. In bed. Alone. Reading a book.'

'Do you have any reason to think he wasn't?'

'No. But equally I have no firm proof to say he was.'

'This is ridiculous. I was alone by then as well. At home. In bed. No one to speak for me. A sight closer to the Ponte San Tomà than Luca too.'

There came that sweet, deceptive smile she had. 'Of this I am aware too. Finish the tale of your night in the Archives, please.'

GODOLPHIN WAS ON US like a shot, barging his way between Luca and me to get to the computer, then running his stubby finger up and down the screen, chortling to himself. I could smell booze on him, and perhaps something else. A woman's perfume. Luca had noticed all this too. I could tell from the look on his face.

'Have you had an enjoyable evening, sir?' he asked in a very pointed fashion.

'A bloody expensive one that's none of your damned business.'

Godolphin stabbed his finger on the laptop screen so hard it rocked. 'You're sure of this?'

Luca glanced at me. I knew what that look meant now. This was my call.

'We're confident this is an accurate translation of the letters.'

'Good work,' Godolphin said, and slapped me hard on the shoulder. 'I knew you were the man for the job, Clover. Old Wolff called it right there.'

'Without Luca . . .'

'Oh,' the man grunted. 'Him too.' A nod to both of us. 'Email me the translations. I'll get them to New York for the contract. To the *Sunday Times* for the story. Front page this weekend. Around the world in hours. Expect calls. This will be the biggest story of your little lives.'

'Is that not a touch premature?' I asked as Luca's face darkened.

Godolphin knew exactly what I meant. All the same, he acted puzzled. 'Why would that be?'

'Because,' Luca declared in a rising, angry tone, 'all you have is a translation of two seemingly ancient letters of obscure origin. Nothing more.'

'I trust Wolff. He's never let me down.'

'But—'

'Why do you doubt their authenticity?'

Luca shrieked, a falsetto cry of outrage. 'We have nothing to confirm it, sir!'

'You're a pair of filing clerks,' Godolphin said with a smirk. 'Not historians. I am, and I tell you I know the truth when I smell it. Look at all the links. Cellini. The Aldobrandini dagger. Michelangelo's behaviour after Florence fell. No one could make up such a web of connections.'

He'd obviously done his research, just like us. Or, more likely, had someone do it for him. Perhaps Wolff.

'That may be so,' I said, trying to turn down the temperature. 'All the same, the authenticity needs to be verified. The word of two . . . filing clerks is not enough for you, surely. Not to strike a TV contract or boast of your discovery to the world.' I hesitated, wondering if any of this was going in. 'These originals need to be examined properly, scientifically, by specialists in the field. The writing, the ink, the paper. Everything must be inspected by people who are trained to deal with them.'

'You're talking months, man.'

'Or years,' Luca interjected. 'Even then, the conclusion may be that no one knows for sure.'

Godolphin found that amusing. 'This is television. As I've explained. Entertainment, vivid, alive. Not your dead, dry academia. Do you not understand? I can be like those idiots I used to try to teach, Fitzroy and Hauptmann, and spend my life earning a pittance reaching a tedious, nit-picking few. Or simplify and amplify, add a touch of theatre to the past and reach millions who'll pay me well for the privilege because that is what they want. That, for them, is history.'

'That,' Luca replied, 'is show business.'

Godolphin glanced at the original documents, now in the glass cases Luca had found in the Archives stores. 'I had thought of keeping you two on for the series. A mistake on my part. You're not fit for prime time. To be frank, I find you rather boring.' He reached out for the cases. 'I will organise the authentication process. I will choose the experts. They will be . . .' he winked, he actually winked, 'decent chaps I know who'll do the decent thing.'

Luca was a sprightly man, a good fifteen years younger than me. He was up in a flash, seizing the two cases, placing them under his arm then reaching for his black cloak and broad-brimmed hat.

'Give,' Godolphin said, gesturing with his fingers. 'They're mine.'

I came and stood next to my friend. Two of us, both slight, neither, I suspect, experienced in fisticuffs at any stage of our lives. In front of us a burly, ill-tempered Englishman full of drink.

'You placed them in our custody. They stay here,' I told him. 'In a safe. You're in no fit state to vanish into the night with such precious objects. If, indeed, that's what they are.'

He scowled, stroked his silver hair. Then patted me on the shoulder and said, 'You're right, of course. I let the occasion run away with me. Keep them here. But tomorrow, gentlemen . . .' he waved a finger at both of us, 'you must join me as guests. Email me those translations. That's all I need. I will arrange costumes.'

'I don't wear costumes,' Luca retorted.

'You're a local. Understandable.'

'I thought we were staff,' I said. 'Filing clerks. Not worthy.'

'Touchy little fellow, aren't you, Clover? I want you both there. I would like you to bring the letters. Then take them back here if you like.' He leaned forward, and once again I caught the smell of hard spirit with a whiff of scent behind. 'Wheels are in motion, boys. Watch them roll.'

Nothing more, then Duke Godolphin made his way a little uncertainly out into the shadowy courtyard beneath the dark shape of the Frari.

'That was an interesting day,' I said. 'I believe we're owed a drink.'

'I believe we're owed a lot more than that.'

'Luca. The man's right. We're archivists. We're not entitled to pass judgement on the authenticity of those letters ourselves. Or likely to find some way of doing so by tomorrow evening.'

'Is that so?' He began packing his briefcase. To my surprise, the letters went in there. 'No drink for me tonight. I have calls to make.' He came close and took my arm. 'Meet me tomorrow morning at Santa Lucia station. We have a journey ahead of us. An interesting woman for you to meet.'

'We're catching a train?'

He grinned, lifted his briefcase. 'We must prepare for Godolphin's *ridotto*.'

'I don't understand.'

'Any more than I. Yet.' He hesitated as we walked out onto the pavement by the bridge. The cocktail bar George Bourne had come to love was there. I could just make him out sitting alone at a table near the door, smiling to himself, lost in something. For once, he didn't look drunk. 'I've never met a brute like Godolphin before. Have you, Arnold?'

'I'm pleased to say not.'

'Best we get him out of here as soon as we can.' He raised his hands and made a choking gesture. 'Before I'm tempted to shake the monster by the throat.'

EIGHT

A Trip to Verona

'You see,' said Valentina. 'Volpetti turning enigmatic again. Did he tell you why he wanted to meet you at the station?'

Not that night. Luca left me hanging. I didn't even get a time until he texted me later. I wasn't minded to complain. He was upset, on several fronts. The fact that he'd got us into Godolphin's grip. The pressure the old man was trying to place on us to rubber-stamp the Wolff letters, if not as authentic – even he couldn't expect that – but as serious historical artefacts worthy of investigation. Enough to seal him the contract with the American network, though what his relationship with Miss Buckley was any more I'd no idea. She was out of sight in her new hotel, with Felicity looking out for her.

There was something else getting to Luca too. My friend was a decent, straightforward fellow, averse to duplicity and complication. He doubtless wondered how Godolphin had come to pick the pair of us and the State Archives as the target for his attention, all on the prompting of the enigmatic, now dead Wolff, an individual he'd never met.

I sympathised, and Valentina's constant nibbling at the edges of his character bothered me.

'He didn't need to. I didn't expect it. We were both exhausted. It seemed we had more work to do. Are you seriously saying you suspect him of some involvement in all this?'

She thought for a second, then said, 'You're all involved, one way or another. My task is to understand how. You said yourself. That he threatened to throttle the man.'

'A turn of phrase.'

'Another. You seem to encounter so many.'

Godolphin was, I said, an aggressive fellow who set out to antagonise. I doubted scarcely a day went by without someone muttering an imprecation about him under their breath.

'There. We're agreed.'

'Valentina. He enjoyed provoking that reaction in others. It was part of his personality. A poisonous one. He didn't want to be liked.'

'To be feared, you think?'

'A little, maybe. Mostly though I feel he wanted to be the boss, the master. To browbeat all those unfortunates who had to deal with him into acknowledging him as their superior. He craved our obeisance. And the less . . .' I stopped. This was an observation that had only come clear to me after he was dead.

'The less . . .?'

'The less he got it, the more difficult and aggressive he became. I got the impression this was his last stab at getting back onto his TV pedestal. There was a desperation about him. A hunger to prove he was still virile, active, important. It was almost tragic.'

She didn't argue with that. Instead she flicked through her notes. 'Interesting you should say "virile". You both thought he might have been with a woman before he turned up at the Archives that night?'

The perfume. It was unmistakable.

'I wondered. Luca, who has more experience in this field, seemed to believe so.'

'But who? It wasn't his wife. She was with Hauptmann and the Fitzroy woman at a concert by Interpreti Veneziani in the San Vidal Church in Campo Santo Stefano. We have confirmation from the internal CCTV. Nor was it Patricia Buckley, who, we gather, stayed locked in her hotel that night. Room service food. What a waste here.'

Perhaps he brought a secret mistress with him, I suggested.

She scowled. 'Don't be so naïve. A mistress entails a relationship.

If we know anything about our late historian, it's the fact that he despised being beholden to anyone except himself. I believe we are agreed here. Godolphin was one of those men who felt the world revolved around him. Connections in which they are supposed to offer anything in return are beneath that kind. The only relationships they recognise are those they conduct through two avenues, money, or power. It was, I think, the first on this occasion. We had a report of a disturbance at an apartment near the Accademia. A woman screaming. A high-class prostitute known to us. It seems she had an argument with a customer. Over what she was willing to do. The customer turned aggressive.'

'You think it was Godolphin?'

'The woman wouldn't elaborate, even to me. They never do. She claimed she'd no idea who the man was. Just that he was English, wealthy, silver-haired, and seemingly a gentleman until they got down to business, as it were. The restaurant across the street said they saw an old man who looked like Godolphin leaving her building in a state of some disorder. My guess is that he fell out with her and was unable to go back to the same pimp. We don't have many in Venice, and those we do harbour tend to deal with wealthy clients who cause them no problems. This isn't Rome or Naples.'

Murder. Prostitution. The prospect of fraud. I felt deeply out of my depth. For a second or two I might even have wished myself back in Wimbledon. It was becoming clear that Valentina Fabbri was not simply questioning the movements and actions of the five people she was keeping in her cells. Luca and I appeared to be on her radar screen for some reason too.

'So,' she said. 'It is now Wednesday. You are going to meet Volpetti for a train journey. By midnight, Marmaduke Godolphin will be dead.'

'I wish he wasn't. I wish he'd just . . . stayed in London and left us here in peace. I wish more than anything that I'd never found those damned letters.'

Her pen scratched at her notepad once more, then came a brief smile. 'But you did, Arnold. So, tell me about your adventure in Verona.' Three quick, hard raps on the shiny table. 'We've been through the preliminaries. We have established the canvas for our fatality. The cast is fixed. The stage is set. The climax we know. Only the denouement remains. A final revelation that is currently beyond my reach.' She glanced at her phone. 'But only just, I feel. I trust you dined well?'

Food. She always wanted to know what we ate.

'Very,' I said, and continued.

LUCA WAS WAITING FOR me at Santa Lucia station with two return tickets for the fast train to Milan. He was carrying his leather briefcase, which, by the looks of him, was heavier than the night before. No flowing Venetian cloak this time, no floppy hat. He was in a business coat with a suit beneath, pinstriped and very smart. I was casual as usual, which is to say scruffy. He looked me up and down and sighed.

'I should have mentioned something about dress. The *dottoressa* can be difficult at times. Still . . .' he patted the valise, 'this will distract her.'

'I'm retired, Luca. Clothes were never something that interested me. Who's the *dottoressa*? Where are we going exactly? And why?'

'Soon enough,' he murmured as we searched for our seats.

I glanced at the ticket. Verona, just over an hour away, was a city I'd yet to visit. Eleanor went there on her own a few times for the opera, something that was not to my taste. She came back loving the place but cursing the crowds of tourists chasing the Romeo and Juliet myth. We had so many places earmarked to visit when we retired. Padua for the Scrovegni Chapel, Vicenza for Palladio, Ravenna for more sights than I could remember. The mountains of Trentino and the Alto-Adige too, not that countryside interested her so much as the urban except that she thought they might make spots to visit during the searing heat of summer. Yet without my wife, I'd found I'd settled into a comforting, solitary indolence that made travel quite unnecessary.

Venice was more than a city, a country even. The longer I stayed, the more it became the boundaries of my life, an entire world of its own, defined by the distant grey horizon of the Adriatic in the east and, in the opposite direction, the soaring mountains, snow-capped now and only visible on clear days, preferably from the campanile of San Giorgio Maggiore. Somehow the list of places to explore on my doorstep, of discoveries to find, seemed to lengthen each day, not grow shorter. I'd not set foot outside the lagoon since that distant day I'd arrived miserable and listless shortly after the funeral. Even the trip to the Lido with George Bourne, where I saw cars and buses for the first time in weeks, had felt like a journey beyond the normal.

Luca stayed silent for a good five minutes as we ran through the industrial gloom of Mestre. Then, once clear of a place I knew he disliked, the train beginning to pick up speed through flat, open countryside on the way to Vicenza, he took off his coat and said, 'Are you looking forward to this little circus tonight?' He frowned. 'A *ridotto*, for pity's sake. The man purloins the cultures of others for his own purposes. For fame and money. It's shameful.'

I had a reasonable idea what a *ridotto* was. A social gathering established centuries before by Venetians of a certain class and kind. A casino too, in the early days.

'It seems to me the man is something of a gambler, Luca. Perhaps it's appropriate.'

He stared out of the window at the lush green fields, then tapped the case. 'And what if he wishes to play with a crooked deck?'

I thought of all the dubious history programmes Godolphin had made over the years. Popular undoubtedly, but so selective with his material most would pass more as fiction than fact. Caroline Fitzroy and Bernard Hauptmann understood that for sure, and perhaps resented the idea that he had abandoned the quiet corridors of Cambridge for television riches and fame. George Bourne doubtless appreciated that Godolphin was a charlatan too. But a charlatan who sold books, which for him was all that mattered. Now all three of them, along with Felicity and the young Jolyon, were about to fall victim to one supreme act of cruelty on the man's part. The academics humiliated, Bourne fired, Felicity and Jolyon abandoned.

'Then I think it's his business. Not ours.'

'Dammit, Arnold!' He was cross, a rarity. 'He's made it our business.'

We'd never argued, never got annoyed with one another. Luca was my best friend in Venice, a kind one who lifted my spirits when I was down and opened many doors that would otherwise have stayed closed. All this he did out of the generous goodness of his heart, for no obvious reward.

I tried to calm things. 'May I ask again . . . who's the *dottoressa?*'

He grinned, and the heat between us vanished immediately. 'Oh! The Great Greta. Someone who may settle this matter one way or another. Dottoressa Rizzo of the Biblioteca Capitolare! You've heard of her?'

'I never dealt much with foreign matters. I thought I'd made that clear.'

'You've visited the Biblioteca, surely?'

'There's so much to see here,' I said as the train began to speed across *terraferma.* 'You really think she can judge the authenticity of these letters?'

'If anyone can give us a quick appreciation.' He seemed surprised by my reaction. 'Don't you want that?'

'There'll be hell to pay if we tell him they're fake. Godolphin will be the one who's humiliated. In front of the very people he hopes to demean himself.'

The downturned mouth, the shrug of the shoulders. 'But if it's the truth, so what? Perhaps Greta will say they look genuine. There's only one way to find out.'

I knew a little of the place by reputation. My friend was determined to fill in the many gaps. The Biblioteca Capitolare had a good claim to be the oldest library functioning in the world. A scriptorium originally, Luca said, a place where parchment books were produced, probably established as early as the fourth century. Over more than fifteen hundred years it had come to house some of the most precious ancient documents still in existence, among them the earliest known copy of St Augustine's *City of God*, dating from the fifth century, and the 'Veronese riddle', a scribble in the margin of a religious document that some regarded as one of the first examples of the Italian language emerging from Latin.

'I can't believe you've never visited professionally, Arnold. Dante studied there. Petrarch not long after. It's not as extensive as our own State Archives, you appreciate.'

Flattered that he would include me in that comment, I said, 'But the Archivio di Stato holds the memories of an entire republic. The Biblioteca—'

'Obscurities. Old ones. Religious ones mostly. Nevertheless . . .'

We spent the rest of the journey largely in silence as the train sped west. Then Verona emerged, or at least a modern part of it, all concrete and busy roads, nothing like the classical city going back to Roman times I'd expected. A disappointment to begin with, though of course, as so often happens in Italy, the train station is set some way from the historical centre.

A ten-minute cab ride took us back centuries, past the outline of the Roman arena where gladiators died and my Eleanor once sat rapt by opera, then along the curving bank of the Adige. I found myself rediscovering that sense of excitement the two of us had when we began to explore Italy more than two decades before. This was the country we loved, a little worn at the seams, but blessed with that extraordinary natural and architectural beauty the locals so often seemed to take for granted. Church spires and domes rose from terracotta-tiled roofs in every direction, a warren of intriguing alleys ran away towards what I assumed to be the city's ancient heart. Across the sluggish river lay two basilicas among winter greenery, one surmounting a distant hill like a temple of old. It was an arcadian view, worthy of one of those paintings of a mythical land found in the Accademia and the Doge's Palace, a peaceful, heavenly idyll designed for the brush of a Carpaccio or – more aptly given where we were – Veronese.

We turned quite abruptly away from the curving riverbank, drove down a couple of narrow twisting alleys and emerged into the piazza – not *campo* here – in front of the city's *duomo*, its Romanesque facade pale and gleaming in the winter sun.

'I never knew it was so beautiful,' I said, standing to admire the cathedral rising above us.

Luca was gazing at a modest door in the adjoining wall. A sign there for the library. 'You haven't seen a fraction of it. When we're inside, let me do the talking.'

GRETA RIZZO MAY HAVE been great by reputation. In person she was a tiny, bird-like woman somewhere between sixty and seventy, with a wry, narrow face, and tied-back hair the same grey as her severe knitted cardigan. She sat at a battered wooden desk of the kind monks might once have used for illumination, peering at a manuscript through half-moon glasses. I had to wonder if the names 'Dante' and 'Petrarca' might be carved into the blackened sides with an ancient penknife.

When we'd walked into her small, brightly lit office, she'd barely looked up from her work. It was a long and fascinating stroll from the modest entrance of the Biblioteca to the river side of the cathedral complex overlooking the broad, slow waters of the Adige. Inevitably

I had to compare the place with the State Archives I knew so well in Venice. Here there was a courtyard too, smaller, but kempt, with a tidy lawn. The shelves of the rooms we passed through were stacked with volume upon volume, spine out. This, I reminded myself, was a library for ancient manuscripts, not an archive with its fonds and filing systems. Luca was to tell me later that Greta could find anything she wished from the Biblioteca's collection by memory, without reference to a single index card.

The atmosphere was quite different too, more that of a monastic institution than a public document service. This extended to Luca's attitude. Usually he greeted those he knew in a friendly, physical fashion, hugs and kisses and kind words. That fulsome welcome he left behind in Venice. He said good morning and got no reply beyond a single raised grey eyebrow. Then she nodded at two chairs by the window, glanced at the work in front of her, and turned to stare very directly at me with eyes the colour of ice. I was reminded of a severe French mistress at grammar school, a woman who would scold you for the smallest of mistakes then forget the transgression immediately and try to teach you something important.

'And who is this you have brought into my home?' she asked.

'Dottore Arnold Clover. A recent resident of Venice, newly retired from the National Archives of Great Britain.'

'Oh,' she said, sharp eyes running me over, and nothing more.

Luca smiled and opened his briefcase. As well as the two framed letters, he'd brought a cake from Tonolo. An expensive-looking one. He nodded at her and placed the creation – cream and fresh fruit, a work of art indeed – on the side of her desk.

'*Grazie*.' She dipped a skinny index finger into the cream, then tasted it with the briefest of smiles. 'You must want a weighty favour, Luca.'

'Your opinion. Which is always something I regard as that.'

The raised eyebrow again. At him this time, not me.

'Dottore Clover and I have come across two documents recently dispatched to Venice. We find them interesting. Don't we, Arnold?'

'Interesting and baffling at the same time,' I agreed.

'He speaks Italian, after a fashion,' Greta noted.

'I do my very best, Dottoressa.'

Luca removed the framed documents from his case and placed them on the desk. She slammed the volume in front of her shut. Dust rose in the bright morning light, dappling the sunshine coming through the long window. We never liked dust much in Kew. It signified carelessness, sloth, a dismissal of modernity. Here it seemed quite natural. Back there, our job was to marshal and categorise the past. The Biblioteca, it appeared to me, was a place that wished to preserve it for eternity, as close to its original condition as possible.

She leaned forward and glanced at the two documents, a cursory look, not a close one. 'I'm very busy. Your delicious present notwithstanding.'

'So are we.'

'By April I may be able to get round to matters other than those that now occupy my time. So perhaps in May I could respond to you . . .'

Luca sighed and looked at me. Of course.

'Dottoressa Rizzo,' I began. 'We have to deliver an opinion of sorts this evening. It's important. We understand that you can't possibly verify the letters so quickly. All we wish to understand is whether they're . . . plausible.'

'You think they're not then?'

'It's a long story,' Luca said. 'And since you are so busy . . .'

'What are you asking me to look at, gentlemen?'

I wasn't going to let him handle that. 'Two letters that appear to have been written by Michelangelo. Signed, as one might expect, Michelagniolo.'

'Good so far . . .'

'One appears to implicate him in the murder of Alessandro de' Medici, to the extent that he designed a dagger for Lorenzino de' Medici for the killing. A weapon made by Benvenuto Cellini.'

That didn't appear to surprise her for a moment. I wondered what might.

'The two did know each other, Dottore Clover.'

'The second implicates him in the assassination of Lorenzino eleven years later in Venice, supposedly for fear of his earlier treachery being uncovered.'

She pulled the frames over, took off her glasses and bent down to peer at them.

'Greta,' Luca said. 'You've worked with this kind of material before. You know his script. You understand the kind of paper. The ink. The—'

'A man's hand is what marks him more than anything,' she interrupted. 'Science is all very well. But the words, the tone, the mood that flows from his pen. That is his mark, as plain as his DNA.'

'And that,' I said, 'is all we need to know. Does this look like him or not?'

She rolled back her chair from the desk and stared at us both. 'In all honesty, I am too busy for these games. If you could come back next week . . .'

'Next week is too late,' I told her, 'if we are to save a great man embarrassment.'

Luca cast me a querulous look and coughed into his fist.

'What is the provenance?' Greta Rizzo demanded. 'Where did this come from? Who supplied it?'

'A man called Wolff,' Luca said before I could answer. 'A dead man. A man of whom we know nothing. Not that it is of any great consequence. If you're unwilling to help, then we must return to Venice and try our feeble best . . .'

He got up to retrieve the letters.

'Wolff, you say?' she repeated, and put out a hand to stop him.

'You know the name?'

Her head went from side to side. 'Come back at four.'

'You know the name?' I asked the question this time.

'Come . . . back . . . at . . . four.'

Luca clapped his hands, as delighted as a child receiving an unexpected present. 'May I show Arnold around the Biblioteca? He will be amazed—'

'No, you may not. Your friend may return another time and one of my people can give him a proper tour.'

'I'd be delighted to,' I said quickly. 'I've never been to Verona before. Perhaps . . .'

She waved a finger. 'The Castelvecchio and San Zeno. I'll walk your English friend round the Duomo and Sant'Anastasia when next he returns. And . . .' her voice rose, 'if I hear you've wasted his time with that stupid so-called balcony, we will cease to be friends.'

A church bell chimed eleven. The sound seemed to ripple the dust in the winter light from the window.

'You seem perplexed. Have I not made myself quite clear?' Greta Rizzo asked.

'Very,' Luca said. 'I was just wondering where to have lunch.'

WE HAD THE BEST part of five hours to kill, yet it vanished very quickly in the company of my knowledgeable guide. First we went to the Castelvecchio, the old castle complex by the river, now a museum, where we wandered through rooms of paintings and military weaponry, admired the view over the river and the medieval bridge there. I tried to talk to him about Greta Rizzo, naturally, and the sudden interest she'd taken when the name 'Wolff' came into the conversation. Until that point, she'd seemed about to turn us down completely. But Luca was having none of it. The Great Greta, he said, was a law unto herself, a marvel when it came to interpreting historic documents, quite unpredictable over every-thing else.

'The last thing one must do with the lady is try to pressure her into a decision,' he declared as we stood in front of a magnificent equestrian statue of Cangrande della Scala, a fourteenth-century ruler of Verona. The chap was leaning back, grinning like a loon on a rather comical horse.

'He seems a cheery fellow,' I said.

'Big Dog?' He cocked his head to one side. 'He was a violent, deeply religious warlord. They all were. Though he gave Dante sanctuary after the Florentines exiled him on pain of death.' We edged round the horse. It was an extraordinary work, particularly since Luca revealed it was designed as a funerary monument. 'They exhumed the chap a few years ago. Turns out he was poisoned with digitalis. Strange, isn't it?'

'What is?'

'Sometimes we do unlock secrets of the past. Sometimes the truths we've believed for years do turn out to be fiction. But . . .'

He left it there and on we walked, by the river, to another fine church, San Zeno. The vast and airy interior reminded me a little of the Frari, the place Lorenzino de' Medici had been buried. There, visible and clearly adored in the crypt, was the embalmed corpse of the city's patron saint, Zeno, an African – his dark complexion was clear from the statue nearby, as was his love of throwing a hook into the Adige as much as he sought to fish for souls. It was past one by the time we left the quiet quarters of San Zeno and Luca hailed a cab for the Piazzetta Chiavica, the little square of the sewer.

An odd destination one might think for lunch. But there was no sewer or smell of it, just a very local restaurant called the Vecchia Fontanina, where he was greeted like an old friend. The place was full of locals enjoying a generous twelve-euro workman's lunch, wine included. I stuck with it and ate nettle pasta to start followed by chicken escalope with vegetables. A vast dish of *bollito misto*, chicken, tongue, *cotechino* sausage and slabs of meat I couldn't identify, turned up in front of my friend.

'Here,' he said, inviting me to dip a piece of bread into the grey sauce that accompanied it. *'Peará.* You'll only find this in Verona. Nowhere better than this place.'

Breadcrumbs, bone marrow, stock and lots of black pepper, he said as he slapped a dash on the soft flesh of the tongue before wolfing it down. I couldn't finish the workman's meal he'd ordered for me, though it was half the size. Luca managed the whole of his lunch with a panna cotta, two coffees and a fennel liqueur.

'We're killing time, aren't we?' I said.

'We are indeed, but no one jails you for that. It would take a brave man to invoke the wrath of the Great Greta by turning up early for her verdict.'

It was three by the time we staggered out. I felt I wouldn't eat another thing for a day or two. Luca swore me to secrecy, then led me round to the via Cappello and let me step briefly into the courtyard where a balcony on the wall marked the site of the Casa di Giulietta, Juliet's House. Not, as he said, that there ever was a Juliet or a Romeo, or that the Cappelli after whom the street was named were the Capulets of the original Italian tale Shakespeare plundered for his play. The place was full to the brim with tourists snapping away with phones and cameras. A queue had formed around the bronze statue of a young Juliet at the back wall. In the balcony above – a sarcophagus erected by the tourist authorities in the 1940s, Luca said – a newly married couple posed for a photographer.

'This is Godolphin's version of history, isn't it?' he grumbled, a little glum for once. 'Fanciful tales invented out of nothing. Love and death. Glory and sacrifice. What was it the priest said? "These violent delights have violent ends." Look at the crowds, Arnold. This is what they seek. What Godolphin wishes to deliver to them. Michelangelo as a newly revealed schemer, spur to a bloody assassination. Think how many of these would pay to see that.'

'If it's not true . . .' I began.

'It won't matter. Those letters could be exposed as guaranteed frauds at the end of all this. Godolphin will have had his fun. Made his ludicrous, flashy TV programme. And you know what? His version will always be the one they . . .' he gestured at the crowd outside the place that was never Juliet's house, 'will swallow. No smoke without fire. The imaginary cat will be out of the bag of lies and there'll be no putting it back. Think about it. I'm not just talking history here. People these days don't want the truth. They just crave something to believe in. That's what Marmaduke Godolphin sells them. History as placebo. Lies that comfort over reality that troubles. And we are his accomplices. Just as he supposes Michelangelo was when it came to the murders of Alessandro and Lorenzino de' Medici.'

He took my arm and there was an anger, a wildness in his eyes I'd never seen before. 'Are we happy with that, my friend? Is that why we're here?'

I laughed and hoped that might lighten the mood. 'We're here to see the Great Greta, aren't we?' I tapped my watch. 'And if we don't start walking, we'll be late.'

His grip tightened on my arm. 'Whatever you say, don't tell her I took you here. *Mi spellerà vivo.*'

'Pardon?'

'Arnold . . . she'll skin me alive.'

GRETA RIZZO WAS AT the same desk in her riverside office when finally we returned to the Biblioteca Capitolare. The light had faded outside. Street lamps, bent iron and attractive, much like those of Venice, had come alive by the Adige. The basilica on the hill was illuminated too, and now seemed even more like a Roman temple of old. She didn't look up as we walked in. We took the seats by her desk, just like before, and waited.

It was three or four minutes before she turned to us, smiling, and said, 'Gentlemen. I apologise.' The Michelangelo letters were in front of her, out of their frames. One at least seemed different. 'I was absorbed. You'd no need to bring the cake from Tonolo, Luca. The delight these . . . objects have brought me . . .' She swept her bony fingers across the pages. 'That was more than enough.'

'They're fake,' Luca declared, and it wasn't a question.

Greta laughed. 'Naturally they're fakes. But no ordinary forgeries. In all my time working here, I've never come across anything so elaborate and skilled. It is quite fascinating. Look here . . .' She gestured to some volumes by the side of the desk. Hefty academic tomes in Italian and English. 'I've gone through the dates, the relationships, Cellini's memoir, the recollections of others such as Giorgio Vasari who knew them all. These two letters are a work of art. Or, more accurately, a work of fine fiction. They re-create a reality that might have been.' Her head rolled from side to side. 'Perhaps even was. I find it unlikely that a fragile, religious individual such as Michelangelo would engage himself in assassination plots. But unlikely does not mean impossible. He was involved in the military planning in Florence against the Pope's forces. He was in Rome, dependent on the patronage of the Vatican, not so long after.'

We knew that already, I said. That the story the letters painted was . . . plausible. There was that word again.

'Indeed,' she agreed. 'But plausible or not, one thing we can be sure of. These . . .' she gestured at the yellowed pages in front of her, 'aren't real. Michelangelo never wrote them. And the fact that I can be so sure of that is fascinating in itself.'

The first clue, she pointed out, was the curious use of the individual 'che', the 'h' running into the top of an extended 'c', with a rising line to form the 'e'.

'The script is an excellent copy of his, in style and individual quirks.

I would accept this oddity of the "che" in the first letter, supposedly written when he was still hankering after Florence. But not in the second, which is meant to be from Rome a decade later, by which time he was settled and had largely left the past behind.'

Michelangelo's handwriting, it seemed, altered the longer he stayed tied to the Vatican. The curlicues and habits he'd adopted in Florence he set aside after a few years, perhaps aware that his time in the city of his birth was over.

'He would never have written that in 1548. Also, the text of the letters, such as this . . .'

Her index finger ran along a line: *I must warn you that I'm barefoot and naked, so to speak, and work for the holy slave master day and night.*

'Michelangelo's words, without a doubt. But from a letter to his father, with whom he had a difficult relationship. I've only looked briefly at the passages – you haven't given me enough time – but I feel certain that a good seventy or eighty per cent of these frauds comes from genuine correspondence the man wrote over the years.'

'You mean,' said Luca, 'someone stole excerpts from his genuine letters and added in the parts that appeared to condemn him for collaborating in the assassination of Alessandro, then, eleven years later, Lorenzino?'

She nodded. 'Precisely. The quote about choosing a wife who is neither deformed nor mean-spirited? Verbatim from some stupid advice he gave to a friend when he was still in Florence. Then there's this . . .'

She pushed the first letter forward and we could see what the difference was. The ink stain in the right-hand corner was almost gone, washed away by some kind of fluid. Beneath was what looked like the stamp of an institution. 'I hope you don't mind, but I took the liberty of removing what was obviously a more recent blot on the paper.'

'What is it?' I asked, pointing at the mark.

'The imprint of the Service historique de la Défense. The national archive of the French armed forces. Which you will find in a castle on the western edge of Paris, the Château de Vincennes. I've no idea how old this paper is. Nor do I suggest you spend time and money finding out. From what I can see, it looks sixteenth century, perhaps even earlier. Not Italian. The texture is wrong. I imagine Vincennes may be able to help there if you wish to pursue this. But gentlemen . . .' with her bird-like hands she pushed the letters across the desk, 'you may remove these objects now. I have to say I've seen a few fakes in my time. None like this.'

'The difference being?' I wondered.

'Because they are no ordinary forgeries, Dottore Clover. So much effort and, yes, talent has gone into making them appear genuine. Into linking real personalities to equally real history. Into mimicking Michelangelo's handwriting, even the style of his quick drawings for the dagger. This requires immense skill. Great and erudite knowledge of Michelangelo, his history, his correspondence, his hand, his drawing. I am full of admiration.'

She smiled, waiting for the inevitable question.

'But?' said Luca.

'But all that effort and aptitude has also gone into making sure this is a forgery that will be detected. At a casual glance, for the half-knowledgeable amateur . . .' Her hand fluttered in our direction. 'A little knowledge is indeed a very dangerous thing. You would doubtless be fooled. Set these in front of any true expert in the field and they're revealed for the deceit they are almost instantly. It's as if this was the perpetrator's true intention. To fool the unwary, only for the trick to be revealed swiftly once the material goes under the microscope of those who know.'

'I suspect,' murmured Luca, 'it was.' He placed the letters back into their cases and stuffed them into his briefcase. 'We're deeply grateful. I feel you deserve more than a cake.'

She clapped her hands and grinned. 'Nonsense. It was a delight. I would have done all this for nothing.' She waited for us to say something. 'You haven't asked me the obvious question.'

'You know the name Wolff,' I said.

A nod. 'I'm glad you noticed. We should be observant in this profession. Six or seven months ago, we received an enquiry by email from an individual who called himself that. He said he was looking to purchase unwanted paper or parchment dating from the early sixteenth century. The fellow described himself as a collector. He liked such things. It didn't matter what was on it. In fact, he preferred it if the pages were blank.'

'Who was he?' I asked.

Greta Rizzo frowned. 'Who knows? All I saw was a name on a single email. An antiquarian from Berlin with specialist tastes, or so he said. I replied that we did not sell such material and heard nothing more. Naturally I alerted the art squad of the Carabinieri. Who wants old blank paper for a legitimate purpose? Nothing was ever done. No crime was committed here. It seems, however, that someone in Paris was more inclined to help the man. You should ask the French. Or Signor Wolff himself.'

'He's dead,' Luca said. 'Or so we're told.'

'Ah.' A frown. 'Then perhaps this is a mystery that will never be solved. It was a most unusual attempt at forgery, I must say. Sophisticated. Erudite. Convincing up to a point, and a deliberate point at that. A fraud designed to persuade the lay follower of history at first glance, then self-destruct once anyone with real knowledge of the subject took a closer look. I've never known anything quite like it.' She looked up at the clock on the wall. 'Time for a break. May I invite you gentlemen for a drink in the Piazza Erbe? I feel I owe you.'

Luca got to his feet and grabbed his briefcase. 'Very kind. Another occasion. We must get back to Venice. It is late.' He came and kissed her cheek, and that surprised them both. 'Arnold and I are greatly in your debt.'

NINE

The Ridotto

'*Peará*. Did you like it?'

I was getting the hang of this now. She never asked the obvious question. Always a distraction, with the real hit to come later.

'For breadcrumbs, bone marrow and pepper, it was quite tasty.'

'You should have eaten horse. *Pastissada de caval*. That's always good in Verona.'

'The English don't eat horses.'

'Very noble. Just battery chickens that never see the light of day. The Veronesi took to horse when they were starving after a siege, nothing to eat but dead animals on the battlefield. In Italy we're made by history and geography. They eat meat and cheese from the mountains. We will always look to the water, the lagoon or the Adriatic. Do not consume horse here if by chance you see it. Do not eat fish in Verona.' She smiled. 'My husband would say, if you go to England, don't eat anything at all. He's funny like that. As is Luca. Another funny man. What did you talk about on the train back?'

There were the pigeons again. The damned things. Clattering on the roof of the Carabinieri station, cooing and flapping. The truth is we barely spoke as the train headed east towards home. It was only when we caught sight of the city, lights glittering across the lagoon beyond the narrow bridge that ran from Mestre into Santa Lucia station, that my friend said something. And that was just 'Who's going to tell him? You or me?'

I volunteered. Luca was a little in awe of Godolphin. Perhaps he even feared the man. I didn't. I knew a bully when I saw one. Besides, this was a problem instigated by an Englishman. It was only right I should be the one to break the news.

'We didn't talk much. There was no need. It was obvious what had happened.'

'The obvious being . . .?'

That someone had spent a great deal of time, talent and money laying a trap for Marmaduke Godolphin, the great television historian, a new and dramatic revelation that would put him back on the screen. This, surely, would be the peak of his long career. Two letters that would convince anyone with a passing knowledge of Renaissance Italy that Michelangelo was party to two famous murders. Except they were forgeries that would be rejected as soon as they were placed in front of a genuine specialist.

'Whoever did this must have been very sure of Godolphin's character,' Valentina said, with her customary canniness. 'This Wolff seems to have assumed he would leap at the prospect without going through the due diligence of a proper historian.'

But as I'd tried to explain to her, he wasn't a proper historian, not any more. That version of himself he'd left behind in Cambridge decades before. Marmaduke Godolphin had abandoned academia for the life of an entertainer. All that mattered was the script, not how much truth lay behind it, as he'd made plain enough to us.

There was a problem in this line of questioning, however, and I felt it was time to raise it.

'Capitano, I'm confused. Yes, there was clearly a conspiracy to dupe Godolphin into believing the Michelangelo letters were genuine.'

'Indeed there was.'

'But what's to say this was anything to do with his death on the Ponte San Tomà?'

A shrug. 'Nothing. For or against.'

'Then . . .'

'I'm merely trying to understand what's happened. To form a picture of events in my head. I like to think in pictures. Don't you?'

'Right now, I'd like to go home and have a lie-down.'

Valentina Fabbri snorted, an odd, almost English sound. 'Don't be silly. You want to know what happened as much as I do. There's free food at Il Pagliaccio too.'

'Oh yes.' I'd put that to the back of my mind.

'But only if you earn it. Tell me about this . . . *ridotto*.'

DUKE GODOLPHIN HAD TO choose the correct location for the declaration of his triumph. There, he thought he'd done his homework, but he was wrong. He'd hired a room in the former Palazzo Dandolo, believing it to be home to the city's original *ridotto*, a social event for the upper crust, who would bicker and gossip and seduce one another around card tables, a kind of aristocratic gambling hall with masks.

In Ca' Rezzonico, the baroque former palace on the Grand Canal, now an art gallery dedicated to eighteenth-century Venice, the period of its decadent decline, I'd seen several fascinating paintings of *ridotti* by Venetian artists like Francesco Guardi and Pietro Longhi. Eye-catching works full of life and colour, gaiety and more than a smattering of the bizarre. The strangest of all being Longhi's depiction of Clara, an unfortunate rhinoceros, paraded in front of a group of Venetians, some masked, one of them holding the sad-looking creature's horn, cut off or shed, no one seems to know. Given my continuing professional curiosity even in the leisure of retirement, I'd researched Clara's story. Seized as an infant in India after hunters slaughtered her mother, the poor creature was paraded around Europe for seventeen years and appeared as a popular feature in the Venice Carnival of 1751, when Longhi painted her. Seven years later, exhibited at the Horse and Groom pub in Lambeth, London, for a shilling and sixpence per viewing, she finally gave up the ghost, the most-travelled rhinoceros of her time, dead in the rough and tumble of a seedy London boozer.

It was a grim, grotesque story, one that seemed to sit quite comfortably among all those paintings of masked Venetians out for the night, desperately seeking money and sex in a republic that would shortly collapse into the hands of Napoleon. This was the Serenissima of Giacomo Casanova, a man Godolphin himself had lauded in one of his many TV series as an intellectual, a great lover of appreciative women, a kind of rock star to be admired amidst the glorious corruption of the time. As even an amateur historian like me knew, the truth was far grubbier. Casanova was, by his own admission, a debauched sexual predator, a rapist who'd bought a thirteen-year-old Russian girl as a slave, committed incest with his own daughter and left her pregnant, abandoned every woman he'd seduced the moment boredom set in, which rarely took long. I wouldn't have been surprised in the least if Godolphin fancied himself as a modern Casanova. The cap would certainly have been a perfect fit.

For once he'd carried out his own research and come to the conclusion that he'd found the place where Longhi painted and Casanova worked the tables, grifting for money and hunting for fresh conquests. Once the Palazzo Dandolo, it was now the Hotel Danieli, a grand off-pink behemoth, its architecture of Venetian Gothic, pointed arches and traceries, reflecting that of the Doge's Palace just a short distance along the Riva degli Schiavoni. The place was beloved of Hollywood stars visiting for the annual film festival, and had housed plenty of celebrities in the past, from Dickens to Byron and Wagner. But it wasn't the principal haunt of Giacomo Casanova. As Luca explained to me on the way, Godolphin had fallen for Venice's habit of using similar names for any number of different *palazzi* owned by the grand families of the day. The real *ridotto* had been in the Palazzo Dandolo di San Moisè, on the other side of the piazza near the Vallaresso vaporetto stop.

Still, we agreed we had sufficient bad news for him already. This was an error that paled in comparison to the fakery of the Wolff

Bequest. The man would be furious enough once he heard our news. All the same, the moment we stepped inside the Dandolo, I felt the hairs prickle at the back of my neck. Behind the almost austere exterior of the building, this was still very much a palace, with a courtyard where a winding staircase of Gothic arches led up to a skylight through which the stars were just visible. I hesitated as we went on. Luca stopped, stared at me and asked if I was getting cold feet. Not at all, I told him. I felt horribly out of place. This was the Venice of luxury, of wealth and influence. The city of Harry's Bar and the Cipriani's exclusive enclave on Giudecca, a world I never visited, nor wanted to. I didn't belong.

'Me neither,' Luca said when I explained. 'But there's more than one Venice, Arnold. You'll begin to appreciate that the longer you live here. For now, this is the version we must deal with.'

An elegant woman in a sleek cocktail dress wandered past sipping what looked like a Bellini. She moved like an extra from a film set or one of those TV adverts for fancy chocolates getting passed around at what looked like a foreign embassy reception. All the same, she smiled at us for a second as she headed off. Luca bowed and smiled back. He could fit in anywhere.

The courtyard and that staircase with its Gothic ornamentation seemed like a tribute to the palazzo of the Doge a short way along the waterfront. Famed artists, writers and musicians had walked those steps. I knew history's ghosts always followed you in Venice, like Lorenzino's shadow making that last journey from Campo San Polo to the Ponte San Tomà that Godolphin had showed us the Saturday before. It was a revelation that they lurked inside this glitzy palace too, a place so brightly lit I felt I ought to be able to see right through them. But no.

'Come,' Luca ordered.

He knew where Godolphin was. The man had booked a function room on the first floor overlooking the Bacino San Marco, a space the Archives used for events from time to time.

There was a uniformed hotel fellow on the door, looking us up and down. He demanded to see our invitations. We had none, of course. So he had to go away and check a list.

'You need your costumes,' he announced.

Through the glass doors we could just make out the group inside. Godolphin on some kind of platform, behind him the dark water crossed by ferries and vaporetti, the disc of a silver moon bright above its reflection in the lagoon.

'We don't,' Luca said quite snappily.

'It's a rule, sir. I've been told. No one allowed in without.' He checked his notes, then went to a coat rack behind him and pointed to two sets of elaborate clothes. 'This for you, Signor Volpetti.' The outfit was all black, plain with a white ruffed collar. 'Scaramouche. You're supposed to powder your face. I have this for your colleague.'

Something black, a voluminous hooded cloak, and that awful white mask I hated.

'Don't be so damned ridiculous,' Luca barked at him. 'Arnold.' He grabbed me by the arm. 'Come.'

'COSTUMES,' VALENTINA SAID.

I waited, wondering to myself, what now?

'Costumes, Arnold. Do you remember what Godolphin had organised?'

'Is this important?'

'It may be. Indulge me.'

At the start of Carnival, during a quiet lunch in the Pugni, Luca had briefed me on the various kinds of dress I would see everywhere on the streets in the weeks to come. Some were modern, the work of fertile imaginations, overly so on occasion. The latest trend seemed to be something called 'steam punk', which as far as I could work out mixed pseudo-Victorian technology with traditional masks and dress.

Luca, for once, wasn't outraged. Carnival, he said, was only traditional up to a point. The Venetians had celebrated it for centuries as a time for lavish food, drink and excess before the austerity of Lent. But the event died out in the nineteenth century and was only revived by the local government in 1979. This, they claimed, represented an effort to restore traditional Venetian culture, though he was adamant it was just a ruse to fill the city's coffers.

Luca regarded the whole affair as nonsense, but I rather enjoyed spotting the difference between all those Carnival masks as I wandered around Dorsoduro. The most common was the simple *bauta*, with its jutting, angular chin that made it an impossibility to eat and drink while wearing it. Then there was the *moretta*, a rather creepy thing, it seemed to me, covering the wearer from forehead to chin, with two circles for eyes. In Longhi's depiction of the unfortunate rhinoceros Clara, one's eyes are drawn away from the poor animal to an elegant woman at the back of the room, staring at the spectacle from behind a pure black *moretta*. The sight lends a disturbing sense of menace to the scene. The less common *gnaga* was a cat mask, so called because *gnau* is 'miaow' in Italian. Luca told me that in centuries past it was often worn by gay Carnival revellers who would throw insults at passers-by, feeling briefly safe behind their anonymity, though they would face cruel punishments if they made their sexuality openly known. Finally there was the mask one saw everywhere in the shops, that of the *Medico della Peste*, the Plague Doctor, with his long beak stuffed with herbs in a pointless effort to keep out the poison of disease.

All of them appeared in the streets and *campi* in those Carnival weeks, and in the Danieli that evening. Godolphin, naturally, had to be different. He wore nothing on his face but make-up, powder and a pair of rouged cheeks. His chosen costume was that of the Doge, a grand red and gold tasselled jacket, a frilly white shirt beneath, and the *corno ducale*, the horned bonnet, again in red and gold over his silver locks. A striking sight, domineering, powerful, as he'd intended.

The rest I could still picture. 'George Bourne was a stout Pantalone in a scarlet suit, long white wig and a black *gnaga*.'

'The costume they used to give to homosexuals. Is that why it was chosen?'

'I don't know. You'd have to ask Duke Godolphin that, and he's dead. Bernard Hauptmann was Harlequin, a suit of diamonds. Felicity was dressed as Vittoria, in rather glamorous rags and a tiara.'

'Vittoria.' A smile. 'Victory, as you say in English. She was in the end, too, wasn't she? Released from the burden of being married to that man.'

'That's a stretch, if you don't mind my saying.'

'Caroline Fitzroy?'

'She had a kind of mob cap and an apron over a dress of diamonds.'

'Like Harlequin's. Colombina, I imagine. A servant. Lowly. Supposedly in love with Harlequin, but in *commedia dell'arte* nothing is ever quite that simple. And the son? The American?'

Godolphin had attempted to make some comment about all of them. He never missed a trick. Jolyon wore a plain grey jacket with purple pantaloons. Patricia Buckley, released from her new hotel, there to anoint the great man's victorious acclamation of the Michelangelo letters, was in a flowing silk ball gown, cream with gold brocade, the front low-cut, pearls around her delicate neck, hair raised up in the kind of style I associated with Marie Antoinette. Eleanor never fussed with her hair, so I've no idea how to describe what I was seeing. It seemed to me that Godolphin had placed the young American on a pedestal, quite deliberately. There was none of the circus or the stage about her dress, as there was about the figures around her. She was there to be admired, ogled on Godolphin's part. Coveted and, in his mind still I imagined, possessed.

I didn't say all that to Valentina. It wasn't necessary.

'Patricia Buckley was meant to be Isabella. A pretty young thing for older men to lust after. Jolyon . . . I don't know.'

'They were the Innamorati. The lovers. Naïve, fickle, given to gossip and the occasional infidelity. Appropriate, don't you think?'

'I've no idea.'

'Of course not. And you, Arnold? What was your costume meant to be?'

'We didn't wear them. We didn't even stop and look.'

'I never realised you were so incurious.'

'Luca had no intention of playing Godolphin's game. Any more than I.'

She picked up her phone and showed me the photo on it. A dark cloak, spread out over what looked like a plain grey office table. 'Remember what I told you. A figure in a black hooded cloak was seen from a distance arguing with a man who could only have been Marmaduke Godolphin by the Ponte San Tomà around midnight. We found this dumped in a rubbish bin close to the Frari the day after Godolphin died. Unfortunately, there's no physical evidence that might help us identify the wearer. That's on your way home, isn't it?'

I blinked, amazed. 'It's one of the busiest routes in that part of the city. As you surely know.'

She fiddled with her phone and brought up another picture. It was a label on the neck of the jacket. A piece of paper attached to the collar by a safety pin. A name there, scribbled in blue felt tip. My name.

I felt myself blushing. The room was too hot. Those damned pigeons kept clattering on the roof.

'You were meant to be the Plague Doctor, Arnold. Did you really not know?'

I held out both my arms. 'W-would you like to arrest me as a suspect as well?'

A smile. A wave of her hand. I knew what that meant by now . . . *On with it.*

* * *

THE MOMENT WE WERE through the door Godolphin dragged himself away from the rest of the party and was on us, jabbing a finger in our faces, flushed, full of drink already.

'Where the hell have you two been?'

Luca lowered his head and kept quiet. I said, 'We need to speak. It's important.'

He barely listened. Instead he snatched the briefcase from Luca's hands. 'I'll tell you what's important. Those letters. They'd better be in here or I swear I'll break your necks, one after the other. What do you think you're playing at?'

'I said . . .'

He opened the case, grinned at what was inside, pulled out the two framed letters, raised them above his head. We were, at that moment, invisible.

'The goods have arrived, people,' he boomed. 'Delayed by Italian tardiness. But now the show may begin.'

I tried to follow him, to persuade him to listen. Luca put out a hand to stop me.

'Let the man have his moment.' He looked at the costumed figures all around, baffled, miserable, all of them, I thought, but still desperate to see the show. 'It's his party.'

'This isn't right. He needs to know.'

'He doesn't want to. It will end soon enough.'

How true that was.

Godolphin went to a raised platform by the window, moving so quickly the ill-fitting *corno ducale* on his head almost fell off. Looking around at this strange circus and the ridiculous costumes the man had provided for them, I was reminded that tragedy and farce were close companions always. It was impossible to discern which of them was uppermost at that moment.

'Why are they going along with this nonsense?' I whispered to Luca. 'Wearing what he tells them? Doing his bidding? Being his captive audience?'

'I thought you said they were his creations at Cambridge?'

'That was four decades ago.'

He seized a couple of glasses of Prosecco from a passing waiter and handed me one. 'Then the force of his personality has not diminished over the decades. Or they just want to see what happens.' He nudged my elbow so hard I spilled my drink. 'Don't you?'

Not really, I thought. I was back in my student days at that moment, trying to draw a line between then and now, to imagine what brought these people here after so many years. Why I was along for the ride too. Godolphin was at the heart of it all, an academic star, a brilliant mind, everyone said, a whirlwind of intellectual activity and creativity. The bright and the ambitious yearned for his attention, but only a few were granted audience and favour. So perhaps Luca was right, and those bonds didn't break, even after all that time and the vitriol the man had dispatched their way of late. He wanted to ridicule Hauptmann and Caroline Fitzroy, that was obvious. His wife and their son he was rejecting too. George Bourne was another cast-off. It seemed he wished to free himself of all the ties that bound him to the past, believing that he could become a new man, with a revived career based in America, doubtless with a fresh squeeze when he could find one now Patricia Buckley appeared to have rejected him. Given that there were forty or so years between them, that was only to be expected, of course. Just not by Marmaduke Godolphin.

This realisation had the oddest effect. I found myself pitying the man. It's not uncommon for people to have a desperate need to be loved. Until I met my Eleanor, I was in that category myself. Not everyone is like Luca Volpetti, floating from arm to arm, free as a bird, happy to be solitary. Godolphin's craving was entirely different. He ached to be envied, to be looked up to as a man who, through his intellect and arduous work, had earned prizes that would always be denied the rest of us. Winning wasn't enough. He had to be seen to triumph, to have that acknowledged by an admiring world. Without the continuing plaudits, he was ordinary, an idea that must have terrified him.

I had to wonder whether the rest of them – Hauptmann, Fitzroy, Bourne, even Felicity and her son – played along with this game because they understood they were witnessing Marmaduke Godolphin's swansong, a final, despairing attempt to cling on to what he felt had made him, the fame, the visible success, the notoriety. Farce and tragedy. Both were captivating. Both seemed to hang in the air in that luxurious room of the old Dandolo palazzo as the lights of the Bacino San Marco twinkled outside the window and a succession of craft large and small criss-crossed gentle winter waves the colour of wet coal, wispy mist beginning to smoke over them from the Adriatic.

There was a large screen in the corner of the room. A beaming middle-aged man with a wide and too-white smile was there, the name of the television network beneath him, behind him an image of New York, skyscrapers and a ragged city skyline. Patricia Buckley's boss, the network CEO, it seemed.

'Quite a show,' Luca whispered.

He was, as always, right.

Godolphin gave a signal. From the side of the room we heard a piercing scream, high-pitched, hurt and angry. Startled, like everyone else, I turned to look. A woman had emerged, young and beautiful in an elaborate gold silk dress, arms flailing, black hair awry, behind her a man in plain historical costume, dark trousers, dark velvet jacket, a chain round his neck. He was angry, she was scared.

'Elena,' the man yelled. 'You bitch. You betray me. You cuckold me—'

'For a finer man,' the woman cried out – Elena Barozzi, it had to be, with her husband, the failed musician and poet Antonio. 'A noble and courageous one.'

Zantani roared, furious, 'And a finer man yet shall see your lover dead!'

It was the same theatre group he'd used before. Much the same kind of crude script too, straight out of some historical soap opera, Godolphin's own words in all probability. There was no sense of doubt or uncertainty anywhere in the brief tale it told. Zantani boasted to his furious wife that he'd received support from Rome, from Michelangelo himself, in seeking revenge on Lorenzino for bedding his wife and fathering her child. A chastened Michelangelo, who was, Zantani claimed, fearful that the loquacious Lorenzino would spill secrets about him that the artist feared might lose him his lofty position, if not his life.

Bibboni appeared, the gigantic snarling, sneering actor we knew already, grinning as he juggled the fancy stiletto from hand to hand. Then his sidekick Bebo, and we were back where we were the previous Saturday, out in the chilly streets around Campo San Polo and the Ponte San Tomà. The handsome Lorenzino de' Medici emerged from the other side of the room, smiling, doomed, oblivious to his impending fate, his uncle Soderini with him. There was much screaming from the beautiful La Barozza. A fight, rather more proficiently choreographed than the words that accompanied it.

Soderini was the first to be wounded, followed, with a wildly histrionic performance, by the murder of Lorenzino. Twice in a week we'd seen this now and there was no doubting the *storia* was real. Only the reasons and machinations behind it were invented, to snare Duke Godolphin into making a fool of himself.

I was grateful the performance wasn't prolonged. So was everyone else in that elegant room over the water. The applause was faint, barely a ripple. But the man on the screen seemed impressed, and it was for him, after all.

'Duke,' he said with a practised smile, 'it's an honour to have you on board. This is going to make our lead historical docudrama of the season. Patty will arrange contracts. You have the media arranged for the weekend?'

'An exclusive in the *Sunday Times*, no less,' Godolphin replied.
'Everyone will be after us when that's out.'

The American nodded. 'Good. Got to change that Passeggiata of
Blood title. Foreign words don't cut it for our audience. I think . . .
The Medici Murders. That'll work.'

The smile on Godolphin's face was as stiff as that of the Carnival
mannequins on display in shop windows throughout the city. 'Cyrus
. . . we can talk about this later, I'm sure.'

'Yeah,' the man said, which was a clear no. 'Good luck with the
rest of your evening. I gotta run. Patty can deal with the details. Give
me a couple of days and I'll get a contract you can sign online.'

The screen turned black. George Bourne said a loud 'Well . . .' then
headed for the bar.

Duke Godolphin held up the two framed letters and began a speech,
a halting one, unprepared it seemed, rambling even, which seemed
out of character. He thanked, quite profusely, those he'd invited for
the occasion, Luca and me too. Then, with a smile, he invited Caroline
Fitzroy and Hauptmann to be interviewed as part of the coming series,
provided he knew in advance what they were going to say.

'The true story,' he went on, 'is clear. The evidence . . .' he
displayed the letters, 'tells no lies. The murder of Lorenzino de'
Medici here in Venice was not the work of Cosimo in Florence or
Charles V as so many . . .' his eyes were on his two pupils who'd
argued their cases in print, 'have erroneously claimed. It stemmed
from a matter of marital jealousy, made possible by the fears of the
greatest artist of his time that his earlier treachery might be exposed.
Our opinion of Michelangelo shall not diminish one whit through
these revelations. In truth, the man, through being more flawed,
becomes more human.'

A heavy silence followed, finally broken by Felicity, who said,
'Congratulations, Duke. If only that worked for you.'

'Fret not, dear,' he replied, waving the documents in her face. 'You'll still get half of everything I earn from these two beauties. The truth, you see, will out.'

The actors from Padua, sensing the awkward atmosphere, bowed to no applause, then exited, grumbling, stage left.

There was no shirking it, no delaying. Had Godolphin agreed to speak to us beforehand as I'd asked, it would have been so much easier. But he chose otherwise.

I strode to the front of the pack and stood before him like an unruly student objecting to a lecture he didn't like.

'I'm afraid,' I said, nervous but determined, 'the truth isn't as simple as that.'

THERE WAS NO POINT in trying to gild what was certain to be a very unpleasant lily. I told Godolphin straight out that we were sure the letters were forgeries. Clever, rooted in real history, but frauds all the same. As the group gathered at my back, listening intently, I went through the evidence, Luca adding his opinion when necessary. The mistakes in the handwriting. The fact that portions of the text had been purloined word for word from existing letters by Michelangelo. The likelihood that the paper was inauthentic. The rest of them stayed quiet, and once again I was struck by the thought that they pitied the man, despite the way he'd treated them of late. Bonds I couldn't comprehend, complex and binding, had been forged in Cambridge, ones that had survived the years notwithstanding. Only George Bourne seemed to find the whole thing funny, and when he made a cruel crack, it was Felicity who turned round and told him to shut up.

When we were done, Godolphin placed the documents on the table by the window and looked at them again.

'And who,' he said, 'are you to say this? Against the word of an antiquarian, Wolff, who's provided me with solid gold before? Two low-grade archive clerks who never rose above the filing cabinets. A pair of nobodies.'

'These opinions aren't ours,' I told him. 'They belong to Dottoressa Greta Rizzo of the Biblioteca Capitolare in Verona.'

'A woman of international repute when it comes to historical manuscripts,' Luca added. 'She thought your forgeries well done on the surface but riddled with deliberate mistakes so they would soon be revealed for the deceptions they are. This Wolff gulled you, Godolphin. He seems to have spent years sucking you in with some minor genuine material so you wouldn't look too closely.'

He walked forward and jabbed a finger on the ink stain washed away to reveal the stamp of the Service historique de la Défense.

'Why else hide the telltale mark? You've been suckered into believing his fairy tale because you wished to.'

'What proof is that?' Godolphin retorted. 'An institution's stamp on a document the provenance of which you're ignorant. It could be there as proof of ownership, the contents ignored for years.'

My dear friend sighed. He didn't have it in him to laugh in Godolphin's face. 'Are you serious? Why would an archive service dedicated to the military come to own a letter supposedly signed by Michelangelo? And ignore it over the years? Why would a convenient ink stain be used to try to cover up the stamp? They're forgeries. Clever, inventive frauds that must have taken much effort and expense. But forgeries all the same, and ones that boast of their duplicity once they fall into the right, expert hands.'

Godolphin started to object again, pathetic protestations.

I intervened. 'The most damning evidence is on file in Verona. Someone using the name Wolff had been calling round libraries and museums trying to buy old paper. The Biblioteca among them. They reported him to the Carabinieri, not that anything happened. Whoever Wolff was—'

'The man helped me! Previous times. Now he's dead.'

'You have no evidence he ever existed,' I said. 'No idea where these papers came from or why they were so carefully hidden alongside all the other junk you acquired. The man played you. For some time, it seems.'

'Why in God's name would he do such a thing?' Godolphin cried. 'The fellow never asked for anything more than pennies.'

'Oh Duke,' Felicity said with a shake of her head. 'You've made so many enemies over the years. And so few real friends.'

He was getting angrier by the second. 'I'm not having this from any of you. Say a word outside these walls—'

Patricia Buckley wasn't taking that. 'Are you kidding me? I've got to tell New York.'

'Tell them what? Two lowly clerks think they know better than Duke Godolphin?'

'In the circumstances . . .' she insisted.

'We have a contract!'

There was a new courage in her now. 'You had a development deal. That's all.' She nodded at the room, the costumes. 'You spent it all on this.'

'Patricia . . .'

She was leaving already. Godolphin was getting redder in the face. He jabbed an accusing finger in front of him, ran it round the room.

'One of you did this. Who was it?'

Felicity sighed. 'Just leave it, will you? It doesn't matter. We've money enough. You're seventy-five. Think of retirement.'

'It's not about the bloody money! Nor will I ever retire.' He prodded the scarlet jacket. 'It's about me. Who did it?' He pointed at Caroline Fitzroy. 'Paris. Was it you?'

She didn't laugh. Just shook her head and said, 'I'd waste my time on this? Think about it. Think what you'd have said to us back in Cambridge if we'd come up with such a cock-and-bull story. You used to be a fine academic, Duke. We all learned from you.'

'We did,' agreed Bernard Hauptmann. 'Then you threw it away. For what?' He walked forward, stroked Godolphin's cheek, showed him the stain of make-up. 'Was it worth it?'

'One of *you* . . .'

Too late. Felicity, Caroline and Hauptmann were heading for the door. Jolyon had vanished too, chasing after Patricia Buckley.

Luca took the letters, then placed them back in his case. Godolphin didn't object. Didn't say a word. Only George Bourne was left, maybe not as drunk as I'd first thought. He swaggered up and prodded Godolphin's chest.

'You know, there might be a book in this, old boy. How the great historian was taken for a ride. You'd need to find out who this Wolff chap was, of course. Doubt it would make TV. Might mean some actual, you know, work on your part. But I could probably put together a modest advance—'

Godolphin leapt at him, fists flying, spitting foul curses, a flurry of vile slurs among them. Bourne was sober enough to step back, laughing. The old man tripped, stumbled onto the carpet, fell over, lay there gasping for breath.

A pitiful sight. I helped him to his feet, got no thanks, naturally, as he staggered to a chair to sit down, wheezing heavily. All the pomposity and confidence were gone. He looked old, weary, lost, defeated.

'I'm sorry,' I told him. 'I wish it were otherwise.'

'Don't patronise me, Clover. You're like the rest of them. Delighted at the idea you might bring me down.'

There was no point in arguing. I couldn't take any more. Still, I don't remember walking down the stairs in that grand old palace, stumbling through the Danieli's ancient revolving door out onto the chilly waterfront. A fine and icy mist was swirling in from the direction of the Lido. The vaporetti moving across the Bacino were nothing more than ghostly outlines, dimly lit. I knew this kind of winter fog by now. It would swirl around the city all night, from *sestiere* to *sestiere*, bitterly cold, feeding its briny presence into everything. The lagoon had so many ways to remind one of its existence, and they varied with every season.

Luca was only a few steps behind. We stood in silence, watching the grey cloud that stood between us and San Giorgio across the water. Then he said, 'You wouldn't believe what that beast just asked me.'

'What?'

'No. I can't. It's too much.'

'If only he'd talked to us beforehand.'

My friend seemed unconvinced. 'Do you think it would have made a difference?'

'Perhaps.'

'It wouldn't. He had convinced himself he was about to be reborn. In truth, he's been conned into engineering his own end.'

I had to ask. 'Who, do you think, was Wolff?'

He frowned. 'I neither know nor care. What does it matter? You heard the wife. There must be an army of foes out there who'll be toasting this moment once they hear of it. This isn't our business and never was. I'm sorry I ever responded to his plea.' He lifted his brief-case. 'These curiosities I'll find a home for somewhere. The rest of the junk this creature Wolff brought us I'll send to the skip tomorrow. Now . . .' He looked upset, as I'm sure did I. 'I intend to walk this off. A stroll to Sant'Elena and then the boat home. That man leaves a nasty taste in the mouth even when he's down. I'm sorry I got you into all this, Arnold.'

'You weren't to know.'

He looked along the waterfront, anxious to go. To be on his own for once. 'I'm sorry all the same. But at least we're done with it now.'

IF ONLY.

Recalling that night in the palatial surroundings of the place where Duke Godolphin believed wrongly Casanova once played the tables made me feel miserable all over again. Valentina seemed to notice, or perhaps she was thinking ahead to the showdown she had planned for us all. A uniformed officer she called Giorgio was summoned, two more coffees ordered, and I was offered the chance of taking mine *corretto*, with a shot of spirit.

I declined. My head was hazy enough after this long and wearisome day.

'You told that very well, Arnold.'

'In what sense?'

'In the sense that you made me feel I was there. Made it real.'

It *was* real. Too much so. I was glad to have it off my chest.

'Now here,' she went on, 'is the problem. Where did you all go afterwards?'

That surprised me. 'I went home. As did Luca. The rest . . . Ask them.'

Again she was checking her notes. 'You walked home?'

'Yes!'

'In what direction?'

I found this tiresome and hoped it showed. By the Accademia bridge, I told her, then through Campo Santa Margherita and back to San Pantalon. There was no other way, except the longer route by the Rialto, and I was too tired for that.

'The fog was awful by then. Our street cameras have little to show.'

'I didn't realise it was my duty to be caught by your cameras.'

She sighed. 'It isn't, of course. In the circumstances, it would be easy for them to miss you. Just as they appear to have missed Volpetti on his walk to Sant'Elena, and then a vaporetto across the water to home. My problem . . .' she flipped round the computer screen to show brief statements from all the others, 'is that I can verify the whereabouts of none of you after this event. George Bourne says he went drinking, to this cocktail bar he loves so much. That is true, though he'd left there before the time we believe Godolphin died. The American woman and the son say they bought a takeaway pizza in Campo Santa Margherita and ate it outside, huddled in the cold, talking. I have no reason to disbelieve them. They're young. I've no evidence to prove they're telling the truth either.'

I thought of the mist that night, a bone-chilling ghostly cloud. It sounded an unlikely tale, though I kept that thought to myself. Not, I suspect, that Valentina needed to hear it.

'Which leaves,' she went on, 'the wife, her lover Hauptmann – past or current, who knows? And Caroline Fitzroy. Who simply say they returned to the hotel and that was that. Someone is hiding something, Arnold. If there's one trick I learned swiftly in this job from my good friend Ugo, who you met this afternoon, it's how to recognise a lie. And how to discern the truth. Which seems to be elusive at the moment. The only thing I know for sure is the roundabout route Marmaduke Godolphin took from the Danieli to his death. Would you like to hear it?'

She tapped at the keyboard, and there he was, caught in his dishevelled doge's costume, stumbling through the Danieli. A man about to die.

HE LEFT THE HOTEL twenty minutes after us. There was CCTV of him in the foyer, stumbling into the revolving door. Old, broken, sad. Freezing soon too, I'd imagine, in that ridiculous scarlet outfit.

Twenty minutes. By this point the swirling mist we'd encountered was turning into the thickest of fogs. From the internal camera you could see him step into it and vanish. Valentina ran me through his movements after that. He was recorded on the camera at the San Zaccaria stop catching the Number 1 vaporetto to Piazzale Roma. An obvious route to the Valier if he left the boat at the San Tomà stop. Though it was clear now that the conversation Luca had had with him was the one about finding a woman for the night. Consolation, comfort, or perhaps just a habit he'd picked up over the years. It was thirty-five minutes on the slow boat from San Zaccaria to Piazzale Roma. Sure enough, the cameras at the busy vaporetto hub caught him coming ashore around eleven o'clock. He was still in his Carnival costume, *bauta* mask around his neck, but the *corno ducale* was gone. I watched as he stumbled onto the jetty, less than an hour of life left to him. A young man followed him. He'd picked up the doge's cap, but all he got was a shake of the head and Godolphin wandered on.

I knew this area reasonably well. It was the place the airport bus stopped, the starting point for most of the many vaporetto lines. Buses and trams thronged the area behind the waterfront, cars queued to get into the busy multistorey car parks along the way towards the bridge back to *terraferma*. A grubby, worldly slice of modern urbanity, necessary, if out of place next to the rest of Venice. A few curious characters hung around there during the day. I doubt it was remotely dangerous, but all the same it wasn't a place I'd choose to linger at night. I could understand why, if pressed, Luca Volpetti might say it was the spot to look for a woman. Not that Godolphin had any luck, it seems. Valentina's officers had been all over, checking out his movements. An elderly man, upset, half drunk, wandering the night in Carnival costume, desperate for company, stood out even there. They'd talked to a cab driver Godolphin had approached asking to be taken to a brothel. A man of impeccable Christian sentiment who remembered very clearly berating a 'rude, drunk, ridiculous English fool' and sending him on his way.

The same happened at a bar near the deserted People Mover that once brought cruise ship visitors into the city back when the monstrous *grande navi* cruise ships docked close by. After that, Godolphin staggered into the night, soon lost in the labyrinth of alleys that stood between him and the Valier. Another camera caught him in the Rialto, where the bright lights of the outdoor bars close to the markets must have appealed as he wandered quite lost, a long way from the straight route home. Again, Valentina's men had interviewed those there, among them a barman who'd refused Godolphin service once he began asking once more about company for the night. Even though I barely knew the man, it wasn't hard to imagine what that might do for his mood.

'And after that . . .' Valentina said, placing her pen on the table, a gesture of finality, 'two things only. As I said, a café worker on his way home reports glimpsing a man in a doge's costume arguing with another in a black hooded cloak by the Ponte San Tomà. Then, in the morning, a body. A famous man no one has reported missing. We fish him out of the water. We go to the hotel and break the news to his wife. To those who knew him.'

Nothing more, so I had to ask. 'What did they say?'

There was a wan, sad smile on her face, and I cursed myself for thinking she was somehow enjoying all this. It was a job. An intellectual challenge she appeared to relish. But a man had died in mysterious, bloody circumstances, and even for a seasoned police officer that, I imagine, must cause some disquiet.

'Let me ask a personal question, Arnold. May I?'

'Do.'

'What did you say when you knew your wife was dead?'

Taken aback, I admitted, 'Nothing that I can remember. It was just the two of us. I would have been speaking to her ghost. I wept. I remember that.'

'No one wanted to speak with Marmaduke Godolphin's ghost.'

'No one,' I said, 'much wanted to speak with him when he was alive.'

She thought for a moment, then sighed in a way that told me something here was personal for her too. 'Grief is a strange thing. A phantom in the shadows, one we all know we'll encounter one day. Just rarely when, or how we'll deal with that moment when it arises. Everyone's different. Only the pain's the same. I've seen people scream and shriek and tear their hair out. I've seen others stay silent, stubborn, refuse to accept it. Denying with heat that anything's changed.'

That last was me after Eleanor died and I was left alone in the house in Wimbledon, surrounded by her clothes, her books, all the physical accoutrements I always thought a part of her. Only to realise they weren't. They were irrelevances, fripperies, pointless dust and debris left behind. The only thing that mattered was gone.

'I've also seen people retreat inside a shell so thick, so opaque they see nothing but themselves, no sight of a world outside that continues regardless,' Valentina went on.

'Which is right?' I whispered.

'There is no right. No wrong. There's only grief in all its many forms.'

'What kind did you encounter when you broke the news to Felicity?'

She hesitated. Then said, 'Not the shrieking, screaming kind, that's for sure. If I were being unkind, I'd have said it was more puzzlement mixed with a touch of shock. But again, that's not unusual. Perhaps it means nothing at all. Although . . .' for once she looked genuinely mystified, 'I also thought she seemed vaguely embarrassed by something. That was new.'

Her phone rang. It was a long call, and whatever news it brought seemed to please her.

'Luca Volpetti has arrived,' she said, not that I'd heard her summon him. 'I have a man newly returned from seeing my pathologist friend at the Ospedale Civile too.'

'Oh,' was all I could think of.

'It's time,' she said, and looked right at me. 'Are you ready?'

TEN

The Circle, Unbroken

Valentina positively bounced out of the office, straight into the welcoming arms of Ugo, her old boss from the bar where we'd eaten those delicious *cicchetti* that afternoon. He was there with a waiter bearing two trays of them: *baccalà*, lagoon shrimp, artichokes, tomato, cheese, prosciutto, *crudo* and *cotto*. My first thought was that perhaps there was a birthday or a retirement party. But no, it was for the group she now described as her 'foreign guests'. Not for me, I was told. I had to save myself for the restaurant. So, it appeared, did Luca, who was standing there looking puzzled and a little nervous.

We followed Ugo and his man down the corridor until we reached a large room at the side of the building – I could see the lights of San Zaccaria through the high windows. Bottles of wine, Campari and a bucket of ice sat on a long bench table much like the ones we'd been using in the archives.

I was beginning to wonder if my head would ever stop spinning.

Soon a uniformed officer was at Valentina's side. He was dispatched to the cells to fetch the remaining 'guests'. Seats for them were arranged along the wall opposite the window. They trooped in, Felicity first, then Hauptmann, Caroline Fitzroy, George Bourne and finally a sullen-looking Patricia Buckley, all weary, jaded, perhaps a touch fearful too.

'Please,' Valentina said, beckoning to the table, where Ugo and his man were making drinks and laying out paper plates for the food. 'I apologise if it appears we've been inhospitable. This has been a strange time for us. A busy time. As I've explained to your friends Arnold and

Luca . . .' a wave in our direction, 'we do not have . . . *events* of this nature in Venice. It's highly unusual. Carnival time too. How inconvenient. So, I wished to invite you to join us here. To make up for any inconvenience, as it were.'

Another uniformed colleague had appeared carrying coats and jackets and a box full of phones and wallets.

'You mean we can go?' Hauptmann asked. 'I'm booked on a flight to New York tomorrow.'

'Try the food and wine,' Valentina replied, ignoring the question. 'My friend and former colleague runs the finest *bacaro* in his part of Castello.'

'True,' said Ugo, handing around plates of food. 'You all look hungry.'

'Thirsty too,' George Bourne announced, and grabbed two plastic tumblers of spritz, shiny red with Campari.

Valentina pointed to the collection of coats and the box of phones. 'Take back your things. I wouldn't want you to leave here without them. You may turn on your phones if you like and check your messages.'

Luca eyed me across the room. I knew straight away what he was thinking. There was more to this than the obvious.

Felicity picked up a bright blue coat from the pile, then a small handbag. Caroline Fitzroy a cheery green tartan jacket and a red bag that clashed. Hauptmann a stylish grey wool coat. Bourne placed his drinks on the table and retrieved an Austrian loden, dark green and expensive, I imagine. Finally Patricia Buckley wandered up to the pile and took the last thing there – a plain black wool coat with a hood – then reached into the box to retrieve her phone.

None of them noticed Valentina watching every movement as they sat down and went through that essential modern ritual of checking for messages.

'Just read them, please,' she said as they stared at their little screens. 'There'll be time to respond soon enough.'

From the look on her face, something had just transpired, though I'd no idea what.

'I guess,' Hauptmann said, 'I have to ask again. Are we about to be released? Can I go home tomorrow?'

'Of course,' Valentina replied with a pleasant smile. 'All I now require of you is one thing. One simple thing. Which I have been denied so far.'

Felicity sighed. Inwardly, so did I.

'The truth,' the *capitano* added.

'We've told you everything,' Caroline protested. 'We went to Duke's idiotic *commedia dell'arte* act. We watched him fall to pieces. Then we returned to the Valier and went to bed.'

'Signora, that is only part. I need the rest.'

'It's the truth!' Felicity cried. 'I knew nothing about poor Duke until the morning, when your people turned up, crawling all over us.' She was, I thought, close to breaking. 'Nothing at all . . .'

'Your son was convinced you'd murdered him.'

That provoked a fierce glare. 'Jo has always suffered from an overactive imagination.'

'Perhaps.' Valentina took a seat and beckoned for first Luca, then me to join her. The obedient uniformed officer with us took out a notebook and a pocket recorder. 'But it's time for this charade to stop. One or more of you must know what really happened that night. Yet when I ask the simple question "where were you?" all I get are evasive half-truths. What you wish me to know. Not what I need to.'

'We really have no idea what you're talking about,' said Caroline.

'Is that so? Let me start with a fact that throws a shadow on your story. Piero . . .'

The officer pulled out his notebook and began to read. 'I talked to the hotel. Your bed wasn't slept in that night, Signor Hauptmann.' He looked directly at Caroline Fitzroy. 'Nor yours, *signora*.'

'In which case,' Valentina went on, 'a question arises. Would you kindly tell me where you were?'

The silence was finally broken by the sound of George Bourne chuckling.

'Oh my,' he said, as he emptied one of his plastic beakers. 'Is it like the old days all over again?'

Hauptmann glared at him and grunted, 'I can explain.'

Felicity put out a hand to silence him. 'No, Bernard. Leave it to me.'

IT WAS A CONFESSION of a kind, one that took me back to distant Cambridge, where I'd watched the Gilded Circle from afar, fascinated, wondering if they really lived the glittering, free, sexually liberated lives the rest of us assumed. I was aware I was never going to be a part of their privileged world, but I was curious nevertheless. And with that curiosity came a degree of gratitude that I'd never find out quite what went on when they closeted themselves together, with each other, with Marmaduke Godolphin, the monarch of their warm, close clique. Something about that privileged bunch never did feel quite right.

I'd felt the same discomfort in that swanky events room in the Danieli, aching to be outside watching the fog roll in over the lagoon rather than triggering the downfall of Marmaduke Godolphin and the wretched denouement of what was supposed to be his apotheosis. Luca felt the same way, I'm sure. We'd witnessed the fellow's dreams dying in front of our eyes with all the accompanying misery, and we were in no small part responsible. If Godolphin had only agreed to talk to me beforehand, we might have persuaded him to hold off on his grand announcement, at least until more opinions could be sought about the letters.

The whole Wolff episode – the secrecy, the fact that the man had never made himself known to Godolphin before dying, the junk that accompanied the two hidden palimpsests – was so bizarre in the first place. Still, I could appreciate why a man like Godolphin would take little notice of two 'clerks' who, in his eyes, had stepped well beyond their brief. Or even the opinion of an expert from the oldest library in the world. He thought he might find some tame scholar to overrule us, but there was enough in the material to make that unlikely. The letters were brilliant frauds, their deceit written carefully beneath the surface, waiting to be found. Palimpsests themselves of a different sort, a modern lie posing over an ancient truth, which was, perhaps, why the mysterious Wolff had labelled them that way. It was as if the whole escapade was one great elaborate joke at Marmaduke Godolphin's expense.

We'd taken little notice as the party broke up. Now, in the Carabinieri station, Felicity, a glass of Ugo's spritz in her hand, gave us a slow and thorough account of the rest of their evening, told in that deliberate, almost lethargic tone she had, one that never changed however extraordinary the circumstances.

BEMUSED, WONDERING WHERE TO go, how to process what they'd just witnessed, they went the wrong way when they left the Danieli. The obvious route home would have been to head to the vaporetto stop and take the Number 1 back to San Tomà. But perhaps they'd have met the furious Godolphin there. That was an experience none of them wanted to face.

Instead, the three old friends from university wandered east along the waterfront towards the Arsenale, then ducked down the alley that led to San Zaccaria. They must have passed the very place where we were all now trapped listening to her recount the night's adventures, fidgeting on our uncomfortable metal chairs. After the church, the lights of the Piazza San Marco had drawn them. The Carnival decorations were still there, along with a handful of visitors in costume like them, a few at tables in the square listening to a piano trio play old jazz.

'God,' Felicity said as they came to a halt outside the basilica. 'This is so touristy.'

The music was well played but hackneyed. All the same, it seemed to cheer them.

'After that performance of Duke's, I'd take anything,' Hauptmann said.

'Me too,' Caroline agreed, and headed for one of the tables beneath a blazing gas heater. 'Let's do it.'

They ordered drinks from a waiter who looked half frozen, laughed at the price when they came. Talked about the weather, Carnival, the journey home, the food. Anything but the subject all three of them wanted to raise.

'It still doesn't settle things,' Caroline said eventually.

Felicity had decided she didn't like her spritz and was ordering a Negroni to replace it. 'What sort of things?'

'We know that Duke's story is rubbish. The idea that a cuckolded husband was behind Lorenzino's murder. And Michelangelo. For pity's sake. How could he have fallen for such a risible idea?'

The other two were silent. Finally Hauptmann said, 'It seems it was well done. Very professionally executed. A neatly considered plan conducted over a period of years. By his greatest fan, or so he thought.'

'It wasn't me,' Caroline declared.

'Ditto,' said Hauptmann.

Felicity shook her head and asked why on earth they were looking at her. 'Everything I knew about history I forgot the moment I was married. Blotted it out, to be honest. I was up the spout and wanted a father for my child. Quite enough on my plate building a career at the Beeb and holding together what family we had.'

No one spoke for a while. No one was sure who or what to believe.

Then Caroline pointed out that the events of the past week added nothing to the central argument. She and Hauptmann were still at odds over Alessandro de' Medici's character. Was he a decent man slaughtered out of jealousy, as she'd written? Or a bloody tyrant deserving assassination as Bernard Hauptmann had claimed in his book?

'Furthermore,' she added, 'the question of Lorenzino – Lorenzaccio, more correctly – and his murder here remains unresolved. You believe Charles V was behind it. I'm sticking to my opinion that it was Cosimo de' Medici, though I admit your case is strong, Bernard. In fact, when I get around to rereading your book with rather more perspective, I may be inclined to change my mind. Which does not happen often. The trouble is . . .' a pigeon flapped close by in the dark, 'you set yourself a direction sometimes and it's damned hard to change it when you're halfway to the destination, all that work behind you. All that labour, that conviction you're reluctant to throw away.'

She smiled and touched his chilly hand out in the breezy piazza. The lamplight glowed, as did the sumptuous facade of the basilica, a low, ornate Byzantine spectre shimmering in the dark.

'So many years we've spent trailing through old paper. Trying to puzzle out something that happened to people we never really knew, all dead centuries ago. Was it worth it? What's the point when Marmaduke Godolphin's fake, showbiz version of history sells by the million while ours gets barely noticed outside the dry and bitchy academic circles in which we move?'

Felicity raised her glass. 'It's what you do, love. Your job. There are worse. I was the ringmaster for Duke's circus act. Best not to question things at times.'

The music stopped. The players marched shivering inside.

'I came into this because of him,' Hauptmann said. 'He was always so full of energy and life, driving you on. Looking for answers. Demanding them of others, pushing us to see how far we could go. Whatever we came to think of him, Duke fired something inside us, didn't he?'

Felicity sniffed at the idea. 'Something that was there all along. He didn't invent it. It was ours to begin with.'

'He did unlock it,' Caroline said. 'Or helped us to do that. And then . . . it wasn't enough for him. Why did he leave it all? For the money? The women? Pardon my asking.'

'Forgiven,' Felicity said immediately. 'He had plenty of money already. Plenty of company on the side too. No. He wanted more. Duke always wants more. The moment he conquers something – a woman, a project, one of his fanciful stories – he's bored and wants to move on to the next. Me. You. Some pretty young girl like that poor American. Even his damned Passeggiata of Blood. There's no such thing as . . . enough. He'd screw the entire world if he could. Then climb back into his telly persona, smile into the camera and make up some new junk to entertain the gullible. Just . . .' she looked round the piazza and there was a gleam in her eyes, so close to tears, 'not any more. He's past it. An angry old man yelling at the moon, and the moon no longer listens.'

She tugged at Hauptmann's sleeve. 'I always wanted to ask, Bernard. Did he ever try it on with you?'

That got a long, deep laugh. 'Of course not. Why do you ask?'

'I wondered.'

'You were married to him. You *are* married to him.'

'And? You can live with someone for forty years, sleep with them when they happen to be around. Wash their dirty clothes. Give them a son. It doesn't mean you know them. The real them. Duke never had secrets. Only things he couldn't be bothered to tell me. I didn't mind. I was comfortable. There were reasons not to leave. Idleness, perhaps.' She hesitated. 'Fear. To be honest, I was glad when he wasn't around so much. I felt I could breathe.'

'Fear of what?' Caroline asked.

'Of being alone mostly. He's got a foul temper, but he's never hit me once. Nor Jo. Not until lately. That was always beneath him. With us anyway. He had plenty of punch-ups elsewhere.'

'No,' said Caroline. 'We were never alone in Cambridge, Fliss. We were young. It didn't happen.'

'Maybe not you two . . . I can be alone in a room full of people. It's not hard.'

'The things we got up to then,' Hauptmann said.

'Did you two ever sleep with each other?' Felicity asked. 'Apologies for the intrusion.' She raised the glass. 'It's the booze asking. Not me. But since this seems to be a night for revelations . . .'

Hauptmann signalled for two Negronis to add to the round. 'Rings a bell.'

A band struck up outside a café along the way.

'Bloody cheek,' Caroline said as the waiter headed towards the bar. 'You know damned well you did, Bernard. When I was going through that phase.'

'What phase?'

'Sleeping with everyone I felt like. Seeing if you were all different.'

'Were we?' he wondered.

'In terms of the varying levels of disappointment . . . yes.'

Felicity snorted and sent Negroni spilling over the freezing table. Two more turned up. The waiter took one look at the odd little party, left the bill on the table and scampered back inside.

'This conversation seems to be heading into rather personal territory.' Hauptmann sounded both worried and curious. 'I wonder if that's wise.'

'I wonder,' Felicity said, 'if we've reached an age where being wise is still required. If we can finally say damn you all. This is who we are. Take it or leave it. Whether that's the *wise* thing to do by now.'

'Like Duke?' he wondered.

'No. Not like him at all. Duke is about Duke and Duke alone and always will be. We were there for each other. Or we were once upon a time.'

Hauptmann took a gulp of booze. 'Since we're asking searching questions, I've always wondered . . . did you two . . .?'

Straight off, Caroline asked, 'Did we what?'

'You know . . .'

'Hook up? Is that the current phrase? Poor Bernard. Can't bring yourself to say it.'

He raised his glass.

'Curiosity got the better of us,' Felicity said. 'Once only. After a ball or something, wasn't it?'

Caroline nodded. 'Definitely. With stuck-up Stephanie from Windsor, if I remember correctly. Isn't she a Tory MP now?'

'Junior minister,' Felicity said. 'Still a pompous cow. Got religion too, or so she makes out. I'd bet her constituency would shriek if they knew what she got up to back then.'

'It's no more than we got up to.'

'We, dear, are not in the public eye. Thank God.'

Hauptmann wore a hangdog look as he stared at his cocktail. 'You've both led rather more adventurous lives than I. There wasn't much in the way of sex after Cambridge. Too busy building a career. Burying my head in books. Reading, writing, all the rest.'

Felicity tapped his hand. 'We've had our flings from time to time over the years. You sound ungrateful.'

'Not at all. I was talking more about the extent of the cast list, not criticising the few poor souls who turned up for the odd performance. Foolish, but there you are.'

There was a moment between them, perhaps of revelation, or a realisation of something they'd come to forget over the decades.

Felicity looked at Caroline.

Caroline looked at Felicity.

Hauptmann stared at his drink and waited.

'Did you bring your magic blue pills out with you?' Felicity asked.

He shook his head. 'Of course not. I'm a sixty-two-year-old professor of history. Not a louche undergrad cruising for an easy lay. They're back in the hotel.'

It was Caroline's turn to prod him in the arm. 'I distinctly remember you having to wander off down the corridor to cadge a condom from one of your mates. That time . . . Planning was never your thing, was it?'

'It was more a rational absence of hope than a lack of preparation, thank you.'

The two women exchanged glances again, then chinked their Negronis together and knocked them back.

'Well then . . .' Felicity said, getting to her feet. 'It seems we have a long night ahead of us. Drink up, boy. Your time has come.'

IT WAS A PERSONAL matter, perhaps an embarrassing one. I could understand why they would have been reluctant to offer it up to a stranger, especially when they were adamant they had nothing to do with the old man's death.

Valentina was less sympathetic. 'I fail to understand why you never told me this, Signora Godolphin.'

'Because it was none of your business,' Felicity replied, straight off.

'Yet clearly it is. I needed to know where you were that night.'

'We were in the hotel.'

'Two of you didn't spend the night in your own room. Naturally I found this suspicious.'

Felicity nodded. So did Caroline. Bernard Hauptmann was going crimson with embarrassment.

'Fair point,' Caroline said. 'We didn't know you were aware of that. Perhaps if you'd asked . . .'

'I just did.'

'And we answered. Would you like more detail? A blow-by-blow account, as it were. It's barely pornographic. Mostly we talked and laughed and joked and tried to pretend we were forty years younger. When physics and mortality kept reminding us sharply we're not.'

Felicity said, voice breaking, 'All the while outside my husband was dying. Or dead. In that filthy canal. All the while . . .'

She stopped, squeezed her eyes tight shut. Caroline edged her chair closer and took her arm, then, when that seemed insufficient, hugged her tight. Luca was watching for my reaction. I could see the two of us were thinking the same thing. This *was* none of our business. We were getting a glimpse into private agonies we'd no right or need to witness. Yet we were a part of the cast, the company of the Passeggiata of Blood.

'You'd no idea . . .?' Valentina began.

'Of course I'd no idea!' Felicity yelled back at her. 'What do you think? I somehow knew Duke was getting a knife in his gut while we . . . while the three of us were in bed together? We were in separate rooms, on separate floors. He insisted on it. Thinking he'd lure Patty there, I guess. I'd assumed he'd come back to the hotel to sleep it off. Or gone chasing some tart for the night. He did that often enough. Even when I was around. You get used to it.'

'Why, *signora*? How do you get used to that?'

A little of the anger subsided.

'If you must ask that question, Capitano, then it's clear that no answer of mine will mean a thing to you. We lived together. We worked together. We tolerated each other most of the time, and if we didn't, one of us made ourselves scarce. When Jo was young, there was no way I could inflict on him the miseries of divorce. When he was older, in some ways it wasn't much different. He's the opposite of his father. Needy. Dependent. Caring. Not that he's really the reason I stayed. Or Duke, for that matter. We were both too busy with other tasks to waste our time on something so petty. Both too lazy to dissolve a dead marriage simply for the sake of burying it.'

The tears came and ran down both her cheeks in parallel, glistening lines.

'Even when there was the matter of the young woman called . . .' Valentina consulted her notes, though I doubted she needed to, 'Julie Dean. Who killed herself after rejecting your husband's attentions and no one cared?'

The tears stopped. Felicity glared at her. 'I never knew a thing about that until it was too late. There was a moment. It passed. For me. For everyone else in Duke's circle. Those moments usually did. You think . . . you really think I had a hand in this?'

Valentina Fabbri paused for a second, then said, 'It was at the back of my mind. No nearer. You and your friends were reticent, evasive. I'm a Carabinieri officer. When people lie to me, I need to know why. It's my job. My calling if you like.'

'I told you why. It was none of your damned business.'

No reply.

'Now . . . may we leave?' Hauptmann asked. 'I really need to pack for home.'

'Very soon,' she said, and made a call on her phone. A minute later, a new uniformed officer arrived, carrying a dark blue plastic bag. The fellow looked pale, scared.

'My colleague is newly returned from the morgue,' Valentina told us. Then she looked at him and asked, 'You unlocked it?'

'Si.'

'The way I suggested?'

He took a deep breath. 'The way you said.'

'Good.' She grabbed the bag and, as the man retreated to the door, pulled out a large smartphone. There were signs of wear and damage, a crack on the screen. 'You recognise this, Signora Godolphin?'

'It looks like Duke's.'

'It was in his jacket pocket when we recovered the body from the water. Still functional. So clever.' She played with the thing. 'Unfortunately, it was locked. As one might expect. But . . .' Valentina looked round the room, 'here is a discovery. A dead man's fingerprint is much like that of the living. When the technical people failed to bring the thing back to life, I sent my officer round to the morgue to see if the hand of our corpse might still do the trick regardless. Behold . . .'

She held it up. The cracked screen was bright and alive. 'It seems

Marmaduke Godolphin made a call not long before he died. But to whom? Let us dial the number.'

Her finger stroked the screen. We waited.

There was a trill from somewhere. Anxious glances. Patricia Buckley began to sob as she pulled a little Samsung out of the pocket of her black coat.

'Signora,' Valentina said, 'I didn't need this really. You picked up your coat here without thinking. Where do you think we found it?'

Only sobs in return.

'At the Danieli, of course,' Valentina went on. 'You left it there by mistake the night of the *ridotto*. Instead you took the Plague Doctor's cloak meant for Arnold here. It is similar, I suppose, and you were upset. Later Godolphin called you and you argued with him on the Ponte San Tomà. Afterwards, when you realised your mistake, you dumped the cloak in a waste bin near the Frari before returning to your hotel.'

Patricia Buckley kept her head down, staring at the bare grey tiles.

'This much I know already,' said Valentina. 'Please tell us the rest.'

I must admit to a sense of mild outrage. She had kept all these people under lock and key for the best part of two days, in spartan conditions. Yet it now seemed she didn't believe at least three of them – Felicity, Caroline and Hauptmann – had anything to do with Godolphin's death at all. Instead she was offended by their lack of candour and determined to punish them for it. I could, perhaps, see her reasoning. What if she was wrong? What if one of them was responsible and she let the guilty party go? They would flee Venice, Italy in all probability, and might escape justice for months, years, for ever.

All the same, it was harsh on her part, and scheming. Her release of Jolyon Godolphin, which had taken me by surprise as much as it clearly had him, seemed more an attempt to disturb the apparent equilibrium of her prisoners than an act of generosity. I was also offended that she had attempted to include Luca and me in her games.

It was obvious now that she'd known for a few hours that the costume cloak of the Plague Doctor that bore my name was taken mistakenly by Patricia Buckley and had, as I'd insisted, nothing to do with me. Yet still I'd had to put up with her searching, accusing enquiries, none of them direct, which only made matters worse. She wanted us all to feel uncomfortable, I imagine, because the more uncertain we were, the more likely someone might make that final, fatal slip.

And here she had it. Patricia Buckley, the young woman Godolphin had been pestering for days, sat in front of us going red in the face.

Ugo began handing round drinks and *cicchetti* as if this was a simple social get-together among friends. I took a glass of sparkling water, nothing more. I was parched and my head was starting to hurt. It wasn't just the faintest ache from that afternoon Prosecco either.

'Patty,' Felicity said, 'you don't need to say a word. I can call a lawyer. There's no point in rushing into anything without advice.'

We watched, we waited for an answer. Nothing.

Valentina reached into the blue plastic bag and retrieved what I imagined was an evidence envelope. It was obvious what was in there. The dagger, the fancy weapon that was part of the so-called proof Godolphin had received to convince him the Wolff Bequest was genuine. We could all see the dark stain of blood along the elegant, finely sculptured blade.

She placed the weapon on the table and the young American shivered, staring at the thing. 'Call a lawyer if you like,' Valentina said. 'But you'll be happier if you talk now. Trust me. The truth may not be quite what you think.'

IT WAS JOLYON GODOLPHIN'S idea. To wander the cold, dark night talking, getting lost, finally finding their way to the Accademia bridge and then into the large, open square of Campo Santa Margherita, where students were out carousing, singing, drinking. Feeling alive.

He'd found a bar there, a place for the young, the music deafening and a cheerful black guy in Rasta clothes behind the counter. Sitting with Jolyon, listening to his feeble attempts to ingratiate himself, Patricia Buckley had finally felt a sense of distance from the strange evening that had gone before. Godolphin's crawling to the TV executives in New York had worked well enough to get him the development money to put together a rough plan for the series. Most of the cash, as far as she could gather, had gone on hosting this curious excursion to Venice, a pointless exercise that seemed to serve primarily as a means of demeaning both his former students and his family. Now that had failed and the man's game plan for a controversial new TV series, streamed by an international network rather than his old home in London, lay in tatters.

She hadn't called New York to tell them yet. Cyrus would not be pleased. The development money was peanuts to the network, but still he hated every wasted penny. Not that her boss had taken to Duke Godolphin personally. There was something about upper-class, snooty Englishmen he loathed. But he'd been willing to overlook that to get a steal on something sensational and snatch the man from the BBC.

In the morning, while New York still slept, she'd put together an email explaining what had happened and why it would now be unwise to proceed further with the project. Part of the blame would come her way, naturally. It wasn't fair. But New York always needed someone to carry the can and there was no other candidate for the fall.

Maybe they'd fire her.

Or demote her to menial duties in the office.

Maybe she didn't care.

Jolyon Godolphin wasn't as loathsome as his father, but he rambled on thinking he was getting somewhere. Not exactly hitting on her, but that was probably because he lacked the courage.

'Damn,' she said, not listening to him much. 'I picked up the wrong coat.'

He felt the fabric, thin and cheap. 'That's one of the costumes. Do you want me to go back to the hotel and get it?'

It was kindness, but with a purpose. Perhaps the Godolphin men always had a secondary plan. In any case, the two of them had already wandered down so many wrong alleys and dead ends, staring at their phones trying to work out the labyrinth of San Marco and find their way to Campo Santo Stefano then the bridge across the Grand Canal. The thought of doing it again . . .

'It doesn't matter. I'll get it in the morning.'

Pizza, he said. There was a takeaway place the students used, just a couple of doors away. They could buy a few slices and sit outside the bar.

Fog was rolling in, dense and grey. It didn't seem to stop the locals who marched through it laughing and joking.

'Food would be good,' she said, and a few minutes later he returned with four floppy slices, plain margherita, courgette flower, salumi and one with aubergine.

She'd almost forgotten about him by the time he came back, a round-shouldered ghost emerging out of the murk.

The pizza was cold but tasted OK. The dampness of the night was seeping everywhere, sitting on the metal table, soaking the furniture, glistening on the cobblestones under the harsh bar lights. She wished he'd go away, but there was one thing she needed to know first.

'Who's Julie Dean?' she demanded.

Jolyon stared at the shiny black stones of Campo Santa Margherita, head down, and muttered, 'Why do you want to know?'

'Because back in the bar, your mother said she wasn't going to let Duke treat me like Julie Dean. I'd like to know what she meant.'

The question hit him, hurt him, and she hadn't expected that. Hadn't wanted it either. 'Why do we have to talk about this?'

'Because I want to know. You were there. In the bar. After that boat ride when . . . After your old man . . .' She left it there.

'Oh, yes,' he said and picked at a piece of meat.

'Oh yes. Who is she?'

'*Was*,' he murmured.

She put her arm through his and pulled him close, guilty, knowing he might read this the wrong way, determined all the same. 'I would like to know.'

He finished his drink and asked if she wanted another.

'Just tell me, Jo.'

He grunted something under his breath, and when he looked at her, she thought she saw a shadow of his father. Cold, uncaring, intent on getting what he wanted.

'If you insist. Julie was a pretty young thing he took a shine to.'

'Thing?'

'That's the way he always puts it. She was a runner. A dogsbody. Unpaid. I was doing less than she was but getting money for it. I liked her. She came from academia or somewhere, dead keen to get into TV. Amazing how many people are. If only they knew. My dad always understands how to use anyone desperate. That's his way in. His *modus operandi*. Control and command. Haven't you worked that out? It's all a game. Fixed for you in advance. All my life I've been surrounded by people making things up. Dad. Mum too. It's like . . . finding everything you do is written by someone else. And we're just players, following his script. I didn't want to do TV at all. I wanted to write. Or teach. But he said I didn't have the talent. I had to do whatever he could line up for me.'

'I was asking about Julie Dean,' she insisted. Not you, she thought.

'I tried to be friends with her. I think that's when he first noticed. He loves stealing things. Especially something he's never valued until he sees that someone else does. I'd really like another beer.'

'I'd really like you to finish the story.'

He winced, looked out into the dense grey cloud ahead of them. 'Dad took her out a couple of times. To talk work supposedly. He kept a flat near Broadcasting House. Like an idiot, she went to meet him there.'

Jolyon Godolphin shrugged. 'I guess you know what happened next.'

'I guess I do,' she whispered.

'Julie was just nice. Came from an ordinary background. Had an ordinary degree. What wasn't ordinary, what Dad didn't appreciate, was that she wasn't going to take being raped by him. Wasn't going to be bought off by a job on the production team. A favour here. A reference there. Lots of them did, more than I know. But not her. Julie went screaming to the management.'

She had to ask even though she knew the answer. 'And?'

He laughed and she wanted to hit him. 'What do you think? A famous TV historian against a desperate twenty-eight-year-old unpaid runner from a council flat in Peckham? I doubt they listened to her for more than five minutes. They made sure to keep my mum out of it. Me too. All I understood was that Julie didn't turn up for work again. We might never have known anything had happened if . . .'

He went quiet.

'If what?'

'If she hadn't thrown herself under a train at Oxford Circus a week after she was fired. Not that it made any difference. Stupid.'

He waited to let that sink in.

She downed the rest of her beer. 'Julie Dean killed herself?'

'Still, Dad sailed on. I'm not sure Mum was ever quite the same with him after she found out. She told me she'd kill him if he ever did that again. Oh . . .' He squeezed her arm, and something in his face told her this evening was coming to a close. 'He did. With you. If he hadn't looked so pathetic tonight, I'd be asking for a ringside seat.'

He got to his feet, then went inside and paid the bill. 'I'm going back to the hotel. I've had enough for one night. Do you want me to see you home?'

He didn't appreciate rejection any more than his father did. Just responded in a different way, with coldness rather than aggression.

'I can find the hotel for myself.'

'Thought I'd offer. Be warned. Dad doesn't like losing. Never had much experience of it. He won't go easily. This is the start of something. Not the end.'

Duke Godolphin, she thought, wasn't going to have much choice. Not after she'd talked to New York.

They parted company at the bridge to San Pantalon.

Patricia Buckley was walking by the canal, peering through the thick fog trying to find the way to her hotel, when her phone rang. She knew it would be him.

When he demanded a meeting straight away, by the Ponte San Tomà, she knew she'd be there too.

BY MIDNIGHT, A SWIRLING grey cloud had swept in from the Adriatic and cast its icy, swamping breath across the lagoon, from Chioggia north to Jesolo. In the streets and alleys around the Frari, the street lights barely shone beyond a few metres onto the frosty cobbles. A handful of late-night strangers still stumbled around, hunting for the way ahead, some in costume, staring hopefully at the small, shining icon of their phone screen, seeking help. Venice, it occurred to her, seemed permanently populated by the lost.

Patricia Buckley was different, good at directions. When she was young, she'd reached the level of cadette in the Girl Scouts until the discovery of boys intervened. The way back to the accommodation the quiet Englishman had found for her seemed simple enough. Turn left at San Pantalon and head along the canal towards Piazzale Roma. The Ponte San Tomà and the hotel Godolphin had chosen for his party lay in the opposite direction, towards one of the quieter stretches of the Grand Canal. He was, he said, waiting for her there.

Four minutes it took her to reach the café called Ciak, a sanctuary she'd found while staying at the Valier, a quiet and friendly spot to escape Godolphin's constant, grasping clutches. The place was closed, lights dimly on. She walked to the bridge and almost bumped straight into him on the steps, close to where the sign for the Casa di Carlo Goldoni hung on the wall of Elena Barozzi's old home, barely visible in the murk. Duke Godolphin stood beneath the faint glow of a single lamp, still in his stupid doge's costume, *bauta* mask loose around his neck. He looked exhausted, drained, more than a little drunk.

The lagoon seemed to be evaporating all around them, the briny heaviness of its mist seeping into her lungs. She was glad she'd had that talk with Jolyon, even if it ended in an uncomfortable parting. For too long she'd been cowed by his father's brash and bullying persona. The way he held his favours over her as a promised gift if she obeyed his will. Or withdrew them with terrible consequences if she denied him. In the end, she'd tried to straddle a middle ground, refusing his attentions while attempting to pacify him with her work, sealing the shift of the Venice project from development status towards a green light, with all the money and contractual obligations that followed. Yet there was no middle ground with this man, and in her heart she'd always known that. Either she gave in fully to his demands, both personal and professional, or she became a foe.

Like Julie Dean.

'I don't know why I came,' she said, before he could utter a word.

'You came because you're interested,' Godolphin replied, his voice low, gruff, for once a touch uncertain.

'Interested in what?'

It was meant to be a smile but looked more like a leer. He came close, brushed the sleeve of her jacket. 'It's cold out here, Patricia. Let's go somewhere private. This room they found you, in your hotel . . .'

'Not a chance.'

That amused him. 'There's always a chance, dear. The question is, are you bold enough to take it?'

'What do you want?'

'You seem different. More . . . forthright. I like that in a woman.'

'Do you?'

'I do. We could go far together. Make a little money. Enjoy one another's company. I could teach you things. Provided we resurrect the Passeggiata. Slightly changed, of course. There's still time. You haven't told Cyrus about that little farce tonight, have you?'

'I was going to wait till the morning.'

'Good idea. Time enough for us to repurpose the package. Make it more enticing.'

She wished she'd never responded to his summons. 'You're wrong there. This deal's dead.'

Closer still, he leaned down and she stepped back from the stink of strong grappa. 'Not yet. The two of us can breathe life into it yet. Make it better.'

She noticed he'd removed from his sleeve the ornate stiletto, supposedly the design of Michelangelo. It gleamed in the waxy yellow light of the street lamp, firm in his fist. There was the briefest snatch of music, hard, crude rap, from a passer-by she couldn't see. The racket disturbed something along the canal, a bird, a rat, rustling, scuttling.

He cocked his head to one side and didn't move. A manipulative man, she'd known that all along in her heart. But she'd allowed him to play her so skilfully she'd scarcely seen it.

'You're better than being a lackey to those creatures in New York. There's a story here. Can't you feel it? Perhaps not the one I envisaged. A darker tale. A mystery within a mystery.'

'About what?'

'About Wolff, of course. The man who sent me this.' The dagger glittered in the yellow light. His voice had fallen a tone. So close he sounded old, asthmatic, not the confident, arrogant figure he portrayed on screen. 'This mysterious charlatan who tried to take me down. Damned near succeeded too. Tried to rubbish poor Michelangelo along the way. It was a clever ruse, you must admit. Hell of a story at the bottom of it. Fakery and fraud. They always make a good tale.' His gaze turned in the direction of the Grand Canal, and the Valier. 'One of those bastards was behind it. The envious. Those of meagre talent. Jealousy's something a man like me must endure. Always have. Between the two of us, we can find out.'

He'd turned the dagger so the hilt was pointed towards her. 'Take it. A gift. A down payment as it were.'

She did, and held the weapon in her freezing hand. Better in her fingers than his.

'Agreed?' he asked. 'I'd happily come to your room and run through some ideas. You won't regret it. I promise.'

Patricia Buckley stood in front of him and tried to peer into his bleary eyes. 'You really don't listen, do you, Duke? We make historical documentaries. I'm not in the market for the story of your vengeance, your bitching over petty details.'

He grabbed the arm of her flimsy black cloak, not noticing how she tried to recoil, or caring. 'There's nothing petty here, love. This could be the making of you. I would be eternally grateful. One good series and we're made for many more. A different style. Finding forgeries, frauds, exposing them. I front it. You're the executive producer. Who knows where that might lead? I am a man noted for his gratitude.'

Even though she couldn't break free of his grip, she had to say it. 'Is that what you told Julie Dean?'

A sudden breeze whipped round them, so cold her fingers gripped the hilt of the stiletto more tightly as the point brushed against his chest.

'They got at you, then?' His voice was cold and full of fury.

'You mean they told me? About a woman you took advantage of? You raped? Who complained and was ignored? And killed herself? Jolyon said—'

'My son's a pathetic idiot who'd be nothing without me. He didn't have the guts to talk to the girl himself. Why shouldn't I? She wanted something. I'd every right to ask for a little in return. That . . .' he shook her shoulder, hard, 'is how the world works.'

'Get off me.'

'That . . .' another shake, harder this time, 'is what a lowly thing like you must do. Don't tell me life's different back in your precious network. Don't tell me the likes of Cyrus and his chums never come calling. Don't . . .' she could feel him pressing himself against her, 'try to tell me you're clueless what you can get if you open those pretty legs.'

'*Don't touch me!*'

But he did, in a way she'd never forget. And that was when the knife seemed to possess a life of its own.

Her arm shot back then forward, the long, thin blade stabbing at the scarlet jacket of a costume doge.

Her fingers failed. The thing clattered on the ground.

Patricia Buckley's hand went to her mouth. Tears seemed to stream out of nowhere, hazing her vision.

Duke Godolphin staggered back against the low metal railing of the bridge, spitting vitriol and curses in her direction.

He was gasping, and even the words wouldn't come right.

Terrified, she turned and ran into the foggy night, arms pumping, tears pouring, cheap black cloak flapping like the wings of a desperate crow. By the gloomy hulk of the Frari she threw the thing into a bin.

Then, sobbing, shivering, wondering, she started on the shambling walk home.

'I KILLED HIM,' SHE said to the hushed group gathered in the Carabinieri station meeting room. 'I'm sorry. I killed him and I should have admitted it. Should have saved you. I was just scared and . . .'

Valentina stayed quiet but kept her eyes on me. This was like the interview with Jolyon earlier. I was the one who was supposed to call out the flaw in the story.

So be it. Though why she was pushing me this way, I'd no idea.

'Th-that can't be right.' I wanted to let Patricia Buckley see the conviction in my face. But her eyes were on the grey tiles and she was weeping. Perhaps my intervention surprised the others. I found they were all looking at me, while I was probably going red in the face.

'Explain yourself, Arnold.' It was Valentina, head cocked to one side like a bird listening for prey. 'What can you possibly mean?'

'You know very well, Capitano.'

'Possibly. But tell me anyway.'

'Because of the circumstances. When he was found, you said. The knife was still there.' It was hard to say without picturing it in my head. 'Still . . . in him. Patricia may have wounded Duke Godolphin. But if she was able to drop the knife, then it's quite impossible she killed him. Someone else must have inflicted that particular blow.'

Valentina clapped her hands twice. 'Sound reasoning. Then who? Who was it?'

'I h-have . . .' I stopped. The damned stutter seemed stuck. 'I have no idea. How could I? All I know is it wasn't this young lady.'

She raised her finely manicured eyebrows, gazing at me and then the rest of them. 'Your English friend is correct. The knife was firmly embedded in Godolphin's chest when we recovered him from the canal. Clearly the man met two enemies that night. It was the second who inflicted the injury that was more severe. There. I said you'd make a detective, Arnold. You shouldn't doubt yourself so much. While you . . .' she pointed a finger at the tearful woman opposite, 'you may have wounded the man, perhaps in self-defence. But you were not responsible for his demise.'

George Bourne walked over to Ugo's table, took a spritz in each hand and returned to his seat. 'Of course she wasn't.' He took a mouthful from one glass, swallowed it, then did the same from the other. 'I'm sorry. All of you. I would have fessed up, as it were. In the end. It's just . . . everything . . .' His voice began to break. 'Everything begins to look so damned stupid.'

THE BAR HE'D ADOPTED was called Il Mercante, a nod towards Shakespeare for those who cared. To the older residents of the city, it would always be the Caffè dei Frari, an elegant establishment dating back a century and a half, little changed in all that time, a peaceful den of subtle mirrors and *fin de siècle* paintings, with a stylish, swirling mezzanine above. All located behind a modest door beneath the eye of the great basilica's eastern front, close to the bridge over the narrow canal that bore the Frari's name.

There, Bourne had felt at home from the storm Duke Godolphin had been building around him all week, a sense of peace he'd decided he'd share with his husband when he got back to London. A return visit to Venice was in order, the two of them this time. The experience with the old man – the tension, the arguments – had got to him so much that, in drink a little, he'd decided to make a fresh start. To see if he could resuscitate their marriage, heal old wounds. Be a little less pompous at times, which was, he knew, simply camouflage for his own insecurities.

The Mercante helped no end, since it was the kind of quiet, intimate institution that surely suited those of a literary and imaginative calling. This wasn't about ordinary booze at all. No off-the-shelf Campari spritzes or substandard, hasty Negronis splashed together with cheap gin and vermouth. Instead, the polite and attentive waitress had talked him through a curious menu divided into three courses, each pairing a unique cocktail with an equally unusual tiny snack.

For openers he'd chosen a salty, smoky *amatriciana* of vodka, dry vermouth and black tea, coupled with parmesan foam, pineapple gel and balsamic vinegar. Both impressed and surprised, he followed this with a mix of Sant'Erasmo artichoke with pear, wine, Martinique rum and St Germain elderflower liqueur, a tiny dish of herb and flower jellies on the side. Finally, as he rolled back on his comfy seat, feeling at one with the world and every soul in it, he finished with the 'dessert', a small tumbler of milk, crushed cornflakes, Russian 'bread wine' and vanilla liqueur, with a sprinkling of different coffees in an ornate dish. It reminded him of the puddings at boarding school, warm and familiar but with a substantial kick beneath the comfort.

He couldn't wait to introduce Ralph to the place. They'd splash out and stay somewhere fancy like the Danieli, queue for the sights, take a gondola, drink coffee in Florian's. Act, for once, like everyday visitors. No need for culture. Simply being there, together, was the aim. To enjoy themselves the way they used to before career and money and ambition began to hammer a spike between their rising positions at rival publishers. Venice might break Duke Godolphin, but the place could surely heal the two of them. Or perhaps, he mused as he downed the last of the creamy pudding cocktail, that was just the drink talking. It was worth a try in any case.

More mellow than intoxicated, he wandered out of the bar after that third course and stood by the narrow canal outside, chilled by the icy fog. The lights of the great rose window across the way were barely visible. He'd yet to step inside the Frari but promised himself he would do so before catching the flight back to Heathrow the following day. The editorial director would be demanding to know what Bourne's star author had to offer next. It would give him no pleasure at all to say . . . not a thing. The Godolphin era was over, along with Duke's flagging TV career. The man's books had been Bourne's source of hits for years, and he had a suspicion that was all that had kept him in a job. Losing that golden goose might mean the end of any meaningful role left for him in publishing. This odd trip had made him realise he no longer cared. Nothing lasted for ever. To delude oneself to the contrary, as Godolphin clearly did, only led to misery, disappointment and pain, for others too. There were more important things in life than forever trying to hit a number on a spreadsheet.

He was coming to feel satisfied with that idea as he ambled in the direction of the Valier when a sudden noise made him stop in the swirling grey cloud. There were voices ahead of him, angry, furious even. One he recognised, a masculine bellow he'd first heard four decades before. The second, American, high-pitched and a little nasal, a woman, he could place when he tried.

Then a scream, two perhaps, pain or rage, he couldn't tell. A shadowy figure flew past in the fog, black cloak flying behind like a highwayman escaping the crime.

Bleary from the long evening and the recent drink, still cheered by booze and his acceptance of the need to attend to both his marriage and his career, he ploughed on through the murk. There was a familiar figure on the bridge, holding the iron railings hard, clutching at his chest.

'I say, old man,' Bourne mumbled as he walked up, struggling to understand what he had come upon. 'Are you all right?'

'Do I look all right?' Duke Godolphin barked back.

'I only asked.'

The dagger the man had been brandishing for his pointless drama was in his right hand. He was holding it against his jacket. There was a rip in the gold and scarlet fabric and a dark stain that might have been blood. 'The bitch stabbed me.'

'What?'

'The American bitch.'

'Christ . . .' It was difficult to think of anything to say that wasn't idiotic. 'Are you hurt?'

'What do you think?'

Bourne bent down to look. Godolphin removed his fingers. There was a cut. Small. In need of little more than a plaster. The man seemed more offended than in real pain.

'You'll live. Let's walk back to the hotel. If you can manage . . .'

Godolphin swore and handed him the dagger, then felt at the wound, wincing. He looked exhausted, out of breath, confused. It had never occurred to him, Bourne imagined, that he would one day edge towards the inevitable feebleness that came with age. Or that a young woman he'd clearly been lining up for himself might jab at him with a knife.

'I will rise from this, you know.'

Bourne was trying to shake all that delicious drink from his head and think clearly. 'Excuse me?'

'I will rise again. When I do, I'll find out which one of you set me up for this outrage. Was it you?'

The man seemed more concerned with his own ego than the wound. 'Duke. You're drunk, you're bleeding and you're babbling. Come on . . .'

'Was it you? Who set up this Wolff scam?'

Bourne could feel himself getting angry, which was not in his nature. 'Oh for God's sake. Put a bloody cork in it. All the crap I've put up with over the years. If I was going to do you harm, I'd have got on with the job long ago. Besides, why should I? What possible reason . . .?'

Godolphin winced at a stab of pain. 'No. Even you're not fool enough to kill the golden goose. Not quite. Without me you'd be out on the street. Didn't Benjamin tell you?'

Benjamin. The boss on high. They never did get on terribly well. 'Tell me what?'

'He was going to fire you a couple of years back. I stopped him.'

There had been a sticky time at work, and it had vanished suddenly, unexpectedly. 'You did?'

'Couldn't face having to deal with some young blade who wouldn't do every last damned thing I asked for. You I could control. A teenage whippersnapper with a scintilla of talent and ambition might be different. I wasn't having it. I told him. Nothing personal, you understand.'

'Too kind.'

A shaky hand waved in the direction of the hotel. 'Kindness had nothing to do with it. One of you's responsible. The Gilded Circle. My acolytes. My creations. I will find out. Then I will destroy the bastard. Utterly. No one does this to Duke Godolphin.'

That was, Bourne suggested, a sentiment for another time. 'Let me get you back . . .'

Godolphin stumbled closer, breathed booze into his face. 'I should have thrown you out in Cambridge. Drunk, lazy, stupid, full of dope.'

George Bourne stepped back and, without realising it, pointed the dagger ahead of him. 'Why didn't you?'

'I couldn't stomach the ripple it might have caused with the others. Their company I enjoyed.'

'And didn't we all know it.'

'For some reason, some lapse of taste, they seemed to like you. Close little bunch, weren't you? Delicate flowers.'

'I never realised you cared.'

'I didn't give a shit. You weren't worth rocking the boat for.'

'Which is why I got a 2:1.'

'No.' Godolphin laughed and prodded him hard in the chest. 'You just weren't up to it.'

Bourne felt the heat rising to his face.

Godolphin lurched closer. 'And look at you now. Thinking you're important. That you matter.'

A laugh, a shake of his head and still the Mercante cocktails wouldn't clear. 'There, Duke, you're revealing your terrible appreciation of character. I'm not so much a has-been as a never-was. I create money and fame for others. Or rather I did. But like you, my time is coming to a close. Come on, old boy. Before you say something else you'll regret. You're tired—'

'Don't "old boy" me.' His voice was loud, bombastic, a slurred version of his TV persona, echoing off the stones where Lorenzino de' Medici died and the walls of the old palace of his lover, Elena Barozzi. 'You were a lousy student. A lousy editor. If it wasn't for me . . .'

They'd never argued over the years. Even when Bourne had told Godolphin his writing wasn't up to scratch. That more work was needed, by a lowly paid researcher if it was down to content. By Bourne personally when, as so often happened, it was a matter of style.

There was a screech from somewhere. A gull. A small boat edged unseen beneath the bridge and pottered off in the direction of the Grand Canal. Venice past midnight was not quite as dead as it appeared.

'You're bleeding, Duke. It's cold. It's foggy. I'm running out of patience. If it's too much to be helped by the likes of me again . . .'

'Again?'

He'd been itching to say this for years. Now, oddly, seemed the time.

'Let me be frank. You may have so many letters after your name, so many chums on high. But I have authors who dance with the English language like Nureyev at the Bolshoi, while you clamber over it like a clod-hopping amateur in hobnailed boots. Not one of them earns a fraction of what you do. God knows how many foul reviews I've saved you from over the years. But that was my job. This isn't. Unless you want to bleed here on your own, you stuck-up, vindictive, hateful old sod . . .'

It came out of the blue. A lunge. A furious yell.

George Bourne remembered then that he'd once seen Godolphin in his cups getting into a fight in a Cambridge pub, wading in like a rugby player pulling furiously out of a ruck to hammer an opponent. Or one on his own side, it scarcely seemed to matter. Only the fury was real for him at that moment.

It had been a sight so shocking he'd buried it deep in his memory, but the recollection returned vividly as the man closed on him, fist circling, spittle flying along with all the curses, the childish insults he'd got so used to over the years.

What happened next, he didn't know. Perhaps Godolphin had forgotten about the knife. Or Bourne brandished it automatically by way of protection. The two men closed, Godolphin punching, gripping him by the collar of his coat, hissing vile abuse all the while.

Then came a groan and a sigh and those bleary grey eyes opened in shock and outrage more than pain.

Bourne stumbled back, breathless, unable to believe what was happening, what he saw. The knife was deep in the scarlet jacket, all the way to the hilt. Godolphin threw his arms wide, staggered back, fell against the low iron railing, toppled over.

He barely made a noise. Only the water did, and that sounded more like the gentle splash of a gondola's *fórcola* than the death throes of a knight of the realm.

'YOU SHOULD HAVE GONE for help,' Valentina said as George Bourne downed the last of his spritz.

He groaned, winced, looked guilty. 'I'd have been calling for an undertaker. I may have little claim to call myself a man of the world. But trust me. I know death when I witness it that close. I . . .' His eyes were glistening, his voice starting to crack. 'I felt the poor bugger leave. Perhaps it was just the flutter of a pigeon in the dark. But something departed. His spirit, dark as it was. Him. The great Duke Godolphin. Dead and gone.' He stared at the empty glass. 'I cannot explain it beyond that. For once, I lack the words.'

He closed his eyes. Tears glistened as they escaped onto his cheeks. 'I regret saying those dreadful things to him. Even if they were true. Even if they were deserved. The trouble is the thoughts that run through your head at such moments. They're either wicked, irrelevant or just downright foolish. Never to the point. Never what you wanted to say. That only comes afterwards, when it's too late.' He looked up. 'Do you know what my first thought was? I told myself: at least that's the last time I need to correct one of the bad-tempered old sod's dangling participles, not that he ever thanked me for it. Oh God . . .'

His head fell forward and he grasped it in his hands. 'If I'd had one more drink or one fewer, he'd still be here.' He looked up at Patricia Buckley. 'You didn't kill him, love. I would never have kept quiet, I promise. Never have let them think it was you. This was my doing. All me. I didn't mean to. Duke just . . . lunged, and there it was.'

The most extraordinary thing then occurred. First Felicity got to her feet and went to him. After that, Caroline Fitzroy and Hauptmann joined them. The three gathered about the sobbing, dejected man like mourners at a funeral. Felicity put her arms around his shoulders. Caroline and the American knelt at his feet. I watched and there I was back in Cambridge, remembering the resentment I felt when I saw the Gilded Circle doing their rounds, always better off, better dressed, better connected, headed to the Elysian Fields or so I imagined, not the drudgery of the everyday that was reserved for oiks like me.

I realised in that one brief moment of epiphany that I wasn't simply jealous because they were more affluent, more privileged, probably smarter than me. They were a family, a tiny, intimate tribe, close, affectionate, connected to one another by their servitude beneath the grand mastership of Marmaduke Godolphin. While I was an invisible outsider, a council house kid from Yorkshire who needed to work behind the bar of a grim pub in town just to make ends meet.

Four decades on, the Gilded Circle still existed. I didn't know what to make of that. To be impressed or not.

'I'll organise a lawyer,' Felicity told him, holding his hand. 'I'll arrange bail. It wasn't your fault, George.'

'No,' said Caroline. 'It wasn't.'

'You weren't there!' His eyes were red, his cheeks puffy.

Hauptmann grabbed another spritz from Ugo's table.

'I don't want that,' Bourne said, shooing away the glass. 'God knows I've had enough to last a lifetime.' He looked at Valentina Fabbri. 'Well, Capitano?' He held out his hands as if expecting to be cuffed. 'You have your confession.'

She didn't move. 'I still don't understand, Signor Bourne. Why did you not tell me this before?' She looked at each of them in turn. 'Why did none of you simply tell the truth?' They kept quiet. 'Three of you shared a bed for the night? Who cares? Against a man's death?'

Felicity snapped, 'I told you . . . it was none of your business.'

'You are too intelligent a woman to believe that, *signora*. And you, Patricia?'

'I thought I killed him!'

'You thought. You didn't know. From what you say, there's a strong possibility you acted in self-defence.' She turned to Bourne, who was wiping his face with a couple of tissues Felicity had provided. 'It's possible the magistrate will think the same of you.'

'I never meant to stab him,' Bourne snapped, glaring at her, suddenly himself again. 'God knows, if I'd wanted to murder an author, I'd have done it long before. Probably with one worse than Duke.'

There was a long silence. Ugo asked if the meeting was over and whether he could clear away the glasses and plates.

'You didn't,' Valentina said, nodding her assent. 'Kill him, that is. Any more than Miss Buckley did.'

ELEVEN

A Phantom in the Shadows

Valentina raised a green folder she'd brought with her. She opened it and spread out on the desk a series of pages and a handful of photographs that after one glance I was determined never to see again. Since everyone else, Ugo apart, felt the same way, she then went through the details one by one.

Godolphin was a man of seventy-five, overweight, with an enlarged liver and a weak heart, quite out of shape. He'd been stabbed twice, the first wound, more minor, Patricia Buckley's. The second was more severe and deeper, though still far from fatal.

'Wait,' Felicity interrupted. 'A stiletto in the heart. You said that. Those were your very words to me.'

'To me too,' said Hauptmann.

To me as well, I thought.

'Ah.' I recognised that sly look on Valentina's face now. 'You English do take things so very literally at times.'

'What the hell does that mean?' Caroline asked.

Valentina's brow furrowed. I thought I saw the shadow of a smirk. 'It means you interpret what someone says in a very direct and straightforward fashion. Shorn of nuance, which is odd, because as I told Arnold here, I find nuance is something the English are very good at, even if you struggle to recognise it in others. May I continue?'

No one seemed moved to object.

'The autopsy has been lengthy and complex, but I'm satisfied, as is the pathologist, that we now have a clear picture of how Marmaduke

Godolphin came to die. The initial blow was mostly dampened by the heavy costumed jacket that must have taken most of the force. A minor wound. One that barely required a stitch. Signora Buckley's. The second should have received medical treatment, without a doubt. That was the injury inflicted when Signor Bourne was holding the weapon. Probably, it seems to me, caused by the man throwing himself on you, though that is a verdict I will leave to the magistrate.'

George Bourne put up a hand to object. 'I think that . . .'

She waved at him to be silent. 'It's taken a while for us to confirm this. The pathologist's verdict – and she is a fine and skilled woman – is that neither of these wounds was the cause of the man's death.' A theatrical pause, then, 'We've examined the bridge very closely to confirm her findings. It's clear that when Godolphin stumbled over the railings – under his own exertions – he hit the stone stanchion on his way down. He was overweight. The whole force of his body was behind the fall. This, I'm told, would have rendered him unconscious immediately and dead seconds after. The likelihood is that he was as good as gone by the time he reached the water. Or perhaps he took a breath or two, enough to put a little water in his lungs.'

She turned to Felicity and there was sympathy in her face. 'The truth, Signora Godolphin, is that your husband was not stabbed to death. Nor did he drown. He died of a fractured skull and a broken neck, the result of a heavy fall from the Ponte San Tomà. There was . . .' she ran her finger across one of the pages in front of her, 'not the slightest possibility he could have survived. Even if you, Signor Bourne, had done the right thing and called for help at the time.'

It was my turn to get the frank gaze.

'I told you this morning, Arnold. We don't have murders in Venice. Outside the fiction of the *gialli*. This was an unfortunate accident, one that appears to have been brought on by the man's own belligerent behaviour and an excess of alcohol.'

There was a pause in which they all looked at one another in astonished silence. This was an outcome that was a surprise to everyone in the room except perhaps Ugo, who whistled as he continued taking out the plates and glasses.

'And when exactly,' Felicity asked, 'did you know this, Capitano?'

Valentina smiled. 'That, *signora*, is none of *your* business. I had every reason to pursue the truth in case one of you had indeed intended to murder him. Or perhaps more than one. I also had every reason to wonder about the strange set of circumstances that led up to his demise, among them this so-called Wolff Bequest. However, the fog has cleared enough for me to reach a conclusion, in the matter of his death at least.'

Bernard Hauptmann bristled. 'All the same, it's a damned impertinence to have kept us locked up here all this time and—'

'Please,' she interrupted him. 'A man died. I needed to be certain who or what killed him. You were in custody because I felt, with justification, there were omissions in your stories.' Again I thought she glanced in my direction. 'There still are. Nevertheless, the facts of Marmaduke Godolphin's death seem to be incontrovertible. He got into an argument first with Signora Buckley, and then with you, Signor Bourne. In both he was wounded, you say because he attacked you. Had you all been candid with me from the outset, this matter could have been settled in a matter of hours. Instead, you chose to stay silent and force me to investigate further, to wait on the judgement of my pathologist and finally to drag the truth out of you. Blame yourselves. Not me.'

She got up and opened the door. 'Patricia. Signor Bourne. We will keep your passports and you must stay in the city until you can be interviewed by a magistrate. I believe this will be a formality, but a necessary one. I think it unlikely they will wish to detain or charge you. But that is not my decision. The rest . . .' she nodded at each of them in turn, 'I trust you enjoy the remainder of your visit here. Good day.'

Luca and I watched them shuffle out, mumbling to one another. Valentina's hand grazed my arm.

'Arnold? Luca? I will be with you shortly. Then we may go to Dorsoduro.'

IT WAS A BEAUTIFUL late-February evening. No fog. No rain, just the faintest breeze to carry the lagoon's salt breeze through the narrow alley that led from the Carabinieri station to the waterfront. Not a cloud in the sky. Above the lights of the neighbouring piazza, the stars were out, along with a moon approaching fullness. From San Zaccaria came the sound of a small choir in practice. The constant traffic on the lagoon joined in with the occasional honk of a horn. I was, finally, back in the city I recognised.

I so wanted to convince myself I was at the end of this curious episode, one that had begun with my genial meal with Luca Volpetti at the back of the Pugni the week before. A leisurely, idle lunch so distant it seemed to belong to a different version of Venice. Perhaps a different version of me.

Luca had vanished, to make a phone call, he said. An assignation for later that evening, I imagined. There always seemed to be one. I was lounging against the wall opposite San Zaccaria, admiring the basilica's ghostly white shape in the dark, when someone's arm slipped through mine.

I was taken aback. Frightened, almost. No one had done that in a very long time. Even Eleanor. Our marriage had subsided into a mostly affectionate form of friendship long before she died. We were more brother and sister than man and wife for years.

'I wanted to thank you.'

Felicity was on her own, eyes glistening beneath the single curling iron lamp above us.

'I haven't done anything, have I?'

'Haven't you?'

'Not that I'm aware.'

'You talked to that woman in there, didn't you?'

I had to admit that was all I'd been doing for the whole day. Explaining to Valentina Fabbri what I knew about the curious events of the past week. Leaving it to her to sort them into order, wheat from chaff, and come to some kind of conclusion. It seemed a minor thing compared to a medical report from a pathologist at the Ospedale Civile, which, I suspect from her attitude, turned up some way through that afternoon.

'Of course you made a difference,' Felicity insisted. 'You found Duke's letters for him, didn't you?'

'Perhaps I shouldn't have.'

'Then we'd still be here.'

'And he'd be alive.'

She slapped my arm. 'It was an accident, Arnold. You heard the woman. Duke brought it on himself. He was a reckless man. You must have said something to her that mattered. While you were with her, we were being grilled by a uniformed officer she kept briefing.' All those phone calls and email messages she'd dealt with. They made sense now. 'I imagine she was checking what you said against our versions, and only then did she come to realise we were telling the truth. Also . . .'

She turned to face me. As alert, as attractive, seemingly as fragile as she'd appeared back in Cambridge, though I was sure now that was an illusion, a false memory, a wish on my part to play the part of the knight errant, rescuing her from all the many dragons that beset her, Godolphin being the worst.

'You were kind throughout. You stood up to Duke when few would. You found Patty that hotel when she needed it. You didn't need to do any of that. We're strangers.'

'Not total strangers. Besides, I'm a solitary widower in Venice. Permanently at a loose end.'

She hesitated, blinked once, then said, 'And now I'm a widow. New to all this. I don't know how to behave. Is that wrong of me? Should I be weeping and howling? How does one mourn a man like Duke? What's the correct procedure?'

I kept quiet. If you had to ask, the question seemed unanswerable.

'Tell me. When your wife died—'

'It was different. We were a happy couple. No great ambitions except to come here and enjoy a few pleasant years of retirement. Very different.'

Perhaps I said that a little sharply.

'I'm sorry. I didn't mean to intrude. I see it still hurts.' She cocked her head to one side. 'I imagine it will hurt for me too. Just not yet. It's still . . . unreal. Duke gone. In such odd circumstances. Poor George thinking he's responsible. Patty the same. He was always destined to make a dramatic exit, I imagine. Dead in the costume of a doge, a stiletto in his chest, one supposedly designed by Michelangelo. If he could have scripted it, I doubt he'd have complained. Only that there were no cameras.'

A tear ran down her cheek and I understood it would be the first of many. 'I simply wish I knew how to react. How . . . how to understand the shape of grief.'

The conversation with Valentina that afternoon came back. There, I had something to say. 'Grief doesn't have a shape. It's a phantom in the shadows, one that comes and goes when it wants. You have to wait and see. It will turn up uninvited, sometimes when you least expect.'

Enough, I thought. The moment was getting to me now.

'Does it still affect you? Losing her?'

'Of course. We spent most of our adult lives together. How could it not?'

My answer seemed to bother her.

'I just feel numb, wrong, as if I'm failing him somehow. That's all. A kind of sorrow. A kind of relief. I never came to hate him. God knows he gave me reason enough over the years. But that was Duke. There was no changing a man like him. A force of nature, or so he thought himself. They always say that when usually it means downright bombastic and a deaf ear just when you'd like them to listen. There were good times. Especially in the early years when we were developing his TV work. In the beginning, he was mostly serious. Mostly accurate, a stickler for facts. It was only later that money and fame and the theatricality of it all took over.' She nodded as she looked down at the cobbles. 'I was responsible in a way. I helped make him who he was. The star performer. I encouraged him because that was what we wanted. Audiences. Awards. If we were dumbing down . . . so what? Entertainment first, reality if it served a purpose. That's what people wanted. Anything but being bored. And now . . .' Her voice trailed off.

'Now?'

'Now I must bury him. Or something. I've really no idea. It may sound strange, but I never gave it a second thought. I always assumed he'd outlive the rest of us out of sheer bloody-mindedness.'

That brought a smile to my face.

'What's so funny?'

'I rather thought that about my Eleanor too.'

'Well, we were both wrong. The dead are dead. It's time to think about the living. I need to sort out Jo. Poor thing. He's been living in the shadow of his father ever since he was tiny. Children never prosper in the dark, do they?'

I wouldn't know, I told her. We never had any.

'You're a sensitive fellow. You'd know.'

She stepped back and looked up into my face. I could smell perfume. She must have put it on before walking out of the station. 'It *was* you who asked me for that dance back in Cambridge, wasn't it? No pretending.'

'Cambridge was a long time ago.'

'Some things seem as clear as yesterday. What if I'd said yes?'

I laughed. 'Then you would have danced with a man possessed of the proverbial two left feet. And found me a timid, impoverished, ordinary young man with a stutter. Someone with no money, no prospects, no great ambition for them either.'

She nudged my arm with her elbow. 'There's more to you than meets the eye, Arnold Clover. I'm not the only one who's noticed. The Dragon Lady of the Carabinieri in there has got your number.'

'H-has she?' I whispered.

Her phone trilled. She looked at a message. 'Jo's waiting.'

I had to ask. 'He really believed you might have killed him?'

She shrugged. 'A long marriage is filled with words one never really means. About love. About hate. Jo's still a child in many ways. A product of a lousy upbringing. My fault just as much as Duke's. More, because I was aware of how we were failing him. I simply didn't have the time or the will to do anything about it. We're all going out for a meal. George and Patty too, when the Dragon Lady releases them. Want to come? It won't be a wake, I promise. I'll get round to that in a while, back in London, when it all becomes real.'

'It never does. Become real, that is. A part of it's always . . . Not a dream. Not a nightmare either. Just fuzzy.'

'I'm paying.'

'Thanks, but I'm spoken for.'

'Lucky them.' She reached into her bag, pulled out a card and secreted it in the pocket of my duffel coat. 'Let's stay in touch. I may come back. I should have spent some time here over the years. It's more interesting, more layered than I realised. It may look like Disneyland with gondolas on the surface. But if that were the case, you wouldn't be here, would you?'

'No.'

I watched her walk off. She shimmied – I think that's the right word

– as she headed towards the piazza, then turned and shouted, her voice echoing off San Zaccaria's old stones, '*Arrivederci*, Arnold Clover. I could teach you to dance, you know. We're not too old for that.'

GEORGE BOURNE AND PATRICIA Buckley were walking out of the front door of the Carabinieri station and rushed to catch up with her as they set off into the night.

The Merry Widow Godolphin, whispered an unwanted voice in my head. Not that she was merry. More reflective. Confused. Lost. The way we all were when someone close died, whatever the circumstances, however fragile the relationship. Numb, to use her word. It was as precise and apt as I might have expected.

'Congratulations,' I said as Valentina arrived. Luca saw us from the alley, put away his phone and came over.

'For what exactly?' she asked.

'For solving your case. Getting to the bottom of it, of course.'

She stared at me for a long moment. Then Luca, sensing the atmosphere, clapped his hands and said, 'Dinner. After that, I have an appointment. The Number 1, I suppose?'

'No,' said Valentina. 'I have a better idea.'

TWELVE

A Stiletto in the Heart

We walked along the Riva degli Schiavoni, past the Hotel Danieli, towards the mouth of the Grand Canal. There were lights in the old prison where Bibboni and his fellow assassin Bebo faced interrogation and torture had they been captured by the Venetian soldiery. Across the Piazzetta stood the two columns where the pair would then have been beheaded or hanged like so many others. For once the Ponte della Paglia was almost deserted, no crowds of tourists taking selfies against the background of the Bridge of Sighs spanning from the Doge's Palace to the place of brutal torment and incarceration. So much history, distant and recent, seemed to be swimming around me at that moment. I would have given anything to have been able to go straight home, leap onto the bed, read a book or listen to Miles Davis and his meandering horn. To drown in solitary mundanity. To feel, like Felicity Godolphin, numb.

Valentina led us past the Giardinetti Reali to the front of Harry's Bar, a place I saw Luca regard with a shudder. There two men in dark winter jackets and raffish gondolier's straw hats emerged from the shadows and greeted her cordially before ushering the three of us onto a *traghetto*, the long, gondola-like ferry used for short crossings. Luca whispered in my ear, 'She fixed this, you know. They wouldn't be waiting around here otherwise, not at this time of night.'

There seemed little my new acquaintance in the Carabinieri couldn't arrange when she wanted.

The pair of oarsmen edged us out into the canal, dodging the heavier traffic, gently rowing towards the arrival pier near the Punta della Dogana. We stood in the middle of the boat, the way locals did. The heavy outline of Salute, subtly illuminated, rose before us, to our left the arrow-like tip of Dorsoduro spearing the Bacino San Marco where the Grand and Giudecca canals began.

Valentina turned to face me. 'We may not have murders in Venice. Mysteries, though. Of those there are multitudes.' The *traghetto* rocked from side to side, washed by the wake of a passing vaporetto. 'In the case of the unfortunate Godolphin, one remains.'

'Wolff!' Luca cried, waving his hands like an excited teenager. There was almost always something admirably puppyish about the man. A bright, unstoppable enthusiasm whenever a new challenge appeared on the horizon. Even Duke Godolphin and his fate failed to extinguish that.

'Precisely.'

I sat down. It was a tourist thing to do, but I was finding it hard to stay upright in the bobbing boat. The last thing I wanted on this strange day was to be fished out of the dark and filthy water by a weary *traghetto* oarsman.

'Was it one of them, do you think? The Gilded Circle?' she asked.

'I doubt we'll ever know, will we?' said Luca, leaping in first, to my relief. 'It seems a terribly vindictive thing to do. To try to sink a man like Godolphin. Unpleasant creature, no doubt, but the man was old. Drowning. On his way out, in any case. I suspect he knew it. That would explain his desperate need to be seen to win.' He shuffled towards me, and I was amazed how well the two of them could balance in the rocking boat, like surfers on dark waves. 'I've met a few so-called stars over the years, you know. The visibly successful. So many of them are unhappy. That's the problem with great accomplishment. You always wonder if and when you might fall from your high and privileged perch.' He slapped my shoulder, out of amity or perhaps just to keep himself upright. 'Best stay in the wings like us. The middle way, the easy path. Though . . . I can't say any of his guests seemed the vindictive sort. I rather liked them, to be honest. Even the American seemed to have a decent side to him once he let it show.'

'Does it matter any more?' I asked. 'You know how Marmaduke Godolphin died. You have two people going to face a magistrate to see if they are to be held to account.'

She waved the idea away with a flapping glove. 'They won't be charged. With what? Minor assault at the most. Godolphin brought his death on himself. Drunk, violent, careless on a bridge with a low railing.'

'Then . . .'

'It probably doesn't matter,' she agreed.

Luca piped up. 'It matters to me! I've taken all this junk into the Archives. I told the boss she was going to get a tidy present we could trumpet to the world. And give the Florentines a bloody nose as well. Instead . . .'

'Throw it all away,' I said. 'Every last bit of it. Let's put this whole affair behind us.'

The jetty was approaching. Dorsoduro. Home just twenty minutes away by foot. But first, the restaurant, the three of us. I was glad of that. I didn't want to spend any more time alone with Valentina Fabbri.

'The trouble is,' she added as we bumped against the planking and got ready to step back onto land, 'I hate dangling threads as much as George Bourne appears to hate dangling participles. Whatever they are.'

'An issue of English grammar.'

I was last off and, being unused to *traghetti*, had to be helped by the cheery boatmen like the foreigner I was.

'English grammar doesn't interest me,' she announced, starting to stride towards the grey bulk of Salute. 'Threads do.'

We struggled to keep up. Valentina dodged by the side of the church, crossed a bridge, entered a dark alley, took us round the back of Ca'

Dario, perhaps the most infamous palace on this part of the Grand Canal for its history of suicides and hauntings. We were soon past the Guggenheim, headed it seemed for her husband's restaurant on the Fondamenta Ospedaleto by a narrow bridge along from the gallery.

She stopped outside, waiting for us to catch up.

'I'm starving,' Luca announced, rubbing his hands with glee. 'Though I must be out by eight at the latest. A rendezvous.'

'You may go for your rendezvous now,' she said. 'Apologies, Luca. Arnold and I need to talk.'

He raised a hand, opened his mouth to speak, saw the look in her eye, thought better of it.

'In that case,' he said with a quick grin, 'I'll be off.'

Valentina Fabbri watched him march down the street towards the Accademia.

'I do hope I haven't upset him.' Then she pushed open the door of Il Pagliaccio. 'After you.'

THE RESTAURANT WAS SMALL, every table booked, most of them occupied already. Mirrors everywhere, fine linen on the tables, the modern decor tastefully elegant, the menu, when I saw it, quite beyond my means. One plate of antipasti alone would have eaten up my daily food budget. Valentina's husband Franco fussed over us at a table for two by the window, some distance from the rest of the diners. He was a handsome, smiling fellow, younger than her, I guessed, slim, dapper and athletic like so many modern chefs. From Milan, not that he could help it, she said.

When his wife vanished to the bathroom, he bent down and whispered, in guttural Milanese tones, 'This is where she brings her criminals before she arrests them.'

I blinked.

'Just joking,' he added with a wink. 'How do you like the wine?'

I took a gulp. It was hazy, with the fizz of Prosecco but different somehow. 'I'm no expert, but it tastes fresh and fruity and . . . quite dry. Flinty I believe is the word.'

'You think it's Prosecco?'

'No. But close.'

He looked impressed. 'A natural wine made with the original process, not the steel vats the big producers use. Re-fermented in the bottle and left on the lees. *Col fondo*, we say. With the bottom.'

His wife was back, listening.

'He has the makings of a connoisseur,' Franco announced.

'Arnold has the making of lots of things. But we're here for this new menu of yours. The antipasti?'

He brandished a handwritten sheet. *Schie, canoce, sarde in saor, cannolichi, baccalà mantecato* and *moeche* along with raw scarlet prawns from Sicily.

'We've had Ugo's *baccalà* already,' Valentina told him. 'I don't want you to feel you're in competition with him. Also, you plan to call this plate "The Delights of Chioggia"?'

'I do.'

'Then you can't have prawns from Sicily. Remove them.'

'Madame,' Franco said with a theatrical sweep of his right arm.

She'd taken off her Carabinieri jacket, done something to her hair while she was gone. White shirt that looked as if it had been freshly ironed, a sparkling necklace, earrings I didn't recall from before, a little make-up. A charming, beautiful woman, a restaurant quite beyond me. It had been an extraordinary day, and it wasn't yet over.

'So, what shall we talk about, Arnold?'

'The food?'

'The food has yet to arrive.'

'Good point.'

'My husband's a wonderful cook, but he lacks a business brain. I keep an eye on money matters, along with my brother. Left to his own devices, Franco would be putting out plates that cost us thirty euros and selling them for twenty. Margins. That's what matters in catering. Much else besides. How much leeway do you have to find a profit? What safety net should one allow?'

'You must be a busy woman.'

'I like busy. So do you, I think. Even in retirement.'

I smiled and raised my glass.

'Do you like opera? Verdi's *Otello* is at La Fenice soon. I could get you a free ticket.'

'Opera was more my wife's thing. Not mine.'

'Of course. Jazz. You said.'

She really didn't miss a thing.

'Shakespeare is so very English. Nuance. Sometimes he gives his plays one name when really they're about someone else. *Julius Caesar*, for example. Who dies near the beginning and leaves the stage to others. Then *Othello*. Which is really as much about Iago, it seems to me.'

'I do recall—'

'Iago. Ostensibly a decent, loyal servant to Othello. Yet there he is, whispering in everyone's ears. "Honest" Iago, forever spreading poison, among his friends, to his lord, who thinks him as trustworthy as his own brother. Why?'

Once again I found myself mired in a conversation I'd not been expecting. 'If I recall correctly, in the play he says he's jealous for being overlooked when it came to promotion.'

Franco returned with the food, two plates brimming with seafood so carefully arranged it might grace the walls of one of the several local art galleries aimed at rich foreigners.

'True,' Valentina said when he was gone. 'But no one believes that, do they? There must be more. Or perhaps . . . nothing. Perhaps that is the truth of Iago. That he is simply evil. Born bad. A dark soul beyond redemption, past explanation.'

She picked up a small soft-shell crab and began removing its spindly legs one by one. I speared a chunk of fish and tried to tell myself I had an appetite.

'Do you find the *sarde* a little too sweet?'

'No. It seems wonderful.'

'A little sweet to me. You have no theory?'

'If I were to offer one . . .' it came straight out, 'I think . . . I believe he must be someone with a genuine grievance. A victim of circumstance. Iago's a foot soldier. A commoner. The kind of man who dies forgotten, buried in a pit in a foreign field, not a grand tomb in Giovanni e Paolo. He's been a loyal follower of Othello on campaigns. Bloody, cruel campaigns. You know the history of Venice. Of the outrages, the massacres in Cyprus and beyond.'

'They were violent times. They were violent men. As were their foes.'

'True. The point is, violence and bloodshed take their toll on the perpetrators as well as their victims. Perhaps Iago's mind was turned by what he saw, what he did on Othello's orders before the story starts, so that by the time the play begins, he's already sickened at the way this slaughter and brutality has brought his master to the heights of Venetian society. His revenge is to bring the same bloody reality home to Othello, to make the man author of his own downfall in the cruellest way possible. By whispering in his ear, scheming behind his back, until he murders his own innocent wife.'

Valentina pointed a mantis shrimp across the table. 'Psychological. Very modern. You were a little like Iago yourself. Whispering in their ears. If you don't mind my saying. Introducing Felicity to the doomed Ursula, who might so easily have turned back after her angelic dream. Telling George Bourne . . . what was it? Oh yes. Nothing ventured, nothing gained.'

She tore the *canoce* in two then devoured the pieces. 'Caroline Fitzroy never got to meet the Venetian lady you had in store for her.

A shame, because I've read a little of Veronica Franco. A fascinating woman. Again, someone who stood up for herself against exploitative men. She deserves to be better known.'

I tried as much of the dish as I could manage. It was astonishing. The problem was my failing hunger. 'I'm not sure what you're driving at.'

She shook her head. 'Nothing. Nothing at all. I was merely noting that a simple, seemingly innocuous word here and there might have substantial consequences. If Godolphin had been exposed as a fraud in the public eye, I imagine those three would have relished the prospect. They'd certainly have done precious little to defend him.'

I was starting to feel too hot. Perhaps it was the room.

'Because of what I said, you mean?'

Before she could answer, Franco was back, beaming, bearing two glasses of a different wine, still cloudy, I saw, still 'natural'.

'How was it?'

'Perfect except for the *sarde*, which I found too sweet.'

'It was all perfect for me,' I added. 'Everything. The best food I've ever eaten in Venice. Or anywhere else for that matter.'

Valentina tapped my arm. 'You don't need to flatter him.'

'I'm not. I'm telling the truth.'

'Good. I like the truth. But you know that already.'

Franco nodded. 'Next we have rice made with little fish we drag out of the mud.'

'Don't say that on the menu, darling.'

'But *darling*, it's the truth!'

Valentina asked me to excuse her for a moment; she had to check something on her phone.

I wished so much I could walk out of there.

I knew I couldn't.

A waiter brought two plates with a circle of what looked like thick porridge, very plain, very creamy, chunks of fish on the surface along with a delicate swirl of oil. *Cucina povera*, cooking for the poor, with an elegant twist, said Franco.

'Tuck in,' Valentina urged me, putting away her phone. 'That's what you English say, isn't it?'

'It is.'

I was halfway through a mouthful when she added, 'Who *was* Wolff, do you think? Arnold? Are you all right? You're choking, dear. Let me pour you some water.'

THE *RISOTTO DI GÒ* was much better than it looked. The rice, Valentina said, was called Vialone Nano and came from Verona. The only variety, she insisted, for a true Venetian risotto, cooked so that it was *morbido*, soft at first try but with an al dente bite at the centre.

While my mind raced for answers, she moved on to an explanation of the lengthy cooking process, one developed mostly by impoverished fishing families from Burano desperate to use a species the finer tables of the city used to shun. How the little gobies had to be teased from their mud burrows, poached gently in wine and vegetable stock, the flesh undisturbed or the dish would be black and bitter. Finally introduced ladle by ladle to the rice, with a finishing dash of parmesan – something I always thought the Italians hated with fish – to enhance the rich creaminess.

It was curious how disturbing a description of an obscure cooking process was to my peace of mind. Of which, I'm sure, she was acutely aware.

'Amazing,' I said, as we were close to cleaning the plates. 'Tell me again how you make it.'

'I just told you, Arnold. Weren't you listening?'

'A lot to absorb. I haven't heard of *gò* before. It's a long way from cod and chips.'

A faint scowl crossed her face. 'Never mind little fishies that live deep in lagoon mud. Let us return to the subject of the mysterious Wolff. Who do you think he – or she – was?'

'Does it matter any more?'

'Dangling threads. I told you. It matters to me. Luca too, though he can remain in the dark.'

I came out with the one suggestion I had. To try to find some of Godolphin's correspondence and trace the enigmatic late antiquarian through that.

'I told you all this afternoon,' she said, and held up her phone. 'We used Godolphin's dead finger to unlock his mobile. Once that was done, I had my people extract everything on it. Contacts. Messages. Emails. Appointments.' She wrinkled her nose. 'Unfortunately, he appears to have changed phones a year or so ago, so nothing goes back further than that.'

'How very clever . . .'

'That's not clever! It's routine. Good practice.' She smiled and leaned forward, even though we were far enough from the other diners for them not to hear. 'I'll tell you clever. A few years ago, we had a significant burglary. Precious items stolen from one of our museums. I had the culprit in jail in days. He left his blood at the scene.'

'Oh . . .'

'You think that sounds obvious?'

'A bit.'

'It was summer. Hot. Sticky. Full of insects. He left his blood in a mosquito he'd squashed against a glass exhibit cabinet on the way out. There was enough for us to establish it was his DNA.'

'That *is* clever,' I agreed, readily too.

Valentina flicked through messages on her phone. 'As to Godolphin's exchanges with Wolff, we know they began some years back. But on this phone we only have messages from nine months ago. A fresh conversation about some exciting find was being established. No mention of the Medici or Michelangelo. Just a worm on a hook, which

Godolphin seemed only too keen to swallow. He was, as we know, desperate for a way back into TV.'

I finished my wine. Another would be along soon for the next course, she said. Then I focused on finishing the risotto. It was excellent after all.

'A few months back, there was an odd halt to the conversation. Godolphin sent a number of emails that went unanswered. It was only in the autumn that Wolff began to respond again. Here . . .' She passed over the phone. 'Read a few. This is curious. Wolff's English is so perfect I can only believe it is his – or her – native language. At the same time there's a change in the style when the conversation resumes. Before, the prose seems more florid, fancier if you like. On its return, we get a practical, everyday tone, one that leads into the promise of a stunning revelation to do with the Medici and Michelangelo. Towards the end, there's the design of the dagger, the one that clearly came from that reference to Aldobrandini. Wolff says he's had it made and will send Godolphin the weapon so that he can admire the artistry for himself. Then one final message in which he announces he's dying, and is sending the material undercover, as it were, here to the State Archives, and recommending your name as someone who might be able to help deal with it. All in the most prosaic and matter-of-fact way, it seems to me. What do you think?'

I flicked through the messages, barely looking at them. A waiter came to remove our plates. Valentina ordered him to tell her husband he needed to check the seasoning on the risotto in future; there was too much salt. He nodded, then laid down fresh cutlery and brought out two glasses of red wine. A Valpolicella Ripasso for the main course, he said, a rich Veneto red that had sat on dried grapes for a while, like its more expensive cousin Amarone, but lighter, and more suitable for the meal to come. That was to be a Rubia Gallega fillet, aged beef from Spain, served with zucchini mint cream, an aromatic salad and a wine sauce.

'I don't know what to think, frankly.'

'I talked to Volpetti about what this clever woman in Verona told you. How the whole prank, if that is what it was, had been put together with such skill. With great historical knowledge to make it seem convincing on the surface, while in truth the vessel was holed from the start by deliberate errors. Ones that would have been immediately obvious to anyone with a deeper understanding of the period.'

The latest course arrived. I stared at mine. Again the plate was as carefully staged as a painting.

'It would require a knowledgeable historian, professional or amateur, to come up with such a ruse,' she went on. 'Of course, the aim was, as Godolphin surely realised in the end, to humiliate him. Not to do away with him. Why go to the trouble? If you wanted the man dead, there were easier ways. I must repeat myself. In Venice we do not have murders.'

'Only accidents.'

'And mysteries, as I said.'

The beef had a tiny Spanish flag stuck into the top, indicating that it was from Galicia, apparently.

'You're silent, Arnold. Do you really have nothing to say?' Valentina prodded and poked at the meat, took a sip of wine, then stabbed at it again before taking a bite. 'No, well, *buon appetito.*'

'Perhaps,' I suggested, 'it's best to accept that life has its dangling threads from time to time. That on occasion it may be best to leave them there.'

'Sound advice. Tuck in.'

The beef was unlike any I'd ever tasted. Mature yet tender. Full of meaty flavour though barely seasoned.

'By the way,' she said, carving through the fillet right to the bloody core, 'I gather from the Metropolitan Police that the unfortunate young woman, Julie Dean, worked in the offices of the National Archives at Kew before moving to Marmaduke Godolphin's television team as an unpaid intern. Did the two of you happen to meet, by any chance?'

I put down my knife and fork, then took a long swig of the heady wine.

It occurred to me that the main course of this meal was me all along, and in my heart I'd always known.

'Once, I believe. No more.'

'Then . . .' She fluttered her hand at me, and I was back there in our little house in Wimbledon, Eleanor dying, staring up at me, her face full of both determination and fear. 'Please tell me. Leave nothing out. After all . . .' with a smile, she raised her glass in a toast, 'we have time before the *dolci*.'

FROM THE OUTSET OF that day when I'd first walked into Valentina Fabbri's Carabinieri office in San Zaccaria, I'd tried my best to act the reliable narrator. She'd asked me to tell her everything I knew, not just about Godolphin and the Wolff Bequest, but also my role in the affair as it wound its way to a final tragic conclusion. And what preceded it, personal details that puzzled me at the time, but since the woman was so insistent, I went along with the idea in any case.

For the most part, I was truthful. The significant inaccuracy – a lie most definitely, though white or not it's for others to judge – concerned the death of my wife. Since such issues are painful and private, I feel I was justified in skipping the details. There were, of course, extenuating, incriminating circumstances. But a man who is intent on self-delusion will always put those to the back of his mind.

Three days before our joint retirement party, seven weeks from taking possession of the ground-floor flat in San Pantalon, Eleanor did not die suddenly in front of my eyes. I was in the kitchen making tea when I heard her scream, then the shocking noise of her hitting the floor. She was gasping and wheezing on the carpet. The ambulance took an hour and a half to turn up. Cuts to the service, I was told. By the time they finally rang the bell, my wife of thirty-six years was dead. Her last breath was in my arms, my tears falling on her terrified face. But not before she told me what she'd been plotting in secret: the downfall and humiliation of Marmaduke Godolphin, a man who had come to represent everything she hated about England and what she felt the country had become. A man she had personal reasons to loathe as well, for his role in the death of poor Julie Dean.

I listened, astonished, ashamed if I'm honest, that my wife would go to such underhand lengths to destroy the man, however much she detested him. I barely knew Julie Dean, a young woman who'd seemed quite timid and frankly unremarkable when she joined Eleanor's department. Then she vanished, off to work for next to nothing for Godolphin, hoping to break into the media world like so many of her age.

Up to that point, I'd no idea Eleanor felt responsible for placing her in the man's clutches. The truth was, she'd provided a glowing reference to get her the job on the understanding it was an opening into the BBC. Nor was I aware the two had remained close when Julie started work and was soon regaling Eleanor with stories about her famous boss. Amusement to begin with, turning to mild horror shortly after. Then matters became darker. Godolphin began to make demands, of the kind women recognised only too well. In return for a full-time position, Julie had to extend to him whatever favours he wanted, when and where he desired them. After she refused and was subjected to physical and verbal abuse from him, she was fired on fabricated grounds. Dejected, terrified by his threats, out of a job, she tried to complain to the hierarchy – avoiding Felicity Godolphin, feeling she might be unsympathetic. But Duke Godolphin went straight to the top with tales about her being a fantasist, sacked for incompetence, with no employment rights since she was an intern without so much as a contract. If anyone was the victim, it was him for having to answer to such outrageous charges. One of his defences, apparently, was that it was ridiculous he would waste his attention on someone as unremarkable as this mousy little thing from Peckham.

The outcome I knew already. It was that five o'clock tragedy on the tracks of the Central Line at Oxford Circus.

Not long after Julie Dean died, a man named Grigor Wolff was born. Eleanor, as I've said, made regular foreign trips for Kew, partly, I suspect, because her boss liked to get her out of the office. A number, it turned out when I later came to examine our finances, were private, paid for out of her own pocket. Through contacts in broadcasting, she was able to discover what projects Godolphin was undertaking and then, in Wolff's name, send him ideas, snippets of information, obscure documents culled from our archives and those of others. They were all leads his normal researchers would have found eventually, but Wolff was able to circumvent the additional work and expense and take the man straight to the material he wanted. All for nothing, out of the heartfelt admiration of his most loyal fan.

From the start, the goal was his eventual disgrace, the humiliation of the supposedly great historian exposed to the world as a charlatan after he fell for a clever forgery. Godolphin would declare Michelangelo to be an accessory to two notorious Renaissance murderers, then be made to look a fool when the true experts examined the so-called evidence.

Eleanor knew her health was failing rapidly, not that she told me about the severity of her condition. I was still in a daydream, waiting on the day we'd move to Italy with all its sights and wonders. Behind my back, with her customary organisational skill, she'd put in place the final elements in her plan to bring down Duke Godolphin. The Wolff Bequest, with its cunning time bomb hidden inside two cleverly forged letters buried in a pile of junk. The details – the dagger she'd had made by a bladesmith she'd found in Warsaw, the letters themselves written by an expert forger she'd found in Fitzrovia – the precise details were unknown to me until, in her papers, I saw the bills. All that remained was to pull the trigger. To send off the emails from the address she'd created, dispatch the stiletto to London as a lure to open the trap. Then, she said, to wait for a desperate Godolphin to set in motion the train of events that would lead him into believing he had, thanks to his distant and late admirer Wolff, come upon a discovery that would place him back on the highest pedestal of TV historians.

But she was dying, in my arms. The light fading in her pained, weeping eyes, the strength in her hands, once so formidable, weakening as I held them. All the years of work, all the effort to construct the public demise of a man she hated, to avenge the suicide of Julie Dean, were about to expire with her.

'Two things you must promise me, Arnold. Two . . .'

I can still hear her saying that. Still see the grim resolve in her glistening grey eyes.

Lost, horrified, scared, I told her to conserve her strength, to be patient, to steel herself and get well. There was time to talk about all this later. Marmaduke Godolphin was the last thing on my mind.

Her wrinkled fingers gripped mine. She didn't say a word. She didn't need to.

'I promise, love,' I whispered. Not long after, she was gone.

The first promise was easy to fulfil. The trap was primed already, the boxes in storage in Berlin ready for dispatch, transit paid for, papers in order. The entire correspondence with Wolff existed on her laptop under a password I found among her papers, in an envelope marked for me with concise and clear instructions on how to trigger the complex scheme she'd set up. She had clearly suspected she might not live to see her plot against the man reach its climax. That would now be my job.

All I needed to do was revive the conversation she'd been having with Godolphin and set the wheels in motion. Then close the deal, as it were, with a farewell message when I got to Venice, saying Wolff was dying and this was his final gift to the historian he revered more than any other in the world. That was the key, you see, the one Eleanor used throughout her conversation with him. The man couldn't resist the adoration of his most ardent fan or begin to believe that someone who idolised him so much could ever wish him ill.

Had Eleanor lived, I imagine she would have offered up her name as the retiree from Kew who might help. Of that I'm sure, since she never told me of the riddle she'd placed on the mythical Wolff's boxes, the hint of how to find the palimpsests. That I had to work out for myself.

No matter. Before I could think straight, I did as she asked and resumed the correspondence with an eager Marmaduke Godolphin. The vessel had sailed under my orders. The bait it offered was rapidly swallowed.

There was silence for two months, a quiet period in which I began to settle into my new home, praying I'd hear no more of Eleanor's scheme. Time, it seemed, in which he managed to squeeze some development money out of the Americans on the promise of an earth-shattering revelation.

Then came that fateful lunch with Luca, and I realised I'd set loose something that was beyond my control.

I'd no idea Godolphin would invite the Gilded Circle to join his private circus. Though when he did, it seemed an obvious idea to whisper words in their ears that might add to his coming disgrace through the resentment and bitterness of his peers. I'd entered into Eleanor's conspiracy. It was only right to follow through. Not for one moment did I imagine he might end up dead. If I had, I would have intervened immediately and told him the truth. As I said at the outset, while I agree with Donne's maxim that each man's death diminishes me, some diminish one rather less than others. I was diminished by Godolphin's demise all the same.

By then it was too late. The path in front of me had seemed a simple one. I never noticed that it forked as I made my way along it. Often choices are made for us, by us even, unnoticed. Either we invent our own lives, our own fabled *storia*, or others invent them for us. As Eleanor invented mine, along with the end of the man she so hated.

It would be hypocritical to say I mourned Marmaduke Godolphin. It would be dishonest to pretend that she, consumed by bitterness, would have done anything but rejoice at the idea of him dead in a Venetian *rio*, a dagger in his chest.

BY THE TIME I'D finished my story, two fancy-looking bowls of *dolci* were on the table. Pannacotta with rosemary gelato, based on a recipe taken from a comedy of Goldoni's, the menu said, perhaps one written in the same small palace where Lorenzino de' Medici used to visit his mistress, Elena Barozzi. There really was no escaping the spider's web of intrigue that had wound itself around me in that short week. Nor did I wish to, if I'm honest. It was what I deserved.

Valentina reached across the table and patted my hand. 'Finish your plate. This English habit you have, of keeping everything trapped inside, is not good for your health. You're in Italy now. Let it free.'

The dessert was wonderful, naturally, especially the ice cream. She kept quiet while we ate. Then, as I scraped the last of it from the bowl, she said, 'You could have refused.'

'My wife, the woman I'd lived with, loved all my adult life, asked me for a promise while she was dying. You think I could have turned her down?'

'Two promises.'

'The second is private. For me alone.'

'You could have said yes and done nothing.'

'That would have been dishonest.'

Franco came over. She told him the new menu was excellent but there were some improvements to be made. She'd talk to him later. I thanked them both. Heaven knows how much that meal would have cost me had I not been Valentina's guest. He placed a plate of fruit on the table, peaches, apples, oranges, with two small, sharp knives.

'From Sicily,' he explained. 'This time of year, we're limited in the north. You must come back in a month or two when Sant'Erasmo begins to prosper.'

'I have a cousin with a small farm there,' Valentina added. 'You need to taste Franco's *risotto de la vigna*. Baby vine and raspberry leaves, asparagus, herbs we grow under the grapes. There's nothing like it.'

'And *carciofi*,' Franco added. 'With Sant'Erasmo one must never forget the artichokes. We live by the seasons, my friend. After a while, you'll get used to it. Winter, spring. Summer, autumn. One cannot hope to buck the time of year. The world is always bigger than little us.'

When he was out of earshot, Valentina asked, 'Are you happy living with yourself now, Arnold Clover? Or still bucking against the season, impossible as that is?'

A fair and inevitable question. 'A man died because of me.'

'That is not the case.' She shook her head very firmly. 'It was an accident. The fact that he was here because of your wife's machinations, and yours, is beyond dispute. But Godolphin placed himself by that bridge. Godolphin brandished that dagger, offended the young American and George Bourne, pounced, seeking a victim for his ire. They are as innocent of his death as you. I don't doubt it. Do either of them look the murderous type?'

How would I know? I was a retired archivist, a filing clerk, in Godolphin's words. A quiet man, logical and curious, who'd spent his adult life categorising and sorting the documents of the past, only to find myself in a conspiracy of my wife's secret making, one that led to an unexpected death.

She picked up the sharp fruit knife and carved out the stone of a peach. It struck me that she handled the blade with great care. Franco wasn't the only cook around. 'When I said there was a stiletto in the heart, it wasn't Marmaduke Godolphin I was thinking of. You wear your remorse like a dark shroud. It was obvious the moment you came through the door. I admire a man who cannot lie easily. There aren't enough of you.' She touched my hand again. 'I also admire a man who can unravel a riddle left on a stash of boxes by his late wife. That was clever, Arnold. You have talents you fail to recognise in yourself.'

I thought of the pigeons cooing everywhere, and how the sound of them kept nagging at me. Of Poe's raven, the recollection that came back to me that morning as I walked, full of dread, across the city to San Zaccaria and the Carabinieri station.

Take thy beak from out my heart, and take thy form from off my door . . .

She was right, of course. I had been carrying a weight of guilt ever since I agreed to place the Wolff Bequest in front of Godolphin, more so when the plot came to life and snared me in its web. His death only made it so much heavier.

'Nevermore,' I whispered.

'Pardon?'

'Nothing. I am responsible—'

'For a prank. A childish, spiteful prank.' A scarlet fingernail wagged in my direction. 'You pressed the starter button. Performed a poor impersonation of Iago to try to get the motor running. To wind them all up so the storm, when it broke, would be all the more intense. That was wrong, and you clearly know it. But . . .' she waved the sharp silver knife, 'you need to remove this from your heart. No one else can.'

I toyed with an apple, heart in mouth. 'You mean that's it?'

'What more do you expect?'

'Aren't you going to arrest me?'

She laughed out loud. 'For what?'

'For . . . something.'

She crossed her arms and gave me a severe look. 'One truth you learn in this job is that people so often find themselves on a strange trajectory, especially when something – their career, their marriage, their life – is coming to an end. It's not fate. It's a direction they take without realising. Duke Godolphin was walking that path. Why else would an intelligent man place all his hopes in a ghost of a character he'd never met, one who seemed to be offering him the world for free?' She leaned across the table. 'Why else would your wife, knowing she was dying, spend all that time concocting a complicated vengeance against a stranger she hated? Coffee?'

'No thanks. It keeps me awake.'

'Best not then.'

She gestured to the waiter, and he brought my coat. Valentina took my arm and led me outside. The night was calm and fresh and cold, the moon so bright it might be electric.

'That was a cruel thing for your wife to do. Passing such a burden on to you.'

'Eleanor was not a cruel woman.'

'I didn't say she was. I said it was a cruel act. That's not the same.'

'No,' I agreed. 'It isn't. You are a very precise and extraordinary policewoman.'

'Nonsense, Arnold. Also, I am a Carabiniere. Not police. And as I explained to you this morning, gender is irrelevant. Now . . .' She guided me beneath the street lamp by the narrow canal. We stood there like parting lovers. 'Here is what will happen. I have a cousin, Paola. She's a librarian at the Querini Stampalia, so you have something in common.'

'No . . .' I was starting to panic. 'I've no need of company—'

'Let me finish! She requires English lessons and will pay twelve euros an hour.'

'But I'm not a teacher—'

'Furthermore, I am placing you on the list of translators we will use when we see fit. The pay is a little higher, the work more rigorous on occasion, with unsociable hours.'

'Valentina! I'm not a translator. Besides, as I've noted already, your grasp of English is excellent.'

She sighed and shook her head. 'How many times will I need to say this? I have no problem with your language. It's your nature I struggle with. Your love of subtle complexity, to which you are yourselves so obliquely blind. Only the English would go to such lengths as your Wolff Bequest. All to right a wrong that should have been dealt with properly in the first place.'

I got a quick, close hug, then she kissed both my cheeks in the Italian way, and it occurred to me at that moment that I now possessed two real friends in Venice. Luca Volpetti and this odd, clever woman from the Carabinieri.

'Your second secret . . .'

'I said. It's mine. I'll deal with it tomorrow.'

'Good. But remember this.' The finger wagged from side to side. 'I look away once. Once only. You will behave now, won't you?'

'Impeccably,' I answered, and without thinking held out my hand.

'Oh Arnold.' She giggled, exasperated. 'We have so much work to do.'

THIRTEEN

Ashes on the Water

The pigeons were out in force the next morning, flocking around San Pantalon, pecking at crumbs in Campo Santa Margherita, wary of the thuggish gulls readying themselves to dive-bomb anyone fool enough to be walking along with a pastry.

They didn't bother me any more.

Santa Maria Gloriosa dei Frari, to give my neighbourhood basilica its full title, was deserted apart from a handful of tourists outside the white marble pyramid of Canova's tomb, the door ever open, a statue of a weeping, shrouded woman hunched by its side. No one took much notice of Titian's more conventional memorial directly across the nave, though to my mind he was the finer, more Venetian artist. But then the Frari, like all the great city basilicas, abounds with graves and monuments. This is a city built on mud and bones, a fact I was aware of with every step.

The place I had to see was the Baptist's Chapel, the first to the right of the altar, named after Donatello's skeletal saint, an animal skin around his shoulders, an agonised expression on his wizened face, a scroll in his left hand reading: *Ecce Agnus Dei*, 'Behold the Lamb of God'. From what I'd learned, it wasn't hard to believe that almost half a millennium earlier, men had buried the bloody remains of Lorenzino de' Medici in secret somewhere beneath these worn grey flagstones. No words to mark the spot, not so much as a small, carved cross. He was an assassin himself, after all, and relations between Venice and Florence would waver from friendship to enmity for centuries to come.

Storia. History or fiction? Lorenzino or Lorenzaccio? He was dead. Did it matter? Not to Duke Godolphin. He would have spun any fairy tale that might put him back on his pedestal, the great storyteller, beloved of the masses. Still, there was a real thread here, from the skeleton that rested in thick, caked earth beneath the Frari floor to a corpse in the Ospedale Civile, waiting on a coffin to England and the kind of funeral reserved for the Great and the Good. This was a nexus in which I'd become entangled. Or rather tangled myself, on a promise to a dying wife.

I'd adored Eleanor unconditionally, which is, perhaps, an unwise way to love. She was everything I wasn't: forthright, quick, cunning too, it seems. I never noticed how much the death of Julie Dean affected her. She hid it well and I assumed, quite stupidly, that my wife, the brighter, more worldly one of us, was simply anxious for the moment the two of us would steal away to Venice and a shared life that might start anew. It was always an illusion. The same kind the doomed Lorenzino may have experienced when he secreted himself in his mansion in Campo San Polo, or the bed of his mistress Elena Barozzi. Safe after all those years of flight, or so he thought. The trouble is, the past, real or invented, tends to catch up with us, and I, for one, lacked the heart and the determination to refuse its siren call.

Still, there was another promise to keep.

IT WAS JUST AFTER nine when I left the Frari and emerged into the searing light of a late-winter morning. Spring beckoned, the hint of a deeper blue to the endless sky, Turner passing the brush to Tiepolo. Coffee in the Adagio, smiles and a friendly word from the women behind the counter. They looked at me in a way that seemed to say they sensed something was on my mind.

Two men, as it happened, Bibboni and Bebo, the near assassins. I felt I could see them now, bolting this way from the Ponte San Tomà, blood on their jackets, Lorenzino's and the unfortunate Soderini's. Somewhere around here, near the grand Scuola San Rocco with its famous Tintoretto interior, close to the place selling *frittelle* fresh from the oven, and more tacky souvenir shops than I could count, they must have fled, wondering if they'd escape Venice alive.

I took the same route they did, through to San Trovaso and then the broad sweep of the Zattere waterfront by the glittering expanse of the Giudecca Canal. There I turned east, past the Hotel Calcina, where Ruskin had stayed while writing *The Stones of Venice* and begun to lose his mind in the belief that Ursula, the mythical saint of Carpaccio in the Accademia, was really his dead love, Rose La Touche. The church of Spirito Santo, brief sanctuary for the terrified pair hiding in the congregation from the city's troops, was shuttered as usual, the wooden door old and battered from decades of neglect. Then life returned at the boathouse named after the Bucintoro, the Doge's private barge, where a crew of women in pink anoraks were manoeuvring their racing skiff with a crane, ready for a morning sortie.

Here, by that broad stretch of water, the air was fresh and sweet, brisk with the aroma of the spring lagoon. There wasn't another soul between me and the Punta della Dogana save a solitary angler casting his line in the shadow of the pillars at the angular cusp. The view here was our favourite in all of Venice, discovered with delight that time, two decades before, we'd stayed in a tent at Treporti. The grandeur of San Giorgio across the Bacino, the columns marking the Piazzetta of San Marco on the opposite bank, the Doge's Palace, the buildings of the Riva degli Schiavoni, the Hotel Danieli and Vivaldi's Pietà – or rather the church that replaced his – running on to the Arsenale. Beyond lay the gardens of the Biennale and, unseen behind San Giorgio, the broader stretch of lagoon between Sant'Elena and the Lido. Here, where tourists posed and pouted for the inevitable selfies, two desperate, bloodstained villains once paid for a gondola to take them across to the Ponte della Paglia and safety with the scheming French.

So many times after that first visit we'd stood at the edge of this promontory, arm in arm like teenagers, dreaming about the life we'd lead when finally we made the move. Did Eleanor know it would never happen? Looking back, I believe so and she was too afraid to say. Not for herself, but for me. I was blind to how ill she was, how inwardly furious about the state of the world. How tortured by the guilt she felt for sending a hapless victim Marmaduke Godolphin's way. The Wolff Bequest was her parting gift, a weapon aimed at the epicentre of her loathing, much like the bow in the hands of Carpaccio's warrior, about to take the life of the fabled Ursula. Though it fell to me to loose the arrow, too late to refuse, too naïve to understand the consequences it might unleash.

Two promises. One kept, with consequences even Eleanor could not have foreseen.

The second was simpler. The small grey metal urn felt clammy as I held it in the pocket of my threadbare duffel coat. Her funeral was modest. In an addendum to her will, she'd urged me not to waste money on the dead, but save it for the future, here on my own. A crematorium ceremony, short, secular, a blur if I'm honest, right to the moment her ashes were handed over, that second promise ringing in my ears.

Scatter me over the Bacino San Marco. Then forget me, dear Arnold. Find the life you should have had.

I scanned the mouth of the Giudecca Canal. A line of *bricole*, the wooden posts used for navigation, rose out of the water like the stumps of a long-dead subterranean forest. The winter sun was low and bright, painting a line of glittering silver across waves dappled by the wake of a ferry headed for the terminal at San Niccolò. On most of the trunks sat cormorants the colour of coal, heads high on narrow necks, beaks long and sleek and shiny. I watched, spellbound, as the nearest turned towards the mottled streak of shimmering light and opened its wings to receive the warmth, like a follower lovingly worshipping the sun. As if hearing some unspoken squawk, the others followed suit. The morning had gathered an avian congregation at prayer to the gorgeous sky.

The little urn turned in my cold fingers as I watched those glorious birds splaying their feathers in the gentle winter rays. I couldn't scatter the dry grey ashes of an Englishwoman on those precious waters. This time, Eleanor, I would refuse.

'*Signore*,' said a voice so close I almost jumped. When I turned, it took a moment to recognise him.

'From the *traghetto* last night,' the man said. He wore a battered gondolier's straw hat, a heavy black jacket and, in bright daylight, the grinning, brutish face of a rugby prop. 'You're the friend of the *capitano*.'

'True. I—'

He gestured at the *traghetto* point. 'You want a ride to San Marco? For free. Valentina is my—'

'Cousin, by any chance?'

He grinned. 'No. My buddy's cousin. They're a big family. It's a quiet day. I'm bored. You look bored too. I can show you the trick of standing upright.' A big wink. 'You won't seem such a tourist then.'

I'll always stick out here. No point in pretending. Or wanting anything else. Regrets were pointless. Just like wishing there'd been some way of telling Eleanor that the only life I ever wanted was the one we'd had together. It wasn't her fault, anyone's really, that so much fell apart in anger and disarray towards the end. That was the path we'd chosen. Or the one that found us. There was no telling which.

Across the Grand Canal, by Harry's Bar, where Valentina had led us, a Number 1 had steered out of the Vallaresso jetty and was mid channel, headed the short distance to the Salute stop. I watched it manoeuvre in the swirling waters as the two of us had done so many times before.

'*Signore* . . .'

'Thanks,' I said, moving already. 'Not now.'

The boat was nearly at the jetty before I realised. I found myself running, breathless, along the pavement, racing along the pier just as the *marinaio* was sliding shut the metal *barcarizzo* gate ready to leave. I smiled at her. She looked back, shrugged, then smiled in return and rattled it to usher me through with a wave.

A quick *grazie*, then I headed straight for the seats in the open stern. Eleanor and I always raced for them, though there was rarely much chance most of the year. In chilly winter, though, the locals believed it madness to sit outside, so the semicircle of hard green plastic seats beyond the doors was quite empty. I took one, back to the glass, facing the churning wake as we pulled out into the canal, the sky a dazzling eggshell blue, the view clear all the way to the ragged green outline of the trees in Giardini.

A sudden breeze caught the burst of the churning propeller, kicking up a splash of spray in my face. A couple of gulls hovered in the air behind the boat.

There was a tiny gap between the seat and the old painted iron of the floor.

There I tucked my little urn.

There Eleanor would stay until the day some zealous cleaner found her. Until then, she'd travel the length of Venice, from Piazzale Roma to the Lido. Whenever I saw one of those ubiquitous vaporetti, I'd remember her, picture the two of us sitting together on the seats at the back, gazing out in wonder at a different world that would one day be our final home.

Promise kept, I got off at San Tomà and stopped at Adagio for a second, warming cappuccino.

The stiletto was gone, the wound remained, but that gentle ache was welcome and deserved. I'd keep it happily all my days.

Hardly had I grabbed my cup than I heard him.

'Arnold! Arnold!' The flamboyant cape, the long scarf, the

broad-brimmed floppy hat. It was Luca, dashing across the paving stones, arms flapping, wide-eyed and brimful of enthusiasm as ever. 'I've been trying to call you.'

How I envied my Venetian friend and his ability to live in the moment. From the excited look on his face, it was obvious that Marmaduke Godolphin and the Wolff Bequest were behind him.

'Coffee?' I suggested. 'My phone was taking a break.'

'Here . . .' He came and pressed a wad of notes into my hand. 'Fifteen hundred each. Five days' work, as agreed.'

'But . . .'

'No buts. Signora Godolphin sent me the money last night and wouldn't take no for an answer, not that I forced the issue. A generous lady. It was there when I checked my account this morning.' He hesitated. 'You wonder what she was doing with him all those years. It's as well I won't contemplate matrimony. It seems I'll never understand it.'

The woman behind the counter waved a dismissive hand in his direction. 'As if any woman would have you, Luca!'

He tapped the side of his nose. 'That, I assure you, Fiorella, is never a problem.'

A brief and cheery argument ensued, one of those happy spats they loved. I listened for a while, bemused, then finished my coffee and got ready to leave them to it.

Luca put out a hand to stop me. 'What will you spend your money on? Something special, I trust. Don't save it. Who knows what tomorrow may bring? These days especially.'

I ran my fingers over my ancient duffel coat, bought all those years ago in a Debenhams that no longer existed.

'Perhaps I need some new clothes . . .'

'Perhaps?' cried Fiorella, creased with laughter. '*Perhaps?*'

Luca stepped back from the counter, sweeping his cape around him like a dancer. 'A *tabarro* for Dottore Clover! A broad-brimmed hat. A scarf. I know just the place. Just the tailor. Just the cloth. We will make a Venetian of him yet.'

'Thanks, but—'

As ever, there was no chance to interrupt Luca Volpetti in full flow. No point in trying.

'So, my English friend . . .' he glanced round the empty bar in a conspiratorial fashion, then leaned in and placed an arm around my shoulder, 'to what strange mystery shall we turn our talents next?'

Author's Note

I am once again indebted to Gregory Dowling for his local guidance and insight into the lesser-known corners of Venice. To Dr Jonathan Davies of Warwick University's history department I owe a spritz or two for guiding me to various sources and places concerning the assassination of Lorenzino de' Medici and its aftermath.

Most of the historical links in this tale – from Benvenuto Cellini's connections with its principal players to Michelangelo's design of the Aldobrandini dagger – are established fact. The red herring of a connection between Michelangelo and the two Medici murders is, of course, a shameless invention on my part. For the real story behind the killings, the reader should turn to *The Duke's Assassin, Exile and Death of Lorenzino de' Medici* by Stefano Dall'Aglio, translated by Donald Weinstein, Yale University Press. This is both detailed academic work and a vivid forensic investigation of the facts behind both the death of Alessandro in 1537 in Florence and the payback assassination of Lorenzino eleven years later in Venice. The author uncovers new documents that show Alessandro's avenger was not his cousin, Cosimo, as was supposed for many years, but his father-in-law, the emperor Charles V.

Lorenzino's justification for Alessandro's killing is available in English as *Apology for a Murder*, Hesperus Classics, translated by Andrew Brown, with an enlightening foreword by Tim Parks. The book also includes a translation of the first-hand account of Lorenzino's murder by Francesco Bibboni, in which he details how he discovered Lorenzino's affair with Elena Barozzi as he hunted down his victim, and the desperate measures he and his accomplice took to escape the vengeance of Venice after the deed was done. Bibboni and his fellow boastful butcher Cellini are among the few people in the real-life part of this drama to have lived to a great age and died peacefully in bed.

Many of the places in this tale are easily visited today. I will leave it to the reader to discover which are real and which pure fiction. Il Pagliaccio is an invention, though the dishes eaten by Arnold and Valentina there I have pillaged from the Bistrot de Venise in San Marco, and the Osteria Al Museo of Burano. George Bourne's cocktails at Il Mercante represent the offerings available around the time of writing and have doubtless been superseded by different exotic concoctions already.

David Hewson
Kent and Venice, 2021